Praise for **New York Times** *bestselling author*
Sharon Sala

"Veteran romance writer Sala lives up to her reputation
with this well-crafted thriller. "
—*Publishers Weekly* on *Remember Me*

"[A] rare ability to bring powerful and emotionally
wrenching stories to life."
—*RT Book Reviews*

"Sharon Sala is not only a top romance novelist, she is
an inspiration for people everywhere who wish to live
their dreams."
—John St. Augustine, host,
Power!Talk Radio WDBC-AM, Michigan

Praise for bestselling author Debra Webb

"Webb's one of the best names in the business when it
comes to romantic suspense."
—*RT Book Reviews*

"Debra Webb is endowed with an incredible
imagination and an impressive ability to create
multidimensional, realistic characters."
—*TheRomanceReader.com*

D1397403

SHARON SALA

New York Times and *USA TODAY* bestselling author **Sharon Sala** has written more than eighty books, and has regularly hit the bestseller lists. She's a seven-time Romance Writers of America RITA® Award finalist and a winner of RWA's Lifetime Achievement Award, five-time winner of a National Readers' Choice Award, five-time winner of a Colorado Romance Writers' Award of Excellence, and has also won many other industry awards too numerous to mention. During that time, she has captured the hearts of countless readers.

She was born and raised in rural Oklahoma and still calls the state her home. Being with her family is her ultimate joy, and she finds great satisfaction in creating her stories, then sharing them worldwide with people who love to read.

DEBRA WEBB

Debra Webb wrote her first story at age nine and her first romance at thirteen. It wasn't until she spent three years working for the military behind the Iron Curtain and within the confining political walls of Berlin, Germany, that she realized her true calling. A five-year stint with NASA on the space shuttle program reinforced her love of the endless possibilities within her grasp as a storyteller. A collision course between suspense and romance was set. Debra has been writing romance, suspense and action-packed romance thrillers since.

Visit her at www.debrawebb.com or write to her at P.O. Box 4889, Huntsville, AL 35815.

BESTSELLING AUTHOR COLLECTION

New York Times Bestselling Author

SHARON SALA

Butterfly

HARLEQUIN®

entertain, enrich, inspire™

If you purchased this book without a cover you should be aware
that this book is stolen property. It was reported as "unsold and
destroyed" to the publisher, and neither the author nor the
publisher has received any payment for this "stripped book."

Recycling programs
for this product may
not exist in your area.

ISBN-13: 978-0-373-18062-2

BUTTERFLY
Copyright © 2012 by Harlequin Books S.A.

The publisher acknowledges the copyright holders of the individual works
as follows:

BUTTERFLY
Copyright © 2000 by Sharon Sala

PROTECTIVE INSTINCTS
Copyright © 2003 by Debra Webb

All rights reserved. Except for use in any review, the reproduction or
utilization of this work in whole or in part in any form by any electronic,
mechanical or other means, now known or hereafter invented, including
xerography, photocopying and recording, or in any information storage
or retrieval system, is forbidden without the written permission of the
publisher, Harlequin Enterprises Limited, 225 Duncan Mill Road,
Don Mills, Ontario M3B 3K9, Canada, .

This is a work of fiction. Names, characters, places and incidents are
either the product of the author's imagination or are used fictitiously,
and any resemblance to actual persons, living or dead, business
establishments, events or locales is entirely coincidental.

This edition published by arrangement with Harlequin Books S.A.

For questions and comments about the quality of this book
please contact us at CustomerService@Harlequin.com.

® and TM are trademarks of Harlequin Enterprises Limited or its
corporate affiliates. Trademarks indicated with ® are registered in the
United States Patent and Trademark Office, the Canadian Trade Marks
Office and in other countries.

www.Harlequin.com

Printed in U.S.A.

CONTENTS

Dear Reader,

This story is about life and what it brings to us. Even with the best-laid plans, it can all go very wrong, and sometimes so fast that you don't even see it coming. When she was just a child, the young woman in this story experienced an incident that damaged her so emotionally, she became trapped in that time. She grew older and grew up, but she never grew out of believing what she'd heard. It wasn't until she nearly lost her life that she found a way out of the past.

We all know the analogy of how patience and time can turn a lowly worm into a beautiful butterfly. So this was how the young woman in my story evolved. Through the love of a good man and the passage of time, she learned not only to accept her worth, but how to grieve for her loss and move on.

This very special story will take you through every heart-stopping moment of being betrayed, of becoming the victim of an act of random violence and of finding love where you least expect it.

It's a murder mystery. It's a story full of suspense. And at its core, it's a very special love story.

I hope you enjoy it.

Sharon Sala

BUTTERFLY

New York Times Bestselling Author

Sharon Sala

THIS BOOK BELONGS TO
THE HOMESTEAD
OF ROCHESTER

I dedicate this book to the butterflies in all of us, and to my Bobby, who made me believe I could fly.

ACKNOWLEDGMENTS

A great big THANK-YOU must go to Pistol Pete Cormican, premier DJ of Dallas, Texas, and one of the most open and generous men with whom it was ever my pleasure to speak. By telephone, he helped me through the geography of his fine city, leading me through the maze of streets and suburbs with patience and ease.

Any physical discrepancies you might find in various locations are nothing more than creative license, and any mistakes are mine, not his.

Prologue

Detroit, Michigan
July 13, Twenty years ago

Sweat ran down the middle of six-year-old China Brown's forehead as she crouched in the cool, dry dirt beneath the porch of her mother's house. Inside, she could hear the murmur of voices and the occasional thud of footsteps as her mother and her stepfather, Clyde, moved from room to room. Every time she heard Clyde's voice she shuddered. It was only a matter of time before he realized his favorite coffee cup was broken. She hadn't meant to do it, but Clyde wouldn't care that it was an accident. He didn't like her any more than she liked him and seemed to look for reasons to reprimand her.

Time passed, and she had almost drifted off to sleep when she heard a loud, angry shout, then the sound of running footsteps coming toward the door.

"China Mae, you get in here right now!" Clyde yelled.

China flinched. He must have found the cup. She'd wanted to hide the pieces, but she'd heard her mother coming and had tossed them into the wastebasket before bolting out the door. Now it was too late. They'd been found.

"China...so help me God, I'm gonna whip your ass if you don't answer me!"

China held her breath. Answer Clyde? No way. He was gonna whip her ass no matter what. Why hurry up the inevitable?

She heard another pair of footsteps—lighter, quicker—then the anxious tone of her mother's voice.

"Clyde? What's wrong?"

Clyde Shubert pivoted angrily, jamming a knobby finger into the woman's face.

"I'll tell you what's wrong. That stupid kid of yours broke my favorite coffee cup."

China heard her mother's swift intake of breath and just for a moment thought about revealing herself. Sometimes Clyde took his anger out on her mother, too. But her fear was greater than her guilt, and she stayed immobile, closing her eyes and praying as she'd never prayed before.

"I'm sure it was an accident," Mae offered, and tried to placate Clyde with a pat on his arm.

But Clyde would have none of it. He shrugged off Mae's touch and cursed aloud before striding to the edge of the porch. China followed his path with a horrified gaze, watching the dirt sift down through loose wooden planks above her head, then blinking furiously when some of the dirt drifted into her eyes. Suddenly her nose began to tickle, and she pinched it between her thumb and forefinger, willing herself not to sneeze.

"China! You get yourself into the house this instant!" Clyde yelled.

China pinched her nose tighter as the urge to sneeze persisted.

"Please…Clyde…it's just a cup."

The sound of flesh hitting flesh was as abrupt as China's exit from the house had been, and she knew without doubt that her mother had just been slapped. The need to sneeze disappeared, replaced by an overwhelming urge to cry. She did neither, instead curling tighter into a ball and wishing she could disappear.

"Today a cup. Tomorrow something else. You're always excusing the little bitch. That's what's wrong with her!" he yelled.

Mae flinched, but held her head high. It wasn't the first time he'd hit her. Doubtless it wouldn't be the last. There were days when it shamed her that she'd let herself come to this, but she didn't have the guts to leave.

"Don't call my daughter names. There's nothing wrong with her! She's just a little girl."

Clyde snorted beneath his breath. "Yeah, and one of the skinniest, ugliest kids I've ever seen. You just keep her out of my face, you hear me?"

China bit her lip as she heard Clyde stomp back into the house. Ugly? She was ugly? Tears welled. She didn't want to be ugly. Her thoughts began to race. Was that why she didn't have any friends? Did the kids down the street think she was too ugly to play with?

"China…where are you?"

Mae's voice startled her, and she almost answered. But a sense of self-preservation kept her quiet, and moments later she heard her mother go back inside.

As soon as she knew she was alone, she rolled over onto her stomach and buried her face in her arms. Ugly. She hadn't known she was ugly. Now it made sense why Clyde didn't like her.

Hot tears welled beneath her eyelids as she lay belly down in the dirt and buried her face in the curve of her arm, her thin little shoulders shaking with suppressed sobs.

The neighbor's yellow cat sauntered into their yard and started beneath the porch, then stopped short, hissing with displeasure as it saw China. Ordinarily she would have jumped and run away, but today she didn't care. Nothing mattered anymore, not even the chance that old Scruffy might scratch her.

The cat sniffed her bare feet, then the backs of her knees, then worked its way up to her face, sniffing and licking at the wash of wet, salty tears streaming down the side of China's cheek.

She gasped and jerked, raising her head too fast and bumping it on the underside of the porch. Scruffy hissed at the unexpected movement and scampered out the other side of the porch to disappear beneath a volunteer stand of Castor beans her mother let grow to keep the moles and gophers out of the yard.

China held her breath, certain that the thump of her head against the underside of the porch had given her away, but when no one came running, she began to relax.

Scruffy seemed to have forgiven her for frightening him and was already in the act of stalking a grasshopper that had landed on a nearby blade of grass. The big cat pounced, and she absently watched the demise of the grasshopper as it disappeared down Scruffy's throat. The cat soon moved on in search of bigger game, leaving China alone with a sense of growing dread. Sooner or later it was bound to get dark, and when it did, she would have to come out. It was a sad but true fact that she was more afraid of the dark than she was of Clyde.

She shuddered on a sob, then wiped her nose on the back of her hand and started inching her way through the dust toward the yard beyond. Just as she reached the edge of the porch, a small brown caterpillar dropped from a blade of grass and began inching its way toward the shade beneath the porch. China hesitated, then rested her chin on her hands, watching in fascination at the undulant movement of the tiny body—at the way it seemed to thread itself between the twigs and pebbles without disturbing a single grain of dust. It was so small. If she hadn't been eye to eye with the little creature, she would never have known it was there.

As she watched, a thought began to occur. If only she could become as small and insignificant as the lowly little worm, then maybe Clyde would never bother her again. And if she was as ugly as Clyde said she was, being invisible would protect her from offending people with her presence. It seemed like a good idea, and she even closed her eyes and tried to think herself small. But when she finally looked up, she was still China and the caterpillar was gone. She crawled out from under the porch and began dusting off the front of her clothes. Some things just weren't meant to be.

She made herself scarce for the rest of the afternoon until the sun began to set. Then, when the shadows in the yard began to lengthen and turn a dark, somber blue, she dawdled through the grass to the front steps and sat, waiting until the last possible minute before going inside to face Clyde's wrath. The hinges suddenly squeaked on the screen door behind her, and she jumped and stood, wild-eyed and poised to run. It was her mother.

"China Mae, where on earth have you been?" Mae asked.

She shrugged and looked down at her bare toes, unable to come up with a suitable answer.

Mae pushed the door open wide. "Well, come on in

then," she said softly. "And go wash," she added. "Your clothes are filthy. What have you been doing?"

"Nothing," China mumbled and slipped past her mother on near silent bare feet.

Mae reached for her child, trying to brush the wayward hair from her little girl's face, but China was too fast. She was gone before she could catch her.

As Mae eased the door shut, she cast a nervous glance toward the living room on her way to the kitchen. Clyde was intent on the evening news and unaware that China was back. All she could do was hope that the meat loaf and mashed potatoes she'd fixed would sidetrack him from going on again about a broken cup.

Staying with Clyde bothered Mae's conscience on a daily basis. It was one thing for her to tolerate Clyde's abuse, but it shamed her that, by staying, she put China in danger, too. Yet leaving was even more frightening. She had no skills and a tenth-grade education, so her choice of jobs was never great. They needed Clyde's paycheck to put a decent roof over their heads.

Inside the bathroom, China pulled the little step stool out from under the sink and stepped up on it so she could reach the faucets. The old pipes groaned as she opened the taps, and she flinched, certain that Clyde would come bursting through the door at any moment and give her a thrashing. In her haste to finish, a goodly portion of the water dribbled down the front of her dress, mingling with the dust to make thin streaks of mud. She swiped at the streaks with the palms of her hands, which only made things worse, and then she had to wash her hands again to get them clean. By the time she got to the kitchen, her legs were shaking and her stomach was in knots. She slipped into her chair without looking up, but she knew

Clyde was there—watching her, waiting for her to make another mistake.

"I thought you told her to wash up," Clyde growled.

China ducked her head as Mae turned, nervously clanking a spoon against the inside of the bowl in which she was dishing up the potatoes.

Mae saw the smudges on her little girl's face and dress, then looked past them to the stiff set of China's shoulders and sighed.

"She's fine. As soon as she's had her supper, I'll give her a bath."

Clyde muttered beneath his breath, satisfied he'd made his point.

Mae set the last bowl of food on the table, then slid into her chair with a heartfelt sigh and gave Clyde a tentative smile.

"I made meat loaf."

Clyde rolled his eyes as he stabbed at a roll. "Hell, woman, I can see that."

Mae frowned, then shrugged. The way she looked at it, she'd made an overture of peace. If he didn't want to accept it, then that was his problem, not hers. She reached for China's plate.

"Here, sweetie, Mama will fix your plate. Are you hungry?"

China dared to look up. The scents surrounding her were varied and enticing, and had she not been so certain that Clyde wasn't through with her, she might have done justice to the meal.

She sighed and then fixed a dark, anxious gaze on her mother's face.

"Not really," she whispered.

"Speak up, damn it," Clyde yelled, and thumped the

handle of his knife on the table, making the dishes and cutlery rattle.

China flinched and moaned and gave her mother a frantic look.

Mae's frown deepened. "I heard her just fine," she told Clyde. "Help yourself to the meat loaf and please pass it on."

Clyde grabbed the platter and defiantly slid over half the slices onto his plate before setting it back on the table with a thump. Then he reached across China's plate for the bowl of mashed potatoes without caring that his elbow just missed hitting her in the nose. She started to slide out of the chair for a hasty exit when Clyde grabbed her by the arm and gave it a yank.

"You sit," he ordered, and then proceeded to spoon a huge portion of mashed potatoes onto her plate. "You ain't gettin' up until you eat every bite."

Mae reached for her daughter's plate. "Clyde, you've given her too much. That's even more than I could eat."

Clyde backhanded Mae, catching the edge of her chin with his ring and leaving an angry gash that quickly started to seep a thin ribbon of blood.

China gasped as her mother cried out, then held her breath, afraid that Clyde would take umbrage with her response. Again she thought of the little brown caterpillar and wished she could just disappear.

Clyde muttered an oath beneath his breath and grabbed a bowl of spinach.

"You got anything to say to me, whelp?"

China shook her head vehemently, her eyes wide with fear.

"That's what I thought," he muttered, then slid a helping of the dark, juicy greens onto her plate as Mae turned away to staunch the increasing flow of blood. Clyde picked up China's fork and slapped it into the palm of her hand.

"Eat!"

China looked up to her mother for help, which angered Clyde even more.

"Your mama ain't gonna help you this time," he warned. "You eat or so help me God, I'll whip your ass until you can't sit down."

Mae pivoted angrily. "You won't touch my daughter."

Convinced that if Clyde hit her mother again, he would kill her, China gave her stepfather a nervous glance.

"It's all right, Mama," she said quickly. "I can eat it."

Across the room, Mae watched her baby girl and knew that, at that moment, China had more guts than she did, and it shamed her.

China looked down at her plate, then up at Clyde as she stuck her fork in the top of the potatoes. An uneasy silence filled the room as she lifted a bite to her lips and then closed her eyes.

Suddenly the back of her head exploded in pain as Clyde hit her with a doubled fist, driving her face into the plate of potatoes and spinach. She came up gasping for air as her fork clattered to the floor. In a panic, she began digging potatoes from her eyes and nose, knowing that to sit blind with the enemy was to taunt death.

"Now look what you did, you ugly little bitch," Clyde snarled, and yanked her up from the chair.

"No!" Mae screamed, and dashed toward the table. But she wasn't in time to prevent Clyde from dragging China from her seat and out of the room.

China was sobbing now, certain she was going to die.

"I didn't mean to break your cup. I didn't mean to break your cup."

But Clyde was beyond reason. He hit the bathroom

door with the flat of his hand and shoved China into the shower stall.

Mae was pounding on Clyde's back with both hands, begging him to leave her baby alone, but he was mute to her pleas. He turned on the cold water faucet. Immediately water came spewing from the shower head and down onto his arms.

In desperation, China kicked and screamed, begging for Clyde to stop, and in doing so, she accidentally kicked him in the eye. With a mighty roar, he grabbed her by the throat and turned her head up to the jets of chill water.

"I'll teach you to mess with what's mine," he yelled. "I'm gonna wash that filth off your face if it's the last thing I do."

Clyde's fingers tightened around China's neck as her view of the world began to spin and then narrow dangerously. Water peppered into her eyes and up her nose, mingling with the tears and mashed potatoes. Choked sobs alternated with frantic gasps for air, and in her peripheral vision, she could just see an outline of her mother's face and the footstool she was holding above her head.

Then everything went black.

Chapter 1

The baby kicked in China's belly as she bent down to pick up her bag, a frightening reminder that she wasn't the only person about to become homeless. George Wayne, her landlord, shifted nervously behind her as he stood in the doorway to the apartment, watching her gather her assortment of meager belongings.

"It ain't my fault, you know. Rules is rules, and you're more than three months behind on rent."

China turned, the bag in her hand, her head held high. "If you'd told me sooner that Tommy wasn't giving you the rent money, I wouldn't have kept giving it to him. I would have given it to you myself."

George Wayne frowned. "That's what you say, but you ain't got no way of provin' that to me. For all I know, you both partied up the money, and when it was all gone, he split on you."

China's heart sank. The fact that Tommy Fairheart,

the father of her unborn child, had disappeared from her life eight days earlier was secondary to the fact that he'd stolen every penny she had to her name when he left. That he had also kept the last three months' rent money instead of paying George Wayne, as China had believed, was, as the old saying went, the last straw.

She gave George a scathing look, pulled the front of her coat as far as it would go across her tummy and shouldered her bag. With her head held high, she moved past George in long, stilted strides, hoping she could get out of his sight before she started to cry.

It was a long walk from the third floor of her apartment down to street level. She made it in record time. But her defiance died when she stepped out the door and turned to face the bitter bite of Texas winter.

Again the baby kicked, then rolled. China placed her hand across the swell of her stomach and shifted the strap of her bag to a more comfortable position on her shoulder. Her mouth was twisted into a bitter grimace, her eyes flooded with tears, but there was determination in her voice.

"Don't worry, baby. Mama will take care of you."

Uncertain as to how that would yet come to be, she started walking. Her plan was to find a church. She'd seen several on the bus route that she rode every day to work. Maybe there would be someone there who could give her some temporary shelter. She had a job waiting tables in a barbecue joint. The pay wasn't much, but the tips were good. All she needed was a place to stay until she could save up enough money for another apartment.

For thirty minutes her hopes were high, but after more than a mile of walking and still no sign of any church, she began to get nervous. Her feet were so cold she could no longer feel her toes, and though she'd dressed as warmly as possible in sweatpants and a sweatshirt and two pairs of socks, her lack of gloves and the bite of the wind against her flesh was taking its toll. And, as if that wasn't enough, to add insult to injury, it started to snow.

Minuscule bits of something that felt more like sleet than snow stung her eyes. She squinted and ducked her head against a cruel winter gust that parted her coat. With shaking hands, she yanked it back over her belly, as if trying to shelter the child she was carrying.

A garbage truck rumbled past her as she paused at a street corner to get her bearings. She told herself that the pain in her lower back didn't matter. The buildings looked festive in their Christmas decorations, but she didn't see anything that resembled a church. As she waited for the light to change, she couldn't help but wish she'd paid more attention to the route the bus had taken instead of putting on her makeup and adding the finishing touches to her hair as she'd ridden to work each day.

"There's got to be one around here somewhere," she said, and headed for a florist on the opposite side of the street to ask for directions.

As she stepped inside Red River Floral and closed the door behind her, the strains of "White Christmas" filled the air. She leaned against the door to rest, letting the warmth envelope her.

"Hi, honey, can I help you?"

China's focus shifted at the woman's approach. She was broad and tall, and had the reddest hair she'd ever seen. It took China a bit to realize that a goodly portion of her height came from the highly teased hairstyle.

"Um…yes, I hope so," China said. "I'm looking for a church."

The redhead grinned. "You lookin' to join it or…"

"No," China said. "I'm sort of lost, and I thought someone there could help me. I saw plenty of them when I rode the bus to work, but now I can't seem to find a single one."

"You ride the bus?" the redhead asked.

China nodded.

"Then why didn't you just get back on that bus and ride it to the church?"

China shrank within herself. Admitting she didn't have a dime to her name wasn't something she was comfortable with, especially to a stranger.

"I missed it, that's all," she said shortly. "Can you help me?"

The redhead's smile shifted slightly as compassion filled her eyes. "Well, sure. We'll go online and take us a look. How's that?"

China smiled. "I would appreciate it," she said softly, and unconsciously patted the swell of her belly as she followed the woman to the back of the store.

While they were in the midst of searching the yellow pages website, a bell jingled, signaling the appearance of another customer, and this time a paying one.

"Excuse me just a minute," the florist said, and moved toward the customer, leaving China alone at the counter.

She scanned the listings, one by one, trying to figure out where she was in accordance with the nearest churches. At this point she wasn't in a position to be picky about denomination; all she wanted from them was charity. She was still looking at addresses when the florist and the customer came to the counter.

"Find what you're looking for?" the florist asked.

China shrugged. "I'm not sure. Are any of these churches nearby?"

The customer, a tall, well-dressed woman in her midthirties, gave China an impatient stare.

"I'm in a hurry," she said, eyeing the florist.

"Yes, I'm sorry," the florist said, and began writing the work order.

"Do you mind?" the woman drawled, elbowing China out of the way in order to set her purse on the counter, then staring pointedly at China's bag on the floor between them.

The woman's attitude was nothing more than another slap in China's face, and for a woman who'd already had one too many blows to her self-esteem that day, it was one too many.

China picked up her bag and headed for the door without getting the address she'd come for.

"Wait, honey!" the florist called. "I'll be with you in a minute."

China paused, then turned, the length of the store carrying the clear, quiet tone of her message.

"Thank you for being so kind."

A frigid blast of wind and its accompanying sleet hit her squarely in the face, reminding her of why she'd sought shelter there. She'd wasted precious time and still didn't know any more now than she had when she went in. She hesitated, considering going back inside, when she caught a glimpse of herself in the store window. Her hair was wild and windblown, her cheeks reddened from exposure. Her all-around appearance was bedraggled. With the bag hanging over her shoulder, she looked like the homeless people she often saw walking the streets. And in that moment, the bitter truth of her situation hit.

She didn't just look like one. She had become one.

Chapter 2

As the sun began to set, China was forced to accept the truth that pride did go before a fall. If only she hadn't stormed out of the florist's before getting the information she needed, she might not be in this fix. From that realization, self-pity moved her thoughts in another direction.

If only her mother were still alive, she would never have gotten mixed up with a man like Tommy Fairheart. Her mother had always had a way of seeing through pretty words to the heart of a person. She'd left Clyde Shubert the day after he had nearly drowned China in the shower. She could still remember her mother apologizing to China over and over as they made their way to the bus station. The determination on her mother's face had been fierce and her faith in men definitely over. Mae wouldn't have been fooled by Tommy's pretty words as China had been.

China sighed as she stopped at a street corner, waiting for the light to change. She stomped her feet and stuffed her hands into the sleeves of her coat. Never would she take being warm for granted again.

As she stood, her thoughts drifted back to Tommy. When they'd first met, he'd been so sweet. In the beginning there wasn't anything he wouldn't do for her. She wasn't so sure she would have listened to her mother—not then. She had been ready for love—for her own life to begin. She was so willing to believe his good looks were a reflection of his soul. Obviously she'd been wrong.

The light changed. Just as she stepped off the curb into the street, a car came around a corner at a high rate of speed, skidding dangerously toward her on the snow-packed street. She jumped back to the curb just in time to keep from being hit as the tires sent a nasty mix of sand, salt and slushy snow onto the legs of her sweatpants.

"You jerk!" she shouted.

The girth of her belly was restricting, and she grunted as she bent down to brush off the mess. This time, when she stepped off the curb to cross, she made a hasty sprint to the other side, breathing a sigh of relief when her feet touched the sidewalk. She started walking. A few blocks back, someone had told her about an all-night mission in the area, and she needed to find it quick. Her lower back was throbbing, her belly was in knots and now her fingers were as numb as her feet.

The streets were well lit, and the bars she was passing seemed to be doing a healthy business. The sounds of holiday music seemed to be everywhere—spilling out of passing cars and from inside different establishments as the patrons came and went. More than once she had to sidestep rowdy crowds standing in front of the doors to continue down the street. The smell of food was making her nauseous, yet she knew she needed to eat.

A few blocks down, the patrons thinned out, as did the quality of the businesses. Her steps quickened as she moved past the varying signs over these darkened doors.

She'd ventured into the Oakcliff area—a place that people in the know called the Sunny South Side. Only it wasn't sunny, and it wasn't a place she wanted to be.

Topless dancers inside.

Lap dances.

Nude Strippers.

The Flip Side.

She'd seen plenty of these places before, but always from within the confines of a car or a bus. Never had her vulnerability been more evident. And just when she thought it couldn't get much worse, three young men stepped out of the shadows of a nearby alley. One grabbed her by the arm and began pulling her toward the darkness.

"Baby, baby, come 'ere to me…I'll show you how to stay warm."

"Let me go!" China cried, then kicked at his shins as she yanked her arm free and began to run.

He cursed in pain and bolted after her, catching her before she'd gone more than a few steps.

China screamed.

Anger slashed across his face, and he drew back his hand to silence her when one of the other men suddenly spoke.

"Let her go, Ruiz, she's got a baby in her belly."

The man called Ruiz snarled, "So much the better for me," and curled his hand in China's hair.

Then the man who'd spoken on China's behalf stepped into the light and curled his fingers around Ruiz's wrist. As the pair glared at each other, it became obvious to China that there was more than a physical struggle going on. The look that passed between the two was more of a challenge for dominance than for doing what was right.

Suddenly the pressure on her scalp ceased. Ruiz had turned her loose. She was free. Hastily, she reached down to pick up the bag that she'd dropped, but the man who'd spoken up on her behalf beat her to it. The look on his face made her take a hesitant step back.

Miguel Hernandez stared long and hard into the young woman's face, looking past the cold that had long ago pinched her features into frozen caricatures, then to the coat that was two sizes too small for her belly.

China held her breath, waiting to see if this savior was going to turn on her, too.

"Where is your man?" he asked.

The question was unexpected, and it cut to the pain China was carrying in her heart.

"I don't have one," she muttered.

The man pointed at her stomach. "Where is the man who put the baby in your belly?"

Her chin began to quiver. "I don't know. He stole my money and left a few days ago."

The man's dark eyes glittered. "Why are you here? It's not safe for a *chica* like you."

"A mission…someone told me there was an all-night mission."

"You have no home."

It wasn't a question. It was a statement. And it cut to China's heart like a knife. She tried to speak, but the words wouldn't come. She found herself staring at him through a thick wall of tears.

"Ahhh, don't cry," he said softly. "Come…" He led her out of the alley and back to the street, then pointed. "See? Just a few blocks away. You are almost there, little mama."

China looked in the direction he was pointing and saw the outline of a lit cross, bright against the skyline of Dallas like a beacon in the dark. It stood silhouetted against the neon debauchery like a lifeline for the lost. She started to shake. It was a normal reaction to the adrenaline rush, but it left her feeling breathless and weak.

"I see it," she said, and eyed her dark-eyed savior nervously.

He almost smiled. "When you get there, tell Father Doyle that Miguel said to treat you right."

"You are Miguel?"

He shrugged, as if remembering that, on the streets, identity was not something one easily gave away.

But China wasn't insulted by his lack of response. She glanced over his shoulder to the pair of men who'd slunk back into the shadows, then back at him. There was something in his eyes that told her he wasn't as far gone as the others. Caution told her to start walking, but she felt guilty at just walking away. Tentatively she touched his arm, feeling the strength of him through the layers of his coat.

"Thank you, Miguel, more than I can say."

A muscle jerked in his jaw, and his eyes suddenly glittered dangerously.

"Just get off the streets," he said, thrusting her bag into her hands, then disappearing into the alley.

China heard an angry exchange of voices and then receding footsteps. With a last nervous glance over her shoulder, she started walking, ever mindful of the snow-packed sidewalks and the baby she carried.

Two blocks came and went, and China's gaze stayed firmly fixed on the cross above the mission. The humble landmark promised warmth and safety and, if she was lucky, maybe some food. Because she was so focused on where she was going, she forgot to pay attention to where she was at.

One moment she was in midstride, and the next thing she knew she'd collided with a tall, elegant blonde in a full-length fur coat. Her bag slid off her shoulder onto the sidewalk as she scrambled to stay on her feet. Certain she was going to fall, she was surprised by the sudden impact of strong, gripping hands on her shoulders, steadying her stance.

"Careful there, honey," the blonde woman drawled. "You don't want to hurt yourself or that little baby in there."

"I'm so sorry. I didn't see you," China said.

The woman's smile was wry, but her drawl held a hint of laughter as she brushed the slight dusting of snow from her fur. Then she patted her hair, as if checking for disarray.

"Obviously."

China straightened her coat and bent to pick up her bag. As she did, she heard someone shouting and then the woman beside her starting to curse. Startled by the sound of someone running through the muck, she spun in fear. A series of lights began flashing, and she screamed. It took a few seconds for her to realize someone was only taking pictures.

To her horror, the blonde suddenly pulled a gun from her purse and fired three shots in rapid succession. The man with the camera staggered, then turned, trying to run. The last shot hit him square in the back. He dropped facedown in the street, sending a small shower of slush into the air as he hit. A pool of red began spilling out from beneath him, discoloring the snow.

China stared in disbelief, first at the blonde with the gun, then at the man in the street. Her mind kept telling her to run, but her feet wouldn't move. Instead, she pressed both hands over her mouth, willing herself not to scream. There had to be a logical explanation for what she'd just witnessed. The man must have been going to attack them. That was it. The blonde had been defending herself.

But when the woman leaned over the dead man and yanked the camera from around his neck, China knew that claiming self-defense would never fly. Pictures might be incriminating, but they were hardly lethal. She took a tentative step backward, and as she did, the blonde looked up, an expression of pure rage on her face, and China knew then that the danger she'd faced earlier with the three men was nothing to what she faced now.

"Please," China whispered, and unconsciously spread her hands across her stomach.

"Well, shit," the blonde drawled, and gave China's belly one last glance before taking aim.

"No!" China begged, and began moving backward. "I won't tell. I don't know you. I don't know him. I won't tell."

"Can't take the chance, darlin'," the blonde woman drawled. "But it's nothing personal."

China didn't feel the first shot, although it knocked her off her feet. The second shot hit high in her shoulder as she fell, ripping her flesh and ricocheting off the pavement beyond as it passed through her body. Pain was muted by the quickening onset of impending unconsciousness. She had a few fleeting moments of awareness, of staring up into the night sky and seeing thousands upon thousands of snowflakes coming toward her, just like the water from the shower all those years ago when Clyde had tried to drown her. Her head lolled to the right as a wave of weakness came over her. From the corner of her eye she could see the outline of the cross, and in that moment she knew she was going to die. Within seconds, the cross began to fade. A single tear slid from the corner of her right eye, and then everything got quiet—so quiet that China imagined she could hear the impact of each single snowflake as it fell against her face. In the distance came the sounds of running feet, but they would come too late.

The darkness was here, waiting for her to catch up.

She was tired—so tired—and so very, very cold.

Her eyelids fluttered once, twice, then closed.

A quiet sigh escaped from between her lips, and then it was over.

The air was warm—without gravity. China was moving without walking—floating toward a distant humming sound—when she heard a child call out for Mommy, shouting for her to wait.

She stopped and turned. A little dark-headed girl, who looked to be no more than three or four, was running toward her and laughing aloud. China smiled. Her daughter. Of course. What had she been thinking? She couldn't go without her. They clasped hands as if they'd done it countless times before and resumed their journey toward the distant rhythmic sound. It didn't seem strange that the child beside her was older than the child she'd been carrying. It was her baby, just the same.

They walked and talked, pointing at a bird sitting on a nearby tree, stopping to smell a patch of wildflowers nestled by the path. The longer they walked, the louder the sound became. Before long, China could just make out the sound of voices, and within a short time, she could hear what they were saying.

"Welcome...welcome. We've come to walk you home."

Joy flooded her as she bent down and picked her daughter up, suddenly anxious to reach them. The child's hair was thick and soft, and it blew against her cheek like

*so many strands of black silk, and then they were there
in the midst of the murmuring crowd.*

"China Mae, I'm so happy to see you, child."

China started to laugh. Mother. It was Mother.

"We're home, Mother, we're home," China said.

*The murmuring began again, only louder, encom-
passed by an ever-growing light. China stood in awe
of the illumination and knew a quiet recognition. Love
filled her as she lifted her face to the light, then everything began to change. Her daughter was in her arms
and then she was not. In fear, she saw her mother carrying her away.*

"Wait," China cried. "Wait for me."

*But the light blocked her path, and she couldn't move
through it.*

"No!" China begged. "Don't leave me here."

*Mae stopped and turned, her granddaughter perfectly
balanced on her hip.*

"It's not your time, China Mae. You have to go back."

*China had no time to protest. One moment she was
standing before the presence of God, and then she felt
herself falling...falling...back to the pain and the cold.*

And she was going alone.

Detective Bennett English pushed his way through
the gathering crowd and then slipped beneath a strip of
yellow crime scene tape, flashing his badge as he went.

"English. Homicide."

The patrolman on duty nodded to let him pass and then
turned his attention to some overzealous onlookers, forcing them back behind the barrier.

Ben shivered as he slogged his way through the muck
on the street, thankful he was wearing his boots instead
of street shoes. He approached a pair of officers stand-

ing near a parked ambulance. One of them was sipping coffee, while the other was using his baton to knock ice from the bottom of one shoe.

"I see you got the luck of the draw tonight, huh, English? Where's your buddy Fisher?"

"Home with the flu," Ben said, then pointed to the bodies. "What have we got?"

One of the officers shrugged. "Dead people," he said, then took another sip of his coffee. "No witnesses. No nothing, which is no surprise around here."

Ben gave the area a quick glance. It was true. This part of the city was not a hangout for Dallas's more law-abiding citizens.

"Hell of a night to die," the other officer said.

Ben frowned. "Is there ever a good time?" he asked, then turned, looking toward the blanket-covered body in the street.

"Do we know who they are?"

"That one's a male. The medical examiner is almost through with him. As soon as he is, we'll check for ID."

Ben nodded, pointing toward the other body on the sidewalk and the paramedics hovering around it.

"What about that one?"

"Woman—mid to late twenties—pregnant."

As cold as he was, Ben felt a deeper sort of chill invade his body.

"Damn," he muttered, as he gave the paramedics a closer look. "So we're looking at three deaths and not two."

Suddenly there was a flurry of activity around the woman. Ben moved closer to the scene.

"What's going on?" he asked.

"We've got a live one," one of the paramedics said, as they began moving her toward a gurney.

Ben's focus shifted. If she lived, it would make getting answers to this mess a whole lot easier. As they pushed her past him on the way to the ambulance, he glanced at her face.

Even with the snow melting on her cheeks and plastering her hair to her head, she was beautiful. She had a small straight nose above lips softly parted, and eyelashes so black and thick they looked like shadows. Her cheeks were pale and pinched from the cold, but the delicate cut of her features was impossible to miss, as was the small, perfect dimple in the middle of her chin.

Ben's gaze moved from her face to the wound near her shoulder. His gaze dropped from that to her abdomen and the wide slash of red staining her coat.

"What about the baby?" he asked.

The medic shook his head as they moved past.

Sadness quickened. He could only imagine her despair if she lived—waking up in a hospital and learning that she had survived while her baby had not. He shifted his stance and looked away, unwilling to pursue his thoughts. He was letting his emotions interfere with his objectivity, and that was something he couldn't afford.

As he watched, the last paramedic climbed inside and reached out to close the ambulance doors.

"Where are you taking her?" Ben yelled.

"Parkland," he said.

Within seconds they were gone, speeding away into the night with a woman in need of a miracle.

Ben took out his notebook and moved back toward the body in the street. The ME was leaving. He caught him at the door of his car.

"Hey, Gregson, got a minute?"

Bob Gregson looked up. "Evening, English. Where's your shadow?"

"Red's down with the flu. What can you tell me about the victim?"

"He died of multiple gunshot wounds. Won't know which one did him in until we do an autopsy, but I doubt it matters. Someone wanted him dead real bad and kept shooting until the job was done."

"Send a copy of the autopsy to my office, okay?"

"Don't hold your breath," Gregson muttered, as he slid behind the wheel of his car. "We're backed up as it is."

Ben empathized with the frustration in the ME's voice, but knowing as much as possible within the first twenty-four hours of a homicide was crucial to solving the case. The coroner drove away as Ben moved back to the body.

"Find any ID on him?" Ben asked.

One of the officers handed him a plastic bag with a wallet and a couple of business cards inside.

"Some guy named Finelli…Charles Finelli."

Ben's pulse surged.

"Wait," he said, and reached down, unzipping the body bag just enough to view the victim's face. He grunted in disbelief.

"You know him?" one of the officers asked.

"By reputation," Ben said. "He's a bartender by trade and a psycho with a camera by night. He's been booked a half-dozen times for trespassing. Thinks he's some sort of Hollywood paparazzi type. Was there a camera on him?"

They all shook their heads in denial.

"Did you search the area?"

"We looked all over," an officer said. "When we first arrived on the scene, we figured this for a domestic situation. You know…a man, a pregnant woman, probably an argument gone wrong. But neither one of them had a gun. We canvassed the area for everything from witnesses to gum wrappers, and if there'd been a camera to be found, we would have it." He motioned toward the sky and the snow still falling. "Even the hookers took the night off, and according to the bunch inside the bar, no one heard a thing."

Ben nodded. "Figures. No one ever wants to get involved. What about ID on the woman?"

"No purse, but she had this bag. We found it on the sidewalk near her body. Haven't had time to go through it."

They handed Ben the duffel bag and moved toward their patrol cars. They'd secured the scene, passed along all they knew to the detective division. It was Homicide's problem now.

Ben tossed the bag into the trunk of his car, along with the plastic bag containing Charles Finelli's personal effects. He would take it all to headquarters as soon as he made a few inquiries of his own inside the bar.

A few officers were still on-site as he stepped inside. It was a sleazy, inconsequential establishment, unremarkable in any respect except for the sign over the door—a bright-blue parrot in flight and the words *The Blue Parrot* glowing a bright neon-orange beneath.

He paused inside, ignoring the smoke and welcoming the enveloping warmth. The underlying murmur of voices silenced almost immediately as several patrons at the bar turned to stare. Their judgment was silent and brief. Moments later they turned back to their drinks, but the silence continued.

Ben stifled a sigh. Obviously he'd already been made, which did not bode well for getting any questions answered. He moved toward the bar.

"What'll it be?" the bartender asked.

"Got any coffee?" Ben asked.

"No."

"Then I pass," Ben said.

The bartender shrugged and started to move away when Ben laid his badge on the counter. The bartender looked at the badge then up at Ben, obviously unimpressed.

"Two people were gunned down in front of your place about twenty minutes ago," Ben said.

The bartender's stare never wavered. "Yeah, so I heard."

"Don't suppose you heard the shots?"

"I don't suppose I did," the bartender drawled.

"Then who called the cops?" Ben asked.

The bartender shrugged. "Some guy came in off the street, said there were two bodies in the snow. I showed him where the phone was. He used it. That's all I know."

"Is he still here?" Ben asked.

"Nope."

"Can you tell me what he looked like?"

"Nope."

Ben had to resist the urge to grab the bartender's shirt and shake that insolent tone out of his voice.

He turned around and raised his voice so that it could be heard throughout the small room.

"Anybody in here see what happened outside?"

Nobody answered.

"Anybody hear anything…like gunshots…or a car speeding away?"

Total silence.

"Well now," Ben drawled. "I want to thank you for your assistance. I know the young woman they just took to the hospital will appreciate knowing how much cooperation you gave toward finding the person who just shot her unborn baby to death inside her belly."

Ben laid his card down on the corner of the bar and

walked out, disgusted with them and with the human race in general. He was halfway to his car before he realized it had stopped snowing. The streets were eerily silent, making the sound of his own footsteps seem ominous as he stomped through three inches of snow. As he unlocked his car, a cat squalled from a nearby alley. Instinctively, he spun, reaching toward the semiautomatic he wore in a shoulder holster under his coat, but there was no one there. Silently cursing Red for succumbing to the flu, he slid behind the wheel and drove away.

Chapter 3

Ben hit the period key on his computer keyboard, then leaned back in his chair, eyeing the report he'd just finished. The shooting down in Oakcliff wasn't the worst case he'd ever worked, but there was something about it that bothered him more than usual. His gaze moved from the computer to the wallets next to his phone. Notifying next of kin sucked.

Charles Finelli's father lived in Krebs, Oklahoma, a small, predominately Italian community known for thriving vineyards and fabulous food. Anthony Finelli had cried when Ben informed him of his only son's demise. After several phone calls he'd learned that there was no one left to cry for China Brown.

He picked up the old red wallet he'd found in her bag and opened it again, as he had off and on for the past hour and a half. It was thin and cracked and held together with a large rubber band. No money inside, and the picture on her driver's license was typical of most—a self-conscious smile in the process of being born—but the tumble of thick, dark hair framing a delicate face was not. Even there, her beauty was evident.

He laid it aside and then leaned forward, resting his elbows on the desk and closed his eyes, and still he couldn't rid himself of China Brown.

Last known address—no longer valid.

He thought of the landlord he'd spoken to earlier. What a jerk, evicting a pregnant woman into the snow. According to the landlord, the boyfriend was a guy named Tommy Fairheart, who'd gotten her pregnant and skipped out on her days earlier, taking all her money with him.

Ben stood abruptly, grabbed his coffee cup off the desk and headed toward the break room. He hoped they both burned in hell.

The coffee was bitter, but it was hot, and for now it was enough. He sipped it slowly, expecting the warmth to envelop him. Instead, the image of China Brown's snow-covered face slipped into his mind. He shuddered instead. God, would he ever be warm again?

He glanced at his watch. It was already morning. He needed to go home, get some food and a shower, at least pretend to sleep. But he knew sleep would be long in coming, if at all. So much about this shooting didn't ring true, and the detective in him couldn't turn loose of the puzzle, not even for the night.

Suddenly he set his cup down on the cabinet and strode to his desk, yanked his coat from the back of the chair and headed for the door. There was something he needed to do before he could sleep.

The nurse on desk duty in the ICU unit of Parkland Hospital was monitoring a patient's erratic heart rate when the doors to the unit swung open. She stood abruptly, eyeing the tall, tousled-haired man with dismay.

"I'm sorry, sir, but you can't just come in here like this. Visiting hours aren't for another hour and…"

He flashed his badge.

"I don't care who you are," she said. "I don't have any patients healthy enough for interrogation."

"I didn't come to talk," he said softly. "I just need to see her."

The nurse frowned. "See who?"

"China Brown…the pregnant woman who was shot."

The nurse's expression shifted, alarming Ben.

"She's still alive…isn't she?"

The nurse nodded. "But her baby didn't make it."

"Yeah, I know," Ben said. "What's her condition?"

The nurse checked the chart. "Critical." Then she gave Ben a pleading look. "Please, Detective English, you have to leave."

He turned, searching the beds for a glimpse of her face.

"Where is she?" he asked.

"Fourth one from the end."

He took an impulsive step forward, then stopped when the nurse touched his coat sleeve, giving his arm a gentle squeeze. "Come back tomorrow."

He hesitated before nodding, his shoulders drooping with fatigue.

"Yeah, maybe I'd better. Sorry for the interruption. It's just that she's been on my mind ever since the—" He stopped, unwilling to bare his soul to a stranger.

"It's a tragedy about the baby," she said softly. "It was a little girl."

Ben nodded. Halfway out the door he stopped and turned. He knew the routine. The baby would have been taken by Caesarian and sent to the morgue for an autopsy, even though it would have been assumed that the shooting was the cause of death. But then afterward…?

"About the baby…"

"Yes?"

"She doesn't have any next of kin—Miss Brown, I mean."

The nurse stood her ground. "I don't know about that, sir. You'll need to check with the doctor who handled the surgery."

"What's his name?" Ben asked.

"Dr. Ross Pope."

"I'll talk to him in the morning," Ben said. "In the meantime, if it matters, I'll take responsibility for claiming the body until Miss Brown is able."

"Yes, sir, I'll make a note of your name for the records."

Ben glanced back at the bed where China Brown was lying, then handed the nurse his card.

"If there's any change—any change at all—I want to be notified. My home and office number are there. Call either, anytime."

She clipped the card to China's chart.

Ben stood for a moment, staring down the length of the room to the woman on the fourth bed from the end, then stalked out as abruptly as he'd come in.

Bobby Lee Wakefield looked good and he knew it. The Armani suit he was wearing fit perfectly, accentuating his slim, wiry build and making his legs look even longer. The thousand-dollar Justin boots he was wearing were an affectation with the suit, but, here in Texas, quite appropriate.

He gave himself one last look in the mirror, smoothed his hands on both sides of his hair to pat down any loose ends and then headed for his desk. Ainsley Been, his campaign manager, would be here any moment to escort him to the Wyndham Anatole, where the press would be waiting. It was an elegant hotel, worthy of the announcement he was going to make. He glanced at his speech, then tossed it aside. He knew the damned thing by heart. He'd been planning it for years.

Bobby Lee Wakefield had come a long way from being a wildcatter's son from Amarillo, Texas. Wearing clothes all through his school years that had been bought from the Goodwill store had not endeared him to any of his classmates, and he'd been far away in the deserts of the Middle East when his daddy finally struck it rich. Coming home to luxury had been as foreign as the jungle he'd nearly died in. He had taken one look at the elegance of their new home and known instinctively that it would take more than an endless supply of money for his family to match their surroundings. Within six months of coming home, he'd enrolled at Southern Methodist University and never looked back. Interning for every politician who would have him on staff had occupied his summers, and by the time he was ready to graduate, he had more than a foot in the door of state government. By the time he was thirty-five, he was serving his second term in the House of Representatives, and by his forty-second birthday he had been elected to a seat in the Senate. Here in Dallas, the city was his. He'd been divorced for years, was wealthy and handsome, popular as hell on Capitol Hill—and he was about to announce his plans to run for president of the United States of America.

His daddy would have been proud.

Just as he checked the time, the door to his office flew back, hitting the wall with a reverberating thud. He didn't have to look up to know who'd just entered, although he turned to face her.

The tall, elegant blonde in white silk sauntered into the

room in a cloud of expensive perfume. His eyes narrowed, and he stifled a curse. Daddy had never known what to do with the woman, and God help him, neither did he.

"Mother, did it ever occur to you to knock?"

Mona Wakefield blew him a kiss and sidled up to where he was standing, pulled her long blond hair over her shoulder and offered him her back.

"Bobby Lee, honey, I do not knock on doors in my own house. Now zip this up for me like a good boy. I want to be ready when Ainsley comes."

Bobby Lee gawked. There wasn't enough back to the dress she was wearing to warrant a zipper, much less anything else.

"Hell's fire, Mother, you are not wearing this to my press conference. You look like a hooker."

Mona shrugged, glancing over her shoulder and batting her eyes.

"Maybe a call girl—an expensive call girl—but not a hooker. Besides, how many sixty-eight-year-old women do you know who look as good as me? I'll tell you how many. None. Now zip me up and stop telling me what to do."

Bobby Lee grabbed her by the shoulders and spun her around.

"You get that goddamned thing off now and put something else on, or so help me, I'll have Waymon lock you in your room. You want to stand by my side and bask in the so-called 'glory' of being Senator Wakefield's mother, then you'd better be wearing something more suited to the occasion."

A dark angry flush stained her cheeks as she stared him in the face. To an observer, they would have appeared quite similar. Their tall, slender bodies were firm, their facial silhouettes surprisingly alike. High foreheads, straight noses, stubborn chins.

Their staring match was a draw until suddenly Mona shrugged.

"You don't like it? Fine. I'll find something else."

She tilted first one shoulder down and then the other, defiantly letting her dress fall down around her ankles in a puddle of white silk. Only after she saw shock replace Bobby Lee's anger did she turn and saunter out of his office as calmly as she'd come in. The fact that she was wearing nothing but high-heeled sling-back shoes, see-through underwear and the white lace garter belt holding up her hose didn't seem to faze her.

Just as she disappeared from sight, the doorbell rang, echoing throughout the downstairs portion of the mansion.

"Jesus Christ," Bobby Lee muttered and grabbed her dress off the floor. Ainsley was here.

He dashed into the hall, grabbed the maid on her way to the door and stuffed the dress in her arms.

"Delia, you make damn sure my mother gets something decent on, you hear? Don't let her downstairs until she does!"

Delia nodded and took the dress on the run. Working in this household was crazy, but the pay was good, and she never got bored.

Bobby Lee hesitated, waiting until he was sure that his mother's bare backside was no longer visible, then he pasted on a smile and strode toward the door.

"Ainsley, you look ready for war, boy," he drawled, affecting his best Texas good-old-boy routine. "Cook has a fine bunch of snacks in the library. Why don't you go on in and make yourself at home? I'll just tell Mother you're here."

Ainsley Been smiled and smoothed a hand down the front of his vest as he aimed for the library. Being hired as Wakefield's campaign manager had been a coup. It would be his first presidential campaign, but if he did this right, hopefully not his last.

"Thank you, Bobby Lee, I believe I will have myself a little snack. I missed my lunch today." He moved on as he'd been directed, unaware of the undercurrents in the senator's household.

Within the hour, the trio was in a white stretch limousine and headed toward the hotel, where the press were awaiting their arrival. Mona was sitting opposite the men, her long legs crossed, her anger still high. She stared out the window, refusing to meet her son's gaze. She'd come downstairs in a two-piece suit, as her son had requested, sauntering across the floor in her black stiletto heels to meet the men. The fact that the skirt was three inches above her knees and the jacket's top button was just below the beginning of her cleavage was bad enough. But it was the fabric about which Bobby Lee was most pissed. Black leather. He was announcing his candidacy for president, and his mother was going to be standing at his side in black leather. All she needed was a whip and a Harley to complete the image.

"Well, now," Ainsley said as the driver pulled up to the front of the hotel. "We're here. Y'all put on a smilin' face and let's knock 'em dead."

Bobby Lee took a deep breath and gave his mother a warning glance. She arched an eyebrow, then smiled.

"Now, Ainsley, I'm here merely to lend support. After all, this is my son's night."

Ainsley smiled broadly. "Yes, it is, and you must be very proud."

Mona looked at her son then, at the glitter in his eyes

and the muscle jerking at the side of his jaw. She gave him a wink. To her delight, she could see him struggling to stay angry.

"Of course I'm proud of him. What mother wouldn't be?" she said.

Bobby Lee shook his head, then grinned wryly. When all was said and done, whatever Mona did, it was going to be done her way or else.

"Thank you, Mother."

"You're quite welcome, Bobby Lee. Now let's go give those reporters something to talk about. Put a smile on that handsome face and strut your stuff."

"Yes, ma'am."

The door to the limousine opened.

Ainsley looked at Bobby Lee and then gave him a thumbs-up.

"After you," he said.

Bobby Lee took a deep breath. By the time he was out of the car, his smile was as wide as his steps were long. He entered the hotel with flashbulbs going off in his face and never looked back to see if they were following. He was on a mission that would not be deterred.

It was ten minutes past seven in the morning when Ben once again approached the ICU. The nurse who'd been on duty last night was gone and another was in her place. Ben flashed his badge and was asking about China's condition as a doctor came in on his morning rounds. Ben took one look at the name tag on the slim, sandy-haired man's lab coat and gave him his full attention. It was Ross Pope, the man who'd operated on China.

"Dr. Pope?"

"Yes?"

Ben extended his hand. "Detective Bennett English,

Homicide Division. I'm handling the case involving China Brown, the woman you operated on last night."

Dr. Pope frowned. "I hope you're here to tell me you have the bastard who shot her in custody."

"No, not yet, but we will."

Ross Pope sighed. "What can I do for you?"

"Grant me permission to see her."

The doctor's frown deepened. "Absolutely not. She's in a drug-induced coma. There's no way she can assist you in your investigation and no guarantee that she will remember what happened when she does wake up."

Ben shook his head. "You misunderstand me," he said. "I don't want to talk to her."

"Are you family?" Pope asked.

"As far as we can ascertain, she doesn't have any," Ben said.

Pope frowned. "Then if she can't talk, why the need to visit?"

Ben hesitated, then glanced toward the ward. He could barely see the outline of her body beneath the sheets.

"Will she live?" he asked.

"Barring any unforeseen complications, I would say yes."

"When will she wake up?"

"When her body has had more time to heal, we will decrease the medications. After that, it will be up to her. She'll come back when she's ready."

Ben thrust his hand through his hair, disheveling the style into spiky disarray. A look of confusion came and went on his face, but he didn't know it. All he knew was that seeing her—touching her—was necessary.

"Look, I can't explain it," he said. "But I keep feeling like I need to be there—maybe it's more for me than for her, but she doesn't have anyone else. From what we've gathered, the father of her baby abandoned her. Her land-lord evicted her yesterday morning, and by nightfall she was near death. Her baby is dead, and she doesn't even know it yet. When she wakes up, well…it just doesn't seem right that she suffer that alone."

Pope's gaze narrowed as he gave Ben a studied stare. He hesitated briefly, then turned to the nurse on duty.

"Make a note on China Brown's chart that Detective English be allowed to see Miss Brown at his discretion." He tapped a finger against Ben's chest. "I'm trusting that you will have sense enough not to abuse the privilege you've been given."

Ben resisted an overwhelming urge to grin. "Yes, sir, that you can."

"Fine, then. Follow me. I'll check on her condition, and then you may have exactly five minutes at her bedside. I'd advise you to be careful of what you say, if anything. We know now that comatose patients often hear what is going on around them without being able to communicate. Keep that in mind. I don't want anything making matters worse for her."

"You can trust me," Ben said.

Pope almost smiled. "Yes…well…it seems I've already done that. Don't disappoint me."

Ben nodded, then followed Dr. Pope to China's bed-side. She was a far cry from the bloody, snow-covered woman he'd seen being taken away in the ambulance last night, and yet not so different after all. She was still so very small. So very silent. So very hurt.

He watched the doctor's every move with interest, not-ing his thorough study of her chart and then the tender manner in which he checked her wounds.

Ben caught a glimpse of pewter-colored staples and winced. He didn't give a damn what modern medicine had to say about the benefits of using metal as opposed to the old-fashioned sutures. They looked grotesque, and he imagined they would hurt like hell. For the first time since this whole thing began, he was glad China Brown didn't know what was happening. At least for now, she couldn't feel the pain of the trauma her body had endured.

With one last warning look, Dr. Pope moved away to check his other patients, leaving Ben alone by China's bed.

Ben took a deep breath and then let himself look, marking every feature of her face for future reference, noting the delicate shape and the dark, winged eyebrows slightly knitted over the bridge of her nose.

He brushed his thumb along the length of one of her fingers. When it twitched, his pulse jumped. Although it was nothing more than an unconscious reaction to stimulus, it startled him just the same. He leaned over and very carefully lifted a strand of her hair from the corner of her mouth, smoothing it back against her head, then whispered very quietly near her ear.

"I'm here, China Brown. You're safe…and you aren't alone."

Rationally, he had not expected anything, but when she gave no reaction to the sound of his voice, his spirits fell. He straightened up, but he didn't move back. Instead, he laid his hand upon hers and took solace in the warmth of her flesh.

The drug-induced coma she was in was allowing her badly battered body to heal. But it was her sanity that Bennett English was most concerned with. When she woke, and Dr. Pope had assured him that this would take place, would she remember what had happened to her? Would she be able to identify the man who'd shot her and killed Charles, aka Chaz, Finelli, or would the trauma and shock of losing her baby and very nearly her life block everything else from her mind? Only time would tell. Unfortunately, time was not on Ben's side. With every passing hour, the chance of finding the person who'd committed the crime grew slimmer.

It wasn't until someone touched his sleeve that he realized his time was up.

"Sorry," he said softly. "I was lost in thought."

"It happens a lot in here," the nurse said. "You can come back later, but for now, you need to leave."

"I'll be back," he said softly, and gave China's hand a soft squeeze.

It didn't make sense, but his heart was lighter as he pulled out of the parking lot on his way to headquarters. Nothing had changed. The woman was still their only witness and, for now, she wasn't talking. But there at her bedside this morning, he'd made a connection with her that he didn't want to lose.

A half hour later he turned down Commerce Street, then pulled into the parking lot of the Dallas P.D., avoiding a melting snowdrift as he parked. He was halfway to the door when his partner, Red Fisher, came striding out and waved him down.

"Saw you pulling in from the window," Red said. "Thought I'd save us both some time and come to meet you."

Ben grinned. "Glad to see you back, but what's the rush?"

Red waved a piece of paper in Ben's face. "I was halfway through reading the report on the Oakcliff shooting when this call came in. You can fill me in on the rest as we drive."

"Where are we going?" Ben asked.

"To see Finelli's girlfriend. She called this morning

to report him missing. When they broke the news to her, she got hysterical."

Ben slid behind the wheel and closed the door as Red got in on the passenger side, still talking.

"Anyway, from some of the stuff she was screaming about, the captain thought we might get a lead on the shooter from her."

"Didn't know he had a girlfriend," Ben said.

Red nodded. "According to her, they've been living together for about a year or so. Maybe she'll know why Finelli was down in that part of town last night."

"Maybe," Ben said, and then turned all his attention to maneuvering through the slushy streets.

A short while later, he pulled to the curb in front of an apartment complex and parked. Gang graffiti was everywhere. On walls, on the sidewalks, even on a couple of parked cars near the back of the lot.

"Jeez," Red muttered. "Rita and I lived in this complex the first two years of our marriage, but it didn't look like this."

"How many years ago was that?" Ben asked.

"Nearly fifteen," Red said. "Garland has changed a lot in the last fifteen years."

Ben thought of China Brown, who became a victim her first night on the streets.

"Fifteen years, hell," he muttered. "A lot can happen between one breath and the next."

Red gave his partner an odd, studied glance. It was unlike Bennett English to be so emotional.

"You all right?" he asked.

Ben shook off his anger and gave Red a grin. "You're the one who's been sick," he said. "Better be worrying about yourself. Now let's go see the lady. What's her name again?"

Red consulted his notes. "Jackie Porter—apartment 610."

Ben rolled his eyes. "Five bucks says the place doesn't have a working elevator."

Red grinned. "I'll give you ten to ride it if it does."

Ben laughed. It was good to have his partner back on the job.

Jackie Porter was still bawling and about ten minutes from a nervous breakdown when her doorbell rang. She jumped reflexively at the sound, then started howling even louder. By the time she got to the door, she was as close to hysterics as a woman could get and not be locked up.

"Who is it?" she yelled, then blew her nose so loud she didn't hear the answer. "Who?" she repeated, then stood on her tiptoes to look through the peephole in the door.

"Dallas P.D., Miss Porter. May we come in?"

She could see their shields and their faces, although it was like looking at them through a fishbowl. Hiccuping on a sob, she undid the locks and the security chain, opened the door, then stepped back to let them in.

"Is it true? Is Chaz really dead?"

Ben steeled himself and nodded.

She let out a wail and covered her face with her hands as Red closed the door behind them. Ben took her by the elbow and led her toward the sofa.

"Please, let's sit down," Ben said.

Jackie Porter fell backward with a plop and reached for a fresh handful of tissues. The men waited while she blew and wiped and managed to compose herself.

"Miss Porter, can I get you some water?" Red asked.

She shook her head. "No, I'll be fine, but thank you," she muttered, then gave her nose a last dainty blow.

"Your name is Jackie, right?" he asked.

She set up a little straighter and wadded the tissues in her hand into a ball.

"It's Jackwilyn Kate Porter, spelled J-A-C-K-W-I-L-Y-N, but everyone calls me Jackie. My mama was a huge fan of *Charlie's Angels* back in the old days. She named me for that Jaclyn Smith woman, and for Kate Jackson, only she spelled it different. Those were her two favorite angels. Mama didn't go for blondes."

Ben wouldn't look at Red. He knew if he did, he might grin, and this visit was no laughing matter.

"Anyway, Chaz and I were supposed to go get some barbecue and then go see a movie last night. At the last minute, he called to tell me he had a hot lead."

Ben looked up. "Hot lead?"

Jackie nodded. "Yeah, you know…if someone famous was out and about in the city, Chaz wanted to be on hand to take photos. He got paid good money for them. I know, because sometimes he had me deposit the cash." She sniffed a bit, then continued. "He was going to be famous like those photographers who work for the tabloids." Her chin quivered as a fresh set of tears began to roll. "I knew something was wrong when he didn't come home last night. He always called if he was going to be late."

Ben had his notebook out and his pen in hand when he spoke. "So you were living together?"

She nodded. "For almost a year."

Ben glanced at his notes. "But this isn't the address that was in his wallet."

"Yeah, I know. He kept his old apartment, but he used it as sort of an office. It was where he developed all his pictures. He kept his cameras and files there, too, I think."

"What kind of files?" Red asked.

"I don't know. About his work, I guess."

"So you know for sure he had his camera with him last night?"

"He must have. The only time he ever stood me up was when he was going to take pictures…and I understood, you know. It was his calling. Chaz was real good at what he did."

A few minutes later, after they'd gotten all the information they could from Jackie Porter, including the key to Finelli's apartment and the make of camera he would probably have been carrying, Red arose from his seat and handed her his card.

"If there's anything else you can think of that might help us find the person who shot Mr. Finelli, please give us a call," Red said. "My office number and cell number are both on the card. Call anytime."

"Thanks," Jackie said, and followed the detectives to the door.

They had started down the hall toward the stairs when she called out to them. They stopped and turned.

"Yes, ma'am?" Ben asked.

"When you arrest the man who did this…will you let me know?"

"You'll know," Ben said.

She managed a smile and then nodded before shutting the door. They heard the sound of four locks being turned. Red glanced at the graffiti on the walls and rolled his eyes.

Ben grinned. "What? You some kind of art critic now? At least it matches the exterior of the place just fine."

Red chuckled and shook his head.

When they reached the elevator, they hesitated, gave each other a questioning look, then headed for the stairs. The idea of two cops being stranded in an elevator in a building like this was something like offering to be targets for some gun-happy gang-banger. Neither man breathed easy until they were in the car and driving away.

"So, what do you think?" Red asked, as Ben braked for a red light.

"I don't know," Ben said. "Finelli didn't have a camera on him when the EMTs got to him. Maybe he was shot for the camera and China Brown just happened to be in the wrong place at the wrong time."

"Yeah...maybe." Red leaned over and turned up the heat. "Or maybe he was playing fast and loose with Ms. Brown. Maybe the kid she was carrying was Finelli's. Maybe Brown's boyfriend found out, they had a fight and he split. Maybe Brown was meeting Finelli to get help."

Ben snorted beneath his breath. "Damn, Red, what the hell kind of flu medicine are you taking? I've never heard so much baloney come out of your mouth at one time since you badmouthed the Slickers in their last Super Bowl."

Red frowned. "Just because I'm not a Dallas Slickers fan does not make me stupid. So I was reaching a little with my last theory. So what. It's possible."

But Ben wouldn't budge. "Not her," he said. "She wouldn't cheat."

"Who? Jackie Porter?"

"No. China Brown."

Red turned in the seat and stared at his partner as if he'd never seen him before.

"Now how the hell do you know something like that?"

Ben shifted restlessly, then shrugged. "Call it a hunch, okay?"

"Did you hear what you just said?"

Ben turned onto the freeway and then glanced at his watch.

"Are you hungry?" he asked.

"I'm always hungry," Red said. "And you didn't answer my question."

"While you're deciding where we're going to eat, I'm going to make a quick stop."

"Where at?" Red asked.

"Parkland Hospital. I want to check on China's condition."

"China? We're calling her China now?"

"Red, we've been partners for the better part of twelve years now, right?"

"Yeah, but what's that got to do with—"

"And have I ever asked you to trust me on something that wasn't right?"

Red sighed. "No."

"Then let this go." Ben took the exit to the hospital and headed down the street with single-minded intent.

Red threw up his hands and leaned back in the seat. "Fine," he muttered, then added, "are you buying?"

Ben grinned. "Maybe."

"Then I'm having steak. Chicken-fried steak."

"I thought Rita had you on a low-fat diet?" Ben said.

"You have your secrets, I have mine," Red muttered.

Ben parked and got out of the car. "I won't be long."

"Oh, no, you don't," Red said. "I'm coming with you. I want to see this woman for myself."

Chapter 4

Red watched his partner's face as they rode the elevator up to ICU. There was a muscle jerking at the side of Ben's jaw, and his gaze was fixed. The car jolted slightly as it came to a halt, and when the doors opened, Ben English strode through them in haste. Red shook his head as he followed. Ben's behavior was bordering on obsessive, and that made Red nervous.

But Ben didn't care what his partner thought. What mattered most to him was catching the person responsible for the murders and making sure China Brown came to no more harm. As they neared the nurses' station, he lengthened his stride. By the time they arrived, Red was all but running to keep up.

"It's a good thing we didn't have to go any farther," Red muttered, as they waited for the nurse on duty to finish her phone call. "I'm all out of breath."

Ben glanced over at Red and grinned. "Too many chicken-fried steaks."

Red glared. "No, I'm just too damned short. You're what…at least a couple of inches over six feet. I'm five-seven. My legs are half as long as yours, and I have to take two steps to your one. Chicken-fried steak, my ass."

Ben glanced down at his partner. "Not so much your ass as your belly."

Red shook his head and then chuckled. It was impossible to get ahead of this man. Before he could think of a good comeback, the nurse on duty hung up the phone.

"May I help you?" she asked.

Ben flashed his badge. "Detectives English and Fisher to see China Brown," he said.

"I'm sorry, but only two visitors at a time in ICU, and there's someone with her now."

Ben spun, staring intently through the glass to the ward beyond. He could just make out the figure of a man leaning over her bed.

"Who is he?"

The nurse shook her head. "He didn't say."

Ben's belly knotted. "That woman is the only witness to a murder. Do you let in anybody who presents themselves?"

The nurse looked nervous. "I don't have any orders to the contrary," she said.

Ben leaned over the desk, his voice hoarse with worry. "Either you go get him out of there now, or I'll do it for you."

She jumped up from her chair and bolted through the doors. Seconds later, she was at China's bedside. Ben had his cell phone in hand and was making a call as the nurse began escorting the man toward the door. By the time they reached the exit, he'd already requested a guard for China.

"Easy, partner," Red said. "It's probably the boyfriend. Remember…the one who skipped out on her. Now and then the jerks do get a guilty conscience."

But the young, thin Latino coming through the doors didn't look like a man filled with remorse. He looked nervous.

Ben stepped in front of him, blocking his way. "Detective Bennett English, Homicide. This is my partner, Detective Fisher. If you'd step this way, we'd like to ask you some questions."

The color faded from beneath the young man's skin, leaving it a pale, ashy gray.

"I don't know nothin'," he said shortly.

"Let us be the judge of that," Ben said, and lightly clasped his arm as they led him toward a nearby waiting room.

As soon as they were inside, they sat him down, then pulled up their chairs so they were both facing him. The implication was plain. He wasn't going anywhere until the officers were through.

"What's your name?" Ben asked. "And how do you know China Brown?"

The young Latino glared, but this time it was anger that fed his emotions.

"¿Hablo Englese?" Red asked.

The man's gaze shifted from Ben to Red, and as it did, a look of disdain replaced his fear.

"Yes, I speak English," he said. *"¿Habla usted español?"*

Red looked a bit taken aback and then shrugged.

"Well, then," the man said, "looks like I'm one up on you."

Ben slid his foot between the young man's outstretched legs and leaned forward. The motion of dominance was impossible to mistake.

"If you two are through with your pissing contest, then

I want some answers. What's your name, and how do you know China Brown?"

At that point, all the fight seemed to go out of the young man. His shoulders slumped, and he leaned forward, resting his elbows on his knees as he looked down at the floor. When he looked up, Ben was surprised to see tears in his eyes.

"Miguel. My name is Miguel Hernandez. I didn't know her. Not really."

"Do you always visit people in the hospital who you don't know?" Ben asked.

"Look, man, it's like this. Me and my home boys were down cruising Oakcliff the other night and this *chica* comes out of nowhere. Ruiz, he starts hitting on her, but I saw her belly." He looked away, then back at Ben, almost defiant. "My sister, she's going to have a baby. I guess I felt sorry for the woman, okay?"

Oddly enough, Ben was starting to believe the man's story. "So you played Galahad, then what?" he asked.

Miguel frowned. "I don't know this Galahad, and I haven't *played* since I was *cinco*...five. I told Ruiz to get lost and then told the little mama to go home."

Ben thought of the woman in ICU. Poor China Brown. She would never be a little mama now.

"Then what?" he asked.

Miguel shrugged. "She said she had no home. I asked her where was the man who put the baby in her belly. She said he stole her money and ran away."

Now Ben was beginning to believe him. This coincided with the little bit they'd learned from China's ex-landlord.

"What was she doing down in that part of town?" Ben asked.

"Looking for an all-night mission. She was cold. She

was hungry. She was looking to God to protect her."
Miguel stood abruptly. His voice was hard, his expression bitter. "God. There is no God. Where was God when the little mama was in danger?"

Ben stood and followed Miguel to a window overlooking the parking lot.

"I don't have any answers for you," Ben said. "But I want some answers from you. Why are you here?"

Miguel spun angrily. "Because I should have walked with her. I thought about it. It wasn't far to the mission from where we stood. I showed her the cross on the building, then I walked away from her. If I'd gone with her, none of this would have happened and her baby would not be dead."

Ben sighed. Guilt. The kid had come out of guilt. He ran a hand through his hair and then glanced at Red. Red just shrugged, as if to say he was on his own. Ben turned back to Miguel.

"Yeah, I suppose that could be true," Ben said. "Or Red and I might be investigating three homicides instead of two if you'd gone."

Miguel shook his head. "Why?" he asked. "Why was she shot?"

"We don't know," Ben said. "Maybe something as simple as being in the wrong place at the wrong time."

Miguel slumped.

"Do you know a man by the name of Charles Finelli?" Red asked.

Miguel looked up. "No, I don't know nobody by that name. Was that the name of the man who was killed?"

Red nodded. "He also went by the name of Chaz."

"Means nothing to me," Miguel said, then gave both men a weary look. "Can I go now? I got places to go, man."

"Got an address?" Ben asked.

Miguel shrugged. "Sometimes I stay with my sister." He gave the men her name and address. "Now can I go?"

"Yeah, sure," Ben said, and handed him his card. "In case you hear anything on the streets."

Miguel frowned. "I don't do business with the 'man,'" he muttered, then took it and stuffed it in his coat. "Only for the little mama, you know."

"Yeah, for the little mama," Ben said.

Miguel got all the way to the doorway then stopped and turned. The look he gave Ben was dark and fierce.

"You catch him, Detective. You catch the man who did this to her."

"We're doing our best," Ben said.

Miguel just shook his head and then made a hasty exit.

Red looked at Ben and shook his head. "Why do I have the feeling that our best isn't good enough for him?"

"Sometimes our best isn't even good enough for me," Ben said. "Now come on. There's a woman I want you to meet."

China was in limbo. Mercifully, her brain registered nothing of what was happening to her, and only now and then did a glimmer of cognizance surface. When it did, it came in the form of flesh-piercing pain and an inability to scream. Her body was healing, but if they'd asked her, she would have said, "Let me die."

Unaware of the countless hours of care she was receiving from the doctors and nurses, or of the persistence of one homicide detective from the Dallas P.D., she lay motionless beneath the covers, tied to machines.

In a way, China Brown was in a chrysalis. All her life, she'd been a victim. First at the hands of her stepfather, Clyde Shubert. Then, throughout her school years, as the kid who was too quiet to speak up for herself. After that, she'd been easy pickings for a man like Tommy Fairheart. He'd told her pretty lies for a place to live and food to eat. The fact that he'd left a part of himself behind hadn't mattered to a man like Tommy, because he had no concept of who he was—only what it took to survive. China had been fair game for the predator that he was.

Before, all the people who'd victimized her had been people she knew—men who were supposed to be taking care of her, men who were supposed to love her. Being the victim of an act of random violence became the next logical step. It remained to be seen what kind of woman would emerge.

The moment Ben stepped into the ICU ward, he forgot Red was behind him. He moved toward China with fixed intent, playing a game with himself that by the time he got to her bed, she would awaken. He needed to look into her eyes. She needed to know that he was there.

When he reached her bedside, he stopped, took a slow shaky breath, then leaned down until his mouth was near her ear.

"I came back, just like I promised," he said softly. "I brought a friend. His name is Red." He straightened up and gave Red a hard stare, as if daring him to argue. "Red, say hello to Miss Brown."

Red shifted nervously. This was weird, talking to someone who didn't even know he was there.

"Hello, Miss Brown. I'm real sorry you got hurt."

Ben nodded, as if satisfied with the way Red had played his role; he touched China's arm, then her forehead. It was cooler than it had been before. A nurse came by on her way back to the desk.

"What's the status on China Brown?" he asked.

The nurse paused. By now, all the staff knew they were cops.

"She's stable, sir."

"Her condition…has it been upgraded?" Ben asked.

She shook her head. "Not yet. She's still listed as critical, but she is holding her own, and that's something to be thankful for." Then she added, "Is there anything else?"

"We're posting a guard outside ICU. No one gets in to see her unless they're okayed by me."

"Yes, sir," she said. "I'll make a note of that on her chart right now."

"Thanks," Ben said, and then glanced at Red. "Well?"

Red looked down at the woman, then back up at Ben. "She's sure small, isn't she?"

Ben laid his hand over her fingers. "Yeah, she's small."

"Looks pretty young, too," he added.

"According to her driver's license, she's twenty-six."

"No next of kin, you say?" Red asked.

"None that we know of."

An awkward silence enveloped the men as they stood on either side of her bed. Finally, Red had to ask.

"Why, Ben? Why this fascination?"

Ben looked up. He started to unload a big set of excuses that had to do with it being part of the job, and then something stopped him. He glanced back at China—at her pale, colorless skin—and remembered the wounds on her body and the loss she had suffered. He started to speak, but the words wouldn't come. Then he cleared his throat and shook his head.

"I don't know," he said softly. "I honest to God don't know."

"Fair enough," Red said.

They stood in silence, each lost in his own set of thoughts. And then something happened.

China drew a deep breath and then moaned. Ben jumped and reached for her face, gently cupping her cheek with the palm of his hand as he spoke.

"Don't be afraid. I'm here."

As they watched, a single tear slipped out from beneath her eyelid and slid down the side of her face. The sight of it hit Ben like a blow to the gut. He leaned down again, his voice harsh and urgent, his own eyes blurring with empathy.

"You cry, girl. You cry all you want, and when you're through and all this pain is nothing but a memory, I will find a way to make you smile. Do you hear me, China Brown? That's a promise from me to you."

Red looked away. This was starting to get to him, as well.

He cleared his throat and muttered, "It's time to go. We've got a killer to catch."

Ben straightened, his expression cold and angry. "And the first place we're going is to Chaz Finelli's apartment. Maybe there's something there that will give us a place to start."

Bobby Lee strode into the dining room and smiled at the maid who was pouring coffee into his cup.

"Morning, Delia. Tell Cook I'd like my eggs scrambled this morning, and bring me some biscuits and sausage gravy, too. I'm a hungry man."

"Yes, sir, Senator. Will your mother be joining you this morning?"

Before Bobby Lee could answer, Mona strolled into the room and answered for herself.

"I'm already here," she drawled. "I'll have fresh strawberries and toast, and bring me some of that herbal tea I like."

"Yes, ma'am," Delia said, and hurried out of the room before the fireworks started. And they would start, of that she was certain, because, although Mona Wakefield was wearing a long silk robe, it was obvious as all get-out that she didn't have a stitch on under it.

Bobby Lee's eyes narrowed angrily as he watched his mother take her seat. As she leaned forward to adjust the hem of her robe, the top gaped open, revealing a goodly portion of voluptuous breast. Bobby rolled his eyes heavenward.

"For the Lord's sake, Mother, tie that robe a little better or put something on under it first. Have you no shame?"

Mona glanced down at herself and shrugged as she readjusted the robe.

"You are such a prude, Bobby Lee. If I didn't remember the pain of birthing you, I would swear you are not my son."

"If only that were so," he muttered beneath his breath and resumed reading the front page section of the *Dallas Morning News.*

"I heard that," Mona said. "And may I please have some of the paper?"

Bobby Lee took a couple of sections from the back and handed them to her.

"The classifieds?" she drawled.

He cursed beneath his breath and handed her another section.

Their banter was so commonplace that neither one of them took much of it to heart. Silence reigned in the dining room for all of five minutes until Delia returned with their food. A few more insults were traded between passing the butter and sugar. After that, they continued to eat while reading between bites. Mona was taking her last swallow of tea when her gaze fell on a small column of news.

"Well, now, just listen to this, Bobby Lee."

He dropped his paper in his lap and looked up with a sigh. "Mother, you know I don't like to be read to."

She wasn't paying him any mind, which didn't surprise him. When had she ever?

Mona cleared her throat and dabbed at her mouth with her napkin, then began to read aloud, hitting only the highlights of the story.

"'Shooting down in Oakcliff...two killed...no witnesses...police at a loss...'"

Bobby Lee interrupted. "The police are always at a loss," he muttered.

"That's not so," Mona said. "You're just mad because you got pulled over last month and ticketed for speeding."

Bobby Lee's eyes narrowed angrily. "The boy didn't know his place."

Mona grinned. "Why, I believe he did. Just because you're a senator, that doesn't make you God." Her grin widened. "That comes afterward...when you're elected president of these United States. Then you can be God."

A grudging smile centered on Bobby Lee's handsome face. "You are a witch," he said. "You know that, don't you?"

Mona arched an eyebrow. "I know nothing of the sort. Now, let me finish," she said, and ran her finger down the page until she found her place. "Oh yes, here's what I was trying to tell you. The man who was killed. It was Chaz Finelli." She made a face. "I never did like that man."

Bobby Lee's mouth dropped. The man's sleazeball reputation for taking scandalous photos of Dallas's rich and famous was well-known. The fact that his mother spoke personally of him made him nervous.

"You *know* Finelli?"

She glanced over her shoulder. "I'm all out of tea. Where's Delia gone off to, anyway?"

Bobby Lee grabbed his mother by the wrist. "Mother, I asked you a question."

"And I heard you," she snapped.

His grip tightened. "Then answer me," he growled. "Goddamn it, I just announced my candidacy for president. I don't need any surprises coming out of the woodwork. Exactly *how* do you know Chaz Finelli?"

"Why would it matter now? He's dead, isn't he?"

Bobby Lee stood, and in that moment Mona was almost afraid of her son. His voice was shaking with fury as he loomed over her chair.

"You talk to me...now!"

Mona shrugged. "It didn't amount to a hill of beans," she said. "I just got a little drunk at the mayor's birthday party last year."

Bobby Lee's mind was racing. He remembered the incident well. He'd pulled in a lot of favors to keep it out of the press.

"And..."

"Oh, hell, Bobby Lee. A woman has needs, too, you know. John Woodley and I were out in the greenhouse when a bunch of flashes went off. We thought they were part of the fireworks for the party until about a week later. John said he got some pictures in the mail."

She gave Bobby Lee a nervous glance. She'd never seen him so quiet—or so angry.

"What were you and John doing in those pictures?"

She grinned. "Well, we weren't counting daisies, Bobby Lee. What the hell do you think we were doing?"

"Jesus Christ," he muttered. "You will be the death of me yet."

"Oh, calm down. John paid him off and got the memory card, too."

"No blackmailer worth his salt *ever* gets rid of all the evidence. Somewhere, I can guarantee, there's a copy of those pictures, and they will show up just when it matters most."

Mona hated being wrong, and like her son, when faced with a problem, dealt with it in anger. She shoved her chair back with a thump and threw her napkin in his face.

"How? By ghost express? He's dead, Bobby Lee. Dead men tell no tales."

Bobby Lee paled. "I've got to call Ainsley." Resisting the urge to put his fist in her face, he pointed at her instead. "You don't leave this house today, do you hear me? If you're ever connected to his murder, then all of this is over…for both of us!"

Bobby Lee stormed out of the dining room. Mona strode to the window overlooking the snow-covered gardens. Icicles hung from the edges of the roof like long crystal spears. A pair of cardinals darted from bush to bush in search of food—as obvious to the human eye as blood on snow. Mona watched their futile search for food without any emotion. When they finally gave up and flew away, she abandoned the view. It was a hard world out there, and in her opinion, it didn't matter how beautiful the birds were. If they didn't have what it took to survive, then they didn't deserve to live.

A thin layer of dust covered the furnishings in Finelli's apartment, as well as three empty pizza boxes stacked on the table with a mummified piece of pepperoni pizza lying on top. There was a small plastic bowl on the kitchen floor with a handful of dried cat food, and another bowl beside it, obviously a water dish that had long ago evaporated. One could only hope that the cat it had been meant for was long gone from the premises. Either that or the stench that they were smelling was the cat. Ben and Red were hesitant to find out.

"Shoot a mile," Red muttered. "Something sure stinks. I hope it's not that cat. Where do you want to start?"

Ben pulled a pair of rubber gloves from his coat pocket and put them on.

"I'll go in the bedroom and work my way forward. You start in the kitchen, okay?"

"What are we looking for?" Red asked.

"Anything that might get a man killed."

"Okay," Red said, and then hesitated. "You got another pair of gloves? I left mine in the car."

"Yeah, I think so," Ben said, and dug through the inside pocket of his coat. "Here you go. Knock yourself out."

With that, both men went their separate ways, looking for answers to a crime that, so far, made no sense.

Time passed as the men moved from room to room. Red refused to set foot in the bathroom, so it was Ben who got left with the job. As he walked through the doorway, the stench they'd been smelling hit him full force. After a quick search of the cabinets and drawers, he decided that it was the sink that was harboring the smell.

It was streaked with grime and hair, and something that looked suspiciously like chemicals. He supposed they were the kind used in developing, but to be on the safe side, he scraped a sample off the sink. Maybe it was residue from a drug lab. If it was, manufacturing amphetamines would go a long way toward explaining why someone had wanted Finelli dead.

There was an assortment of bottles, mostly chemicals, in the cabinet beside the sink, and Ben was beginning to believe this had been Finelli's darkroom. He moved them around, reading each one label by label, but could find nothing that looked out of place. Yet when he set one of them down, the sound seemed hollow. He shoved several bottles aside and tapped on the bottom of the shelf once more. Again the thumps seemed to echo.

"Hey, Red!" he yelled. "Got a minute?"

Red appeared at the door.

"Yeah, what's up?"

"You got your flashlight on you?"

Red pulled a small flashlight out of his pocket. "Like the Boy Scouts, I'm always prepared."

Grinning, Ben took it from his partner and flipped the switch. He leaned closer to the cabinet, aiming the beam of light at the cabinet floor. Almost immediately, he could tell that it had been altered from its original design. Quickly he took all the bottles out of the cabinet and set them in the sink, then took out his pocket knife and stuck the point at one end of a crack.

"Whatcha got there?" Red asked.

"Don't know," Ben said. "Maybe nothing." But he continued to dig. Within seconds, something popped, and all of a sudden the floor of the cabinet was in his hands.

"Would you look at that?" Red said, and leaned closer, peering over Ben's shoulder. "Is something in it?"

Ben aimed the flashlight into the opening. "Son of a…"

"What?" Red asked. "What's in there?"

Ben began pulling out photos, along with a couple of manila envelopes, and he'd only skimmed the surface of the stash.

Red's eyes widened. "Oh, man. Would you look at these? Hey, isn't that Sonny Harold of the Dallas Lone-

Stars with the needle in his hand? I thought he was on probation."

"He is," Ben said.

Red held up another. "And this one…the naked woman riding that mechanical bull. She looks familiar, but I just can't…"

"The mayor's wife," Ben muttered. "And I must say, I've seen her looking better."

"Jesus!" Red said. "Where do you suppose he got these?"

"With that famous little camera he was never without. You know…the one that's missing. Without doubt, I'd say we've got, at the least, a good hundred or so reasons for murdering Finelli. The question remains, which one of these creeps did the deed?"

Chapter 5

Aaron Floyd slapped his desk with the flat of his hand and tossed the list he'd been handed back to Ben and Red.

"Jesus Christ! Do you two have any idea what a mess this is going to make?"

Anger was thick in Ben's voice as he answered his captain.

"Yes, and ask me if I care. Those people in the photographs caused their own set of problems. Finelli exacerbated them and it got him killed. We're just trying to find some justice for the stupid bastard, not that I'm sure he deserves it, but China Brown damn sure does."

Aaron Floyd wiped a hand across his face, then ran it through his hair, giving himself time to calm down. He took a deep breath, and when he spoke again, his demeanor was apologetic.

"I didn't mean that the way it came out," he muttered. "Hell, yes, I want the shooter caught, and if he's on this list, then we'll find out." He glanced back at the list and then shook his head. "The mayor's wife? Larry Dee Jackson? Ariel Simmons?" He rolled his eyes as he repeated her name. "Ariel Simmons is one of those TV preachers, for Pete's sake. For now, keep your questioning discreet until we find out who's got an alibi and who doesn't. If this gets out, we'll have the Dallas city government, the Country Music Association and even God on our ass if this gets mishandled. I don't want to set the police department up for a lawsuit, do you hear me?"

"Fine. We'll make sure we don't step on too many toes or ruffle any more feathers than we have to," Ben snapped. "But I think it needs to be remembered that we've got a victim who's hanging on to her life by a thread, a woman who has yet to hear the words, *your baby is dead.* When she wakes up—and she *will* wake up—do you want to be the one to tell her that we still don't know who killed her child because we were afraid to make somebody mad?"

Before Aaron Floyd could answer, Ben picked up the list of suspects and strode out of the office. Red shrugged apologetically.

"This one just got to him, Captain. He'll be all right."

"See that he is, or I'll put someone else on the case."

"That won't be necessary," Red said, and left quickly before he unloaded what was on his mind, too. He was as ticked off as Ben. The way he looked at it, if the stupid fools hadn't gotten themselves into these messes, then there wouldn't be any incriminating pictures to worry about. His mama always said if you lay down with dogs, you were bound to get fleas, and after looking at the pictures they'd pulled out of Finelli's stash, it would take more than flea baths to solve their itches.

"Ben, wait up," Red said, as he grabbed his coat and followed his partner out the door.

Ben spun, his face tight with anger. "Politics suck. If

you know the right people, or have enough money, you can buy your way out of just about anything."

"The captain said if you don't pull it together, he's going to put someone else on the case."

"He'll play hell trying," Ben said. "You driving, or am I?"

"Me."

Ben tossed him the car keys and strode out the door. Red shook his head and followed.

Twenty-four hours later, they'd eliminated fifteen of the forty-five names on the list. Some of the people had been out of town when the incident occurred, others had unshakeable alibis. But they had all been appalled to learn that there were still existing pictures of their indiscretions.

At the moment, the man they were interrogating was less than happy to see the picture of himself and the teenage hitchhiker he'd picked up, having sex in the backseat of his car, as naked as the day they were born.

"Sombitch!" Jody Franklin had roared. "I paid that little weasel good money to get these back. He assured me I had them all, including the negatives."

"Obviously, he lied," Red said. "When was the last time you saw Mr. Finelli?"

Jody grabbed a cigar from a box on his desk, bit the end of it off with his teeth and spat, sending the bit of tobacco flying.

Ben watched without speaking. Jody was so furious, he half expected the man's cigar to light on its own. That kind of anger could easily escalate into something more—something deadly.

"Mr. Franklin?"

Jody Franklin glared at Red. "I heard you the first

time," he snapped. "I'm thinkin'." He lit his cigar, taking several long puffs until the end of the cigar was glowing; then he circled his desk and sat down with a grunt and buzzed his secretary to come in. "Eileen, bring me last year's calendar."

A few moments later, a short, well-dressed woman entered the room, eyeing the detectives with curiosity.

"Any particular date you want me to look up for you, sir?"

"Yeah. When did I go to the Fort Worth livestock show? It was sometime last spring, but I don't remember the exact date."

Eileen ruffled through the months, running her finger down the dates on individual pages until she found what she was looking for.

"Here it is. May 12 through 15. You stayed at the Hilton."

"Thank you, Eileen. That will be all."

The secretary exited. As soon as the door had closed behind her, Franklin strode to the window, a wreath of smoke following him as he walked.

"It was May 15, my last night in Fort Worth. The little bastard showed up at my hotel, handed me a copy of that picture you have there and said if I didn't give him ten thousand dollars, he was going to mail copies to my wife, my daughters and my mother." He spun, his face dark with anger. "My mother, for God's sake! She's eighty-four years old. The shock alone would have killed her."

"Did you pay?"

Franklin shrugged. "Hell, yes, of course I did. Money wasn't the issue. I would have given him double without thinking twice. I got the negatives and all the prints." His eyes narrowed as he glanced back at the picture lying on his desk. "At least I thought I did."

"And you haven't seen him since?" Ben asked.

Franklin took a long puff of his cigar, then blew a couple of smoke rings before answering.

"We don't run in the same social circles, Detective."

"Where were you last Friday?"

Franklin took another long, thoughtful puff. "Oh, yeah," he muttered. "Squiring my wife and youngest daughter to see *The Nutcracker* ballet." He grimaced. "Damn boring, dancing around on your toes and all, but you know how it is…sometimes you do what you have to do."

"We'll have to verify that," Ben said.

For the first time since they had walked into his office, Jody Franklin looked scared.

"Check with the box office, they can verify we were there. Call Mayor Devlin. We sat next to him and his wife. Just don't call Mary Sue. I don't want to hurt her."

"Should have thought of that before you screwed a kid young enough to be your daughter," Ben snapped.

"Hell," Franklin muttered. "Give me a break, Detective. I'm not gonna lie and say I didn't wish the little bastard dead a hundred times, but I swear to God I didn't have anything to do with his death."

"We'll be in touch," Ben said. "Oh…and don't leave town."

Franklin was pale and sweating as they left his office.

Red grinned as they reached the elevator. "It just goes to prove that being rich doesn't necessarily mean you've got brains to go with it." Then he glanced at Ben. "What do you think? Was he telling the truth?"

Ben shrugged. "Probably. It will be easy enough to find out. As for the brains part, it's for damn sure Jody Franklin could have used some more and a measure of good sense to go with them."

"Now what?" Red asked.

Ben glanced at the list. "We've got time for a couple more before—" His cell phone rang. "Just a minute," he said.

"Ben English."

"Detective English, this is Dr. Pope. You asked to be notified if there was any change in China Brown's condition?"

Ben's heart skipped a beat. "Yes?"

"As you know, we've been decreasing the sedatives for some time now. And, as you also know, her wounds are healing nicely."

Ben interrupted. "You didn't call to tell me this," he said. "What's wrong?"

"She's failing," Dr. Pope said. "Her vital signs aren't good."

Shock spiraled, sending Ben into a panic. After all of this, surely God wouldn't let her die.

"This doesn't make sense. If everything else is as you said, then why is this happening?" Ben asked.

"I suppose there could be all sorts of explanations," Dr. Pope said. "But my personal opinion is, I don't think she wants to live."

Ben groaned. "I'm on my way."

"What's wrong?" Red asked.

Ben bolted inside the elevator before the door was completely open and quickly punched the Close Door button, then the one for the lobby. Red made it, barely, snatching his coattail before it got caught.

"Come on, partner, talk to me."

It was all Ben could do to say the words aloud. "They're losing China Brown."

"That's too bad," Red said. "We lose her, we lose our only witness."

Ben snapped. "She's more than just a witness, damn it."

Red grabbed Ben's arm. "That's just the problem, buddy. She's not. Whatever you think you're feeling is all in your mind. She doesn't know you exist."

"Shut up. Just shut up and get me to the hospital, and then you're on your own for the rest of the day. I'm not leaving her until I know she's going to be all right."

The elevator stopped. The doors opened. Ben strode out into the lobby of the office building and began moving toward the entrance at a jog.

Red caught up with him at the curb. "Wait! Ben, wait!"

Ben turned. "What?"

"What if she doesn't pull out of this?"

Ben took a deep breath, then another, trying to answer without making a fool of himself, then realized he'd already done that a hundred times over since this whole thing had begun. His shoulders slumped, and for a moment he looked away. Then he lifted his head and gave Red a cool look.

"Are you driving, or am I?"

"I will," Red muttered. "I want to get there in one piece."

China was drifting. There was a place between cognizance and oblivion that let her hide without effort. All she had to do was focus on the dark and everything else would fade—even the muscle-racking pain that dug into her sleep. It was a place of safety—a place where reality did not exist. When she thought about it, which was rare, she knew she was in a hospital. Now and then there were even flashes of ugly memories that reminded her of why she was there. Those were the times when she felt herself slipping, and slipping was something she longed for, more and more. Remembering was a pain worse than anything physical.

And she would have gone long ago except for that voice that kept pulling at her to stay. In a way, she was reluctant to turn loose of the connection. The tenderness in his voice and the gentleness of his touch were things she'd once longed for. But it was too late—too late to care, too late for everything of this earth. Nothing mattered but finding peace, and when China Brown had faced the barrel of that gun and felt the bullet that ripped her child from her body, she'd accepted the fact that her peace would not be on earth. Now all she wanted to do was go home.

Ben was out of the car and running before Red had come to a complete stop. All the way into the hospital, he'd been unable to think past his panic. His breath came in short, anxious gasps as he entered the elevator, and when it stopped, he found himself running down the hall to the ICU.

At the sound of his footsteps, the nurse on duty looked up.

"Dr. Pope called me," Ben gasped.

"Yes, sir, he's inside waiting for you."

Ben dropped his coat and gloves on a nearby chair and kept walking, knowing that if he stopped, he wouldn't be able to move.

Dr. Pope was standing at the foot of China's bed. He looked up when the doors opened and motioned for Ben to come.

God, don't let this be happening. He nodded to Dr. Pope. "Thank you for calling me."

"It seemed important to you. I was glad to do it." Pope

looked at China and then down at her chart before moving to her bedside.

"Talk to me," Ben said. "Why is this happening?"

The doctor took Ben by the arm and pulled him aside so that their voices could not be heard by any of the patients.

"The human mind is a powerful and mysterious thing. We know very little about the intricacies of how it works, but basically, I would say she's just not fighting it any longer."

Ben's belly rolled. "She wants to die?"

Pope glanced at China and then shrugged. "It amounts to the same thing."

Ben looked at her then, absorbing the delicate perfection of her face. He moved to the bed, touching her arm, then her wrist, barely able to feel the thin, thready pulse. His voice was shaking, his gaze begging Ross Pope to change his prognosis.

"Don't let this happen."

"It's out of my hands," Pope said.

"And there's nothing you can give her?"

"Medically, I've done all I can. The rest is up to the lady." Then he patted China's leg and gave Ben a sad smile. "I've got to finish rounds. If I'm needed, they'll page me."

Ben suddenly realized that the allotted five-minute ICU visit was not going to be enough. How could he reach China if she couldn't hear his voice?

"I'm not leaving," he said.

Ross Pope nodded. "I didn't think you would. I've already given orders that you be allowed to stay for as long as you want. But you have to be very quiet. There are other patients whose care depends on it."

"Yes, I promise."

"Well...goodbye then," Dr. Pope said, but Bennett English's focus had already shifted to the woman in the bed.

"It's me," Ben said softly, and stroked her cheek from temple to chin with the tip of his finger. "I told you I'd be back."

The only answer he got was a slow but steady beeping from the monitor hooked up to her heart.

"I saw a robin today in a tree outside my apartment. Soon winter will be a thing of the past. I can help you, honey, but you have to wake up."

Beep. Beep. Beep.

Ben bowed his head and closed his eyes. *God give me the right words to say before it's too late.* He took her hand and then inhaled slowly.

"China. China Brown. Can you hear me? If you can, then squeeze my hand."

Beep. Beep. Beep.

"I know it's difficult. You've been very, very sick, but you're getting better now. I know you can hear my voice." He gave her fingers a gentle squeeze. "That was me, squeezing your hand. All you have to do is move a finger, just one finger, and I'll know you're listening."

Beep... Beep...

There was a long pause before the beeps resumed, and the fear that shot through Ben's body left him weak and shaky. He was losing her, and he didn't know what to do. His voice was trembling when he began to speak.

"There are doctors and nurses who have worked very, very hard to make you well. There are policemen who are working day and night, trying to find the man who hurt you. You think you're all alone, but you're not. You're not alone, China. You have me. I'm here. All you have to do is squeeze my hand."

He clasped her fingers, willing his warmth into her hand.

Beep. Beep. Beep. Beep...

Again the monitor skipped the count of two heartbeats before resuming a steady rhythm. Ben could feel her life slipping away before his eyes, and the thought of never seeing her smile made him crazy. He leaned down until his mouth was only inches from her ear, his voice harsh and ragged with fear.

"Damn you, don't you quit on me! Do you hear me? I haven't quit on you. You at least owe me the courtesy of doing the same."

Beep-beep. Beep-beep. Beep-beep.

He didn't know whether the irregularity was a good sign or a bad one, but either way, he'd committed himself.

"That's all right," he said. "Get mad. I'd like nothing better than for you to open those eyes of yours and tell me to take a hike. If that's what it takes, then get mad. Do anything but quit."

Beep-beep. Beep. Beep. Beep.

Ben breathed a little easier. Needing to touch her, wanting her to feel him, he began stroking her hair with his other hand as he searched for a way to reach her. As he stood, racking his brain for something wise to say, he saw tears welling at the corners of her eyes. The breath slid out of his body as quickly as if he'd been punched. All at once he understood.

"Oh, honey." He gave her fingers another gentle squeeze. "You know, don't you? You know your baby is dead."

The monitor beeped erratically a couple of times. Ben was so focused on the sounds that he missed the movement of her fingers against the palm of his hand.

"I'm sorry," he whispered, and without thinking,

leaned down again, this time kissing the side of her cheek. "I'm so, so sorry."

Beep... Beep... Beep.

The length of time between the sounds seemed to Ben like slow sobs. It wasn't until he straightened that he felt a tremble in her hand. His gaze slid to the delicate length of her fingers against his palm.

"China? Can you hear me? If you can, move your fingers for me."

At first he saw nothing, and then ever so slowly, one finger rose, followed by the one beside it.

"Thank You, God," he muttered, as she rubbed the tips of two fingers against his skin.

"That's it!" he cried. "I knew you could do it! I knew you weren't a quitter."

Instantly the motion stopped, and the message was as clear as her silence had been before.

"You aren't!" he argued. "No one who's fought this long to stay alive would be a quitter. Move again for me, China. Prove it to me."

Beep-beep. Beep-beep. Beep-beep.

"Damn it, no!" he growled. "You don't do this! You don't do this to me! If you quit now, you're letting a man get away with murder. Is that what you want? Is it, China?"

Beep-beep-beep. Beep-beep-beep.

"I don't believe it! I don't believe you. You loved that baby you were carrying. Now help me find the man who killed her."

China drew a slow breath and Ben held his as he waited for her to exhale. If she didn't, he wasn't certain but that he would die right here and now, with her.

Then she exhaled, and it sounded to Ben like a sigh. As she did, her fingers curled ever so slightly around the palm of his hand, as if grasping to hold on to life. Quick tears blurred his view of her face.

"That's what I wanted to hear," he said softly. "You just hold on, honey, until you feel strong enough on your own to let go. After that, I'm making you a promise that, together, we'll bring your baby's killer to justice."

Beep. Beep. Beep. Beep. And so the monitor danced, slow and steady, all through the night.

Sometime later, a nurse brought him a chair and scooted it beside China's bed. Gingerly, he sat without breaking his hold on her hand. Hours passed and his eyes became heavy. He laid his head down on his arm—just to rest, just for a minute.

He woke at daybreak and for a moment lay without moving, listening to the sounds of the changing shift and the footsteps coming and going as a new set of nurses checked patients' vitals, dispensing gentleness and kind words with the medicine. It took a moment for him to realize that China Brown was no longer holding his hand. Instead, sometime during the night, she'd thrust her fingers into his hair.

Even after he lifted his head to check the monitor by her bed, he imagined he could still feel the imprint of her fingers against his scalp. The strong, steady beep of the heart monitor was a welcome sound. He stood and stretched, raising his arms stiffly above his head and then arching his back before laying a hand against her cheek.

"Good morning, sweetheart. Just for the record, I got your message. You're going to be okay, and so am I. I'll be back, and when I come, I promise to shave. I don't want to look like a wild man the first time you see my face."

Then he leaned over and kissed her again, feeling the warmth of her cheek against his lips. Just as he started to raise his head, he hesitated. With no more than an inch of space separating their faces, Ben moved a bit to the right and kissed her again. This time, right on her mouth.

When he left the ICU, he was smiling.

Bobby Lee tossed the morning paper down onto the dining room table, took a slow, satisfying sip of his favorite coffee, then leaned back in his chair, surveying all that was his.

The opulence of his home was evident, but tasteful, a perfect backdrop for a man who would be king. The festive red and green of Christmas hung from every corner, evidence of the expensive decorator Mona had hired. Bobby Lee had the poor-boy-makes-good syndrome going for him, as well as being a certifiable war hero. His eyes narrowed as he thought back to his years in the military. At the time, he wouldn't have given a plug nickel for his chances of coming home alive, never mind in one piece. If anyone had asked him about the notion of using those years as a springboard into politics, he would have laughed in their face and called them crazy.

He chuckled beneath his breath and then shook his head as he took another sip of coffee. Life could be a bitch, but it could also be beautiful, and right now, his world was full of beauty and light.

"Bobby Lee! Where are you?"

The bubble of perfection popped as the screech of his mother's elevated voice echoed throughout the halls. Goddamn it! Wouldn't that woman ever learn? Ladies did not shout. He bolted from his chair and stalked to the doorway. Mona was standing in the hall, pulling on a pair of elbow-length gloves and preparing to let loose with another shout when he spoke.

"Must you shout?" he snapped.

"If I wanna be heard," she drawled, and sauntered toward him on three-inch heels.

His eyes narrowed with disdain as he absorbed the outfit she was wearing. It was velvet, red and short, with a faux fox collar framing her neck and face. Her gloves were longer than her skirt, and her buxom torso was zipped into the jacket so tightly that one sneeze could prove a disaster.

"Where are you going?"

"Out."

"Not good enough," he said.

She rolled her eyes. "Shopping?"

"Is that a statement or a question?"

She tapped a finger against his chest, angrily punctuating her words with each impact.

"I am your mother, not your child. You do not tell me what to do or where to go, is that understood?"

He grabbed her finger in the midst of a tap and then, ever so slowly, began bending it back toward her hand.

"You are a walking time bomb. I will do what it takes to keep your ass out of trouble, even if that means locking you in your room. Is that understood?"

Pain shafted up her arm as she screamed and yanked away.

"You're hurting me!" she cried. "How dare you?"

Bobby Lee moved closer—so close that he could smell the peppermint flavor of her mouthwash.

"I'll do more than hurt you if you fuck up again, Mother dear."

Mona blanched. "What the hell do you mean?"

Bobby Lee smiled, and in that moment he had no way of knowing how like his mother he looked.

"You think you're so smart. You figure it out."

Mona pivoted angrily. Unwilling for him to see how

his words had rattled her, she stalked toward the door, her legs pumping beneath the tight red velvet like well-oiled pistons. When she got to the door, she turned and shouted, "You son of a bitch!"

He grinned. "You should know."

The door slammed behind her with a solid thud, rattling a picture on a nearby wall. Bobby Lee stood for a moment, thoughtfully staring after her exit, then shrugged and went back to his coffee. He had a meeting to attend and no more time to dwell on the oversexed woman who'd given him life.

Chapter 6

Ben English was in good spirits as he and his partner pulled up to the gates of Ariel Simmons's estate on the south edge of Dallas. Red pointed to the massive iron angels on either side of the entrance.

"Unless she's got one hell of an explanation for the picture of her that we found in Finelli's apartment, she's going to be needing more than two of those fellows," he said.

Ben shrugged as he pressed the button on the call box.

"Maybe it was just a poor choice of Halloween costumes."

Red grinned. "Black leather, a whip and iron spikes, maybe…but I don't think that man in manacles was part of the costume."

Ben nodded. "Yeah, and if Finelli hadn't written her name on the back of the photo, chances are we would never have been able to identify her. Looks a damn sight different than the slender blonde angel who appears on television four nights a week."

The iron gates swung open.

"So let's go talk to the angel and see what she has to say for herself," Red said.

Ben put the car in gear and drove through. Yet when they were ushered into Ariel Simmons's living room by a uniformed maid, their perception of her changed again. The room was all crystal and steel, with sharp angles in the furniture and freeform sculptures that made no sense.

"Man," Red muttered. "What do you make of this?"

Ben stood with his hands in his pockets as his gaze jumped from one corner of the room to the other, and while he would have been the first person to agree that taste was subjective, the first word that came to mind was, *wasteland.*

"It looks like the set of a bad sci-fi movie," Ben said.

"Gentlemen, how may I help you?"

The woman's voice was startling in its clarity and power. They turned toward the sound, facing the tall, angular woman silhouetted in the doorway. Her white-blond hair was shorter than Red's. Pale-blue leggings accentuated her shapely legs, while the embroidery at the hem of her poet's shirt brushed the tops of her knees. Blue ballerina shoes covered her feet, and a bulky gold chain served as a belt, molding the shirt to a very small waist.

Ben flashed his badge. "Detective Bennett English, Homicide. This is my partner, Detective Fisher." Red offered his badge as identification, too.

As Ariel walked toward them, Ben tried to superimpose the woman in Chaz Finelli's picture onto her face and couldn't quite make the connection. Had they made a mistake?

"So, Detectives, to what do I owe the pleasure?"

"Maybe you'd like to sit," Ben said. "This may take a while."

Ariel smiled and glided past them, moving like a

dancer across a stage. When she sat, Ben was aware that, once again, she seemed to be playing a part.

"All right, I'm sitting," she said. "Now, how can I help you?"

Ben sat on the sofa directly across from her chair and then laid the picture on the table between them.

"Explain this."

If he hadn't been watching her so closely, he might have missed the look of shock that came and went in her eyes, because when she looked up, her expression was suitably disgusted.

"A woman in need of God," Ariel said, and touched the picture with the flat of her hand. "Tell me her name, Detective English, and I will pray for her."

Red shifted nervously beside Ben and gave him a questioning glance, but Ben knew her poise had been shaken.

"According to Charles Finelli's files, her name is Ariel Simmons."

Ariel gasped and clasped both hands to the sides of her face. "Have mercy!" she cried. "Surely you gentlemen could not believe that lascivious woman is me? You know my truth. You know God is love."

"Actually, Miss Simmons, we don't know your truth, which is why we're here. Now can you tell us where you were around 10:00 p.m. on December 11?"

"I was on television. Check your listings," Ariel said, then stood abruptly and sailed past them to a phone on a nearby table. Angrily, she punched in a series of numbers. As she waited for someone to answer, she turned toward the men, giving them a fairly good rendition of a woman wronged.

"Look, Ben," Red muttered, "the captain will have our hides if we tick off the religious right on this case.

Maybe it isn't her. After all, that woman in the picture has dark hair."

But Ben didn't answer. He was too busy watching Ariel Simmons's face.

"Langley, I need you," Ariel said. "It's an emergency. Something terrible is happening—just terrible. I'm about to be slandered, and I want protection. Yes, just get over here as soon as you can."

She hung up with a flourish and then pointed toward the door, something Scarlett O'Hara might have done in banishing Rhett Butler from her life. It was all a little too exaggerated for Ben to believe.

"Gentlemen, I believe you can find your way out."

Ben shook his head. "Not until you answer a couple more questions."

"I don't have to answer anything. I know my rights, and I will not be blackmailed by some—"

Ben moved, pinning Ariel between his glare and the front of her desk. He kept thinking of the woman who'd come so close to death last night, and of the baby she'd lost. Even Charles Finelli, as low as he was, hadn't deserved to be gunned down in the street like a gutter rat.

"This isn't blackmail, lady, it's murder," Ben said. "Now you can talk to us here, or you can come down to the station. Either way, you *will* talk to us until we're satisfied with your answers or we decide you're lying. In which case you *will* be needing that lawyer you called when we read you your rights."

Ariel paled. Her eyes darted from one man to the other. Ben imagined he could see the wheels turning as she decided how to play her next scene. Suddenly she became teary-eyed and bowed her head as if humiliated and shamed, then staggered back to her chair before sinking into its depths.

"I'm sorry, so sorry, but you must understand. This was such a shock. Of course that sinful woman is not me. I preach God's message, not Satan's. I'll help you if I can."

"You're quite different in person from the woman on TV," Ben said. "Your hair is short, and your clothes are nothing like the gowns that you wear on your show."

Ariel gave him a tremulous smile. "Praise God, dear sir. If you've seen my broadcasts, then you have heard the Word. Of course, my image is all important. But I make so many public appearances that it becomes difficult to maintain a perfect coiffure, so I wear wigs. I have several, you know. As for the gowns, well…" She shrugged.

"All part of the image, right?" Ben said.

She nodded and sighed, then leaned over and pulled a tissue from a box before using it to blot her tears.

"Did you know Charles Finelli?" Red asked.

Ariel was a little startled when the question came at her from another source, and again Ben saw her composure slip, but it was so fleeting it almost escaped him.

"I'm sorry…what was that name?"

"Finelli. Charles Finelli."

"No, I can't say that I do," Ariel said. "But I meet so many people in my ministry. If you had a picture…"

Ben pulled one out of his pocket and dropped it in her lap.

"Dear Lord!" Ariel gasped, and covered her eyes.

It was the one of Finelli lying in the street after he'd been shot.

"The poor man. And you say he was murdered?"

"He was also a blackmailer," Ben added. "According to the files he kept, a very successful one. How much did you pay him for the pictures he took of you?"

Ariel's eyes narrowed as, once again, her saintly countenance began to fade.

"Again I tell you that woman is not me, nor did I pay any money to Chaz Finelli."

Ben went still. He could feel Red looking at him, but he wouldn't take his eyes off Ariel's face. He leaned down, bracing himself with a hand on either arm of her chair. Her breath was warm against his face as he spoke.

"A few more questions, and then we'll be gone," he said.

She looked up, meeting his gaze head-on.

"I thought you didn't know the murder victim," he said.

"That's right, I don't."

"But you called him Chaz. Only the people who knew him best called him by that name, and since I didn't tell you that little bit of information, I'm inclined to believe you've been lying."

All the blood drained from Ariel Simmons's face. Her eyes widened in fear as her lips went slack.

"And there's something else you should know," Ben said softly.

"Wh-wh-what?"

"I don't like being lied to. Did you have Charles Finelli killed?"

"No, and I don't care what you like," she blustered. "Now get away from me before I call the police."

Ben smiled, and it was not a pretty smile as he waved the picture of Finelli beneath her nose. "We *are* the police, and if I find out you're responsible for this, all the prayers in heaven will not save your lying ass. Do we understand each other?"

"Get out," she muttered.

Ben straightened. "Don't leave town," he said. "Don't bother to get up. We'll see ourselves out."

Once they were outside, Red took a deep breath and then scratched his head as he looked at Ben's angry face.

"I think that went well," he said.

"Just get in the car," Ben muttered.

For the first time in days, China was physically aware of her surroundings. She felt pain. She felt cold. She felt the nurses' hands as they ministered to her needs. Sometimes she even understood what they were saying, but the flashes of cognizance didn't last. Her awareness would fade with the onset of a fresh wave of pain, or from the contents of a hypodermic syringe being administered intravenously. Each time she started going under, there was a part of her that resisted. She kept remembering that voice promising to help find her baby's killer, and all she had to do was wake up. If she didn't, the man behind the voice might forget, and if he did, it would be the end of any hope of justice. She knew they would never find the person responsible for the shootings, because they were looking for a man.

She struggled with the thought, but the sedative was too strong and her pain was too sharp, so she let herself slide into oblivion—one more time.

"Where in hell did you get that?"

Ben put the picture he'd just shown country singer Larry Dee Jackson back in his coat pocket.

"Why? Did you think you'd bought them all?"

Larry Dee wiped a shaky hand across his face and then dropped to the side of his bed.

"I paid the son of a bitch more for it than I did for the Renoir hanging in my house back in Nashville."

"Then I take it the blonde in the picture isn't your wife?"

Larry groaned beneath his breath. "No." He grabbed Ben's arm. "You've got to keep this under wraps. If my wife finds out, it'll be the end of my marriage." Then he covered his face with his hands. "I can't lose my wife and kids. I love them."

"Should have thought of that before you got naked with another woman," Ben said.

"Oh, man," Larry muttered, and stood abruptly. "I need a drink."

"Not until you answer some questions," Ben said. "Where were you around 10:00 p.m. on December 11?"

"What day was that?" Larry asked.

"Last Friday."

"I was in the hotel having an early night. My flight came in around 3:30 p.m. and I was tired."

"Can anyone vouch for that?"

Larry Dee began to sweat. "Hell, I don't know. I had room service about six. Made a couple of calls, then watched a movie on pay-per-view."

"Any late-night visitors, like maybe the lady in the picture?"

Larry Dee looked away and then shrugged. "I'm not saying."

"You do know that Texas has the death penalty?" Ben asked.

Larry Dee turned pale and then shuddered.

"I swear to God I didn't have anything to do with that man's murder."

"I need more than your word," Ben said. "So, how about it? Did you have any visitors?"

Larry shook his head. "Sorry, I don't kiss and tell."

"Look, Jackson, the time to play gentleman would have been when you had the option of keeping your pants zipped and going home to your wife. You made a choice.

Now you face the consequences. Either you tell me now, or we'll take this discussion down to the station."

"Christ almighty, Connie's gonna kill me."

Ben's interest piqued. "Is this Connie capable of murder?"

Larry looked like someone had just goosed him in the butt.

"Oh! No! Hell, no! That was just a figure of speech."

"Poor choice of words," Ben said.

Larry Dee poured himself a generous belt of whiskey, downed it neat, and then turned to the two detectives.

"It's Connie Marx."

Red stopped writing in the middle of a word and looked up.

"*The* Connie Marx, WFAL anchorwoman on the evening news?"

He nodded.

Red whistled beneath his breath and made a couple more notes as Ben shifted his line of questioning.

"Did Miss Marx know that Charles Finelli blackmailed you?"

"Yeah. He got the both of us, actually. Took me for double what she had to pay, though. Said I had more to lose than she did."

"Was he right?" Ben asked.

Larry sighed. "Oh, yeah." Then he added, "What are you going to do?"

"Find a killer, Mr. Jackson."

"Can you keep this under wraps—I mean about the picture?"

"We aren't advertising the names on this list. But if it were me, I think I'd play it safe and confess my sins to my wife and hope for the best. I'd say you have a better chance of coming out on the good side if you do that than if she reads about this mess in the papers."

"Oh, man," Larry muttered, and poured himself another drink as the detectives left.

Once Ben and Red exited the hotel room where Jackson was staying, Ben slipped his notebook into his pocket and pulled out the picture of Larry and the blonde.

"Let's see if we can catch her at the television station and then call it a day, what do you say?" he asked.

Red nodded. "I'm all for that. I could go for a steak and a hot shower. Rita was making apple cobbler when I called her at noon. Want to come over? We can always throw another steak on the grill."

Ben shook his head. "No, but thanks for asking. I'm going to swing by the hospital before I head for home. I didn't get much sleep last night."

"You're moving into dangerous territory with her, you know that," Red said.

Ben started to argue, then nodded instead. "Yes, I know, but it's too late to pull back now. I made promises to her."

Red frowned. "What are you going to do if you can't keep those promises?"

"One thing at a time, buddy. One thing at a time. She's alive, and for now, that's enough."

"Miss Marx, there are two detectives asking for you."

Connie Marx looked up from the script of the night's broadcast and frowned. She didn't know the short, red-headed man, but she recognized the tall one on sight. English. Ben English. He'd been the primary detective on the Whitman kidnapping last year. She stood, then went to meet them.

"Detective English, it's been a while," she said, offering him her hand.

"Miss Marx. This is Detective Fisher, my partner. We need to ask you some questions."

She smiled wryly. "That sounds serious. And here I thought you'd come by to invite me to the policemen's ball."

The fact that Ben didn't return her smile was warning enough that she wasn't going to like what they'd come to say.

"So, what's up?"

Ben took the picture of her and Jackson out of his pocket.

Her expression froze as she stared in disbelief. When she looked up, her eyes were filled with fury.

"I didn't think you were the voyeuristic type," she snapped. "Where did you get that?"

"From Charles Finelli's apartment," Ben said.

"That sorry, lying little bastard," she muttered. "Someone should have shot him sooner and saved us all a lot of trouble."

"So you know he's dead," Ben said.

She rolled her eyes and then waved her script beneath his nose.

"Yes, I know he's dead," she said. "It's what I do for a living."

"Where were you on December 11 at 10:00 p.m.?"

"Home. Nursing a case of the flu."

"That's not what Larry Jackson said."

Ben could tell she was shocked. But her shock soon turned to anger, and she exploded in a fit of rage.

"We have nothing more to say to each other, and you get the hell out of my face. I've got a show to do. If you have any other questions, you can contact me through my lawyer, is that understood?"

Red glanced at Ben. "Didn't take that well, did she?" he asked as she sailed out of the room in high gear.

Ben put the picture back in his pocket. "No, she didn't, but it's about what I expected of her. She's a real bulldog. Doesn't give an inch."

Red nodded. "Would she have someone killed?"

Ben hesitated, trying to imagine Connie Marx hiring a hit man, then shrugged. "Last month, I would have said no. But after seeing the picture, I couldn't hazard a guess. I know that if the picture gets out, she's probably unemployed."

"Would you kill to keep your job?" Red asked.

"People have killed for a whole lot less, and we both know it," Ben said. "Let's get out of here."

"Sure I can't talk you into coming home with me tonight? Rita would love to have you."

"No, but thanks anyway, okay?"

Red sighed. "Tell China Brown I said hello."

"I will." Then he added, "Hey, Red?"

"Yeah?"

"Don't worry, okay? Everything's under control."

Music rocked the walls inside the secluded cabin on Lake Texoma. The tall, leggy blonde sat before her mirror, putting the finishing touches on her makeup. Just a last brush of blush, then one more touch of eyeliner at the corner of her left eye. When she had finished, she leaned back, giving herself a final assessment, then slowly smiled. Yes, she was beautiful, but makeup was an art, accentuating that which was already pleasing to the eye.

"Honey, you are a knockout," she murmured, then

stood and danced her way to the closet and the white, beaded dress hanging on a blue silk hanger.

As she lifted the dress from the hanger, she shivered in sudden ecstasy. God, but she loved the feel of silk between her fingers, and on her body—and between her legs. She stepped into the dress, then pulled it over her hips, slowly sliding her arms into the sleeves. Just the feel of that fabric against her skin turned her on.

The words to the Rod Stewart classic, "Do Ya Think I'm Sexy?" were her anthem. She sang along with the song as she zipped up her dress and stepped into the matching heels.

A quick glance at the clock told her it wouldn't be long before her date would be here. A shiver ran up the back of her spine as she thought about his hands touching her. God, but she loved the feel of a man's hands on her body as much as she loved the feel of silk. It made her sick to her stomach, thinking how close she'd come to losing all of this. She had no misgivings about what she'd done to Chaz Finelli. The little bastard never did know when to quit. Besides, the game he was playing was dangerous. What happened to him was nothing more than a job hazard. She did regret having to shoot an innocent bystander, but not enough to lose any sleep. This was a tough world, and she was as tough as they came. Survival of the fittest was her motto, and to hell with anyone who got in her way.

The song rocked its way to silence, and for one blessed moment she closed her eyes, savoring all that was her world. Secrets were dangerous, but danger also added another frisson of excitement to the game.

Suddenly the sound of tires rolling on gravel became apparent. She moved to the window. Although it was dark, the cat's-eyes headlights on the sports car were a

signal that her date had arrived. She'd heard about his pre-
dilection for…how could she put it? Unusual sex? All it
had taken was one phone call and he was hers. Through
the window, she saw him get out of the car. He paused,
smoothing back his hair and brushing something from
the front of his coat before moving toward the door. She
smiled to herself as the doorbell began to ring. The stupid bastard. He might be rich and kinky, but before the
night was over, he would know her in a very special way.

Captain Aaron Floyd was nursing a headache and the
beginnings of what felt like the flu when Detectives English and Fisher knocked on his door.

"Come in," he said, and then winced at the sound of
his own voice. "Give me some good news," he said, as he
opened a drawer and took out a bottle of cough medicine.

"China Brown is getting better," Ben said.

"That's good, but not the news I was referring to," he
said, then tilted the bottle to his mouth, rather than use
the little plastic cup that also served as a lid. He swallowed and shuddered as he replaced the lid and put the
bottle back in the drawer. "God, I hate winter and everything that comes with it."

Both detectives wisely chose not to comment and
waited for him to continue.

"Okay," Floyd said. "Tell me where we are on this investigation. I'm getting some flack from up above."

"Dang, Captain, you mean even God's in on the case?"

Floyd rolled his eyes and then blew his nose. "Shut up,
Fisher. I don't feel good enough to put up with your crap."

Red grinned.

Ben leaned forward, his elbows on his knees. "We've
been as discreet as possible without undermining our investigation. Beyond that, I don't give a good damn. Be-

tween the adultery, the drugs and the perversions, the
people involved brought it on themselves."

"Amen," Red echoed. "And what sticks in my craw is
the fact that not a damn one of them even blinked about
the money they paid Finelli. It was getting caught that
pissed them all off."

Floyd nodded. "Yeah, but when the mayor's involved,
it puts a lot of heat on a lot of people. So, what do we
know?"

Ben handed the captain a list of names. "The ones that
aren't crossed out are the only people who don't have
iron-clad alibis. The ones with a red mark beside them
are the ones who have no one to corroborate where they
were. The others had people who could vouch for them
part of the night, but not all of it."

Floyd scanned the list. "Ariel Simmons? Wasn't she
on television that night?"

"Taped show," Red said. "Which she forgot to mention when we asked."

Floyd moved to the next name. "Connie Marx?"

"Said she was home with the flu," Ben offered. "Turns
out Larry Dee Jackson says she was in his hotel room
with him. Either way, one of them is lying, maybe both."

"What about Bo Milam, the real estate developer?"

"In a jet on his way to Las Vegas. It checked out."

"And the others?" Floyd asked.

"About the same story, but we're still working on these
two." Red pointed to the bottom of the page. "One's a
banker. One's a plastic surgeon. Neither one has an alibi
worth a damn, and we've got a couple of guys checking
them out."

Floyd looked up. "Okay, keep at it," he said. "Let me
know as soon as something breaks."

"Captain, about the guard we put on China Brown…"

"What about it?" Floyd asked.

"I'd like to continue it 24-7 until we know who we're looking for. If word gets out that we've got a live witness to this, her life won't be worth a damn."

"How are you handling that, by the way?" Floyd asked.

"With a little deception. The newspaper account said two people were killed. Finelli and someone whose name wasn't being released until notification of kin. We're counting on the shooter to assume that China was the other death, since she's the one who got shot. The fact that it was her child instead of her might not occur to him, and as long as he thinks she's dead, she's safe."

"Okay, I'll back you on this," Floyd said. "Continue the guard. But after she's released, that's another story. She was homeless, right? We don't have the budget to put her up in a hotel with round-the-clock guards until we bring in the perp."

Ben was already ahead of the issue. "There won't be any problems. I'm taking her home with me."

Floyd forgot the headache and every other ache in his body as he bolted up out of his seat.

"The hell you will," he said. "You're already over the line with this."

"I'm not planning to kidnap her. I'm just offering her a safe place to stay."

"That's a conflict of interest. I won't allow it."

Ben stood his ground. "I'm not a lawyer. I'm a cop. What I do on my own time is my business as long as it's not illegal."

"I don't like it," Floyd said.

"Objection noted," Ben said. "Is there anything else?"

Floyd glared at Ben English. Ben returned the stare without comment. Floyd was the first to look away.

"You mess this up and I'll have your ass," he warned.

"It's already messed up, Captain. I'm just trying to do something right. It's the least she deserves."

"Then go catch me a killer," Floyd said.

Chapter 7

It was noon the next day when they got their first break in the case, and then it was just by chance. A man named Tommy Fairheart had been booked into jail the previous night on a drunk and disorderly. Ben weighed the odds on how many men would have the same name and not be the man who'd walked out on China, then decided to see for himself. He grabbed Red on the way out of the men's room and together they headed toward the city jail.

A short while later Ben stood outside the interrogation room, staring through a one-way mirror at the man inside. His clothes were fashionable but rumpled. His sandy-blond hair was just a little too long, and, except for a weak chin, Ben had to admit women probably found him handsome. Even though he'd spent the night in jail, he seemed unfazed by his situation. He was smiling and laughing and playing his con, even while Red was interrogating him. Ben wanted to hurt him—to make him suffer the way China was suffering.

When Red turned and stared directly toward the mirror, nodding slightly, Ben's muscles tensed. It was their prearranged signal for Ben to appear. Red had Fairheart at ease. It was time for Ben to nail his ass to the wall.

When the door opened, Fairheart looked up, a smile still on his face. Compared to the trouble he'd been in before, a drunk and disorderly was nothing. The fact that they were interrogating him made no sense, because no crime had been committed against the bar owner. However, he was willing to go along with their game, as long as it got him released.

But the detective who entered didn't return Tommy's smile, nor did he seem inclined to do so at a later date. Tommy shrugged it off and leaned back in his chair, waiting to see what came next.

Ben walked up behind Fairheart, then stopped. Fairheart looked up into the mirror at the man standing behind him. Their gazes met and locked. After a moment, Fairheart's smile began to slip.

"What's going on here?" he said, and looked at Red for an answer.

"My partner doesn't have anything else to say to you," Ben said. "But I do."

"Oh...I get it," Fairheart said and then smirked. "This is good cop-bad cop, and you're Satan himself, right?"

Ben spoke, his voice low and angry. "Shut up, Fairheart. I'm the one asking questions, understand?"

Fairheart shrugged, although he was beginning to get nervous.

"So ask," he blustered, and leaned back in the chair, balancing it on the back two legs.

"Sit up!" Ben ordered, and pushed the man into an upright position. The chair hit the floor with a thump.

"Where were you at 10:00 p.m. on December 11?"

Fairheart's belly began to knot. Fuck! How had they

found out? He would have sworn there was no way they could trace him to the robbery in Dallas Heights.

"I don't remember," he said. "What day was that?"

"Friday."

"Oh, yeah, I guess I was at the movies."

"What did you see?"

"I forget."

Ben circled the table to face him, then leaned down, bracing his hands on the surface.

"You've got to do better than that. Do you own a gun?"

"No," Fairheart blustered, thinking of the 9 mm semi-automatic back in his apartment. "Besides, what does this have to do with having a little too much to drink? All I did was break a couple of chairs."

"Not a damn thing, actually," Ben said. "This is about the two people who were murdered down in Oakcliff on December 11. You *have* heard of the area, right?"

Now they had his attention. Fairheart would have been the first to admit he was a con man, but a killer? Never. Yet he also knew that plenty of men went to prison for things they didn't do.

"Oakcliff is a pretty big area. Where did the murders take place?" Fairheart asked.

"The Blue Parrot sound familiar?" Ben asked.

Fairheart shook his head. "I've heard of it, but I haven't ever been there. Look, Detective, I didn't have anything to do with any killings, and I don't hang out in places like that. I don't swing that way, if you know what I mean."

"You saying The Blue Parrot is a gay bar?"

"All I'm saying is, you go in there, you better be careful who you come out with. You get it? There's a little bit of everything going on in there."

"Yeah, I get it," Ben said. "And we both know you like women, don't you, Fairheart?"

Tommy shrugged and then grinned. "What's not to like about them? I'm all man and then some."

"Oh, we know what kind of man you are," Ben said. "You're a liar and a thief. You use women, and when they don't have anything left to give, you walk out on them, leaving them to deal with the mess you've left behind. Is that a fair assessment?"

Fairheart shrugged again.

Ben slapped the table with the flats of both hands. "Answer me, you son of a bitch, or I swear I'll—"

Red laid a hand on Ben's shoulder. For the moment, it was enough to steady Ben's anger.

"So I'm not the marrying kind, so what?" Fairheart asked. "Since when is that a crime?"

Ben leaned forward until there was less than a foot between their faces.

"For starters, since you stole money from China Brown."

Fairheart sighed with relief. "Is that what this is all about? Well, it's her word against mine. Besides, she's gone."

Ben's heart skipped a beat. The information he had from China's landlord had Fairheart skipping out about a week before she was evicted. How could he know she was gone unless he'd seen her afterward—like maybe on the street, in front of The Blue Parrot?

"Gone where?" Ben snapped.

"She's not at the apartment anymore, that's all I know."

"And you know why, don't you? She's not there because maybe she went looking for you after she got evicted. She was six months pregnant with your kid and needed a place to stay. She got all the way to the South Side, didn't she? Only you didn't want to be found. You got into an argument on the street in front of The Blue

Parrot, and you shot her—twice. And then someone started taking pictures of what you'd done, and you shot him, too."

Fairheart needed to throw up. "No! God, no! I didn't shoot China. I didn't even know she got shot. I don't kill people, man. I drink too much, and I don't like to be tied to one woman, but I'm not a killer. I swear to God, I'm not a killer. I'm not the one who killed China, and I don't know anything about another man. As for the kid being dead, so what? At least the system won't be hounding me for the next eighteen years to pay child support for some brat."

Before Red could react, Ben had taken Fairheart by the neck, yanked him out of his chair and slammed him against the wall.

"Help!" Fairheart screamed. "Get him off me!"

Red grabbed Ben's wrist before he threw the first punch, but it was all he could do to hang on.

"Ben! Ben! Don't ruin your career over this piece of shit!" he cried.

Ben cursed, turning loose of Fairheart as if he'd suddenly ignited and stalked to the other side of the room.

"That's police brutality!" Fairheart shouted. "You're looking at a lawsuit that will—"

Red put his hand against Fairheart's chest, and the quiet tone of his voice was more frightening than any threat he might have made.

"You're not going to sue anybody, because there's not a mark on you, and you are going to sit down and be quiet," Red said. "And while you're there, you need to think about all the dangers a pretty boy like you faces behind bars."

Tommy Fairheart had a sudden urge to urinate. He'd been in jail before, but never for any length of time and never in a maximum security prison. If they nailed him for murder, he wouldn't survive inside, and he knew it.

"I didn't kill anybody," he repeated.

Ben turned, and the look on his face was deadly.

"Then prove it," he said.

Fairheart sighed. Copping to a B and E, breaking and entering, was a hell of a lot better than being sent up for murder. With any luck, he would be out within a year. Besides, it wouldn't be so bad, being inside during the winter months. A warm bed, three squares a day and clean clothes. It was beginning to sound better and better.

"I can prove where I was," he said.

Ben shoved his fists in his pockets to keep from putting them in Fairheart's face.

"Keep talking."

"There's this house over in Highland Park. You can check with Robbery. They'll tell you. I was there on December 11 around nine-thirty in the evening. I pawned the take at Frankie's Gun and Pawn Shop the next morning. There isn't any way I could have been on the south side if I was robbing a house in Highland Park, right?"

At that moment Ben knew he was telling the truth, and the knowledge made him sick. Even if they were going to put Fairheart behind bars, they were back to square one with the murders. He couldn't get Fairheart for murder, but he *could* get him for money.

"I noticed on your booking sheet that you had a little over twelve hundred dollars on you when you were picked up."

Fairheart shrugged. "So?"

"So I'm thinking that you've just gotten an attack of conscience over the way things have turned out." Ben looked up at his partner. "Hey, Red, didn't I just hear

Fairheart say he was planning to give that money to the county to pay for burying his child?"

Red grinned. "Yeah, that's what I heard."

Tommy Fairheart bolted to his feet. "Hey, man, you can't do that to me. I need that money for my bail and I—"

Ben took one step toward him.

Fairheart began to back up, holding his hands in front of him like a shield.

"Wait…wait…yeah, that's fine with me. After all, I can always get more." He couldn't resist bragging. "There are plenty of lonely women. China Brown was an easy mark. I didn't hit her. I never hit my women. I treated her good when I was with her."

"And when you left, you destroyed her," Ben said. He pointed at Red. "Call Robbery. Get someone over here to take him to booking, and don't forget to have lover boy here write a letter of intent about the money before he leaves."

Now that everything was beginning to calm down, Fairheart began to regain his bluster.

"You don't scare me," he said, as Ben opened the door.

Ben turned. "You should be afraid," he said softly. "Very afraid. Stay away from China Brown. If you come near her again, I will bury you so deep in the paperwork of the Texas justice system that you'll never see daylight again." He walked away, not trusting himself to stay any longer.

Fairheart glared after the man's back, then turned his fury toward Red.

"That was another threat. You heard him," Fairheart argued as Red began to handcuff him for transport.

"I didn't hear a damned thing," Red said.

Ben walked all the way back to Homicide by himself. He needed to put distance between himself and that man before he did something he couldn't take back. But when he got to his desk, the note by the phone darkened his mood even more.

Call the coroner.

He punched in the numbers, although he suspected what the message would be. Red walked into the room just as he disconnected. He grabbed his coat from the back of his chair and slipped his cell phone in his pocket.

"What's up?" Red asked.

Ben paused. "China Brown's baby...the coroner just released the body to the next of kin."

"I thought she didn't have any kin," Red said.

"She doesn't," Ben muttered, and headed for the door.

"Where are you going?"

"To talk to China. I need to ask her where she wants the baby buried."

"She can't talk," Red argued. "Besides that, you can't just waltz in there and ask her something like that. She doesn't know about the baby. The news could kill her."

"She does know," Ben said. "And she can talk. She just hasn't wanted to yet. I'm taking the rest of the afternoon off, okay? If the captain needs to get in touch with me, he has my number."

Before Red could argue, Ben was gone.

Someone was washing China's face and brushing her hair, and she wanted to tell them they'd just gotten soap in her eyes, but she couldn't summon enough initiative to argue. Early that morning she'd heard a man—a doctor, she thought—giving orders regarding her care. They had upped the antibiotic and lowered the pain medication. She wanted to tell them they were crazy. If they hurt in as many places as she did, they would shoot themselves full of painkillers and never stop.

A loud noise sounded in the hallway outside, and China jumped. The reflex was instinctive—the sound too much like a gunshot.

"I'm sorry, dear," the nurse said, and patted China's arm in an effort to calm her. "You're in a hospital. You're safe. Don't be afraid. There's a policeman on guard outside the ward, and you're doing just fine."

She struggled with a sigh. Safe? She would never feel safe again. Her mind gave up the struggle to stay awake, and she drifted off to sleep. Sometime later she awoke but could not bring herself to the point of opening her eyes. The last thing she'd seen was that woman pointing a gun at her, and then the snow falling into her eyes. She was afraid to look—afraid of what she might see. So she lay without moving, listening to the murmur of nurses' voices and the occasional moan from a patient nearby.

She was drifting again, lost in a place between reality and denial, when she heard another sound—that of footsteps coming toward her at a steady pace. Her heart skipped a beat. She knew those steps. She knew his voice. It was the promise man.

The adrenaline rush of wanting to wring Tommy Fairheart's neck was subsiding as Ben exited the elevator and started down the hall to the ICU. Normally he looked forward to these visits, but not this afternoon. Instead, he felt sick to his stomach. There was so much he needed to know, and she was the only one who could help them. Guilt had a good foothold in his conscience as the nurse at the desk waved him into the ward. What if Red was right? What if this visit made things worse instead of better? He shrugged off the thought. This woman was a fighter. She deserved the right to be a part of these decisions. For all he knew, it was the only thing keeping her alive.

Then he saw her face, and the tension begin to ease from his body. Just a few more steps. Finally he was there.

"Hello, China."

He stroked the length of her arm, testing the warmth of her skin as he touched her.

Although her eyes were closed, there was something different about her. It had to do with the posture of her body, or maybe the tilt of her head upon the pillow, almost as if she were listening. He slipped his hand beneath her fingers, letting them rest on his palm, and then gave them a gentle squeeze of hello.

"It's me. Ben. It's been a few hours since we last talked, and a lot has happened that I knew you would want to know. We found your friend, Tommy Fairheart."

She inhaled slowly. Ben looked up just in time to see a muscle twitch in her jaw.

"Okay, maybe he's not your friend anymore, but we found him, just the same. At first we thought he was the one who shot you, but he has a pretty good alibi. Just don't give up on us, okay? The investigation is still going strong."

She sighed, then seemed to be waiting for him to continue.

"There's something we need to talk about."

He hesitated, uncertain of how to begin. She was so small and so hurt, and the thought of causing her more pain of any kind was abhorrent. Yet it was her child, and she was the one on whom the decision should rest.

He cupped the side of her face, tracing the curve of her cheek with his thumb.

"China, you do understand me, don't you?"

Within seconds, she nodded slightly. The communication, scant though it was, was beautiful to Ben. He wanted to laugh, then he wanted to cry. Instead, he patted her cheek and then brushed a few strands of hair from her forehead.

"That's good, honey, so good. Now, do you think you can do something for me?"

She didn't move, but he could feel her pulse jumping.

"Will you open your eyes for me?"

China's heart was pounding inside her chest so hard that it felt like it might explode. Her fear was so great that she couldn't find the words to say no.

"Please," Ben begged. "I promise it will be okay."

She sighed. The promise man—back with another promise. Did she dare to trust him? Did she dare to trust herself?"

"I need your help," Ben said softly. "We need to bury your baby. I don't know what you want me to do."

A moan slid out from between her lips, followed by the onset of tears. Both the sound and the sight broke Ben's heart. He didn't know whether to apologize and leave, or cry along with her.

"I know, honey…I know," Ben whispered. "I'm sorry. Do you want me to leave?"

When her fingers curled around his wrist, he took it as a no.

"Okay, then," he said. "I'm here. You just take your time. When you're ready, we'll talk."

He looked around for a chair, but before he could move, he heard her take a slow breath. He looked down. Her eyelids were fluttering, then opening to accommodate only the briefest of glances, as if the lights were too bright for her eyes.

"Here, China. I'm here."

She turned to the sound of his voice and then stilled. Ben felt as if he'd been waiting all his life to look into her eyes.

China's memory quickened. Light. She'd almost forgotten there was a world beyond the darkness of her mind. Shadows danced before her eyes, coupled with intermittent flashes of brilliance. Her eyelids were dry against the corneas, and she blinked several times until it was no longer painful. She could feel his breath on her face and the rock-steady beat of his heart beneath her fingers.

"Mama," she said, and didn't even recognize the sound of her own voice.

Ben frowned. Was she more confused than he'd imagined? Her mother was dead. Surely she wasn't asking for her.

"I'm sorry, China, but your mother can't be here."

She licked her lips and then slowly shook her head no.

Ben was even more confused. "I don't understand," he said. "What are you trying to tell me?"

"Baby…with Mama."

Suddenly Ben understood. "You want the baby buried beside your mother?"

Immediately the tension in her body relaxed and she managed a nod.

"Can you tell me where she's buried?" Ben asked.

"Rest…"

At first Ben didn't understand as his mind raced toward a dozen different conclusions.

"I know she's at rest, honey. But I need to know where she's buried. Is she in Dallas?"

Her eyes opened a little bit more, and then she was looking at Ben English's face. Ben caught himself holding his breath. Her eyes were blue—a deep, stormy blue—and her gaze reflected such sorrow he couldn't find the strength to speak. He waited, naked before her gaze.

"Restland."

"Oh…Restland Cemetery on the north side of Dallas?"

She nodded, then closed her eyes.

"I understand. Your mother is buried there, and you want the baby with her."

China's answer came out in whisper.

"Yes."

"Will you trust me to do this for you? Will you do that, honey? I promise to make it special."

Tears welled, coming all the way from a broken heart to China's eyes. The promise man—so full of promises. Why couldn't she have met a man like this before it was too late?

"Ah, God," Ben murmured. "I didn't mean to make you cry any more. Forgive me?"

She curled her fingers around his wrist and then sighed. She was tired—so very tired. She wanted to sleep, but there was something she needed to tell him, only she couldn't remember what.

Ben could tell her endurance was just about gone, but he didn't regret a moment of his visit. Today was the first day since he'd seen her lying on the sidewalk in front of that bar that he felt positive she would recover.

"I'm going to let you sleep now," Ben said. "You did good today, really good. I'm so proud of you, China. Just remember, we're still hard at work on your case, and we will find the man who shot you. It's just a matter of time."

Suddenly China's eyes flew open. She remembered what it was that she'd been wanting to say.

"No," she muttered, and dug her fingers into his wrist.

Startled by her vehemence, Ben frowned.

"No? You don't believe we'll find him?"

"No," China said, her voice little more than a whisper. "Not a him."

Ben froze. What she'd just said was something they'd never considered.

"China, are you saying the person who shot you was a woman?"

China's eyes were drooping. She was fighting an overwhelming urge to sleep, but he had to understand that they were looking in the wrong places. Her head lolled to the side. She could hear the promise man's voice, calling to her from far away.

Ben was frantic. "China...sweetheart...just one more time. You can do it, I know you can. Are you telling me that the person who shot you was a woman?"

He saw her take a breath. Her lips parted. He stared at her mouth, waiting for the word to emerge. Finally a whisper came, so faint that he had to bend down to hear.

"Yes."

His eyes narrowed as shock shot through his body.

"I heard you, honey. I understand. Now rest. I'll be back tomorrow. I promise."

When China heard the words "I promise" she smiled in her mind, though the smile never reached her face.

Ben straightened abruptly. Satisfied that his visit had done China no harm, he touched the side of her cheek one last time and then walked away. This changed everything, and Red and Captain Floyd needed to know as soon as possible.

"Senator Wakefield, you'd better turn on your television and take a look at this."

Bobby Lee glanced up as his aide, Duffy Melton, entered his office, then picked up the remote and hit the Power button.

"What channel?" he asked.

"Breaking story on all channels, I think," Duffy said.

As the picture began to emerge, Bobby Lee could see news crews and an ambulance, as well as about a dozen of Dallas's finest cordoning off what appeared to be a crime scene.

"What's the big deal?" Bobby Lee asked.

"Tashi Yamamoto was found dead in his car in a bank parking lot. They think it was a robbery. His wallet and jewelry are missing, and they're saying he died of a gunshot to the head."

Bobby Lee frowned. "Tashi Yamamoto of Yamamoto Industries?"

Duffy nodded. "One and the same. This is going to play hell in South Dallas. That factory employs over a thousand of your constituents. If they close down that plant, we've got a whole lot of people out of a job, and in this economy, that's not good."

"I never met the man," Bobby Lee muttered.

"No, sir, but you know the rumors about him. He didn't come to Texas often, but when he did, he was almost a recluse. People said he was into a lot of weird stuff…perversion…things like that."

Bobby Lee shrugged. "I was taught never to speak ill of the dead, so just drop it. By the way, where's that EPA file on the Ellis Fishery? Damn agency, always meddling into hardworking people's business. Find it for me, will you? I promised Edward Ellis that I'd see to it they didn't shut him down."

"Yes, sir," Duffy said. "I'll be right back with it."

As Duffy left, Bobby Lee's frown deepened as he glanced back at the television screen. He hated surprises, but he hated turmoil more. With a muffled curse, he aimed the remote at the television. When the screen went black, he tossed the remote aside and stalked to the sideboard to pour himself a drink.

Chapter 8

The information Ben received from China set Homicide into an uproar. Now the forty-five names on the original list had to be looked at from another angle, and within the space of three days, the investigation had Dallas society into an uproar. The media had been told nothing, but it was inevitable from the number of people involved that something would eventually leak. China Brown had been moved from the ICU into a private room with a guard posted outside her door. No one went in or out who wasn't on the list, and Ben's anxiety grew. The longer it took to find the killer, the more difficult it would be. And if word got out that the Dallas police had an eyewitness, China's life wouldn't be worth a dime.

The men who'd been eliminated earlier were still in the clear, but now their wives were not. Before, the women in Finelli's pictures who were without good alibis had been put more or less in the background of the investigation. Now they were prime suspects. Four teams of detectives from Homicide were working the list, going from one household to the next and raising more hell in

Dallas than the annual rivalry of the Texas A&M–Oklahoma University football game.

High on the list of suspects were anchorwoman Connie Marx, Shelly Milam, a local real estate developer's wife, and televangelist Ariel Simmons. Their alibis were vague, and they had no one to corroborate their whereabouts on the night of the shootings. After learning she was a suspect in a double homicide, Connie Marx had been put on temporary leave by her boss. She was so angry at the Dallas P.D. that she was threatening to hire a lawyer. The fact that Larry Jackson claimed she was with him was tainted by the fact that there was no one else to verify their story. In the eyes of the police, being lovers *and* suspects more or less negated whatever truth there might be between them.

Two other detectives were trying to find Shelly Milam, who'd served her husband with divorce papers after he'd been interviewed the first time around. All they knew at this point was that she'd flown to Alabama to be with her family and wouldn't be back in Texas until next week. They were in the process of notifying the Selma, Alabama, police department that Mrs. Milam was wanted for questioning in two murders and asking their help in locating her.

Since Ariel Simmons's earlier claim that she was broadcasting her show had been disproved, Red and Ben descended upon the woman's home with renewed fervor. Only this time, Ariel's lawyer was present.

"Looks like she's got company," Red said, as he parked in front of Ariel Simmons's door.

The black Jaguar already in the driveway spelled money, and the vanity plate below the bumper, ILUV-

2SUE, was a mobile advertisement for the lawyer who owned it.

"More like reinforcements," Ben said. "Let's get this over with. I promised China I'd come by this evening before I drove out to the ranch."

"Going to see Mattie?" Red asked.

Ben nodded, then grinned. "Yeah, tomorrow's my day off, and Mom's been giving me heck about how long it's been since I've been home. Thought I'd better check on her and the place while I've got a chance."

He rang the doorbell.

Within seconds, a man answered. From the cut of his suit and the Rolex on his wrist, Ben assumed this would be the lawyer.

"Detectives English and Fisher to see Miss Simmons," Ben said.

"This way, gentlemen. And for the record, I'm Herb Langley, Miss Simmons's lawyer."

"For the record, she's going to need one," Ben replied, and was satisfied to see the back of Langley's neck turning red as he escorted them down the hall.

As they entered the library, it was obvious that Ariel had been awaiting their arrival. She was in character, from the long blond hair to a soft, flowing white dress. At their approach, she looked up from the chair where she was sitting and laid her hand on her Bible, as if to hold her place while she greeted them.

"Do sit down," she said softly, and then bent her head and closed her eyes as she murmured a quick, silent prayer.

When she looked up, her face seemed illuminated, her eyes wide and bright with unshed tears. She sighed, then closed her Bible and laid it aside, giving them her full attention.

"I was told you have some more questions for me, so I've asked my lawyer, Herbert Langley, to sit in. I'm sure you understand."

Neither detective seemed impressed with her change of manner or appearance, and it aggravated Ariel greatly, but she didn't let it show.

"Now, what can I do for you gentlemen?"

Ben pulled out his notebook and went straight to the point.

"When we were here before, you told us that on the night Finelli was murdered, you were doing a live broadcast. We have since found out that the show that night was taped at an earlier date."

Ariel's hands fluttered up from her lap in an awkward sort of way, as if they were connected to the strings of an apprentice puppeteer.

"You are so right, and I apologize for the mistake. You see, I rarely air anything that's not live, and I suppose in my shock at that horrible photograph you showed me, I just forgot. Of course, when I checked my calendar, I realized what I'd done and told Langley immediately. Didn't I, Langley?"

"Yes, you certainly did," he said. "And, as you know, before I could contact the police department and inform them of the error, your people contacted my client instead. The accusation that she is in any way connected to that horrible woman in the photograph, or to the murders, is absurd."

"That's all well and good," Ben said. "But we need more than an apology from Ms. Simmons. We still need to know where she was that night."

Ariel smiled, although in truth she wanted to scream. This was all Finelli's fault. If the stupid little bastard hadn't chosen to meddle in things that were not his business, none of this would be happening.

"I was here, in my home," she said, and then the tears that were glittering in her eyes began to slide soundlessly down her face. "I was preparing my sermon for the Sunday broadcast, and I'm afraid my only witness was God." She leaned forward. "Will you take God's word, Detective English?"

"Of course," Ben said. "Tell him I'm listening."

A dark flush spread across her cheeks. "You jest about God's word? How dare you?" She looked to her lawyer, holding out her hands in supplication. "Langley, how am I to deal with unbelievers?"

Ben's patience had been thin when they started this conversation, but it snapped when she started to emote.

"Look, lady, can the drama, okay? My religious beliefs are not on trial, but you very well could be if you don't come up with a better alibi than that."

Ariel stood abruptly, her saintly persona gone. "I have nothing more to say to you. Either arrest me or get out of my home. And be warned, I intend to go on the air and tell the world of the evil that is trying to drag me down." She was in full swing now, beginning to pace back and forth in front of them the way she did onstage. "That picture you have of me is a fake. Someone has put my face on another's body. Langley says it's a simple matter to do such a thing nowadays, and I won't be railroaded into submission. God is my strength. I accept this as a trial of my faith. God will be with me through the wilderness of this horror, and I will prevail."

Ben stood. "Sit down, Miss Simmons. We're not through until I say we're through. Yes, faking photographs is easy, but it's also easy for an expert to detect, and so far, our experts haven't found any discrepancies."

Ariel sat, her fury evident. "Langley, do something," she muttered.

"Are you going to arrest her?" Langley asked.

Ariel shrieked. "You're supposed to be helping me, not them!"

"Shut up, Ariel, you've said enough," Langley said. The woman's shock was evident, but she hushed. Langley looked up. "Okay, men, we've all got our cards on the table. Miss Simmons was in her home preparing her sermon. She can't prove it, but can you prove otherwise? Do you have any witnesses who say they saw her in Oakcliff that night? No, you don't, or she would already be under arrest. So where does that leave us? In the clear, that's where." He stood. "Now, my client has cooperated fully with you people, and if you aren't going to arrest her, then I suggest it's time you take your leave."

Both men stood. Ben gave the preacher a calculated look, then left her with a parting shot.

"We're going, but I want you to remember something, lady. Lies have a way of coming back and biting you on the ass, so you better watch where you sit."

When Langley got up to follow them out, Ben stopped. "Don't bother," he said. "We can find our own way."

Ariel Simmons was arguing with her lawyer before they got out the door, and when they were halfway down the hall, they heard her starting to shout.

Red grinned. "Right about now, old Langley's earning every penny she pays him."

Ben shook his head. "There isn't enough money on earth to pay me to work for a woman like her. She's lying, Red. But how in hell can we prove it?"

"Do you think she did it?" Red said.

"I don't know," Ben answered. "Only China can help us with that one. Yesterday, when I went to see her, she talked to me for almost five minutes before she went back to sleep. I keep wanting to push her for answers, but then I remember how she looked that night, all pale and still, with the snow falling on her face." He shuddered. "I thought she was dead."

"She came close," Red said. "But that's the operative word. *Close* is not the same as *over*. You said it yourself, she's getting better every day. When she's ready to do more, you'll know it. Right now, be grateful for small favors. At least we know the shooter was a woman. Now all we need is a name."

China was awake when Ben came into her room. The sight of his smile did things to her heart that she would rather not face. No use wasting time caring about a man ever again. They were full of pretty words—until they were through with you.

"Hey, there," Ben said, as he reached her bedside and set a little Santa Claus doll on her table. "It's just a feel-good thing," he said, pointing to the doll. "Good to see you awake. How have you been doing?"

"All right," she said, and when he touched the side of her face with the back of his hand, she told herself he was only feeling for fever. But when his hand turned and he cupped her cheek, she didn't know what to think.

Ben was elated that she was recovering, but there was a drawback he hadn't expected. Before, he'd touched her without thought. Now she was obviously not receptive to the notion and while he understood her distrust, it hurt him just the same.

"That's good," Ben said, and took off his coat and laid it at the foot of her bed.

China wiggled her toes beneath the weight and decided it felt comfortable after all.

"Do you feel up to taking a look at a few pictures?" he asked.

"Of what?" China asked.

"Possible suspects."

China's eyes widened as she stared at the pictures he took out of his jacket pocket. She wanted the woman found, but the thought of seeing her again made her sick with fear.

Ben saw the look and instantly understood. "It will be okay, honey. They're only pictures."

China bit her lip and then reached for them. "Yes, I'll look at them."

"Good."

He laid them in her lap, spreading them out until she could clearly see all six. Almost immediately, she pointed to three of them.

"Not her, or her, or her," she said.

Ben picked them up and put them back in his pocket. "What about the other three?"

China picked them up one at a time, looking intently. One was of Shelly Milam. There was a resemblance, but she couldn't be sure. Twice, she went back to two of them—one of Ariel Simmons, one of Connie Marx. Finally shook her head.

"I can't be sure. There's something about these two that looks familiar, yet not exactly right."

Ben knew that a lawyer would have a field day with that remark. Both women were recognizable in their own right, which could be why China was confused.

"Take your time," he said. "Try to remember what she—"

She looked up. "I don't have to try. That woman's face is forever etched in my mind."

"Sorry," Ben said, and then picked up the pictures and put them back in his pocket. "It was worth a try."

"No, I'm sorry," she said. "But their hair is different, and it was dark, and the woman was wearing some kind of evening dress under a full-length fur coat."

Ben took Ariel's and Connie's pictures out of his pocket again and laid them back in her lap.

"Picture them wearing a wig like the woman who shot you and then tell me if the features fit."

China looked again, fingering one, then the other. Finally, she shook her head.

"I just can't be sure."

Ben's hopes fell, but he didn't let on. "That's all right. Don't think this brings anything to a halt, okay?"

"Okay."

"Well, I'd better get back to work. Red's at the dentist. I promised to pick him up before noon, and he reminded me earlier that it's my day to buy lunch."

China listened intently but without comment. It would seem that Ben English kept his promises to everyone, not just to her.

"You going to be all right?" Ben asked. "Is there anything you need?"

"No, thank you, I don't need anything." *Except peace.*

Ben hesitated, wanting to hug her goodbye, but having to settle for a smile and a wave instead.

"We'll talk soon."

She nodded, glanced once at the smiling Santa doll, then drifted off to sleep.

Outside, the holiday spirit was in full swing. Nurses went about their duties wearing Santa Claus hats, and a group of children from a private elementary school sang carols out in the hall.

China awoke just as a little boy began his solo verse.

His voice was clear, a pure tenor that would one day give way to maturity, but for now it wrapped around a verse with such purity that she felt shattered all the way to her soul.

Away in a manger,
No crib for a bed,
The little lord Jesus,
Lay down His sweet head.
The stars in the bright sky
Looked down where He lay.
The little lord Jesus,
Asleep on the hay.

The image of a baby—any baby—was too much for China to bear.

"Oh God," she whispered, and then she started to cry.

Two days later, China was sitting up when Ben walked into her room. When the door opened, she flinched, relaxing only after she recognized who it was.

"You startled me."

"Sorry," Ben said, and strode quickly to her bedside. "Should you be sitting up like that? You don't want to—"

"I walked from the bed to the bathroom today."

Without thinking, he cupped the side of her face. "Oh, honey, that's wonderful news!"

The familiarity of his palm against her cheek made China nervous. It wasn't the first time he'd touched her in this way, but today it felt different—less impersonal. She looked at him, frightened by the power in his gaze, and caught herself holding her breath.

For a moment, neither of them moved. China was the first to look away, and she shivered as she fidgeted with her sheets. This was something she wasn't ready to handle—might never be able to handle again. Right now, any intimacy with a man, no matter how innocent, was impossible. There was nothing left inside her but the need to get well and the need for revenge.

Ben saw the look on her face. At that moment, if Tommy Fairheart had been within reach, he would have beaten him senseless. Damn that man to hell and back for what he'd done to China Brown. He decided that a change of subject was in order.

"Has your doctor been in today?"

To his surprise, she hesitated, then began to tremble.

"China?"

"What?"

"What did Dr. Pope tell you?"

"That he will release me in two or three days."

Ben frowned. "And that bothers you?"

She shrugged.

He eased down on the side of her bed and laid his hand on the covers. Her legs were shaking beneath them as if she'd gotten a chill, but he knew she wasn't cold.

"China, we've come too far in this together for you to quit trusting me now. What's wrong?"

She bit her lip and then looked up at him. "After all this time and no notice, I know I've lost my job. I have no money or home. When they release me from the hospital, I will have no place to go."

He wanted to take her in his arms and kiss away all the pain, but it would only make things more complicated than they already were.

"I'm sorry. I should have told you sooner," he said. "That's already taken care of. I'm taking you to my mother's until I'm certain you're safe."

"Oh, but I couldn't impose on—"

Ben shook his head and patted her leg. "If you knew my mother, you'd know better than to say that. She's a widow, and I suspect she's often lonely. She lives by herself in a great big house out in the country and will welcome the company, trust me."

She shook her head, still not convinced. "What if that woman—the woman who shot me—what if she comes looking for me?"

"You'll be fine. I have someone who's going to play bodyguard for the both of you. He's an ex-cop and an old friend of the family. He'll be happy to have an excuse to hang around my mother, anyway."

China was intrigued in spite of herself. "He's in love with her?"

Ben grinned. "Probably, but I'm staying out of that. Now don't worry. You just concentrate on getting well. I'll have Mom call you before you leave the hospital. You can say hello over the phone, and maybe you won't feel like such strangers when you do finally meet."

She hesitated, then sighed. "It shames me to admit that I don't really have a choice."

Ben tilted her chin to meet his gaze.

"We all have choices, China. Some are better than others, but none of them are wrong, they're just choices, okay?"

She nodded, and when he moved his finger from her chin, she felt as if her gravity shifted. The thought made her angry, but only with herself. He didn't really mean anything to her except a means to an end. He was a cop. He was sworn to protect her. The fact that he was willing to go a few steps farther was good for her. As her mother used to say, she shouldn't look a gift horse in the mouth.

"Then tell your mother I'm grateful," she said.

"Tell her yourself when she calls," Ben said. "Now

I'd better let you get some rest. I'll see you the day after tomorrow."

Her heart skipped a beat. A whole day without seeing him? In spite of her unwillingness to admit he mattered to her, he'd become her safety net.

"Okay, sure," she muttered, and willed herself not to cry.

Ben started to leave, but there was something about her silence and posture that bothered him.

"Is there anything you want to tell me—anything you need?"

She didn't answer.

"China."

She looked up.

"You can trust me. I promise," he said.

Tears welled anew. The promise man. He had yet to let her down.

"No, nothing is wrong. I've been crying a lot the last couple of days for no reason. Dr. Pope said it's my body readjusting." She bit her lip and then met his gaze. "You know, after the baby and all. I guess my hormones are all messed up."

If she'd punched him in the belly, he couldn't have been more dismayed. What the hell had he been thinking? Of course something was wrong. She was grieving for her child.

"Another thing I should have told you. I found where your mother is buried. Tomorrow your daughter will be beside her."

China started to shake. "Thank you," she mumbled. "I—" And then she covered her face with her hands. "Please let this be a nightmare and please let me wake up."

Ben groaned. Seconds later he was at her bedside and cradling her in his arms.

"Ah God, honey, your grief is breaking my heart. You might not need to be held, but right now, I need to hold you."

She cried herself to sleep in Bennett's arms.

Ben stood on the porch of the ranch house where he'd been raised, listening to the occasional bawl of a cow searching for her calf and the sound of the big rigs shifting gears on the highway a few miles east. Last night had been great. His mother had been so happy to have him, cooking all his favorite foods and dragging out picture albums and talking about his childhood as if it were yesterday. He'd waited too long to come visit and wouldn't do it to her again.

Tomorrow he would report back to work, which also meant that he would see China again. Although he was less than an hour from Dallas, he could easily imagine himself in another world.

He folded his arms across his chest and then leaned against the porch post as he looked up at the sky. The night was cold, but the sky was clear. The lights from the house behind him made patches on the floor of the porch like cold pats of butter on dry toast. The television was on in the other room, and he could hear his mother chuckling at the antics of the situation comedy she was watching.

A fresh wave of guilt hit him gut first. His mother laughed alone every night. He should be in there sharing the laughter with her. But there was a loneliness inside him that not even a mother's love could heal. He would crawl into his bed tonight and sleep alone, as he slept every night. He was thirty-six years old and had been engaged only once, twelve years ago. The engagement had lasted six weeks. To this day, he couldn't remember who'd broken up with whom. All he knew was, it was the

smartest thing he'd ever done. He wanted a family, but
with the right woman, not just because he was lonely. He
wanted a marriage like the one his parents had shared.

Immediately, his thoughts moved to China. He didn't
know a damn thing about her except that she'd put her
faith in someone who'd let her down. He didn't know if
she liked to dance. He didn't know her favorite color or
what she liked to eat, and yet he'd bonded with her in a
way he'd never done with any woman before. However,
what he felt—or thought he felt—for her was moot.

"Bennett, darling, you're going to freeze."

He turned. His mother was standing in the doorway
with a worried expression on her face.

"You're right, it's colder than I thought," he said, and
followed her back inside.

Mattie English paused in the hallway to look at her
son. There were shadows beneath his eyes and a grimness
to his mouth she couldn't remember ever seeing before.

"Son?"

"What?"

"Is everything all right?"

"I'm fine, Mom. Sorry I'm not better company. I've
got a lot on my mind."

She slipped a hand beneath his elbow and walked him
back into the living room.

"Put another log on the fire, will you, honey?"

"Sure," he said, glad to have something concrete to
do. He moved the fire screen aside and dropped another
log on the fire. When he turned, his mother was on the
sofa. She patted the cushion beside her.

"Come sit with me," she said.

He sat.

"Is it work?" Mattie asked.

Ben hesitated, but he knew better than to lie to her.

"Yes."

"Are you in trouble?"

"No, no, Mom, nothing like that. I'm sorry if I worried you."

"I've just never seen you so distracted. Do you want to talk about it?"

He looked at her and almost smiled.

"I think I'd better," he said. "Especially since I've more or less involved you in the problem."

Mattie grinned. "As long as it has nothing to do with a bake sale, we're in business."

He laughed aloud. It was an old family joke, dating back to a time when he'd volunteered her baking prowess for a bake sale his Cub Scout pack was having, and at the time, Mattie had had one arm in a sling and the other in a cast.

"No bake sales," he said. "I promise."

"Then talk to me," she said.

Ben took a breath. How to explain? There was only one way—from the beginning.

"It started two weeks ago, with a shooting in Oakcliff. A man was murdered, and a woman was shot and left for dead."

He glanced at his mother, aware that this could get touchy, because she had miscarried and lost the only child she would ever carry. The fact that they'd adopted him when he was only days old rarely crossed his mind. But if China was to stay here, this had to be said. His mother needed to know what she was going through.

"The woman was pregnant. The baby died."

"Oh, Ben," Mattie said, and then leaned over and took him by the hands. "It's all right, sweetie. I'm not that fragile, you know. Losing your father was the hardest thing I've ever had to bear, and I survived that. Keep talking."

"Okay, but remember, you asked for it."

She nodded. "So, this case…it's one of yours?"

"Yes."

"The woman who was shot…will she live?"

"For a while it was touch and go, but she's doing great now. In fact, that's part of what's been bothering me. The day she was shot, she'd just been evicted from her home. Long story short, her boyfriend dumped her, stole all her money and left her flat. She's now the only witness to a murder that is becoming a bigger mess with each passing day, and in a few days she's going to be released, but with nowhere to go. I need to keep her safe." Then he added, "I care what happens to her, Mom, and I'm about to ask a very big favor of you."

Mattie could see what was coming. "Is she nice…you know…decent?"

"As far as we can tell, she's an innocent. She's distrusting of men, but, Mom, she's so tiny…I guess *fragile* is a better word. And she's beautiful, only the oddest thing about that is, I don't think she knows it."

Mattie knew her son. She'd never heard him speak of a woman in this way. The last thing she wanted was to see Ben get mixed up with someone sordid. In her opinion, the best way to oversee the situation was to be in the middle of it. Ben might be smitten, but she would reserve judgment until she'd seen for herself.

"Bring her to me," Mattie said.

"You'll have to put up with Dave being around, too," he warned.

Mattie felt herself flushing. "Oh, Ben, he makes me nervous," she muttered. "Always fiddling around, trying to help me do stuff. I've been taking care of myself for years. I don't need him to do anything for me."

"She's a witness to a crime, Mom. The guard is neces-

sary. Dave Lambert is a retired cop. He's nearby. He's volunteered. If China comes, he has to be part of the deal."

"China? Surely that's not her real name?" Mattie
asked, envisioning some tawdry stage name for a strip-
per act.

He grinned. "Yes, ma'am, it is. China Brown. Her
mother, Mae, is deceased, or you could take the name
business up with her."

Mattie frowned. "I didn't mean there was something
wrong with it. It's just different, that's all."

"And so is she," Ben said. "So it's all right? I can tell
her you said it's okay?"

"I'll tell her myself tomorrow. What hospital is she in?"

"Parkland."

"I'll call her room. We'll talk."

Ben's grin spread. "Come here to me," he said, and
held out his arms, giving her a hug when she scooted
nearer. "I know what you're thinking, but you'll see for
yourself. She's about the least dangerous woman you'll
ever meet." Then his mood shifted, and his smile slipped.
"I buried her baby today before I drove to the ranch.
There was no one there but me and a preacher I didn't
know. Help her, Mom, because I damn sure don't know
how."

In that moment, Mattie felt a connection with the
woman she had yet to meet.

"It will be all right, son," she said softly. "Time heals
a lot. Maybe we'll heal each other. Who knows?"

Chapter 9

"Bobby Lee! Bobby Lee! We'll vote for you!"

Bobby Lee smiled and waved at the trio of giggling women across the street from the television station as he and Ainsley Been got out of his car. WFAL Channel 7 was doing a special interview on him and his recent announcement to run for president, and he was running late.

"I'll hold you to that," he called out as he entered the station.

A harried producer was waiting for him at the door.

"Senator Wakefield, thank goodness! You're on in five minutes," he said, and began miking Bobby Lee as they walked.

"Well, now," Bobby Lee said. "And here I thought I was late." Then he added. "This is my campaign manager, Ainsley Been."

The producer nodded a quick hello and then hustled the men into the studio, where Ronnie Boyle, the evening anchorman, was winding up the national news.

"Just have a seat," the producer said quietly.

Ainsley Been handed the producer a sheet of paper. "This is a list of questions the senator will respond to."

"You're restricting us as to what we can discuss?"

Bobby Lee frowned at Ainsley, then patted the young man on the back.

"Hell no, boy! I'm an open book. You just tell Boyle to ask away, you hear?"

"Thank you," he said. "Now step this way. We need to get you seated."

Ainsley started to argue, but Bobby Lee shook his head, then strode onto the set, taking a chair as if it were a throne and he the reigning king.

Granted, there weren't any real time bombs in Bobby Lee's past—except possibly his mother, and most everyone in Texas knew Mona Wakefield, or at least knew of her and accepted her as the colorful character she was. Bobby Lee's past *was* his ticket to stardom. His war record, his football prowess, his dedication to government from an early age—he was a man's man in every sense of the word, yet wealthy, unattached and handsome enough to set every woman's heart aflutter. However, it could not be forgotten that the senator was no longer just a Texas boy made good. He had moved into the national arena, and it remained to be seen how Mona Wakefield would fare.

Normally Connie Marx would have been doing the interview, but since her suspension from the network, her coanchor, Ronnie Boyle, was sitting in as host on the guest segment of the broadcast.

"Good evening, Senator," Boyle said, and shook Bobby Lee's hand as he took a seat opposite his guest.

Bobby Lee nodded and smiled.

"You're on in two," someone said.

Boyle nodded without taking his eyes from Bobby Lee.

"Are you comfortable, Senator Wakefield?"

"Yes, I'm fine," Bobby Lee said.

Boyle nodded again and began readjusting his mike, then glanced down in his lap to refer to some notes he was holding.

Again nerves twitched in the pit of Ainsley's belly, but he told himself to stay calm. After all, what the hell could happen?

In the background, someone began counting down the time.

"Five…four…three…two…"

Ronnie Boyle looked up and smiled straight into the camera. "Welcome back. We have a special guest in the studio this evening. One of Texas's finest, our very own Senator Bobby Lee Wakefield." Boyle turned his smile to Bobby Lee. "Senator, you recently announced your candidacy for president of the United States. What was it that led you to the decision to run?"

Bobby Lee leaned forward just a fraction, giving the impression that he was imparting confidential information. The expression on his face was warm but serious.

On the sidelines, Ainsley breathed a sigh of relief. He should have known better than to worry. When it came to the media, Bobby Lee was a consummate professional.

"Well now, Ronnie…you don't mind if I call you Ronnie, do you?" Bobby Lee asked.

"Of course not," Boyle said. "We're all among friends here."

"That's what I want to hear," Bobby Lee said, and began to talk.

On the other side of the city, Mona sat cross-legged in the middle of her bed, her gaze fixed on the television screen. She was listening to her son with an absent air. Most of her attention was focused on what he was wearing and how he looked. After a couple of moments, she began to relax. He looked just fine, and that Boyle fellow didn't know it yet, but Bobby Lee was guiding the interview right where he wanted it to go.

Minutes passed as Mona's mind wandered to the future and a much more momentous occasion than a local television interview. She leaned back against the headboard of her bed and closed her eyes, picturing her son standing on the steps of the White House and taking the oath of office while she stood at his side. She would wear white—no, maybe she would wear red. It would show up better on national TV. And she would wear a hat. She looked good in hats, and it was cold in the capitol in January.

Then her thoughts refocused on the show, and she glanced back at the screen just in time to hear Boyle changing the subject from national platforms to local politics.

"Senator, I'm sure you're aware of the recent death of Tashi Yamamoto. There's a rumor that the company he owned here in Dallas will fold. If it does, a lot of your constituents will be out of a job. Do you have any information that might alleviate the worry for all those families?"

Bobby Lee tilted his head sideways just a bit, giving himself a thoughtful appearance. He knew it made him look good. He'd practiced just that very pose for years to get it right.

"That was a tragedy, for sure," Bobby Lee said. "Unfortunately, I've not been contacted directly regarding any decisions from Mr. Yamamoto's company, but my sympathies go out to his family, and to the people who might be affected by the company's closing." Then he looked straight into Boyle's eyes, well aware that the camera would make it appear as if he were talking to the viewers themselves. "This is proof of how violence in this country affects us all, even indirectly. If I'm elected president, I intend to do everything in my power to change this country's thinking on capital punishment. Too many repeat offenders are released back into our society."

Boyle glanced ruefully at the producer, who was indicating that time was up, then skillfully wrapped up the interview. When it was over, Bobby Lee stood and took off his mike, dropping it into the chair in which he'd been sitting.

"Fine job, Mr. Boyle," he said, and shook the man's hand.

Ronnie Boyle nodded and smiled. "You made it easy."

Bobby Lee smiled. He never tired of having his ego stroked.

"We covered a lot of bases in five minutes," Boyle said.

"There's a lot going on in this country."

"You're right about that," Boyle said. "Especially here in Dallas."

Bobby Lee looked confused. "Are you referring to Yamamoto's death?"

"That and the Finelli scandal."

Bobby Lee's expression blanked. "Yes, well, I have another appointment in a few minutes. I must be going."

Boyle followed him off the set. "How do you think Dallas is going to come out of the mess?" he asked, and then lowered his voice a bit as he continued. "I mean, after all, this thing goes all the way to the top of the city's business and social ladder."

Bobby Lee's heart began to pound. He'd heard all about the police interrogations and the pictures they'd found in the murdered man's apartment. He'd lost sleep wondering if his mother would show up in any of them, then wondering how many people he would have to buy off to make sure the pictures disappeared if she did.

"Yes, I suppose it does, although I'd rather not comment." He grabbed Boyle's hand and gave it a vigorous shake. "Thank you again, son, for a fine interview." Then he looked at Ainsley. "Have the driver bring the car around. We're through here."

He walked away without looking back, leaving Ronnie Boyle to wonder why the senator's jovial manner had so suddenly disappeared.

The television on the wall was on, but the sound had been muted. A plate of congealing chicken and noodles was on the table near China's bed. The bowl of Jell-O was half-eaten and most of her milk was gone. She'd eaten because they'd insisted, not because she was hungry. Her appetite for everything except revenge was gone. Ever since Ben English had challenged her to get well, she'd focused all her energies on doing that very thing, and for one reason only. She wanted the woman who'd shot her to pay. Maybe then she would learn how to live with some measure of peace.

As she lay there, someone suddenly laughed aloud outside her door, and the sound hurt her heart. It seemed obscene that the world still turned when hers had all but stopped. She felt caught in a vacuum without any way out. Everything seemed pointless and frightening. During rounds this evening, Dr. Pope had told her that if she continued to progress, she would be released the day after tomorrow. The idea of moving beyond the safety of this small room and the guard at her door was horrifying. What if the moment she stepped outside the hospital door the killer shot her again? It could happen easily enough, and the killer certainly had good reason to want her dead. After all, she was the only person who could identify her.

"Oh, God, help me get through this," China whispered, and turned her face to the wall.

Within moments, the phone beside her bed began to ring. Her heart jerked with fright. Who could be calling her? No one even knew she was here. And then she thought of Ben. She hadn't seen him since the day before yesterday. Maybe he was calling to check on her. Wincing as she extended her arm, she picked up the receiver and held it to her ear.

"Hello?"

Mattie English took a deep breath. The soft, broken sound of the word was not what she'd been expecting.

"Is this China Brown?"

Suddenly the face of the woman who'd shot her flashed before her eyes. What if it was her? Frightened, China hung up, then pulled the covers up to her chin, as if the simple act would keep her safe.

A few seconds later the phone rang again, shattering her nerves and sending her into a panic. She opened her mouth to scream for help, but nothing came out. All she could do was lie there in fear. On the fifth ring, a nurse entered.

"Honey, your phone's ringing off the wall. Can't you reach it?"

Without waiting for China to speak, she picked up the receiver.

"Miss Brown's room. May I help you?"

China was holding her breath when the nurse handed her the phone.

"It's Mattie English. Says she's Detective English's mother. Do you want to talk to her?"

"Oh, my God," China muttered, and started to shake.

She'd forgotten that Ben's mother was going to call. She'd hung up on Ben's mother. She reached for the phone.

"Hello?"

Mattie started talking before China could hang up again. "I should have identified myself. I know you've been through a terrible ordeal, but I'm told you're making wonderful progress."

"Yes, ma'am," China said.

"Ben tells me you're going to be released soon."

"Yes, ma'am."

Some of Mattie's doubts began to slip. *Ma'am.* At least the girl had been raised to respect her elders.

"The reason I'm calling is to second the offer Ben made to have you come stay with me for a while—at least until an arrest can be made."

China hesitated. "He said something to me about it, but it's such an imposition for you, having a complete stranger in your home."

Mattie smiled to herself and relaxed even more.

"Oh, honey, these days I'm lonesome more than I care to remember. It will be good to have another voice in this house besides my own."

Tears unexpectedly filled China's eyes. It had been so long since she'd felt welcome anywhere that the empathy got to her.

"I suppose Ben told you I had nowhere else to go."

When the girl's voice began to shake, Mattie's empathy changed to sympathy.

"Yes, he did, and he told me the reasons why. I'm so sorry for your loss," she said softly.

Tears spilled down China's face. All she could do was nod, even though she knew Mattie could not see her.

When Mattie thought she heard a choked sob, her last bit of reserve disappeared.

"You go ahead and cry all you want to," she said. "I know the pain of what you're going through. I miscarried my only baby two months before he was due and I wanted to die. I think I tried to die." Her voice shook with remembered pain. "But the damnedest thing happened."

"What?" Mattie managed to ask, intrigued in spite of herself.

"First, I discovered that it's impossible to die from holding your own breath."

China almost smiled.

"And," Mattie continued, "I'd worked too hard on the nursery to take it all down. I wanted to be a mother more than anything on this earth, so my husband and I adopted a baby boy. It took a couple of years, but my Ben was worth the wait."

"Ben is adopted?"

Mattie smiled. Even though China's voice was still shaking, she could hear true interest in the question.

"Yes. Turned out pretty well, considering how much my husband and I spoiled him, don't you think?"

China closed her eyes, trying to picture the big man she knew as a baby someone hadn't wanted. The image hurt her heart.

"Yes, ma'am."

"Well, now, if you're going to be sleeping under my roof, you need to know one thing right now. I won't answer to anything but Mattie. None of that ma'am stuff, you hear?"

This time, China did smile. "Yes, ma'—I mean, yes, Mattie."

"That's better," she said. "Now, don't you worry about another thing. Just get well. I'll see you soon."

"All right," China said. "And thank you."

"You're welcome, honey," Mattie said. "Oh…almost

forgot. Do you have any allergies, or any horrible dislikes to foods?"

"No allergies, and the only thing I dislike about food is not having any."

Mattie's laugh tickled China's ear, making her smile widen.

"Good," Mattie said. "You've got a sense of humor. I can tell we're going to get along just fine. Get some rest. I'll see you soon."

China hung up the phone, the smile still on her face. Sometime during her conversation the nurse had gone, taking the tray of uneaten food with her. China glanced up at the television and the muted screen, then toward the window. The skyline looked the same, but there was an intangible difference in how she felt. She closed her eyes, willing herself to sleep, but the longer she lay there, the more restless she became. If only...

The door opened. She heard the swift intake of someone's breath, and she turned her head.

Ben. It was Ben. Once again her promise man had come through.

"You came," she said.

The door closed behind him as he moved toward her bed.

"I said I would."

China almost smiled. "Yes, I know."

They stared at each other without speaking. Ben felt as if he'd been away for a week instead of only one day. He wanted to take her in his arms and feel the warmth of her skin against his face, but he couldn't. Whatever he was feeling for her had nothing to do with reality.

China was silent, uneasy with her feelings. She kept staring at his face and the tenderness there—remembering how safe she'd felt within the shelter of his arms.

Suddenly he moved, and she panicked. If he came any closer, she might do something stupid, like throw herself into his arms.

"Your mother called me."

Ben stopped at the foot of her bed and then shed his coat, tossing it on a nearby chair.

"So, what did you think?"

"That she's very nice."

Ben breathed a quiet sigh of relief. "Yeah, she's that, all right."

China hesitated, then added, "She told me about her miscarriage."

Ben was surprised but didn't show it. He managed a nod. When China gave him another speculative look, he would have bet his next month's wages he knew what she was thinking.

"She said you were adopted."

And he would have been right.

"Yep, when I was about a week old. I was given up for adoption when I was born. That's about all I know."

"Does it matter to you…not knowing?"

He shook his head. "Being a cop, I've seen just about every sordid aspect of life that people can bring upon themselves. I feel thankful my mother didn't have me aborted and, if there was trouble in her life, had the good sense to give me up to shelter me from it. My adoptive parents couldn't have been any better. I consider myself blessed."

"My mother loved me very much," China said. "She left my stepfather because he was mean to me. She protected me from everything bad up until the day she died." China sighed. "That was almost five years ago, just after my twenty-first birthday, and there isn't a day goes by that I don't think of her. When I died…she was there, waiting for me," China said, and then looked away, shocked that she'd revealed something so personal.

For a moment Ben couldn't speak. China had spoken so casually about dying that it took him aback.

"When you died?"

China shrugged and looked away.

Ben scooted onto the edge of her bed and took both her hands in his.

"I'm not making fun of you. I just didn't know."

China looked up, her eyes swimming with tears. "I knew what had happened, but it didn't seem to matter. My baby was with me. I could hear voices welcoming me, then I saw people. My mother was there, smiling and calling my name." She took a deep breath and then shuddered. "Oh, Ben, He made me come back, said it wasn't my time. Only He sent me back alone."

Ben groaned and then took her in his arms, cradling her gently against his chest.

"But you're not alone anymore. I'm here for you. I'll always be here for you. I promise."

Her promise man had done it again. China closed her eyes and gave herself up to him—just for a moment, just long enough to remember what being safe felt like.

They sat without moving—him testing the boundaries of his emotions while China absorbed the scent of his aftershave and the feel of his hands cupping the back of her head.

And then she moved.

Ben found himself staring at her eyes, then the slight flare of her nostrils, then the curve of her lips.

The next thing he knew, he was kissing her.

Gently.

Slowly.

Imprinting the shape and texture of her mouth onto his brain.

Then again.

Urgently.

Desperately.

Wanting more than she was ready to offer.

He was the first to break away.

"China, I—"

She put her fingers on his mouth, then shook her head. "Don't. Don't say anything…please."

He stood abruptly and shoved his hands in his pockets as he strode to the window, needing to put space between them before he made a complete fool of himself. Had he frightened her? He was almost afraid to turn around and look. Would she change her mind about staying with his mother? Ah God, not that. The killer was still out there, and he had to know she was safe.

He turned, intent on offering an apology, but she was looking away. Although he knew he'd embarrassed her, he saw something on her face that stopped him cold. He stared, trying to figure out what was different about her. And then his heart skipped a beat. Her cheeks were pink. Her eyes were flashing. And by God, she was almost smiling.

"You going to be all right about staying with my mother?"

She looked up. "Will you be there?"

He hesitated, then nodded. "As often as I can."

Satisfied with his answer, China folded her hands in her lap.

"Then yes, if you're there, I will be all right."

Moved by the simplicity of her answer, for a moment he couldn't bring himself to speak. Suddenly he knew if he didn't leave now, he was going to make an even bigger fool of himself. He grabbed his coat and began putting it on.

"I'll see you tomorrow," he said. "Call if you need me."

China nodded, her gaze following his every movement. He was almost at the door when he stopped and turned.

"Why?" he asked.

"Why what?"

"After what Fairheart did to you, why do you trust me?"

"Promises," she said.

Ben wondered if he looked as confused as he felt. "Promises?"

"You're a smart man. You figure it out," China said. "Would you turn out the lights when you leave?"

"What? Oh...yeah, sure," Ben said, and flipped the switch as he opened the door. Then he looked at her again. She had rolled onto her side and closed her eyes. Just for a moment, before his eyes adjusted to the dark, he thought he saw someone standing beside her bed. Then he blinked, and the image was gone.

"Sleep tight, honey. I'll see you tomorrow."

Her voice reached for him from across the room.

"Do you promise?"

"Absolutely," he said.

He was still smiling as he started down the hall. It wasn't until he reached the elevator that it hit him. Day by day she'd been judging him on the promises he made against the promises he kept. A shudder racked him as the thought slid through his mind. *Please, God, I don't ever want to let her down.*

That night, despite the underlying, inevitable noise of a hospital, China slept—without nightmares, without fear—just like she'd slept as a child, knowing her mother was near.

She woke the next morning as a nurse barged into the room with a tray of pills and carrying a sprig of mistletoe, which she promptly pinned on China's pillow.

"Something to dream on, honey," she said, and then poured some water and handed China her pills to take.

"They'll be bringing your breakfast soon," the nurse said. "Do you need help getting up and getting to the bathroom?"

"No, I can do it," China said.

"Fine, then," the nurse said. "Ring if you need me."

China made her way to the bathroom and back, ever conscious of the light-headed feeling she always had when she first stood. She hated being weak and depending on others for her care. But she was alive, which was something, and she would recover fully, Dr. Pope had promised her.

Before she got back into bed, she vaguely remembered Ben leaving one of his cards and dug through the stuff in the table drawer until she found it. Her legs were shaky, so she got back in bed before reaching for the phone, but her intent was strong. Last night, in a dream, she'd seen the woman's face again—so clearly that she'd imagined the warmth of her breath upon her own face. She'd watched her expression change from rage to a complete disregard for human life, and there was something she had to do while the image was fresh in her mind.

She glanced at the clock. It was a little before seven. Maybe she should try the home number first. She punched in the numbers, then waited, counting the rings.

Ben was just getting out of the shower when the phone began to ring.

"Well damn," he muttered, then grabbed a towel and

wrapped it around his waist as he made a run for the phone.

"Hello," he said, a little breathless from the dash through the apartment.

China hesitated. He sounded out of breath and busy, and it suddenly occurred to her that his personal life might include a woman. Her mind went from that to picturing her phone call disturbing them in the act of making love.

"I'm sorry...I shouldn't have called so early. I'll call you later when you—"

"China...honey...is that you?"

"Uh, yes, but I've obviously caught you at a bad time and I can—"

"I was in the shower, that's all," he said quickly. "What's wrong?"

Her fingers curled around the receiver as she tried to picture him wet and naked. The image came through all too quickly and clearly, and she immediately bit her lip in order to focus on the pain instead of Ben.

"Nothing's wrong," she said. "But I had a dream about the woman last night, and in the dream, I saw her face so clearly. Does your department have an artist? You know, someone who can draw faces of people from a description?"

"Yes, and that's a good idea. In fact, Red and I had discussed it before, but I didn't think you were up to it."

"I want to do it," China said.

"Then it will be done. Give me a couple of hours to get everything worked out, and then we'll come to your room."

China began to relax. "All right. Uh...Ben?"

"What, honey?"

"Thank you."

"No, honey. Thank you. See you later, okay?"

"Yes, later."

She hung up and then sat quietly, contemplating what she'd just done. For the first time since the incident, she didn't feel so much like a victim, and it felt good—damn good.

Chapter 10

China was sitting up in a wheelchair when Ben and Red arrived. Another officer was right behind them, his arms full of computer equipment.

Ben went straight to where she was sitting. He wanted to hug her but had to settle for a smile.

"Good morning, China. This is Officer Matt Avery. Just as soon as he gets set up, we'll start recreating the shooter's face."

China had expected an artist with a sketch pad, not a laptop. "You do it with a computer?" she asked.

The officer looked at China and grinned. "Just wait until you see what I can do with this thing," he said.

Ben shed his coat and began helping Avery set up his equipment, while Red sidled toward her breakfast tray.

"Good morning, Miss Brown," Red Fisher said, and then pointed to her tray. "You didn't eat your toast."

"I got full."

"Do you mind?" he asked, and picked up the toast, as well as a packet of jelly, and gave it a liberal smear before taking a bite.

Ben rolled his eyes. "For God's sake, Red, if you could see yourself."

Red shrugged and then took another bite.

"So, we can assume Rita still has you on that diet," Ben muttered.

"Yeah, but the damned thing doesn't work," he muttered around his last bite of toast.

"I wonder why?" Ben drawled, and then looked at China. "As you can see, I can't take him anywhere."

China laughed and then almost immediately was flooded with guilt. How could she be laughing at a time like this? She looked down at her hands and then at a hairline crack in the corner of the room near the window, making herself focus on anything to keep from crying.

Ben moved away from Avery and then squatted down before China's wheelchair.

"Don't," he said softly.

She wouldn't look at him. "Don't what?"

"Don't play that game with yourself. It's wrong."

"I don't know what you're talking about."

"Survivor's guilt. I've seen it time and time again." He turned her chair, making her face him. "What happened was not your fault. You weren't on the streets by choice, and you didn't pull the trigger. The fact that you didn't also die when everyone else did is a miracle, not something of which to be ashamed."

Her chin was quivering, her eyes blinded with unshed tears. In her mind, she knew he was right, but it was her heart that was having difficulties in letting go of the guilt.

"China?"

"Yes, I know," she said. "Hand me some tissues, will you?"

He handed her the box from the table and then walked

away, giving her time to wipe her eyes and compose herself again.

A spoon clinked against a bowl. They all turned to look at Red.

"What?" he mumbled. "It's perfectly good oatmeal. Oatmeal is healthy. Give it a rest."

This time, when China laughed, it was easier, and when the last echo of the sound was gone, a large measure of her guilt had gone with it.

"I'm up and running, Detective English."

"Are you ready, China?" Ben asked.

She nodded.

"Good," he said, then wheeled her over to the table where Avery was waiting.

"The program Officer Avery works with has literally thousands and thousands of combinations of facial features from which to draw. You tell him what you saw, and he'll start with a face similar in structure. Between the two of you, you'll fine-tune the features individually until you're satisfied with the composite of the perpetrator's face. Understand?"

"I think so," China said.

"Anytime you get tired or want to stop for any reason, you just say so. The last thing we want to do is endanger your health."

"Okay."

He laid his hand on the back of her head and then allowed himself one stroke of the thick, dark length of her hair.

"Just relax, honey, and do the best you can."

The feel of his hand on her head and then the back of her neck was distracting, but when he moved away, she felt abandoned.

"Miss Brown?"

China turned. "Sorry," she told Avery. "What do I do?"

Avery smiled. "Talk to me. You'll see how this works as we go. We're going to start with the shape of her face and an approximate age."

China frowned, trying to remember exactly. "The street was almost deserted. There were lots of dark places and shadows, but we were standing in front of a bar, and there were so many Christmas lights that I got a pretty good look at her—twice. Once when we bumped into each other and then when she aimed the gun at—"

She stopped and shuddered.

"Take your time," Avery said. "I know this is hard."

"I'm fine," China said. "As for her age, it would be a guess, but I will say she wasn't young."

"By that, do you mean she was middle-aged?" Avery asked.

"I mean she wasn't a twenty-something, or, for that matter, a thirty-something, either. She was a very beautiful but mature woman. Maybe in her late forties. Her face was oval, I think, with a strong chin and a straight nose. Very regular features."

Ben stood aside, watching the screen as a face began to take shape.

"Hey, partner, I'm going to run down to the gift shop a minute," Red said. "I need some antacids."

"Just don't come back here with chocolate on your breath or I'm telling Rita."

"Jeez, can't a man have a simple snack without starting a revolution?"

He ambled out of the room, leaving Ben to watch over the proceedings.

Ten minutes passed. Red returned and took a silent stance beside his partner. Soon a half hour had gone by.

Avery's quiet but persistent questions were pulling things from China's memory that she hadn't known were there.

One eyebrow that arched slightly higher than the other.

Lips that were less than voluptuous.

By the time an hour had passed, she was pale and shaking. When she suddenly slumped forward, Ben called a halt.

"That's enough," he said, and started to push her wheelchair back toward her bed. But China grabbed his arm.

"No, wait," she said. "I need to finish this, and it just isn't right. There's something wrong." She stared at the screen, taking apart the woman's face one feature at a time.

"Maybe her forehead was higher," Avery suggested. He typed in a series of commands, and the forehead of the face on the screen morphed into another face altogether.

"No, go back to the way it was," China said. "It's not above the nose. It's something around her mouth, but I can't—" She gasped. "Her upper lip. That's it. Her upper lip. Make it longer and add a deep indentation. The way it is now makes her face too soft."

Avery's fingers flew over the keyboard, and a new feature was added to the face.

"Yes!" China cried. "Yes. That's her! That's the woman who shot me." Her voice broke. "That's the woman who killed my baby girl!" She covered her face and started to cry.

"Wrap it up," Ben ordered.

Avery did as he was told. Whatever else had to be done could now be done at headquarters. Red began helping pack up the equipment, while Ben wheeled China back to her bed. Within moments they were alone. She started to stand, but Ben stopped her.

"Let me," he said softly, and lifted her out of the chair and then into bed.

She was limp with exhaustion and so tired of crying. "I did it, didn't I, Ben?"

Ben straightened her legs and then pulled the covers up past her waist. There was a knot in his throat and rage in his heart. God would have to have mercy on the shooter, because he never would. He smoothed her hair away from her face and took a deep, calming breath before he trusted himself to talk.

"Yes, honey, you did it, but are you all right? Should I call a nurse? Are you in pain?"

He was reaching for the buzzer when she grabbed his wrist.

"No. No nurse."

"You're sure?"

She nodded. "I just need to rest."

"Then close your eyes."

Her eyelids fluttered, then fell, as she took a deep breath. Within moments, her breathing had slowed. Ben watched until he was certain she was falling asleep; then he turned out the light over her bed and leaned down and kissed the side of her cheek.

"Sleep tight, China. Sleep tight, and don't let the bedbugs bite."

He looked back as he reached the door, assuring himself that she was all right, then made a quiet exit. But his goodbye had slipped deep into China's subconscious, dredging up an old, but sweet memory from her youth.

"But, Mommy, I don't want to go to bed."

"School tomorrow, China Mae. Now close your eyes and think sweet dreams."

China wiggled beneath the covers and closed her eyes, but sleep wouldn't come.

"Sing to me, Mommy. Sing me one song and then I can sleep."

Mae Shubert smiled. "If I do, will you promise to be quiet?"

"Yes, Mommy, yes, I promise."

The sweet sound of Mae's voice filled the room.

"'Amazing grace, how sweet the sound. That saved a wretch like me. I once was lost, but now am found. Was blind, but now I see.'"

She sang one verse and was halfway through the second when she realized China was asleep. She stopped, leaned down and pressed a kiss on her daughter's forehead.

"Sleep tight, China doll. Sleep tight and don't let the bedbugs bite."

China smiled in her sleep. It was good to see her mother again.

Mona Wakefield paid the cab driver and then hurried into the Galleria to get out of the cold. Her pantsuit was fashionable but less than suitable for the December weather. The fabric was too thin to protect her from the piercing wind gusts, and while she could have worn any one of the dozen or more coats that she owned, she hadn't wanted to be burdened with hiding what she'd worked so hard to present—namely herself. The smug expression on her face was partly due to the fact that she was about to embark upon her favorite thing, which was shopping, and also due to the fact that she'd eluded Bobby Lee's watchful eye. She shifted the strap of her purse to a more comfortable position on her shoulder and set off down the mall with purposeful strides. The aroma of cinnamon and popcorn filled the air, reminiscent of the upcoming holiday. As she strolled from store to store, she took great pleasure in the surprised glances and second looks her appearance was eliciting. God, but she loved the fame, even if it was secondhand.

Bobby Lee slammed down the receiver and then turned with a jerk and pointed a finger at Ainsley Been.

"Delia says my mother is not at home. You told me she was taking a nap."

Ainsley paled. "But that's what she told me she was going to do when I stopped by the house to pick up that file I left yesterday. Besides, I'm not her keeper, and what's the big deal? Maybe she decided to go out. She's a grown woman. Surely she doesn't need your approval before she makes a move."

"Big deal? What's the big deal, you say?" He grabbed Ainsley by the lapels of his suit and pulled him to within inches of his face. "If you want to ride my coattails all the way to the White House, then you'd better learn to become her keeper. You don't know what hell Mona is capable of, and by God, you better hope you never find out."

Ainsley's eyes bugged and his mouth dropped. He'd never seen Bobby Lee so upset.

"Okay, okay," he muttered, and peeled himself out of Bobby Lee's grasp. "I'll see what I can find out. Meantime, you settle down now, you hear? You wouldn't want the media to get wind of the fact that you think your mother needs a keeper."

He escaped without further comment, thanking his lucky stars that all he'd gotten were new orders. For a minute there he'd thought Bobby Lee was going to hit him.

Bobby Lee strode to the window overlooking downtown Dallas. This should have been a time of regrouping. The senate was not in session, and the family business more or less ran itself, although he showed up at the office now and then, as he was doing today. The oil business wasn't as profitable as it had once been, but Wakefield Industries had diversified years ago. The Wakefields might not be old money, but they had a whole hell of a lot of the new stuff. Yet for Bobby Lee, it was never enough. It wasn't about money; it was about power. He liked to play games, like buying industries on the brink of bankruptcy and then selling them for huge profits. In the old days, before he'd become Senator, his peers had called him a shark. The fact that he made money was almost incidental to the joy he received in being in control. Now he'd embarked upon the ultimate power trip, and God help anyone who got in his way—including his mother.

It wasn't even noon, and Connie Marx was pouring herself another drink. She tossed it back with a grimace and then poured herself another as she resumed her pacing between the wet bar in her living room and the computer she kept in her bedroom. The blinking screen mocked her, as did the text she'd typed days before. It was a letter of resignation that she had yet to hand in, and therein lay her dilemma. Delay could mean the end of her career. If she quit, she could begin that book she'd always been going to write. Then later, when things cooled off, which they were bound to do, she could wend her way back into broadcasting, maybe with a bestseller under her belt. But if she waited and wound up getting fired, she would never work in the business again.

"Goddamn it," she muttered, and downed her drink, then spun and threw the empty shot glass at the wall, hitting the picture of Larry Dee Jackson right between the eyes. "It's all your fault, you amorous jackass. If you'd kept your big mouth shut, none of this would be happening."

Within seconds the phone rang. Startled, she spun and ran to answer. It had been days since she'd talked to anyone, including Larry Dee.

"Hello?"

"Hey, Connie, it's me, Ronnie Boyle."

The familiar voice of her coanchor was surprising. He had never called her at home. In fact, they didn't even like each other. At least, she damn sure didn't like him.

"Ronnie."

Boyle caught the cautious tone in her voice and knew he was going to have to play loose to make this work.

"Just thought I'd check in and see how you're doing. We miss you, you know."

"Really?"

He grimaced and tried another tack. "Look, Connie, I want you to know I think you're getting a raw deal. No one believes you had anything to do with the shootings. I mean…hell, you report stories like that, not cause them, right?"

"Look, Ronnie, I appreciate the call, but I'm kinda busy. Thanks for—"

"Wait!"

She sighed. "What?"

"How about an exclusive? Are you really having an affair with Larry Jackson? He's news, Connie, and we both know it. The public has a right to—"

"Who the fucking hell are you working for—Channel 7 or the tabloids? As for the public, they can go straight to hell with you."

She hung up the phone and then yanked the jack from the wall and threw the phone across the room.

"Damn you, Boyle, damn Larry Dee, and damn you Chaz Finelli for starting this mess. I hope you're in hell, because it's where you belong."

Ariel Simmons took a deep breath and then exited her dressing room, making her way from backstage toward the podium and the awaiting crowd. Tonight the congregation had spilled out into the parking lot of the amphitheater where her broadcast was being held. Many of those in attendance were regulars—people who believed in her ministry—and then there were the others who'd come to see the woman who was under suspicion for murder. She'd heard the gossip. Everyone knew about the picture of her in leather and brandishing a whip. They'd come to see the woman who preached the Word on Sundays and played with the devil on Saturday nights. Damn Chaz Finelli. She still didn't know how he'd gotten that picture, but there was nothing she could do but bluff her way through. Commandment or not, she would gladly shoot Chaz Finelli a thousand times over if it would make this all go away.

"Sister Simmons, are you ready?"

She turned. Her producer was watching her. Even he was treating her differently. The rage that had been bubbling within her began to boil over. She'd come too far from the backwoods of Mississippi to be stopped now.

"Yes, I'm ready," she said, and strode onto the stage, her pale-blue gown floating about her ankles like clouds too low to the ground.

The murmuring crowd was suddenly silent as Ariel thrust her hands upward, as if beseeching God to hear.

"I am being tested!" she cried, and before anyone could

react, she doubled up her fists and shook them toward the crowd. "Satan is trying to silence the Word. He's poisoned the minds of the law and the media and all of you who doubt me now. He's putting evil in my path at every turn, but hear me now!" Her voice rose to a scream. "I will not be overcome! God is my sword. He is my shield. I am an innocent lamb, but I will not be slaughtered in Satan's name."

Then she fell to her knees, her long blond hair falling over her shoulders and onto the stage as she prostrated herself before the crowd.

They came to their feet as one, crying and shouting. The people began wailing and praying aloud, shamed that they'd believed, even for a minute, that this delicate angel of God could be guilty of even one measure of the gossip being spread.

Ariel lay immobile, her face hidden beneath her arms. When she felt the floor shaking from the thousands of stomping feet and heard the wailing of the crowd, she smiled.

Rod Stewart music rocked the walls of the cabin as the woman strutted before the cheval mirror standing in the corner. The red silk against her skin and the long blond hair brushing against her neck were aphrodisiacs. But the music was her anthem—her high. And there was only one thing she needed now to complete the mood. She paused before the mirror to stare at the picture she'd taped to the surface. Dark eyes stared back at her from a chocolate-brown face. It didn't matter to her what color a man's skin was as long as he had what it took to set her on fire, and from everything she'd been told about this man, he was a walking flame and none too picky about who or what turned him on. She liked that in a man—someone who was willing to experiment.

"Hurry, my darling," she whispered, then touched herself lightly, fondling herself, sliding her hands between her legs.

The loose silk of the caftan wrapped around her hands as she pressed them against her body, and she closed her eyes and let her head fall back, playing out the sexual fantasy of a man's hands upon her. It felt good—so good. The blood began to pulse within her to the beat of the music. She opened her eyes, watching her own face as she began to pleasure herself.

Suddenly the lights of a car swept across the wall behind her, and she stilled, her heart pounding, still cupping herself. A slow sigh slid from between her lips, and then she smiled.

"Just in time," she whispered, and headed for the door.

Just after daybreak, the nude and lifeless body of LaShon Fontana was found near a Dumpster in Garland. The media arrived at the same time the coroner's car pulled up.

"Christ almighty," someone said. "Tell me it isn't so. Tell me that's not Fancy Feet Fontana."

But it was. All six feet five inches of pure muscled perfection—pride of the Dallas Slickers and the best running back in the league for three years straight—with a bullet through the back of his head. Four hours later they found his abandoned car at a convenience mart with all his clothes inside. A few hundred workers had mourned the death of Tashi Yamamoto, and only then because of losing their jobs, but the state of Texas and the nation had gone into mourning over Fontana's death. The Garland police department was overwhelmed with media camping

on their doorstep. But it wasn't until late that afternoon
that the real shit hit the fan. Someone in the Dallas crime
lab got curious and ran a test on the bullet that killed Fontana to see if it matched the bullet that killed Yamamoto.
It did, and not only that, they also got a match on one of
the bullets they had dug out of Chaz Finelli. The police
commissioner then ordered a series of tests to be run on
all the unsolved murders in the Dallas-Fort Worth area
with similar profiles. By nightfall, there were six matches.

Ronnie Boyle broke the story on the 10:00 p.m. news.
Even the death of Fancy Feet Fontana took second place
to the fact that there was a serial killer in their midst.

Connie Marx sat on her living room sofa with a bottle
of Scotch between her legs, a shot glass in her hand and
tears streaming down her face. Last month, this would
have been her story. She would have been the one covering the updates. But thanks to Chaz Finelli, she was part
of the sordid affair. She poured herself another drink and
then tossed it back as if she were taking medicine. With
each passing minute, her rage and sense of injustice grew.
If Chaz Finelli hadn't already been dead, she would willingly have killed him.

Homicide was in an uproar at the Dallas P.D. The governor had called the commissioner, expressing his concerns over the recent revelations. A tactical meeting had
just taken place in which Captain Floyd had established
a task force on the Finelli and Yamamoto murders, with
Ben English as the primary and Red Fisher as second in
command. Everyone who wasn't already tied up on serious cases had been ordered to give this top priority. All
information was to be shared with both the Garland police department and the Arlington police departments,

since they, too, had open cases that were now connected to the whole.

The picture that Avery and China had made the day before was being distributed to every police department in the area and had also been released to all the media. By morning, that face would be in every newspaper and on every television station in the area.

That was the good news.

The bad news was that, inevitably, someone would ask who'd given them the ID.

China was no longer safe.

Chapter 11

Mattie English alternated between pacing the floor and staring out the window. The sun was setting, and she still hadn't heard from Ben, although she'd left two messages for him to call. Ever since she'd heard last night's news, she hadn't been able to get China Brown out of her mind. The poor girl had to be terrified, knowing that she was the only witness to a serial killer. It also occurred to Mattie that by having China stay with her, she was putting her own life in danger, but she couldn't bring herself to say no. The memory of the heartbreak she'd heard in China Brown's voice was stronger than her fear.

Just as she passed the phone, it rang. Startled, she jumped, then grabbed the receiver.

"English residence."

"Mom, it's me."

"Ben, what on earth is going on? Is China all right? Has the media gotten wind of her identity?"

"She's fine, and thank God, no. Look, Mom, I think maybe we need to rethink this visit. Having her on the ranch could put both of you in danger."

"We'll be fine," she said. "Dave will be here, remember? Besides, I've lived in the shadow of life for too long. A little excitement might be just what I need."

Ben snorted lightly beneath his breath. "Mother, we're not talking about a trip to Six Flags, we're talking about a serial killer. I love you. I don't want you hurt."

"What about China? How do you feel about her?" Mattie countered.

There was a moment of total silence, and then Ben completely ignored both her questions.

"The only way this is happening is if the both of you are under twenty-four hour watch. Dave will watch you during the day. I'm staying there at night."

"That's quite a drive to make each morning," she said, reminding him that it was more than half an hour from the ranch to the city.

"I think you're worth it," he said. "Both of you."

Mattie pursed her lips. She'd been right all along. There *was* more to Ben's feelings for China than duty.

"That's it, then," she said. "When can I expect you?"

"As soon as it gets dark. I don't want to take a chance on some snoopy journalist recognizing me, then seeing me with a convalescing woman and putting two and two together."

"I'll be waiting," Mattie said. "Drive safely, Bennie. I love you."

"I love you, too, Mom," he said.

He was frowning when he hung up the phone. Bennie. Hell. She hadn't called him that in years. She must really be worried. Well, it was his job to make sure she didn't have anything to worry about. He put on his coat, then picked up a handful of files and dropped them on another detective's desk as he walked by.

"Merry Christmas," he said. "The captain has taken

me off everything except the Finelli case. If you have any questions about my notes, just yell."

The detective rolled his eyes and then grinned. "How loud?"

"At least let me get out of the station," Ben said, and then added, "Thanks. I owe you big time."

"I won't let you forget it," the second detective said.

But Ben already had. His thoughts were on China and getting her out of Parkland Hospital unobserved. He also needed to talk to her doctor and make sure that everything about China Brown's stay at that hospital ceased to exist—at least for the time being.

China was dressed and waiting for Ben to arrive. Tonight she was leaving the sanctity of the hospital, and she was more than a little bit scared. After all the hospital gowns, it felt strange to be wearing her own clothes again, even though they'd been in the closet in her room since she'd been moved out of the ICU. It had been a battle of wills not to cry as she'd pulled up her sweats. The last time she'd worn these clothes, they'd been tight across her tummy. Now there was no baby, only a long, healing scar. She'd managed her pants, but had to ring for help from a nurse to get her sweatshirt over her head. She had several months of rehabilitation ahead of her before her arm would be back to normal, but Dr. Pope had assured her that it would eventually heal. Until then, her infirmities would be constant reminders of the ordeal she so badly wanted to forget.

She walked to the door and peeked out, hoping to see Ben coming down the hall, but all she got was a polite nod from the guard stationed outside her door.

"You'd best keep the door closed, miss," he said quietly.

China sighed as she let it shut. How long would this

enforced imprisonment last? What if they never caught the killer? Would she have to stay in hiding for the rest of her life? Overwhelmed by the thought of the troubles ahead of her, she crawled back into bed. Wincing a bit, she rolled over on her side and closed her eyes, but sleep wouldn't come. Her thoughts were full of what lay ahead. Not only was she going into hiding, but she would be doing it with strangers. Trust had always come easy to China—too easy. But that was before. Now, everyone was a threat. Except for Ben English. So far, he'd proved himself trustworthy in every way. Ben. Her promise man.

And with the thought, in he came, carrying a sack and striding through the door with purposeful intent and flanked by three uniformed officers, her doctor and a nurse pushing a wheelchair.

"It's time," Ben said.

China started to sit up and then groaned. Immediately Ben was at her side.

"Here, honey, let me," he said, and scooted his arm beneath her shoulder and lifted her to a sitting position. "Okay?"

She nodded.

Dr. Pope stepped forward and put a hand on her knee. "You're a remarkable woman, Miss Brown. I'm sorry we met under these circumstances, but I can truthfully say that it would have been my loss had I never known you."

"Thank you, Dr. Pope, for everything you've done for me."

Ross Pope smiled, then glanced at Ben. "They're ready for you now, and you're ready to go. If you have any concerns, you know how to reach me. Continue the pain medicine I gave you, and I'll call in a prescription for you, which Detective English has assured me he will see that you get. Take care and God bless."

Impulsively, China wrapped her arms around the doctor's neck.

"You saved my life," she said softly. "I won't waste it."

"Let's get you in the wheelchair," the nurse said.

"I can walk," China said.

The nurse shook her head. "Hospital rules."

"It's cold outside," Ben said, and handed her the sack.

She looked inside, and then her eyes filled. It was a new coat. She hadn't thought once of the condition of her old one, but it dawned on her that it had probably been ruined by bullet holes and blood.

"Oh, Ben."

He took it out and held it up for her to put on.

She put one arm in and then the other, enveloped by the weight and warmth of the blue wool. When she stood, the hem of it reached the backs of her knees.

Ben reached for the edges and buttoned it up.

"Good, it fits," he said, and let the hood hang down her back. He added quietly, so only she could hear, "It's the color of your eyes."

While she was still digesting the fact that he'd been thoughtful enough to provide her with a coat, she had to accept the fact that he'd also picked one out that matched her eyes.

She sat down in the wheelchair. Ben picked up her bag, then set it in her lap as the nurse began pushing her toward the door.

"Just a minute," Ben said, and opened the door and stepped out into the hall, looking first one way and then the other. "Okay," he said. "Bring her out."

Everything seemed to move past her in a blur. Flanked by the uniformed officers, with Ben taking the lead, they headed for the service elevator at a fast pace. China's last few impressions were the scent of antiseptic, the sound of someone laughing, and a television playing too loudly in a room somewhere down the hall, and then they were in the elevator. All too soon they'd reached the ground floor.

Again Ben was the first to step out, and as he did, China realized he had taken his gun out of his holster. The sight of it in his hand made her sick. The urge to bolt and run was strong, but where would she go? Then sanity returned, and she closed her eyes and took a deep breath. These people weren't the enemy. They were here to protect her.

"Okay," Ben said shortly. "Bring her out."

Seconds later they were in a parking garage and headed toward a light-gray sedan. A cold wind whipped through the area, and China was grateful for the warmth of the coat.

"Easy, honey," Ben said, as he helped her into his car.

The absurdity of the moment seemed surreal. The wind on her face. The scent of leather from the interior of his car. The satiny comfort of the coat lining. The uniformed officers outside the car with weapons drawn. She wasn't just being released from the hospital. She was going into hiding.

She had settled in her seat and was buckling the seat belt across her lap when Ben got inside. Almost immediately the car seemed smaller. His presence beside her seemed threatening until she happened to catch him looking at her for assurance. When she gave him a tentative smile, he seemed to relax.

"I know this is tough for you," Ben said. "But in my business, there's no such thing as being too cautious."

"It's all right. After all, you're doing this for my benefit."

"Good," he said. "Now here's the deal. I'm taking you straight to Mom's. It's already dark, so we won't be spotted. The ranch is isolated enough that you can pretty much move about as you feel like it. You just won't be leaving the ranch until we've caught the killer. So far, your identity is protected, but we can't take any chances, understand?"

She bit her lower lip and then nodded.

"Are you feeling all right?" Ben asked. "If you're uncomfortable, you can lie down in the back or—"

China laid her hand on his arm. "I'm fine."

"I won't let anything happen to you, China. I promise."

"I know."

The trust in her eyes humbled him and, at the same time, scared him to death. As she leaned back in her seat and folded her hands in her lap, he started the car, waved off the officers and drove out of the parking garage into the night.

Within the hour Ben was pulling into the yard of his childhood home. He killed the engine, then glanced over at his passenger. She'd fallen asleep before they'd cleared the streets of Dallas, and he'd played a game with himself all the way to the ranch, pretending that they had been together for years and had been out on the town, and then, on the way home, she had just fallen asleep. It was frightening to accept that this woman was stealing his heart.

As he sat, she began to stir, then slowly opened her eyes.

"Are we here?"

"We're here. Welcome home."

He got out and circled the car, intent on helping her inside. But China was still trying to absorb the sweetness of the invitation he'd given her.

Home.

He'd welcomed her home.

What would it be like to have a home with this man,

to never know uncertainty or hunger again—to feel safe and loved?

China shuddered. Loved? Where had that come from?

Ben opened the car door and slipped a hand under her elbow.

"Easy does it, honey. I'll get you in the house and come back for your bag."

"All right," China said, and scooted to the edge of the seat before allowing herself to stand.

Stiff muscles protested as she braced herself against the sharp bite of the wind. Almost immediately, Ben put himself between her and the blast, and then slipped an arm around her shoulder.

"Lean on me," he said, as they started toward the house.

China wouldn't look at him or let herself comment. She was too taken aback by the notion of doing that very thing. She was only here because she was valuable to them as a witness. Leaning on Bennett English would be all too easy to do, but she had to remember that one day this would be over, and when it was, his duty to her would be over, as well.

As they reached the porch, the front door swung open. China had a moment's impression of a gray-haired woman in blue jeans and a red flannel shirt, a Christmas wreath hanging on the front door, and then she was whisked inside.

"Mother, this is China Brown. China, this is my mother, Mattie English."

In typical Mattie fashion, she held out her hand. "Welcome to my home. You look chilled. Let's get that coat off you and come in by the fire."

"Thank you, ma'am," China said.

Mattie stopped. "No *ma'am,* remember? Call me Mattie." She looked at Ben. "Well, what are you waiting for… Christmas? Go get her bag and take it to her room. I put her in the east room."

"Yes, ma'am," Ben said, then winked at China. "I swear her bark is worse than her bite."

"Get," Mattie said. "And don't dawdle in the doorway. You let in too much cold air." She took China's coat, hung it on a rack in the hall and took her by the elbow. "Can you walk all right, dear? We'll go slow."

"I'm okay," China said. "Just a little stiff. The pain is pretty manageable now. Not like before."

Mattie hesitated, giving the young woman a careful look. She wasn't very tall, probably no more than four or five inches over five feet. Her hair was thick and dark and looked as if she'd been cutting it herself for years. Her face had a fragile, delicate beauty that made her seem weak until Mattie looked in her eyes. That was where her strength shone through.

"You're a tough one, aren't you, girl?" Mattie murmured.

"I've had to be." Then she looked a bit nervous. "At least, I have been up until now. Ben thinks I'm in danger."

"Ben is a good man and a good cop. He will see that you're protected."

"Yes," China said. "He promised not to let anything happen to me. He's a man who keeps his promises."

Mattie nodded, for the moment satisfied with her houseguest.

"Now, let's get you a chair by the fire. I made some hot chocolate earlier. Would you care for a cup?"

A pensive smile broke the somberness of China's face. "Mother used to make hot chocolate for us on cold nights."

Mattie nodded. "Sounds like a smart woman."

"Yes, ma'am, that she was."

"Mattie! Not ma'am. Now put your feet up on this stool and close your eyes. I'll be back in a bit with the chocolate."

China did as she was told, thankful she wasn't having to make any decisions.

The warmth of the fire and the peacefulness of the house lulled her. Once again, she dozed. When she woke, Ben was coming into the room carrying a tray with the mugs of hot chocolate. Mattie was right behind him with a plate of cookies.

"Smells wonderful," China said, as Ben handed her a cup.

"One lump or two?" Ben asked, holding out a bowl of miniature marshmallows, rather than cubes of sugar.

Surprised by his playfulness, China slipped into similar character as she peered into the bowl. "They're rather small."

Ben grinned. "Then allow me," he said, and dropped a handful into her mug, then handed her a spoon. "Knock yourself out, kid."

Mattie sat on the sofa sipping her chocolate and watching them spar, wondering if they knew how obvious they were—wondering if they knew they were falling in love.

Within the hour, China caught herself nodding off. Ben saw her and got to his feet.

"You're done for, honey," he said softly, and lifted her out of the chair and into his arms.

China woke abruptly. Embarrassed that Ben was doing this in front of his mother, she began to argue.

"I can walk."

"Humor me," Ben said, and headed down the hall toward her room.

Mattie watched, again without comment. But she'd

seen enough to know that her son was in over his head. This woman was part of a case—a witness to a murder— and he was falling in love.

Ben carried China into the room she'd been given and then set her down on the edge of the bed.

"Your things are on that chair," Ben said. "There's a new toothbrush in the bathroom drawer and fresh towels in the cabinet beneath, although I laid one out for you for tonight. Do you want to shower tonight, or in the morning?"

"I'll shower in the morning," China said.

"Don't try to do it by yourself," Ben said. "When you're ready, give us a yell. Mom will be glad to help."

China nodded. "She's really nice—your mom."

Ben smiled. "Yeah, she's pretty great."

"I think she wishes I wasn't here," China said; then, embarrassed that she'd even brought it up, she added, "Not that I blame her."

Ben's smile stopped. "Why would you say that?"

China's face flamed, and she looked away, unable to meet his gaze. "I think she wishes…I mean, I think she believes that I…that we…"

Ben turned her head, making her look at him.

"And that would be bad?" he asked.

China shook her head. "Yes…no…well, from her point of view, yes. But it's okay…I mean, I don't blame her for being concerned. You're her son. Of course she would want the best for you."

"And why would that exclude you?"

China's chin quivered once, and then she shrugged.

"Get real, Detective. I'm homeless and involved in a very ugly crime. I'm obviously not too smart or I would never have involved myself with someone like Tommy Fairheart and I'm not much to look at."

Ben was flabbergasted. He didn't know what to respond to first, but the most obvious was her reference to her looks.

"Who told you that?" he snapped.

"Told me what?" China asked.

"That you weren't much to look at? Was it Fairheart, because if it was, I can—"

"Oh, no," China said. "I've known that all my life."

Ben couldn't believe what he was hearing. She wasn't kidding. She really believed she was homely.

"Who told you that?" he repeated.

China looked up at him then, a little surprised by his anger.

"Clyde."

"And who in hell is this Clyde?"

"He was my stepfather, until my mother divorced him."

Ben stood abruptly. "Was he blind? For that matter, honey, are you? Don't you know how beautiful you are?"

China was stunned. All she could do was shake her head.

"Well, you are," Ben said shortly. "Now get in bed before I say something we'll both regret, and remember, if you need anything during the night, just call out. My room is right across the hall."

He strode out of her room, leaving his anger behind him.

China sat without moving, reliving the last moments of their conversation over and over until her mind was reeling. Finally she made her way to the adjoining bathroom and started to undress. As she did, she caught a glimpse of herself in the mirror and stopped to look, then abruptly looked away.

Ben had lied. There wasn't anything pretty about her, and she could prove it. If she was beautiful, as he'd claimed, then why did men treat her as they did? From her earliest memory, men had ridiculed her, beaten her and lied to her. It would take more than words to make her change her mind.

She got her nightgown from her bag and then began to undress. Painfully, she managed to get her sweat-shirt over her head. She laid it on the side of the tub and was reaching for a washcloth when she caught another glimpse of herself in the full-length mirror hanging on the back of the door. Her eyes widened in quiet horror as she touched her breast and the red puckering scar above it. Then her gaze slid lower, to the beginning of the scar that showed just above the waistband of her sweats. With shaking hands, she pushed the elastic down, then down some more, finally stepping out of her clothes until it had been completely revealed. Her tummy was almost flat again—a painful reminder of what she'd lost. But it was the fiery scar down her belly that put everything into perspective.

Damaged goods. In every way that counted, she was damaged goods.

In a rush of panic, she grabbed her nightgown and yanked it over her head. Ignoring the pain of sudden movement, she wouldn't look at herself again until she was completely covered. Only after she felt the night-gown brushing against her ankles and had buttoned the last button would she turn and face herself in the mirror.

The look on her face was not unlike that of a deer caught in the headlights of a car—frightened, but rather fatalistic. She reached for her washcloth again and let the water run until it was warm. Methodically she washed her face, brushed her teeth, then her hair and then turned out the light. Carefully she made her way to the bed and crawled between the covers. The pillow was soft, the mattress and fresh bed linens smelling of springtime—nothing like the antiseptic smell of the hospital. A strong gust of wind rattled the windows on the other side of the room. She pulled the covers up to her chin and closed her eyes. Down the hall, she could just hear the murmur of voices as mother and son continued to talk. Somewhere outside these walls, a killer was waiting for another chance to finish what she had started.

In the back of China's mind, she could almost hear her mother calling out to her.

Sleep tight, China doll. Sleep tight and don't let the bedbugs bite.

She started to cry, and once the tears began to fall, they just wouldn't stop. She had survived thus far, and even if she somehow managed to survive the rest of this horrible mess, there was nothing in her future but loneliness. And right now, it was the loneliness that was hardest to bear.

Betty, Ariel Simmons's maid, was just coming into her bedroom with some tea when Ariel sneezed several times in succession and then moaned softly as she reached for some fresh tissues and tossed the others into the trash.

Betty quickly set the tea tray aside and rushed to Ariel's bed.

"Miss Simmons, do you want me to call your doctor? You sound just awful."

Ariel managed a pitiful smile and shook her head. "No, dear, I will be fine. A good night's sleep will help, I'm sure."

"But you look feverish."

Ariel put a hand against her own forehead and sank back against the bank of pillows behind her.

"I suppose I am, a little, but this past week has been draining on my spirit. Satan always comes at you when you're at your weakest, you know. Just put the tea here by my bed where I can reach it and hand me my Bible. I'll read a bit before I go to sleep. It will be better medicine than any pills the doctor could bring."

Betty's eyes teared. "Yes, ma'am. You're right. Will there be anything else?"

"No, dear. You go on to bed now, you hear?"

"Yes, ma'am."

She exited the room, closing the door quietly behind her.

The moment she was gone, Ariel sat straight up in bed and checked the time. It was five minutes to ten. Betty's routine was set in stone. She would sneak her three shots of whiskey that she thought no one knew about, and by ten-thirty she would be out like a light. And that was what Ariel was counting on.

She flung her handful of tissues into the trash and jumped out of bed, her "illness" disappearing as miraculously as it had appeared. Dressing quickly in dark clothing and tennis shoes, she pulled a black stocking cap over her hair and made her way downstairs. The grandfather clock in the hallway began to strike as she reached the last step.

Perfect. Betty would be sound asleep. But just to make sure, Ariel made a quick sweep through the kitchen and down the hall to the servants' quarters. She could hear Betty's snores before she reached the door. Pivoting sharply, she retraced her steps, disarmed the security system and slipped out the front door. Her car was too recognizable to take, so she slipped through the hedge to the garage in back and quietly rolled a small black motorbike out onto the street before she started it up. The power of the engine between her legs made her shudder with want, but this was no time to give in to her lust. She sped off into the night.

Hours later, on the other side of the city, a small fire suddenly sprang to life inside an abandoned warehouse. Within minutes a wall of flames was devouring the guts of it, destroying everything in its path. The first fire trucks arrived on the scene with a noisy blast of sirens, drowning out the sounds of the motorbike's exit.

It was 3:00 a.m. when Ariel Simmons slipped back into her house. She reset the security alarm, double-checked Betty's room to make sure she was still asleep and then sauntered up her stairs. She stripped off her clothes and tossed them in a bag of clothing that was going to Goodwill, took a shower to wash the scent of smoke from her body and crawled into bed.

Without saying her prayers, she closed her eyes and fell fast asleep, secure in the knowledge that she could never be linked to that picture again. The leather, the chains, even the black silk and whips, had just gone up in smoke.

Chapter 12

"Good morning, Senator. How would you like your eggs?"

"Morning, Delia," Bobby Lee said. "I'm thinking I'll have my hen fruit poached today, and bring me some bacon and toast, too."

"Yes, sir," Delia said, as she poured him a cup of freshly brewed coffee. "You just sit yourself down and enjoy your paper. I'll be back shortly."

"Thank you, Delia," Bobby Lee said, as he reached for his cup.

"Oh, Senator…is your mama awake?"

"I don't think so," he said. "Just go on and tell Cook to fix my food. If Mother comes down before I'm through, I'll ring."

"Yes, sir," Delia said, then set the coffeepot down and left.

Bobby Lee took a careful sip of the brew, then leaned back in his chair and opened the paper. A woman's face was centered right below the headline which read "Serial Killer at Large." The coffee hung at the back of his throat as he forgot to swallow. When he gasped in shock, the coffee rerouted itself through his nose. The paper fell to the floor as he grabbed for his napkin, saving his clean shirt and suit from stains as the scalding liquid seared the hairs inside his nose.

"Jesus Christ!" he yelped, and dabbed at himself until he was certain all the coffee had been blotted.

He picked up the paper again, his horrified gaze fixed upon the woman's face. How could this be? In the midst of panic, his mother walked in.

"I heard you cussin' all the way down the hall. What's got you riled up so early in the morning?"

"Burned my mouth on hot coffee," he muttered.

"Poor baby," she said, and sauntered toward the side-board to pour herself a cup.

The fact that she was actually dressed this morning should have been a relief. But her clothes or lack thereof were the least of Bobby Lee's worries. He stared at her then as if he'd never seen her before—at the long blond hair falling over one shoulder, at the mouth a shade too thin to be truly sexy, at her large, puppy dog eyes and the thrust of her chin. Feature by feature, her face would have been unremarkable, but together, somehow they were a thing of beauty—and a damn sight too close to the woman in the paper for his peace of mind.

He knew that it was only a stroke of luck that his mother had never been implicated in the Finelli investigation. By her own words, she had not been recognizable in the picture that Finelli had used in his blackmail. And it had been another stroke of luck that John Wood-ley had come up with a fail-safe alibi for the night of the murders. The fact that Woodley had known enough to keep his mouth shut about the woman he'd been with had been entirely due to a phone call from Bobby Lee himself. This, however, was another kettle of fish.

Mona flashed him a smile as she sat down. In that moment, Bobby Lee knew what to do. He laid the paper aside and then reached for her hand.

"Mother, I want to tell you something."

Mona was surprised but pleased by the tenderness of his gesture. More times than not they were fighting, and she did love her son more than life.

"What is it, Bobby Lee?"

"Lately, with the stress of the announcement and all the stuff that goes with it, I confess I haven't been myself. I feel I've been short-tempered with you, and I regret it and want to make it up to you."

Mona beamed. "Now, honey, you don't have to do any such thing. Mothers understand about things like that. You know you're my pride and joy. I would do *anything* for you. *Anything.*"

It was the *anything* that made him nervous.

"I know, and I for you," he said. "I have a surprise."

Mona clapped her hands. "Oh, Bobby Lee, you know how I like surprises."

He grinned. "Yes, ma'am, that I do."

"What is it, Bobby Lee?"

"I know Christmas is still a few days away, but I want to give you your Christmas present early. How would you like a two-week vacation at the spa of your choice? Have daily massages, go shopping at all the best places, play tennis or even lie around a pool all day if that's what you want?"

Mona was ecstatic. Next to shopping, pleasing herself was her favorite thing.

"Oooh, Bobby Lee, it sounds perfect. To get away

from this awful old cold weather—I can't think of anything I'd like better."

"Wonderful," he said. "Then it's decided. When I get to the office, I'll have Duffy get your reservation. How about L.A.? You can do Hollywood. Shop on Rodeo Drive, do the town up right."

Mona squealed.

He grinned and then gave her a casual glance, as if assessing her features.

"You know what else you should do while you're down there?"

"What?"

"Have yourself one of those makeovers. If I'm going to be the next president, I want you shining by my side."

Mona began to frown, uncomfortable with the idea that she didn't look perfect. But Bobby Lee had been ready for that. He wasn't through piling on the bull.

"You're such a beautiful woman, Mother. I want your best qualities accentuated, and where better to do it than in Hollywood, where perfection is a business? What do you think?"

When she looked at it from that angle, it made perfect sense.

"I think you're the best son a woman could have," she said.

Bobby Lee leaned back in his chair, his scalded nose forgotten. When his mother came back, she would look nothing like that woman in the paper, and that would be that.

China had been awake for some time when she heard the sounds of people stirring outside her door. Although she could not distinguish what they were saying, she could tell that there was great love between mother and

son. The tone of Mattie's voice was teasing yet gentle, and
Ben's laughter proved the camaraderie between the two
was comfortable. It made her homesick for her mother.
They'd laughed like that—before Mae had died.

Footsteps faded. She supposed they had moved to
the kitchen. Ben would soon be leaving for Dallas. The
thought of not seeing him again until nightfall had her
rolling out of bed. As she stood, it dawned on her that
she wasn't as sore as she'd been the day before. So Dr.
Pope had been right. Her body was healing. She sighed.
If only it were that easy to heal a spirit.

She made her way to the bathroom, taking time to pick
out some clothes to wear for the day. There was a shower
to take and hair to brush—things she'd once taken for
granted and dashed through without thought. Now she
had to plan her moves so as not to cause herself pain.

The warm water felt good on her body. The light, peppering spray was like a body massage, loosening tight
muscles as well as her nerves. By the time she emerged,
she was feeling much better. When she reached for a
towel, she realized that the full-length mirror had fogged
over. So much the better, she thought. At least she
wouldn't have to face the hideousness of her physical self.

A few minutes later she emerged from the bathroom
wearing an old shirt and jeans. The last time she'd worn
the jeans was back in the spring, before her belly had
started to grow. They were loose on her frame, evidence
of the weight that she'd lost during her hospital stay.
The shirt had seen better days, but the snaps were what
sold her. They were easier to fasten than pulling another
sweatshirt over her head. Carrying her socks and a band
for her ponytail, she left the anonymity of her room.

Although her entrance was silent, Ben seemed to sense

her arrival before she spoke. He looked up. China braced herself.

"Good morning," he said. "How did you sleep?"

Mattie turned around, a pancake turner in her hand.

"Welcome. I hope you brought your appetite," she said. "Breakfast is almost ready."

"The bed was very comfortable, thank you. Something smells good."

"Good," Ben said, although he noted she hadn't really answered his question. A comfortable bed did not necessarily make for a good night's sleep. Then he noticed she was carrying her socks and shoes. "Need some help?" he asked, and was up before she could answer.

She hesitated, then handed them over. "Yes, I'm sorry to have to ask, but—"

Ben's voice was almost angry. "Don't apologize for something that's not your fault."

She took a seat at the table as he knelt before her. Once she glanced up at Mattie, a little nervous as to how the woman would construe her son on his knees before her. But Mattie seemed focused on taking eggs out of a skillet. China looked down at Ben, watching the gentle way in which he pulled up her socks, then reached for her shoes. As he turned, she noticed a backward swirl in his hair right at the crown. Without thinking, she touched it.

"I'll bet you had a time keeping that combed when you were a little boy."

The touch of her hand in his hair gave Ben the shivers. To his relief, his mother spoke, saving him from making a fool of himself.

"That cowlick, you mean? I'll show you some pictures later. You should have seen it. Are you familiar with the little boy who played Alfalfa on *The Little Rascals?*"

China smiled. "The one with the freckles across his nose and the piece of hair that stood up like a flagpole?"

Mattie chuckled. "That's the one. Well, Bennie's hair was a little like that, only it didn't stand up stiff and straight, it was a great big curl."

Ben finally found his voice. "Yeah, and I gave Pete Farmer a black eye for calling me a sissy."

Mattie laughed aloud. "I remember. That summer your daddy took you and got your hair cut so short we didn't even have to comb it."

China grinned. By that time, the awkwardness had passed.

"Did I tie them too tight?" Ben asked.

China wiggled her feet inside her tennis shoes, then shook her head, and as she did, the heavy fall of her hair slid across her forehead.

"Mattie, when you've finished there and before we eat, would you mind doing my ponytail? My arm is still a bit too stiff to do it right."

"I can do that," Ben said, and took the ponytail band from her hand before either one of them could argue.

China was a bit startled. She hadn't expected him to volunteer for such a girlie thing.

"I...um, you don't have to."

"Don't get all sexist on me, woman. Just because I'm a man, doesn't mean I can't do this right."

"I didn't mean...I just thought that..."

Mattie grinned. "Don't you apologize to that man, dear. He's just teasing." Then she waved her finger at Ben. "Be nice. You'll scare her off before we've had a chance to make friends."

Ben snorted lightly. "Just what I need. Two women instead of one to make me dance through hoops."

"But, Bennie, you dance so well," Mattie said, and began serving the food that she'd cooked.

"Are you tender-headed?" Ben asked.

"No," China said.

"Good," he said, and thrust his hands into the thickness of her hair and began combing it back with his fingers.

Instead of feeling awkward, the rhythm of his hands against her scalp was oddly soothing. She closed her eyes and gave herself up to the pleasure.

"At the back of your neck or up higher?" he asked.

"The back is fine," China said.

A few quick twists and he was through.

"Breakfast is ready," Mattie said, as she carried the plates to the table. "I hope you like your eggs fried hard. Can't stand to look at a runny yolk."

China hid a smile. Mattie was outspoken, but somehow, it suited her.

"They look good," China said.

"You get choices around here," Ben drawled. "But food isn't one of them."

Mattie arched an eyebrow at her son. "You've managed to survive on my cooking all these years."

"And it's good cooking, too," he countered. "Now, may I have my food so I can eat and get to work?"

Mattie plunked his plate in front of him and then kissed his cheek. Ben grinned and then glanced up at China, who was looking as if she didn't know whether to laugh or pretend she wasn't there. He winked. Almost immediately, he saw her relax. As soon as he was satisfied that their teasing hadn't upset her, he dug into his food.

China picked up her fork, then realized Mattie had yet to sit down. She laid down her fork and folded her hands in her lap just as Mattie turned toward the table with a platter of toast.

"Aren't you hungry?" Mattie asked.

"I'm waiting for you," China said.

Touched by the girl's thoughtfulness, Mattie hurried to the table and set the platter down.

"Help yourself," she said. "Bennie, pass the jelly."

Ben rolled his eyes as he reached for the jar. "Only if you quit calling me Bennie."

Mattie looked a little startled, then grinned. "Sorry. Was I cramping your style?"

China grabbed the pepper shaker and began peppering her food so she wouldn't have to look at Ben's face. But she could tell by the ensuing silence that he was probably giving his mother a disgusted look.

Soon the mood lightened and the meal commenced.

Ben was at his desk, digging through the mounds of paperwork that seemed to grow on a daily basis. But it was difficult to concentrate, knowing that when he went home, China would be there. Maybe not officially waiting for him, but there just the same.

"Hey, Ben, is Bo Milam's wife officially off the suspect list?" Red asked.

Ben looked up. "Yes, according to China, even with a wig and a lot of makeup, she's about a foot too short to be the shooter, remember?"

"Oh, yeah," Red said, and then laid aside the file. "Good. At least that's one less face to consider." He stretched, then got up from his desk. "I'm going to get some coffee. Want some?"

"Yeah, thanks," Ben said absently, and handed Red his cup without looking up.

A few minutes passed before it occurred to him that

Red hadn't come back. He looked up, searching the room for his partner's face, but he was nowhere to be seen. He stood and stretched. He liked being a cop, but not the paperwork that went with it.

Suddenly he saw Red come rushing into the room. Wherever he'd been, he'd left both of their coffee cups behind.

"Did you have to pick it?" Ben asked.

"Pick what?" Red asked.

"The coffee beans."

"Oh! Yeah, that's right. Dang, where did I leave those cups?" Then he shook his head, as if reminding himself why he'd been hurrying in the first place. "Never mind about the coffee. I ran into Jones in the hall, and you'll never guess what he told me."

"Jones who?" Ben asked.

"Mike Jones—from the bomb squad."

An image of a short bulldog of a man emerged from Ben's memory. "Oh, yeah, that Jones. So, what's the big scoop?"

"He had a call early this morning to go to a big fire down in the warehouse district. At first they thought it might have been started by a bomb, because someone said they heard a loud explosion. But it was later determined that the fire had been burning for some time before it detonated some stored chemicals."

"And how does that impact us?" Ben asked.

"Jones said his buddy with the fire department said it was arson, but that's not the kicker. It's who the warehouse belongs to that he thought might interest us."

"And the winner is…?" Ben drawled.

"One Ariel Simmons, that's who."

Ben jerked. "The hell you say."

"Jones also said that there was some real strange stuff in that fire that didn't burn up."

"Like what?" Ben asked.

"Like a pair of manacles and chains attached to a wall that didn't completely burn, and he said there were also the remnants of what looked like a bed."

"Wouldn't it be interesting to find out what Ariel has to say about this?" Ben asked.

Red was already putting on his coat. "I knew you'd say that," he said. "I already told Captain Floyd we're paying her another visit."

Ariel was playing the role of patient to the hilt. Betty had made two trips to her room since breakfast, bringing honey and lemon tea for Ariel's cough, and then the morning mail as soon as it came. She was fielding all of Ariel's phone calls as she'd been instructed to do, so that if questions arose, there would be no doubt in anyone's mind that Ariel Simmons was ailing.

Just before noon, the doorbell rang. Ariel heard the chimes echoing in the downstairs hall and fluffed her hair just a bit to look mussed, then pinched her nose several times to give it a red, stuffy appearance. She grabbed a handful of tissues and then flopped backward into the nest of pillows behind her, then yanked and kicked the bedclothes to make it look as if she had suffered a long, sleepless night. Satisfied that she was now in character, Ariel waited for the inevitable knock on the door.

"I'm sorry, Miss Simmons, but there are two detectives who insist upon seeing you."

"If they want to risk my contagion, they are welcome to come up, but I'm not feeling well enough to come down."

"Yes, ma'am," Betty said. "I'll go tell them."

Within minutes, another knock came. Ariel smirked. Just like moths to a flame, they obviously couldn't resist seeing if she was really indisposed.

"Come in," she croaked, and then lowered her eyelids to half-mast as the door opened. "Detectives, forgive me for not greeting you properly, but as you can see, I'm a bit under the weather."

Red glanced at Ben, trying to judge his expression to see if his partner was as uncomfortable as he was. But Ben's face gave away nothing of what he was thinking. Red waited for his partner to make the first move.

Ben was quietly judging the scene before him. Granted, Ariel Simmons was in bed, but other than a half-empty cup of tea and a few tossed tissues, he could see no signs of illness. There was no cough medicine in sight, no pill bottle on the table, and there were no signs of illness or fatigue on her face. She didn't appear feverish, although she was playing it to the hilt, and her eyes were clear and glittering with interest. He decided they were being had and refused to comment on her condition.

"We had a few more questions for you," he said.

Ariel frowned. At the least, she had expected a word of apology from them.

"If you must," she said. "But please don't draw this all out. I'm not well."

Ben nodded. "So you said."

Ariel's color rose, but not from fever. She scooted herself up to a sitting position.

"Ask away."

"One of your warehouses burned down last night. The firemen found some interesting items in the fire. Items that relate to the picture Chaz Finelli had of you—items that would punch a lot of holes in your claim that the picture in question was faked."

Ariel's heart skipped a beat. "I'm sorry, but I don't know what you're talking about. I have no business that has need of a warehouse. You must be mistaken about the ownership."

"No, there's no mistake," Ben said. "The deed on the property states it belongs to the Simmons Ministry."

Ariel shook her head, still maintaining a perplexed attitude. To throw a little reality into the moment, she managed a sneeze.

"Bless you," Red said.

"Why, thank you," Ariel said, and gave him a smile.

"About the warehouse?" Ben persisted.

Ariel shrugged. "I really don't know," she said. "However, I will tell you that my ministry receives hundreds of property donations during any given year. I suppose it's possible that one of my viewers donated such a building in God's name, but I have no knowledge of it. I will give you my accountant's name and number. He could clarify that for you better than I. I don't bother myself with such things. I'd rather focus my energies on the Word."

Red wrote down the accountant's name and number as she gave them out, but Ben wouldn't let go.

"Where were you last night?"

Ariel gave them an indignant look. "Not again!" she cried. "Must I constantly prove myself to you people? Don't you have someone else you can harass?" Then she picked up the phone by her bedside and buzzed for Betty to come up. "I was in bed last night, suffering from this cold or flu or whatever you call it. Betty was here. Ask her yourself."

As if on cue, Betty knocked and then entered. "Yes, ma'am, how can I help you?"

"These men have some questions they want to ask you."

She turned. "Yes?"

For all it was worth, Ben asked the questions, but in his opinion, the woman could easily be lying on her employer's behalf.

"Betty, is it?"

The maid nodded.

"Okay, Betty, can you tell us what time it was when you last saw Miss Simmons last night?"

The maid frowned, trying to remember. "I brought her some honey-lemon tea for her throat just before ten. She was as ill as she is now, so I left her alone to sleep."

"Do you live on the premises?" Ben asked.

"Yes, my rooms are directly off the kitchen downstairs."

"Are you able to hear anyone coming or going?"

"Yes, definitely. My bedroom is next to the garage, and I heard nothing."

Ariel gave both men a triumphant glance. "That will be all, Betty." She waited until her maid was gone; then she glared at both men. "Before you ask, yes, that's my car out front, so if I had driven it, there's the possibility Betty would not have heard it. However, it's been parked out front since the day before yesterday. It has not been moved, and with all your snoopy technology, I'm sure there's some mechanic or something who could verify that. Now, if you gentlemen will let yourselves out, I need to rest."

Ben knew she was lying about the fire. He could see it in her eyes, which made him suspect she was lying about everything else. With the right wig and makeup, she could be the woman China had seen. He knew she wore wigs, she'd admitted as much, and she had been lying about everything else from the start of their investigation, but at the moment, he didn't have any leverage to make her break.

As they started to leave, he saw she'd been reading the *Dallas Morning News,* which meant she'd seen the picture on the front page. He reached for the paper, then tossed it in her lap with the headlines facing her.

"Interesting likeness, isn't it?"

Ariel turned pale. "You can't be serious! That woman doesn't look anything like me."

"I don't know about that," Ben said, then elbowed his partner. "What do you think, Red? Does that look like Miss Simmons?"

Red squinted his eyes, pretending to study her face.

"Well, with the right wig and makeup, I think she could pass."

Ariel's belly lurched, and for the first time since she'd taken to her bed, she really began to feel sick.

"Get out," she moaned. "Just get out and leave me alone."

Then she bolted from her bed and into an adjoining bath, slamming the door behind her. The sounds of retching were too real to be faked.

"What do you think, partner?" Red asked.

"I think we hit a nerve."

Chapter 13

Mattie English was all out of sorts, and China had done her best to stay out of her way. The moment Dave Lambert had arrived at the ranch, Mattie's good humor had fled. As an outsider, it seemed obvious to China that they cared for each other, but she didn't know enough about their history to question what kept them at odds.

However, Dave and China had hit it off from the start. The retired cop was gruff but gentle with her. At least she knew where she stood with him. But it would seem that Mattie did not. She couldn't be in the same room with him without making a caustic comment about one thing or another. China went to her room to escape the consequences of both their bad tempers.

By noon, Mattie was frazzled and snapping constantly at Dave. Finally China overheard the confrontation as Dave's patience ended.

"Damn it to hell, Mattie, I know you don't want me here. You've made that blatantly clear. But this isn't about you. It's about that young woman in there. I made a promise to your son, and I aim to keep it, which leaves you with two choices. Put up or shut up."

China held her breath as the silence lengthened. Then she heard a pan bang against the cabinet as Mattie uttered one word.

"Fine."

"Fine what?" Dave asked.

"You figure it out," Mattie said, and that ended that.

China smiled. Although she wasn't really tired, she decided that she would stay in her room rather than get in the middle of their cease-fire. A small bookcase beneath the window held an assortment of books. She knelt before the shelves, searching the titles for something to read. As she looked, she heard an approaching car and pushed aside the curtains to look out.

It wasn't Ben's car, although she hadn't really expected it to be. It was too early for him to come home. With no knowledge of Mattie's daily routine, she watched out of curiosity. The car came to a stop at the end of the walk leading to the house. The sun was glaring on the driver's side of the windshield, so for a moment, she couldn't see who got out. Then the driver moved into her line of vision.

It was a tall, slender woman wearing dark slacks and a knee-length coat, with a fur-lined hood pulled tightly around her face. A large bag hung awkwardly on her shoulder, while sunglasses disguised a good portion of her face. As China watched, the woman ducked her head and started toward the house at a run.

Staggered by a sudden panic, it was all China could do to get up. She bolted out the door, calling Dave's name as she ran.

The fear in China's voice yanked Dave out of his chair. He came around the corner on the run, his gun drawn.

"What?" he yelled.

She pointed toward the door.

"A tall woman—running toward the house. I—"

Mattie was there within seconds. "What's wrong?"

"China said there's a woman running toward the house."

At that moment a series of rapid knocks sounded on the door, and then it flew back against the wall, rattling the ornaments on the Christmas tree standing in front of the picture window.

Dave turned, his gun aimed.

China screamed.

Mattie began to shout as she ran toward the woman. "Don't shoot! Don't shoot. It's the Avon lady."

Almost immediately, Dave recognized his neighbor, Patsy Reynolds.

"Damnation, Patsy. You almost got yourself shot."

Patsy's face mirrored her confusion. "I knocked," she mumbled, as her bag slid to the floor. Her eyes filled with tears as she looked at Mattie. "I was in a hurry. I needed to pee."

Overwhelmed with relief, China started to laugh as Dave began to curse even more.

"Well, you know where the bathroom is," Mattie said.

Patsy shook her head. "I don't need to anymore. Guess I got it scared out of me."

This made China laugh even harder. Patsy didn't know whether to be insulted or glad no one was angry that she'd come in without an invitation.

Mattie stifled a sigh, although it was funny. Dave looked as if he'd swallowed a bug as he holstered his gun and stalked out of the room.

"Have a seat, Patsy. You'll have to excuse us, but we've been under a little stress, and you just got caught in the middle."

Patsy Reynolds sat, but on the edge of the chair, in case she needed to make a quick getaway.

"Y'all must have really been mad," she said, eyeing the doorway where Dave had disappeared. "He had a gun."

This sent China into convulsions of laughter, and she waved herself out and escaped to her room.

"Who's she?" Patsy asked, as China left.

Mattie rolled her eyes. "Oh…she's family. Distant… but family, just the same."

Back to business, Patsy nodded, then reached into her bag. "Here's the latest brochure. We've got a special on hand cream—the kind you like. And if you buy two tubes, you get the third one free."

The last thing Mattie wanted was to look at Avon products, but considering what could have happened a few moments ago, she decided the least she could do was spend a few dollars for hand cream. It was a whole lot cheaper than flowers for the poor woman's funeral.

Connie Marx stood at the window of her Highland Park apartment, contemplating her life. She'd had her last drink more than two days ago, after accepting the fact that she'd brought every damn thing that was happening to her down on her own head. A Mississippi sharecropper's daughter, she'd spent most of her life dreaming of success, and she'd had it all—until she'd messed around with someone else's husband.

All during her days of self-pity, when she'd stayed lost in the whiskey, an old memory had stayed in her head. Just after her sixth birthday, it had started to rain. It rained for five days straight. The river below their house began to flood, and just before sundown, their house was swept away by the waters. Her daddy had stood on a rise above the river with a look on his face that she had never before seen; then he sat down with his head between his knees and began to cry. Two days later, he hung himself from the rafters of his brother's barn, ending his worries, but exacerbating theirs. In a fit of blind grief, her mother had packed up all five of her children and set out walking. They walked all night and most of the next day before the children began to cry, begging her to stop. So she stopped.

But she never managed to get up. Someone passing by on the road reported a woman and five kids were in some sort of distress. Just before nightfall, a couple of police cars drove up and loaded the kids in one car and Connie's mother in the other. They never saw her again. In later years, she learned that her mother had gone quietly insane and died one night in her sleep. The weakness of both her parents, to just quit on themselves and the children they'd brought in the world, had been something Connie kept to herself. She'd prided herself on being strong and focused, with her eye always on the goal ahead and never on her personal self.

But then she had met Larry Dee Jackson, and the suave, sexy superstar had sweet-talked her right into his bed. In one fit of passion, Connie Marx had traded her dreams for pleasure.

For a while she'd wallowed in self-pity and had even contemplated ending it all herself. But that was before the dream—before she remembered the dark, bloody face of her father as he swung from the rafters, his eyes bulging, his lips slack and swollen, and the puddle of pee on the ground below his feet. She'd come out of her bed with a gasp. In that moment, a plan was born.

Now she paced the living room of her Highland Park apartment, waiting for Detective English to return her call.

A few minutes later, her telephone rang. With a strong sense of déjà vu, she picked up the receiver.

"Hello."

"Miss Marx, this is Ben English. I have a note here that you called."

Connie's fingers tightened around the receiver in her hand.

"Yes. There's something I need you to do for me."

Ben had never had a murder suspect ask him for a favor before. To say he was surprised would have been putting it lightly.

"Yes?"

"I want to take a lie detector test, and I want you to set it up for me. I didn't kill Chaz Finelli, and I want you to prove it."

Ben was stunned. The vehemence in her voice was not faked, nor was her confidence in herself.

"You know that such a test is not admissible in court," he said.

"Yes, but I also know the weight one carries in the public eye, and I will not be dragged through any more of the mud Finelli made of my life. He's dead. I'm not sorry, but I didn't do it."

"When can you come in?"

"Today, tomorrow, you name it."

"It's just after one. Let me make a few calls and I'll get right back to you," he said. "Oh…I suppose I should tell you, you might want your lawyer present."

"No. I just want this over."

A distinct click sounded in Ben's ear. Frowning, he hung up and headed for the captain's office. He knocked once, then opened the door.

Aaron Floyd was on the phone. He waved for Ben to come in and then quickly hung up.

"What's up?" he asked.

"I'm not sure," Ben said. "It could be a ploy, but I think she sounded sincere."

"Who sounded sincere?" Floyd asked.

"Connie Marx. She wants to take a lie detector test—today, if it can be set up. What do you think?"

"Go for it," Floyd said. "Call her back. Tell her three o'clock, and tell her where to go. I'll set it up."

"Yes, sir," Ben said, and backed out of the office.

Five minutes later, the call had been made. Ben left a note on his partner's desk, then made a quick call home. This might make him late, and he wanted to be sure Dave Lambert would be there until he arrived.

His mother answered the phone.

"Hey, Mom, how's everything going?"

"You don't want to know."

The hair rose on the back of Ben's neck. He didn't like the sound of her voice.

"Has there been a problem? Is China okay?"

Mattie snorted. "Oh, she's fine. I can't say the same for Patsy Reynolds, and Dave hasn't spoken to either of us since noon, but other than that, we're just great."

He frowned. "What happened to Dave, and how does Patsy Reynolds come into the scenario?"

"She would be my Avon lady, remember? Dave nearly shot her today. I don't think she'll ever be back, and I do like that hand cream they sell."

Ben almost dropped the phone. "Shot her? Why the hell would Dave want to shoot the Avon lady?"

Mattie sighed. "Looking back, it was sort of funny, but at the time, no one but China saw the humor in the situation. Anyway, China came out of her room like a scalded cat, said some woman was running toward the house. Dave pulled his gun just as the door flew open. It was Patsy. But she wasn't trying to hurt anyone, she was

just in a hurry to use the bathroom. Oh…it was all such
a mix-up, and then—"

"China! Is she all right? It didn't frighten her, did it?"

"Frighten her? Oh, hell, no. She laughed herself silly,
that's what she did. And the longer it went on, the harder
she laughed. Dave is embarrassed and mad, but he's been
mad ever since he got here. China has spent the afternoon
reading. Every time I go check on her, she grins. It's just
been hell. Tomorrow is bound to be better."

Throughout the story his mother was telling, only one
thing stuck in his mind. China had laughed. He would
have given a lot to have heard the sound. Then he remembered why he'd called.

"I may be a little late. Tell Dave not to leave until I
get there."

"Oh, fine," Mattie said. "This should finish off the
day just right."

Ben grinned. "Tell him I'll honk twice when I drive
up so he won't shoot me by mistake."

"We're not talking," Mattie said.

Ben's grin faded. He'd expected something like this.

"Somebody better be talking when I get there," he said.

"We don't always get what we want, my dear son. Just
get yourself home before you completely ruin what is left
of my world."

"Yes, ma'am," he said. She hung up in his ear.

Ben sighed as he hung up. That was the second time a
woman had hung up on him within the last half hour. He
hoped it was not a portent of things to come.

Connie Marx came out of the interrogation room with
a defiant stride, her head held high, her shoulders back
and soldier straight. Ben was waiting for her at the end
of the hall.

"You passed," he said.

"That's because I'm innocent," she said shortly. "Now call off your dogs, or I will get myself a coyote-mean lawyer who'll take you and everyone connected with the Dallas P.D. to the cleaners. Do I make myself clear?"

"There are no dogs on your trail, Miss Marx."

Connie looked startled. "What do you mean?"

"Didn't you see the sketch in today's paper?"

"I haven't read a paper in days," she muttered.

He handed her a copy.

She unfolded it, scanned the headline, then the face below. Her eyes widened in disbelief.

"She doesn't look like me," she said.

"No, ma'am, she doesn't."

She took a deep breath. "You mean you don't consider me a suspect anymore?"

"That's right."

"And you let me rave on about that test, then let me take it, knowing it wasn't necessary?"

"I wasn't aware you hadn't seen the paper, Miss Marx. Look at it this way. You've cleared yourself in the eyes of the world by volunteering to take the test. Passing it was a plus."

Her voice began to shake. "Has anyone called my place of employment to let them know I am no longer a suspect?"

"No, ma'am. It's not something we normally do."

Connie lifted her chin. There was another wall she had yet to climb.

"I have a favor to ask."

Ben hesitated. "You can ask. I can't guarantee anything."

"When all this breaks, I want an exclusive."

Ben had to admire her. "I'll do what I can," he said.

"That's enough," Connie said, and then began to walk away.

"Miss Marx?"

She stopped and turned.

"Where can you be reached in case I need to make that call?"

"At home. I'm not going back to Channel 7 with my tail between my legs. I will go back with the scoop of the year and a raise in salary, or flip burgers for the rest of my life."

Ben gave her a quick salute. She smiled grimly and then headed for home. More than halfway down the hall, she saw the elevator begin to open. When Larry Dee Jackson emerged, a huge smile on his face and his arms open wide, beckoning for her to come in, she couldn't believe her eyes.

"Connie, sweetheart! I saw the paper. Now everyone will know you couldn't be the killer. I've been looking for you all over. Your lawyer told me where you'd gone. It's over, isn't it, baby? It's all over."

She stared at him, trying to figure out what she'd ever seen in the man. Other than a pretty face, he was as shallow as they came. He'd given up her name to the police, then abandoned her when she became a suspect. Now he was back with that take-me-to-bed smirk on his face? She didn't think so.

"Oh, it's over, all right."

She slapped him hard, taking pleasure in the pain against her own palm, then stepped inside the elevator and rode it down alone.

Ben saw it all from a distance and even winced when she slapped Jackson's face, yet he couldn't help thinking the man deserved it. That was one incident when Jackson hadn't been able to pay out to make everything right.

Then Ben thought of China, and of his mother and Dave and the mess waiting for him there. It was time to go home.

Around six in the evening, the scent of something wonderful cooking and guilt that she hadn't offered to help prepare it drew China from her room. As she walked down the hall, she could hear the murmur of voices coming from the kitchen and hesitated, but they didn't sound angry, so she kept on going. Just as she reached the doorway, she heard Mattie laugh. It was a quiet, intimate chuckle between old friends, and she smiled. It would seem that the ruffled feathers had been soothed, at least for the time being.

"Am I too late to help?" she asked.

Both Dave and Mattie looked up. Mattie waved her in.

"Figured we'd scared you out of ever coming out," she said.

China figured she'd laughed enough for one day and just smiled.

"I wasn't scared. I just thought it prudent to stay out of the line of fire."

Dave grinned. "Told you she was a smart one."

Mattie waved a spoon toward the table. "Sit down, honey. There will be time enough for you to work later, when you've recovered some more. This was your first full day home from the hospital. You're bound to be a little bit weak."

"I've rested," China said. "And since you're all about honesty here, I have to tell you that I feel very guilty about invading your lives like this. I know if it wasn't for Ben's insistence, you would not have been forced into this situation."

"No one forces me to do anything," Mattie said. "So sit."

Dave got up and pulled out a chair for her. "You may as well do as she says," he said. "She won't hush until she has her way."

China sat.

Mattie muttered something beneath her breath as she turned back to her cooking but managed to keep her thoughts to herself.

China glanced at the clock, and Dave saw her.

"Ben called earlier. Said he would be late," he said.

China blushed. "I wasn't...I mean I didn't..."

He chuckled. "You know what they say about protesting too much."

"Now I know why Mattie feels the need to tear a strip off you from time to time," she muttered.

His chuckle deepened.

"David Wayne, leave her alone," Mattie snapped.

Dave hushed, but his eyes were still twinkling as he leaned back in his chair.

An awkward silence rose between them, and China was thinking she should have waited to come out after all when the sound of an approaching car altered the mood. Two short blasts from the car horn followed.

"That's probably Ben," Dave said. "I'll go see."

China's heart skipped a beat. Suddenly the thought of his deep, booming voice and the tenderness of his touch was more than she could bear. She started to bolt when Mattie turned, aiming a spoon at her to punctuate her order.

"You can set the table now," she said. "Silverware is in the top drawer on the left of the sink."

"Yes, ma'am," China said and got up.

Mattie sighed, laid her spoon on the cabinet and then

walked over to where China was standing and gave her a hug.

"Honey, I'm sorry I've been so hateful today. It had nothing to do with you. There's old business between Dave and me, and you just got caught up in the middle."

The warmth of Mattie's hug and the sincerity in her voice were enough to make China want to cry. Instead, she swallowed the lump in her throat and managed a smile.

"I figured as much," she said. "And you didn't hurt my feelings."

Mattie grinned and playfully tweaked the end of China's nose. "Good. Then the next time you call me 'ma'am,' I'm going to stuff a sock in your mouth."

China laughed aloud.

And that was the first sound Ben heard as he walked into the house. It stopped him in his tracks, leaving him weak and wanting, and in that moment he had to accept the fact that he was in love with China Brown.

"About time you showed up," Dave said.

Ben blinked. He hadn't even seen Dave standing there.

"Shut the door, boy," Dave said. "You're letting in a whole lot of cold air."

"Oh, yeah, sorry," Ben muttered, and came the rest of the way inside, shedding his coat and gloves as he moved toward the hall closet. "How did everything go today?" he asked.

Dave snorted. "Oh, I'd say pretty good, except for the fact that I almost shot the Avon lady."

Ben grinned. "I heard."

Dave frowned. "Then why the hell did you ask? Just to see if I'd tell you the truth?"

Ben chuckled and then slapped his old friend on the back.

"Confession is good for the soul. You taught me that, remember?"

Dave grinned wryly. "Yeah, but that was because I caught you smoking a cigar behind your daddy's barn. There's a big difference between sneaking a smoke and plugging your neighbor."

"Heard she was in a hurry to use the bathroom," Ben said.

Dave's grin widened. "After I pulled my gun on her, I doubt she made it in time."

"Wish I'd been here," Ben said. "That would have been something to see."

"Wish you'd been here, too," Dave said. "A houseful of women makes me nervous. Now come on, boy, let's go see your mama before she comes looking for us."

"Is China okay?" Ben asked.

The smile slid off Dave Lambert's face. "You're pretty gone on her, aren't you?"

"There you are," Mattie said, as she came into the room. She gave her son a welcoming hug. "Supper is ready. We'll have it on the table in five minutes."

"Smells good," Ben said. "But I want to say hello to China before I change."

"Oh, she's—" Mattie started to say, but Ben walked off before she could finish.

"He's in love with her," Dave said.

Mattie frowned.

"What?" Dave asked. "I thought you liked her?"

Mattie shrugged. "I like what I know about her well enough, but she's only been here a day. I've wanted Ben to settle down for years now. After all, he's in his thirties. But I don't know what I think about a woman like her."

"She seems decent enough," Dave said.

"Only months ago she was living with another man

and having his baby without being married. When she got shot, she was homeless. Now she's the only person who's seen this serial killer and lived to tell about it. That's not exactly the kind of woman a mother wants her son to marry."

Dave looked at Mattie and then shook his head. "How soon you forget," he said.

Mattie's color rose and her chin jutted. "I don't know what you're talking about."

Dave took her by the shoulders. His voice was quiet, his grip firm.

"You stayed married to a man you didn't love out of a sense of duty. You cheated yourself and me out of a lifetime of happiness. Your husband hadn't been dead more than a week when we made love, and you've never forgiven me for it. Judging that girl is a little beneath you, don't you think?"

Mattie's face fell. Her eyes glittered with unshed tears. Truth was a hard thing to face.

"I've got to get supper on the table," she said. "Go wash your hands."

"I think I've been here long enough for one day," he said. "I'm going home."

"You walk out that door, don't bother to come back," she said quietly and then walked away.

Dave stared for a moment, then went to wash his hands.

Chapter 14

Ben entered the kitchen and found China at the cutlery drawer.

"Mom put you to work?" he asked.

The deep voice startled and, at the same time, excited her. Reacting normally around this man was becoming a difficult thing to do.

"I offered," she said quietly, and moved toward the table, her steps slow and measured.

Ben watched her through narrowed eyes. She was sore. He could tell by the way she moved.

"You've been up too much today," he said, and took the cutlery out of her hands and began laying it in place around the table.

"I've been in my room almost—"

Ben looked up and grinned. "Yeah, I heard you lit out for parts unknown after Dave tried to shoot the Avon lady."

She grinned in spite of herself. "I shouldn't have laughed."

"Sounded pretty funny to me," Ben said.

"It was all my fault. I panicked. They just reacted to me. It nearly got a woman shot."

Ben shook his head. "Dave's too good a cop to shoot an unarmed suspect, even if she was carrying."

"But she wasn't armed," China said.

"She had her Avon bag."

China giggled. "And I laughed."

Ben couldn't quit staring. Since he'd known her, she'd either been suffering from pain or grief. This playful side was a surprise and a joy.

China straightened a spoon, then moved to another place and switched the knife and fork to opposite sides of the plate while still trying to explain.

"I think it was all just a reaction to my relief...you know...realizing that the woman wasn't here to kill me after all. It was right after she said she needed to pee that I started to fall apart."

Ben chuckled.

China grinned. "I tried to stop laughing, I swear I did. But things kept going from bad to worse, and Dave was so mad, and Mattie was yelling, 'Don't shoot, don't shoot, it's the Avon lady,' and...well, you just had to be there." Then she laughed aloud.

Her laughter stopped him cold.

"Jesus," he whispered.

China froze. Something had changed, and she didn't know what had caused it. When Ben began to circle the table toward her, she started to get nervous.

"What?" she asked. "What did I do?"

He touched her face, tracing the shape of her mouth with his fingers. It was soft, so damned soft.

"The laughter," he mumbled. "It changes you."

Suddenly embarrassed, she tried to turn away, but he wouldn't let her.

"It probably makes me look stupid. My eyes are too big and my mouth is too wide, anyway."

Ever careful of her injuries, he took her by the shoulders and turned her back around to face him.

"Look at me, China."

He had given her no choice.

"Your laughter is beautiful, just like you, and it makes me ache with envy, knowing I wasn't the one who made you smile. I don't know how, but one of these days you'll learn to believe in yourself."

He moved away, knowing that if he stayed this close any longer, he would be kissing her.

China's heart was pounding—her thoughts going crazy. God, how she wanted to believe him, but she'd looked in the mirror, she'd seen the flaws for more years than she cared to count.

And then Mattie came striding into the kitchen with her head up and fire in her eyes, and the moment to question him was lost.

"I'm going to change. Be back in five," Ben said quickly, and left.

China sensed Mattie's mood. Uncomfortable being alone with Ben's mother, she sat down, hoping the silence would make her invisible. But to her surprise, Mattie suddenly turned and smiled.

"Hope you're hungry, dear," Mattie said. "I think I made too much chicken and dumplings."

"Oh! One of my favorite foods," China said. "I haven't had it in years."

It was the perfect thing to say. Mattie began talking companionably, as if they'd been working together all their lives, and by the time the food was on the table and everyone had gathered round, the atmosphere in the room was comfortable and light.

An hour or so later, after the food had been eaten and the dishes were done, Dave left for the night. Mattie moved to the living room, settling in her favorite chair with the remote at her elbow and her knitting in her lap, leaving Ben and China alone in the kitchen.

"Want to take a walk?" he asked.

The idea of getting out, even for a short while, was exciting.

"Yes, very much," she said.

"Get your coat."

She jumped up too quickly and winced.

"Take your time, honey," Ben said. "I won't leave without you."

Excited about doing something normal rather than hiding in fear, she went to the front closet to get her coat. Mattie looked up from her knitting as China slipped her coat from its hanger.

"We're going for a walk," she said.

Mattie nodded approvingly. "It will be good for you," she said. "You'll sleep better after getting some fresh air."

"We won't be long," China said.

"Take as long as you like. Ben won't let you come to harm."

China hurried back to the kitchen, where Ben was waiting, but with a new sense of peace. Seven little words, but they had made all the difference in her world. *Ben won't let you come to harm.* His mother was right. Ben would take care of her, and not just because he was a cop and it was his job, but because he'd promised.

Ben helped her put on her coat, pulled the hood up close around her face and fastened it beneath her chin.

"Don't want you getting chilled."

"I'm tough."

He paused, staring intently at her face. "Yes, you are, aren't you, honey?"

Pinned by the shadows in his eyes, China shivered, and then the moment passed. He took her by the elbow and led her out the back door. Earlier, the wind had stopped. Now the air was cold and still, and as they stepped off the porch, the grass crunched beneath their feet. She took a deep breath and then looked up at the sky. Only a few stars were showing, which told her the storm front that had been predicted earlier was probably moving in.

"Are you warm enough?" Ben asked.

She nodded, then remembered it was dark and added a yes.

"Better take my hand," Ben said. "Some of the ground is a little uneven. Above everything else, I don't want you to fall."

She slipped her hand in his without thinking about the consequences, yet as soon as they touched, the awareness between them came back.

"We'll make this quick," Ben said. "When you're stronger, we'll stay longer, but a short walk to the barn and back should be enough for tonight."

The silence between them was oddly comfortable. As they walked, China became aware of a dark shadow looming in the distance. This had to be the barn. As they neared, a horse suddenly nickered. She jumped.

"It's just Cowboy," Ben said. "He's my horse. He's twenty years old and has never lived anywhere but this ranch."

A sense of poignancy swept over China. How strange that she was homeless but Ben English's horse wasn't. She shrugged off the self-pity and made herself smile.

"Can we see him?" she asked.

"That's a given," Ben said. "He knows we're com-

ing. If we don't show up with a treat or two, he'll sulk
for a week."

"Oh, but we didn't bring anything with us."

"I have some sugar cubes in my pocket," Ben said. "I
got them while I was waiting for you."

"I've never petted a horse before," China said.

Ben stopped, pretending great surprise. "And how long
have you lived in Texas, lady?"

"Almost twenty years."

"Someone has neglected your raising, honey. Allow
me to intervene."

China was smiling as they entered the barn, and although the building was open at both ends, there was a
sense of warmth and shelter. She shoved the hood away
from her face as Ben flipped a switch, flooding the barn
with light. Immediately, a big sorrel with a white blaze
on his face stuck his head over the door of his stall.

Ben laughed. "Yeah, I see you, fella. We're coming
as fast as we can."

China was beside herself with excitement. Before Ben
could stop her, she hurried ahead. Ben started to caution
her. Cowboy didn't like strangers. But there was something about the silence of the horse and the woman as
they took each other's measure that told him this would
be different. He stopped and took a deep breath, savoring the rare communication between the pair.

China was entranced. The animal's dark-brown eyes
were fixed upon her face, its nostrils slightly flared as it
explored her scent. And then Cowboy nickered softly, as
if saying hello. China looked to Ben for approval. When
he nodded, she extended her hand. The soft, velvety pull
of the horse's lips tickled the palm of her hand, in search
of the favored treat. Ben slipped her a cube, which she
promptly extended.

When the horse took it out of her hand without touching her skin, she sighed with delight.

"His nose…it's so soft," she whispered.

"He likes you," Ben said.

There was childlike excitement in her voice. "He does?"

Ben nodded. "He doesn't let just anyone pet him."

China shivered with delight. "Do you have any more sugar?"

Ben handed her what he'd brought, watching as the big horse daintily nibbled up his treats.

"That's all," China said, when the last one had been eaten.

Just as if he understood, the horse tossed his head and then surprised her by nuzzling the side of her face and then gently pulling at her hair.

When China gasped, Ben thought she was afraid and moved to step between them.

"No," she begged. "He's not hurting me. He's loving me, isn't he?"

Pain twisted his heart. "How can you blame him? You'd be easy to love."

She turned then, her eyes wide with disbelief. "You mean easy prey, don't you? After all, look at what I let Tommy Fairheart do."

"No, that's not what I meant, and don't put words in my mouth. You didn't *let* that heel do anything to you, honey. You were his victim. He's a con man. He looks for innocent young women…lonely women. He feeds them a line and takes them for what he can get and moves on." He moved closer, his voice softening. "It's not a mistake to want happiness. It's not a crime to fall in love, and I'm sorry he hurt you—more than you can know."

She glanced at Ben, then looked away. "Maybe so, but it doesn't make me feel any less stupid."

"Do you still love him?"

"Absolutely not," she said, and moved away. "That part of our relationship had been over for months. Even before he stole my money and left. I just didn't know how to let go of the man who was my baby's father."

Ben couldn't deny the relief he felt. At least he wasn't going to have to fight that, too. And fight he would. He'd already decided that she was worth whatever it took.

"That's good," Ben said. "It makes my job a whole lot easier."

"How does my hating Tommy Fairheart have anything to do with protecting me?"

Ben moved closer then. "I'm not talking about that job," he whispered, as he cupped her face with his hands. "I'm talking about teaching you to trust me. Without trust, there's no love, and, honey, I want you to love me more than I've ever wanted anything in my life."

China's eyes widened, her lips parting in surprise.

It was what Ben had been waiting for. He lowered his head, centering a kiss in the middle of her mouth. Her head fell back against his arm as he cradled her against his chest. He felt her shock, then her lips trembling against his. She was sweet, so sweet, and so damned scared. When she moaned, he instantly pulled back.

"Don't be scared," he begged. "Not of me. I would never hurt you." He nuzzled his lips against the side of her neck. "Never."

She stared up at his face. The tenderness was there. She'd expected it. But there was also a passion she didn't know how to take. Her hands were shaking as she lifted them to her mouth. She felt branded and wondered if the imprint of his lips could be physically felt.

Ben was scared he'd ruined everything by coming on so strong. It had been too soon. What the hell had he been thinking?

"China…honey?"

She shook her head, as if coming out of a daze.

"Never?" she asked.

Ben exhaled on a shaky sigh. "God yes, never ever."

"You promise?"

He nodded. "Have I ever broken a promise to you?"

She bit her lower lip, then shrugged. "Not yet."

At that moment, if Ben could have put his hands around Fairheart's throat, he would have throttled him. He stifled the urge to react in anger, but it came out in his voice anyway.

"China."

"What?"

"Don't make me pay for someone else's mistakes."

"I—"

"You've been out long enough," he said. "It's getting late. Tomorrow's another day."

Their walk back to the house was silent. When they got inside, Ben paused to lock the door behind them. China watched him, wondering if she'd ruined everything between them, then deciding that it was all in her head, because there was nothing to be ruined. He'd kissed her. That was all. No need to wrap herself around a future that couldn't possibly exist.

"Give me your coat," he said. "I'll hang it up for you."

She handed him the coat, then stood, unwilling to end their evening.

"Thank you for the walk…and for Cowboy…and…" Unable to speak of the rest of what had happened, she ended her thanks with a shrug.

The last of his anger faded as he saw the panic on her face. His voice gentled, his smile forgiving.

"You're welcome."

She was on her way out of the kitchen when Ben called out to her.

"China?"

She spun, unaware of the anxiety in her voice. "Yes?"

"Do you need any help getting undressed?"

"No, no, I can manage."

He shoved his hands in his pockets and nodded.

She started to leave again, but there was something inside him that hated to let go. He called to her again, and again she turned.

"Yes?" China said.

"Sleep tight. Don't let the bed bugs bite."

The tension on her face began to fade, replaced by a slow, timid smile.

"Yes. You, too," she said softly, and then left him standing. She couldn't bring herself to look back for fear the look of hunger she'd seen on his face would still be there.

Long after the house was quiet and everyone had gone to bed, China sat in a chair by her window, staring out into the night. Her thoughts were on replay, from the time Ben had tied the hood beneath her chin to the moment he'd told her good-night. She kept remembering the feel of Cowboy's nose on the palm of her hand and Ben English's mouth upon her lips. One had tickled, the other had made her knees go weak. What was she to do? She couldn't be falling in love. She was in enough danger already without giving another man entry into her heart.

But then she reminded herself that Ben wouldn't hurt her. He wasn't that kind. He was a man who kept the promises he made. All she had to do was learn to believe in herself as much as she believed in him.

The woman opened her closet and reached in for a gown, letting her fingers run lightly over the satins and silks before choosing one of red chiffon. She dropped it over her head, sighing in satisfaction as the fabric slid the length of her long, slender body. It hung loose from the decolletage—a diaphanous nightgown that swept the floor as she walked. She stepped into a pair of red mules and then put on the matching robe, tying it in a neat, dainty bow.

As she passed the stereo, she punched Play. At once, the throbbing bass of a rock-and-roll band reverberated against her skin. She shivered as the sensation went all the way to her bones. Dancing her way toward the dresser in long, sensuous strides, she paused to give herself a critical stare, then reached for the wig on a nearby stand. With a practiced hand, she flipped it over her head, then pulled it down around her ears. The new haircut made it fit a little bit loose, and she tugged on the cap until it finally settled in place. This time, when she swung around to view herself in the full-length mirror, she liked what she saw. The only problem was, no one would see her like this. It was too dangerous to play the game anymore.

She frowned. The music played on, but she wasn't able to respond as she normally did. She kept picturing that woman on the front page of the *Dallas Morning News*. Damn it all to hell, how had they done that? She would have sworn there wasn't a living soul who'd seen her face. She'd been so careful, never leaving a witness to tell about her little games.

A shiver ran up her spine as she remembered Chaz Finelli coming out of nowhere and the flash of his cam-

era as it caught her in disguise. Thank God she'd had her
gun with her. She'd made short work of Finelli and his
damned camera. The cops would never find it. She'd removed the memory card from the camera and set it on
fire, then tossed the camera into a Dumpster on the other
side of town. It had been unfortunate about that woman—
the one with the baby in her belly. Then she shrugged. It
was survival of the fittest. She'd worked too hard to get
where she was to toss it away on sentimentality.

Suddenly angry, she stomped over to the stereo and
turned it off, then began yanking off her clothes and tossing them all around. When she was through, the woman
from the mirror was no longer recognizable. She washed
her face until it was devoid of any makeup, dressed in the
clothes she'd worn to the cabin and turned out the lights
as she left. In a week or so, after the New Year had been
rung in, she would start a quiet investigation. She had
money and power and friends in high places. Somehow
she would find out how the police had come up with that
picture. There was too much at stake to take any chances
of being found.

Christmas Day dawned with a gray, cloudy sky. China
buried her nose beneath the covers, reluctant to emerge.
This day hadn't meant much to her since her mother's
death, but she had looked forward to the Christmases she
would have had with a child. Shopping for toys, pretty
dresses and bows for a little girl's hair. But the dream
was gone now, like everything else she had treasured.

A knock sounded on her door.

"China, are you up?"

"No," she said.

He opened the door. "But you're awake."

"I am now."

"Good," he said. "I wanted to give you your present."

"But I didn't get you anything," she said.

"Of course not," he said. "You're in hiding, remember?"

"So that makes me exempt from giving gifts?"

He tugged at a lock of her hair, then sat on the edge of her bed.

"In this instance, yes." He laid a small box in her lap.

"That doesn't seem right," she said, although she was interested enough to sit up.

"Open it," Ben urged. "Please."

She began to remove the ribbon, then the paper. A few seconds later, she opened the lid and lifted the figurine out.

"Oh, Ben." Her eyes filled with tears.

"I know," he said. "But when I saw it, I knew it was yours."

"It's perfect," she said. "Even though it makes me sad, it's also a reminder of where she's at."

Ben sighed with relief. It was exactly what he'd been trying to convey.

She lifted her arms, then wrapped them around his neck.

"Thank you," she said.

"You're welcome," he whispered, and stole himself one Christmas kiss. "Mom's making biscuits. Do you feel like getting up to eat?"

"I wouldn't miss it," she said. "Just give me a few minutes to get dressed."

"If you need any help, just holler."

She nodded. He winked and then left, leaving her alone with the gift she'd unwrapped. The porcelain angel was perfect in detail, right down to the folds of fabric on her pale-pink gown, but it was the infant she was holding that broke China's heart.

She picked it up again, holding it to the light coming in through the window. Sadness swept over her in one crashing wave after another as she read the small inscription at the base of the statuette.

Someone to Watch Over Me.

It hit her, as she studied her gift, that this could also be symbolic of her relationship with Ben. In a way, she was the infant, helpless to fight all that was facing her now, and he was the angel, holding her safe to his heart. He was pledging his life to keep her safe.

All through the day, she kept the thought in her heart.

Ben tossed aside a file he'd been working on and then leaned back in his chair, eyeing his partner at the desk opposite his.

"Hey, Red, are you taking Rita out tonight?"

Red looked up and frowned. "No. Why?"

"It's New Year's Eve, for God's sake. This time tomorrow it will be a whole new year. That's something to celebrate."

Red looked nervous. "She hasn't said anything."

Ben rolled his eyes. "She shouldn't have to."

"So you think I'd better come up with a plan?" Red asked.

Ben grinned. "If it was me, I would."

Red folded his arms on his desk and leaned forward.

"So, lover boy, if you're so on the mark, exactly what do you have planned for you and the china doll?"

Ben's grin faded. "That's different. She just got out of the hospital, and we're not dating. Besides that, I could hardly take her out, even if we were. She's in hiding, remember?"

"Yeah, I guess. But it seems like you could do something. I mean, she's really had a rough month."

They went back to work, but the seed had been planted in Ben's mind. A short while later, he called home. His mother answered.

"Mom, it's me. Just checking on everyone."

"We're fine. China is napping, and I'm considering it. Dave is puttering around out in the barn, looking for something to fix a broken shutter."

"Tell him there's some stuff in the last granary on the right."

"Okay, I will," Mattie said. "Will you be home late?"

"No, and that's why I'm calling. Have you started anything for supper?"

"Not yet. I don't know why, but I just can't get in the mood. I'll come up with something before the evening is over."

"How about if I bring something home? Maybe Chinese? It's New Year's Eve. Thought we might have a little celebration of our own. Tell Dave he's welcome to stay and see the New Year in if he wants."

Mattie was silent just a moment too long.

"What?" Ben asked.

"Well, Dave sort of asked me out to eat tonight. I told him I'd see."

Ben's pulse jumped. A whole night alone with China. He couldn't have asked for anything more.

"For Pete's sake, go, Mom. We don't need baby-sitters. I'll bring Chinese for us, and you and Dave go kick up your heels."

"He said there was a dance at the Elks lodge, although I probably should say no. I don't have a thing to wear."

"Mom, for the last time, accept his invitation. If you won't do it for yourself, do it for me. I know you get lonely out there by yourself. Nothing would please me more than to know you had someone in your life."

He sensed her embarrassment, but to his delight, she finally agreed.

"Good, it's settled then," he said. "Tell China what's going on when she wakes up. And if she doesn't like Chinese food, somebody better call me before I get off work. I can always pick up something else."

"All right, son," Mattie said. "And thank you."

"No, Mom. I should be thanking you for putting up with all of this."

"You already did. And if the truth be told, I admit that I'm enjoying the hustle and bustle of someone else in this house."

"Is China opening up to you any?"

"Not about personal things, no. But we get along fine. There's just one thing that bothers me about her."

"What's that?"

Mattie hesitated, then blurted it out. "Did you know that girl thinks she's ugly?"

Ben frowned, remembering the day she admitted that her stepfather, Clyde, always said she was homely.

"Yes. It's hard to believe, isn't it?"

"She's absolutely stunning. All that black hair and those big blue eyes. I can't imagine what has happened in her past to make her think something like that."

"Just be patient with her, Mom."

Mattie chuckled. "You're the one who tries my patience. I hardly know she's here."

Ben smiled. "Hey, I do what I can," he said.

Mattie laughed. "Come home safely."

"Yes, ma'am. I'll be there around six-thirty or seven."

Chapter 15

Mattie was behaving like a teenager, tossing one out-fit after another aside while trying to find something to wear for her date with Dave. She'd dragged China into her room on the pretext of asking her for advice, but truthfully, she felt guilty about going out, and she wanted someone to talk to—to keep her mind off what she was about to do. All these years, the guilt of making love with Dave when her husband had been dead only a week had weighed heavily on her conscience. Rationally, she knew it had happened because of a need for emotional release, an affirmation that she was still alive although her hus-band was not. And instead of accepting the weakness for what it was, she'd blamed herself and Dave for something that was no more than an act of desperation.

"So, what do you think about this one?" Mattie asked, holding up a dark-navy sheath.

China frowned. "Too somber. I like the dark pink one better."

Mattie groaned. "I can't make up my mind."

China smiled. "Yes, that much has been obvious for the past fifteen minutes. May I make a suggestion?"

Mattie threw up her hands. "Anything!"

"You go shower and fix your hair, and let me pick out what you'll wear. When you're finished, you come out and put on the outfit I've laid on your bed. You put it on without fussing and go out and have a wonderful time."

"Oh, no," Mattie moaned. "My hair! I'd completely forgotten. How am I going to wear my hair?"

China got up from the chair and pushed Mattie toward the bathroom.

"Go away," China said. "You're making me nervous. Do your hair like you always do. Pretend you're going to church or something. It's not going to matter to Dave what you look like, and you know it. He'd be happy if you went in what you're wearing."

Mattie looked down at her rumpled jeans and sweater and then sighed.

"You're right. Oh lordy, you're right."

She started toward the bathroom, then stopped.

"China...dear?"

"Yes?"

"Thank you."

China grinned. "It was my pleasure."

Still Mattie hesitated. "You know, when I was younger, I'd always planned on having a large family, at least three children, maybe more. When I lost my baby, I lost my dream. Adopting Ben was the best thing we ever did, but as I look back on the years, I wish we had adopted a dozen. I always wanted a daughter. Someone like you would have been perfect."

She gave China a quick hug and then escaped to the bathroom, leaving China speechless.

Someone like me? China walked to the mirror. The

woman looking back at her was all eyes and too thin.
And when she thought about what she looked like beneath her clothes, her stomach knotted. *No one would
want someone like me.*

But as she moved about the bedroom picking up the
clothes Mattie had tossed aside, the sweet words of praise
kept echoing in her heart. Even though she didn't really
believe them, they'd been nice to hear.

When Mattie came out a half hour later, her hair in
hot rollers, her robe flapping about her ankles, China
was gone and her room had been picked up. One complete outfit was lying on her bed, with matching shoes
on the floor beneath it.

Mattie sighed. It was the most daring outfit she owned.
A black dress with a rather audacious neckline. The shoes
were gold, but with nearly flat heels, which would be perfect for dancing. Even the little black shoulder bag lying
next to it was just large enough for a compact and lipstick
and a few dollars for emergencies.

With an anxious heart, she began to dress. But by the
time she had finished her clothes and her hair, her anxiety had turned to excitement. She looked at herself in
the mirror and then did a quick pirouette. For a woman
pushing sixty, she decided, she looked pretty darn good.
Then she heard the sound of a car driving up and glanced
at the clock. That would be Ben. The plan was to leave
now with Dave, go to his place so he could change, and
then the evening would start from there. She grabbed
her bag, gave herself one last look, then opened the door.

As she passed China's room, she noticed her door was
ajar. Wanting to thank China again, she peeked in. China
was sitting in a chair by the window, her hands folded
in her lap in quiet repose. Mattie started to speak when
China turned. The tears on her face said it all.

"Oh, sweetheart," Mattie said. Moments later, she was at her side. "Is there anything I can do?"

"No. You look beautiful."

"Somehow this seems wrong," Mattie said. "I'm going out to a party, and you—"

"This isn't about me," China said. "This is about you and Dave and a lot of wasted years, okay?"

"Okay," Mattie said, then held out her arms. "How do I look?"

China smiled. "Like a woman in love."

Mattie looked a little stunned. "I don't want to look that good," she said. "At least, not just yet."

"Time is precious. Let yourself be happy."

"I'll be late coming home, but I promise to be quiet," Mattie said. "Tomorrow is Ben's day off, so we can all sleep in. Take care of yourself, dear, for me, as well as for you."

"Yes, I will," China said, touched by the woman's concern.

Mattie kissed her goodbye and then waved again as she left.

The room seemed empty after she'd gone. China turned back to her post at the window, although it was already dark outside and there was nothing to see but an occasional set of headlights from a passing car on the road beyond the ranch. The sudden yip of a coyote on a nearby ridge sent a shiver up her spine, and she had to make herself stay still, although she was haunted by an image she couldn't forget. Her child—a child who had never known the sweetness of a single breath of air—lay alone in the dark, in a box, very deep in the ground. In her heart, she knew the baby was with God, but she hadn't been able to turn loose of that pain. Maybe if she'd had a chance to say goodbye…

As she sat, she heard laughter from the front of the house and then, a few minutes later, the sound of a car leaving the yard. That would be Mattie and Dave, off for the night. She struggled with herself, trying to unload the depression. Ben would be looking for her any minute, and she didn't want him to see her cry.

She got up from the chair and washed her face, then contemplated brushing her hair. But the effort was still too painful, so she gave up the thought. As she was leaving the bathroom, it dawned on her that she and Ben would be alone. She shivered. There was no denying the fact that she was attracted to him, and as good as he'd been to her, she was afraid to trust her own judgment. Then she heard him calling.

"China? Where are you?"

She lifted her chin and walked out of her room.

"I'm here," she called.

He met her just outside the kitchen. "Wait," he said. "Close your eyes."

"Why?"

"I have a surprise."

She smiled in spite of herself. "Really?"

"Yes, really. Now close your eyes and hold out your hand."

She did as he asked, letting him lead her into the kitchen.

"Okay," he said. "You can open them now."

She smelled the surprise before she saw it, and still her delight was real.

"Oh, Ben, Chinese? I love Chinese food."

"Great. I wasn't sure what you liked, so I got a little bit of everything."

She smiled as she saw all the boxes. "That's for sure. How many boxes are there, anyway?"

"I'm not sure. Maybe thirteen or fourteen, counting the one with the fortune cookies."

"Oh, I love those. Let me see."

"No fair," he said. "They come last. Now sit your sweet self down. I'm the chef tonight."

China sat, and as she watched him digging through the boxes with such pleasure, her mood began to change. Dejection shifted, giving way to brief moments of peace. For tonight, it was enough.

"Here," he said. "You have to eat with chopsticks."

"I don't know how."

He grinned. "Neither do I. But tomorrow is a whole new year, and we should have at least one new skill to go with it, don't you think?"

"It's a grand idea, but chopsticks? Don't you think something enlightening would have been more in order?"

"After the day I've had, this is just about all the challenge I care to handle."

China tried to pick up a bite with her chopsticks. When it fell back on her plate, she frowned.

"Yes, I see what you mean."

"Want a fork?"

"No," China said. "I can do this." She bent to the task.

Ben watched for a minute, admiring her concentration. When she suddenly crowed with delight and got a bite of stir-fried shrimp in her mouth, he fell a little bit further in love. The meal continued in the same vein, with more laughter and jeers and the occasional flight of a bite of stir-fried rice. It wasn't until China opened her fortune cookie that the evening changed.

She was smiling as she broke the cookie in two. When she pulled out the fortune, she waved it beneath his nose in a teasing fashion.

"Mine will be better than yours," she said.

He grinned. "We'll see about that." He broke his open as well and began to read.

"'You are having dinner with the woman of your dreams.'"

"It doesn't say that," she muttered.

"It does. Here, read it for yourself."

She looked, then sat back in disbelief. "You made that happen."

"No, I didn't. I swear," Ben said. "Read yours. If I'd fixed it, it would say, 'You are having dinner with the man of your dreams,' right?"

"I guess," she muttered, and turned hers over to read.

She scanned the bit of paper and then went suddenly pale. It fell from her hands as she got up from the table and quietly left the room. Ben picked it up and read it.

There is a thing you have left undone.

He read it again, still uncertain as to what had upset her, then went to find her. She was back in her room, sitting in the dark. He went to her. Her face was in shadows, but he could tell she was crying. Tears were thick in her voice.

"China, I don't understand."

"I know."

"Then talk to me. I can't help unless I know what's wrong."

"My life is out of control."

"I know, but it won't always be."

"I've always taken care of myself, and I feel so helpless, even worthless."

"No, honey. Never worthless."

"You don't know. You can't understand. I don't belong anywhere. I don't have an address. I don't have a job. There is no one alive who remembers anything about me. I let myself fall for some pretty words. I let myself get pregnant, and then I let that baby die. I wasn't even there when she was put in the ground." China stood suddenly, her voice rising as she continued to talk. "Do you know how that makes me feel?"

Ben hurt for her in so many ways. "No, but you can tell me. You can tell me anything and I will understand."

She grabbed him by the arms, her fingers digging into his flesh.

"I play at being all right. I pretend that things are getting better. But I need to see my baby. I need to see the place where she's at. I don't know anything about the… about how you…" She took a slow, shuddering breath. "Tell me what you know, and trust me, whatever you tell me can never be as bad as what I've imagined."

Ben was afraid—so afraid of what he was about to do. But China was right. She, above everyone else, had the right to know what had happened to her own child.

"You're sure?"

She nodded.

"She was very, very small, a little over three pounds, I think. The coroner said she died instantly."

"How?"

"One of the bullets ricocheted off a rib and into her."

China moaned.

Ben took her in his arms. "I picked out a little white casket with an angel on the lid. We wrapped her in a pink blanket."

China sighed. "To keep her warm."

It was all Ben could do not to cry. "Yes, it would have kept her warm—very warm."

She laid her face against his chest as the panic began to recede.

"I need to see," China said.

"Cemeteries are locked after dark, and taking you

there in the daytime would be a risk I'm not willing to take."

"It's not your risk to take, it's mine," China said.

Ben tensed. She had asked nothing of him until now. But this? Should he dare?

"Please," she begged.

He sighed. "They will unlock the gates at sunup. I'll take you then. Most of the city will probably be sleeping off the aftereffects of ringing in a new year."

"Thank you. Thank you so much," China said.

His voice rumbled deep against her ear. "Don't thank me yet. I won't rest easy until this is over."

She looked up at him then. "Now you know how I feel."

Midnight came and went. A couple of hours afterward, Dave brought Mattie home. Ben heard the car drive up, and a few minutes later the front door opened, then closed. He heard his mother pause in the hallway, probably to take off her shoes, because afterward he could no longer hear her footsteps. A bit later, he heard the bedsprings creak as she crawled into bed.

He got up then, walking barefoot through the house, checking all the doors and windows one last time, but he knew that no amount of caution in this house was going to offset the danger of taking China back into the city, yet he could not refuse her. Until she said her goodbyes, she was never going to heal.

As he passed her room, he noticed the door was half-open. He stopped and looked in. She lay on her back with one arm outflung, the other beneath the covers. He hesitated, then walked to her bed, lifted the covers and gently put her arm beneath the warmth. She sighed, then started to turn, wincing aloud in her sleep as pain pulled her back. Without waking her up, he put a hand beneath her back and helped her turn. She settled into a comfortable position with a soft, quiet sigh.

Ben straightened, satisfied that all was well, and then paused at the foot of her bed to watch her sleep. In the dark, she looked a bit like a child, but he knew there was a strong, resilient woman beneath all that pain. He gripped the footboard with both hands until the tips of his fingers ached. There in the dark, in the quiet of the night, he made her a promise to keep.

"I will bring that woman to justice. She will pay for all you've lost if it's the last thing I ever do."

Then he closed her door and went back to his room. Sunup would come far too soon.

The gates of Restland Cemetery were already open as Ben slowed the car down to turn in. Except for a few brief comments, he and China had not spoken to each other on the way into the city. He glanced at her now. She was pale and quiet—almost too quiet. But they'd come this far. It was too late to turn back.

"I'm not sure if I remember the exact spot," Ben said. "It may take me a couple of minutes to find the place."

"I remember where Mother is buried," China said. "Take the second gate and turn right at the third road."

He did as she said, and soon memory began to return. A few minutes later he saw the new grave just up the slope and stopped.

"This is as close as we can get with the car," he said.

China looked. The pile of freshly turned dirt was like a sore upon the earth. It would take time for it to settle, just as it would take time for the pain of loss to settle within her.

Ben jumped out quickly and ran around the car to help

China out. The air was cold, the sky cloudy and over-cast. He pulled the hood up over her head and handed her his gloves.

"Here, honey. Put these on. They'll be too big, but they'll keep your hands warm."

She held out her hands as if she were a child, too numb to do anything more than what she was told. The soft-ness of the fine leather and the lingering warmth inside the gloves made it seem as if Ben were actually hold-ing her hands. She folded her arms across her chest and then took a slow breath. Ben slipped a hand beneath her elbow to steady her.

"Are you ready?"

She paused, then looked up at him, her eyes full of unshed tears.

"I have to do this alone."

He hesitated, uncertain. But when she started across the dry, brittle grass, he found himself standing and watching her go.

For China, everything seemed surreal. The sound of the grass crunching beneath her shoes. The cry of a hawk somewhere high above her in the sky. That particular scent that cold air has when it's almost too cold to breathe. The hammering of her own heartbeat, thumping in her ears. And the dark musky smell of earth that had been recently disturbed.

She stopped at the edge of the mound and stared down at the grave. The tiny marker and the name, Baby Brown, were evidence enough of her loss. The child had not even been named. Subconsciously, her hands splayed across her stomach as they had so many times before. But this time her belly was flat and the bulge was in the earth at her feet. Her gaze shifted to the small headstone just to the right of the dirt.

Clara Mae Shubert—A good mother—Rest in Peace.
She shuddered. Rest in peace. And in that moment, a knowing came upon her. That was what she'd forgotten. For her baby to rest in peace, she had to let go.

She closed her eyes then, remembering the moment of her death, and the journey they'd taken together. Her baby wasn't here in the ground. She was already gone.

With aching regret, she lifted her head. As she did, the sun broke from behind a cloud, and the unexpected warmth on her face was like a kiss. She looked up beyond the horizon to the bit of blue peeking through the clouds and let go of what was left of her guilt. It *wasn't* her fault she'd left her daughter behind. There was a reason she'd been sent back—to help find the woman who'd killed her.

She turned then, searching for the man who'd brought her. He was standing beside the car, and even from this distance, she could see the concern on his face. Despair shifted, just enough to let in the memory of their shared kiss.

The promise man.

China began to retrace her steps, and as she did, she saw him move away from the car and start toward her. Another measure of despair fell away from her heart. Whatever she had to do, Ben would be there. She wouldn't have to do it alone.

One day led into another, and then another. Ariel Simmons was touring the country, taking the Word to the masses and battling a growing sense of depression. She'd done everything she knew to protect herself from the fallout of Chaz Finelli's murder, but it didn't seem to be working. Too many people believed in the old adage of where there's smoke, there's fire, and she was suffering the consequences. Hate mail came on a daily basis. Obscene phone calls were a constant recurrence. Instead of leaving it behind, her shame traveled with her. She was losing weight and taking pills and praying as she'd never prayed before. But nothing seemed to work. No amount of prayer could rid Ariel of the guilt of what she'd done.

Connie Marx had all but gone underground. She had become a recluse in her own apartment, living off her investments and biding her time as she researched everything she could about Charles Finelli, as well as the killer's other victims. She spent her days clipping items from the newspapers regarding the ongoing case and taping every soundbite of television coverage. When the case blew open—and she knew that it would—she was going to be ready.

Mona Wakefield was missing from the compound of Dallas society, preparing herself for a comeback. She had convinced herself that a new hairstyle and new clothes would remove the old problems in her life.

Bobby Lee was back in D.C., circling among the movers and shakers of the nation's government and basking in the glory of his growing popularity. In his mind, the past was past. He'd tied up all the loose ends of his problems and was concentrating on the task at hand—that of becoming the next president.

But they weren't the only ones who were trying to put the past behind them. From the day they'd come back from the cemetery, China had been a changed woman. Her body was healed, her heart in the process of repair. Her bouts of depression were all but gone, and she grew stronger with every passing day.

A month passed, and then another, and while no one was watching, spring appeared.

* * *

"I'm going to the barn," China announced, and sailed out the back door before anyone offered to accompany her.

Dave started to follow when Mattie caught him by the arm.

"Let her be," she said. "There's no way anyone can sneak up on this house. You'll see them coming long before they arrive. Besides, something tells me that the danger has passed. There haven't been any killings in months. The woman is probably long gone to another state."

"I'll keep my distance," Dave said. "But I don't know about everything being over. In my experience, a serial killer can't stop. It's part of the pattern that drives them to kill in the first place."

Mattie frowned as she watched China stride off the porch.

"I've come to love that girl," she said. "I couldn't bear it if anything ever happened to her."

Dave put an arm around her shoulder and gave her a quick hug.

"You aren't the only one who loves China. Your son is so far gone he doesn't even know it."

Mattie sighed and then looked up at Dave and patted his cheek.

"Thank you for being here," she said.

He grinned. "Never thought I'd hear you say those words."

"Go find something to do," Mattie said. "I'm too busy to fight with you."

His chuckle followed her as she left the room.

Meanwhile, China was in a world of her own. The day was mild, although there was a fairly brisk breeze. She'd pulled her hair into a loose ponytail to keep the wind from yanking it in tangles and had a pocketful of Cowboy's favorite treats. Today she'd seen buds all over the lilac bush in Mattie's backyard, and she stopped again, testing the fat round buds with the tip of her finger. As she did, she saw a small brown worm inching its way up a stem.

Time stopped. In her mind, she was a little girl of six, hiding from Clyde beneath the porch and watching a brown caterpillar wend its way through the grass. Then she'd felt like that worm. Brown and ugly, of no consequence to anything in the world. She'd tried to make herself small, hoping to hide from Clyde. It hadn't happened.

She still felt small and of no consequence, a homely little thing that mattered not at all in the world, but something was changing inside her. She no longer wanted to hide. It was a day for new beginnings, and it made her heart beat fast, as if something wonderful awaited her just out of sight. She moved on, anxious for her playtime to begin.

As she entered the barn, she blinked several times in succession, allowing her eyes to adjust to the dimmer light. Down the aisle and then out in the corral beyond, she could see Cowboy. She whistled and then started to run. He came to meet her at a trot.

"Hey, baby," she crooned, and began to climb, straddling the fence panels as she dug in her pocket for his treats. He nuzzled at her hands, and she laughed. "Give me a minute," she said. "I've got them here somewhere."

Eagerly, he took the first one out of her hand and was begging for the second before he'd swallowed the first. She laughed as he ate, and when they were all gone, she slipped off the fence and onto his back without benefit of bridle or saddle. Then she stretched out, aligning her upper body along the length of his neck, held on with her legs and threw her arms around his neck. He stood in the sunshine, accepting her affection as easily as he'd taken the sugar.

"You big, old, pretty baby," China whispered.

A horsefly buzzed around Cowboy's head. But other than a twitch of his tail, he didn't move.

Ben found her there, half asleep on the back of his horse with the sun hot against her back. Breath caught in the back of his throat as he watched them. From the first, their bond had been magic. It was as if the old horse had sensed all her wounds, both physical and mental, and given her his complete devotion. China had returned it a thousandfold. Even if she was shy about returning affection to people, she gave her love without question to the old, gentle horse.

Quietly, Ben walked up to the corral and climbed the fence. Cowboy nickered softly. Ben smiled.

"Yeah, I see you, boy, and don't start making excuses. She has you as buffaloed as she has me."

China roused at the sound of his voice and sat up sleepily, her hair loose and wild about her shoulders, her lips tilted in a half smile.

"I almost went to sleep," she said.

"I saw you," Ben said. "There wasn't any almost to it. Now come here to me, sweetheart. I don't know how long you've been out here, but you're getting too much sun."

China felt the back of her neck. It was hot.

"Oooh, you're right," she said, and held out her arms.

He lifted her off the horse and held her until she was steady on the fence rail. Then she climbed down herself, brushing off the bits of horse hair and hay from the front of her shirt.

"You're home early."

Ben nodded. "Took a half day of personal leave."

China really looked at him then. He had already

changed from the clothes he wore to work and was in an old pair of boots and jeans and a soft denim shirt.

"Are you sick?"

"No, just tired and missing you."

The words wrapped around her heart. She gave him a bashful smile.

"Really?"

"Yes, really," Ben said, and then took her in his arms. "How are you feeling?"

"Good," she said.

"Not sore anymore—anywhere?"

"No. I'm completely healed."

"Good," Ben said. "Then come with me. I have a surprise."

"Where are we going?" China asked.

"Not far."

Her eyes were dancing with excitement, and she was trying to imagine the surprise, when he came to a sudden stop no more than thirty feet from where they'd started.

"Is this it?" she asked, looking around at all the open doors and empty bins.

"Nope," he said. "We're going up," he said, pointing to the ladder built against the wall.

"To the loft?"

He nodded. "You first. I'll go behind, so I can catch you if you fall."

If I fall. China sighed. Safe. She always felt safe with this man.

"What's up there?" she asked.

"You'll see when you get there."

Stifling a nervous giggle, she began to climb.

Chapter 16

As China reached the opening, a pigeon took flight from the rafters and disappeared out the window. She paused, peering cautiously around the vast open space to make sure there were no more surprises.

"You okay?" Ben asked.

"Yes, just making sure," she said, and climbed the rest of the way through, leaving him to follow.

It was even warmer up here than it was down on the ground. There was an old mattress leaning against the wall, with a tarp draped across it. A pile of burlap sacks lay in one corner, a pair of hay hooks hanging on the wall above them. An incubator had been pushed against the wall, a dinosaur from the days when Ben's parents had actually hatched their own baby chicks. Other odds and ends of ranch history lay about the area. It was like walking into someone's attic and looking at bits and pieces of their lives.

"What's this?" China asked, as Ben came up behind her and picked up the item she was looking at.

"It's a sad iron. That's what my grandmother used to

iron their clothes before electricity came to the country. She heated it on the woodstove and then ironed until it cooled and then heated it again. I think there used to be a couple of extra bottoms to the thing. You know, two could be heating while she was using one and then she would unfasten the cool one and clip another one on."

"Makes you think the good old days maybe weren't so good after all," she said, and then turned, her eyes dancing with excitement. "You said you had a surprise?"

He smiled. "Yes, over here." He took her by the hand and led her toward the far corner of the barn. "You have to be quiet, though. Old Katie doesn't much like strangers."

China's eyes widened apprehensively. "Old Katie?"

"Shhh," Ben whispered, and then pointed at a wooden crate.

China leaned over and at first saw only a jumble of magazines and papers. Then a crumpled pile of papers suddenly moved and a cat peeked out from beneath. Ben lifted the paper off the cat and laid it aside, revealing the secret beneath.

"Oh, Ben."

The reverence in her voice said it all. There in the middle of the crate lay a calico cat nursing a litter of babies. When the cat saw them, she hissed.

"Easy, old girl," Ben said, and then grabbed China's hand before she could reach out and touch her. "Don't try it, honey, not when she's feeding the babies."

"Oh, right," China said, and took a quiet step back, but she couldn't take her eyes off the box and the four tiny squirming babies the old cat was nursing. She stood there for a while, staring intently at the scene, then announced, "We have to name them, you know."

Ben grinned. "Yeah, I guess we do. Why don't you pick the names? Old Katie won't mind."

China kept staring, looking for differences in their markings, but without holding them, it seemed impossible.

"They all look like her," she said.

Ben laughed. "Yeah, Old Katie has a tendency to mark her babies all the same."

She studied them some more and then suddenly smiled. "I know. We'll call them Eeny, Meeny, Miney and Moe."

Ben chuckled. "But which is which?"

"With those names, it won't matter."

Ben laughed. "Come on, honey, we'd better let Old Katie alone for now."

"Can I come back?" China asked.

"Sure, but not too often, or she'll just get nervous and move them and then you won't know where they're at."

Her eyes grew round. "Really? She would do that?"

"Yeah, it's part of her mothering instinct—a way she protects her young."

China flinched as if she'd been struck and had to take a deep breath to continue. "I can understand that. Keeping them safe is all that matters."

Ben saw the look on her face and silently cursed himself for all kinds of a fool. He touched her arm, then her face, wanting to wipe away the sorrow.

"China, sweetheart, I'm sorry. I didn't think when I—"

She put her fingers on his lips. "Don't. There's no need."

He took her hand and lifted it to his lips. The sensation of his mouth against her palm did funny things to her heart, and an ache began to grow in the pit of her stomach that had nothing to do with grief. She tried to say his name, but all that came out was a groan.

Ben lifted his head and then froze. He'd prayed for

this day—for that look on her face—and now that it was here, he was afraid he would do something that would make it disappear.

He laid her hand on his chest, letting her feel the rapid beat of his heart, and watched her eyes widen in disbelief. He touched her face, trailing his thumbs across her lower lip and then tunneling them through her hair.

He pulled her close, and when she didn't resist, he went a step further and cupped the back of her head. When she wrapped her arms around his neck, he slanted a slow, tender kiss across the middle of her mouth.

She sighed and took another step toward him, until they were completely aligned and she could feel the imprint of his body.

"You make me crazy," Ben whispered. "Crazy in love."

She looked at him, at the hunger on his face. For her. It was for her. The knowledge was exhilarating and powerful.

"I want to make love to you, China. I need to see joy on your face and know that I put it there."

He kissed her again, and China melted against him. Suddenly she was in his arms and he was carrying her across the floor toward the mattress leaning against the wall. With a kick, he sent it tumbling. It landed on the floor of the loft with a muffled thud, sending up a cloud of dust that neither one of them seemed to mind. He laid her there, then stretched out beside her.

Like a magnet, she turned toward him, pulling him close. It had been so long—an eternity—since she'd felt so alive. She was out of control, and it just didn't matter.

Ben traced every inch of her face with his kisses, memorizing the shape of her lips, the texture of her skin and the silent plea in her eyes as his hand slid beneath the waistband of her jeans.

Then suddenly she was rolling off the mattress and scrambling to her feet. Her hands were shaking as she clutched at her shirt, holding it close around her neck.

"I'm sorry, I'm sorry. I can't let you see the… It's too awful to—"

Ben stood. The pain in his voice was too obvious for her to ignore.

"All you had to do was say no. I would never hurt you," he said, and started to walk away.

"No, wait!" China cried. "Not like this. I don't want you to think I didn't…that you—"

Ben turned, confused and more than a little bit hurt.

"Then what? Tell me, China. What the hell went wrong?"

She turned loose of her shirt, then dropped her head, unable to see the disgust on his face.

"It wasn't you, it's me," she whispered, touching her breasts, then her stomach. "The scars…they're terrible… so ugly. I can't even look at myself. How can I—"

Ben cursed. His anger startled her, and she gasped and took a sudden step back.

"You think I'm so shallow? You think I don't know the consequences of what happened to you?"

"Not shallow, not you. It's me. I—"

"Stop it," Ben muttered, and took her by the shoulders, making her look at him. "I've seen your wounds. I saw them the night they picked you up off the street. I saw them in the hospital when your belly was nothing but a long line of staples. I sat by your bed and prayed for you to open your eyes and talk to me, and not one Goddamned time did I think to myself that what had happened to you made you less of a woman."

Horrified by what he was saying, China wanted to run.

She couldn't look him in the face and know that he'd seen a part of her that even she couldn't face.

"Don't you turn away from me," Ben said, his voice rising in anger. "Don't you do that to me. You can hide from yourself, China Brown, but you don't hide from me. I'm not afraid of what's beneath your clothes. You're the one with the problem." She watched in horror as he suddenly ripped off his shirt and threw it on the floor.

"If you're so turned off by scars, then you'd better see mine." He lifted his arm and then turned. The light caught and held on the thick, jagged pucker of flesh across his ribs.

"Car bomb, my rookie year on the force. Every time I look at that scar, I remind myself how blessed I am to be alive."

China jerked as if she'd been slapped, knowing how deep the wound must have been to leave such a horrible mark.

"Oh…my…God."

He took one look at the horror on her face and knew it was over. Tired of fighting a losing battle, and tired of being the only one in love, he reached down to pick up his shirt when she caught his hand.

"You shame me," she whispered, and laid the palm of his hand against her breast. "Please. Help me. Teach me to love myself as much as I love you."

Joy spread within him in quiet increments. "Teach you? I can't teach you anything, China. All I can do is love you. The rest is up to you."

"Then bear with me, Bennett." She lowered her head and began unbuttoning her shirt.

He stopped her with a touch, then a kiss. "Let me," he begged. She dropped her hands to her sides and looked down at her feet.

"No fair," he said softly, tipping her chin up to meet his gaze. "If you have the courage to confess your love, then you have to follow it through. Test me, China. See the look on my face and know the truth in my heart."

So she did—watching him with a steadfast gaze as he undressed her, one piece of clothing at a time. When he was through, he took off the rest of his clothes and then stood before her, unashamed of his obvious need.

"Beauty is in the eye of the beholder, China Brown, and to me, you are the most beautiful woman in the world. I've loved you far longer than it made sense to care. You took me into your heart. Will you let me the rest of the way in?"

She held out her hand, and he took it, letting her lead him back to the mattress. Then she pulled him down beside her and took him into her arms.

"Make love to me, Ben."

He rolled, covering her body as he captured her mouth with his own. Time ceased.

The old cat in the corner was through nursing her kittens and now slept with them curled all around her. The pigeon China had frightened away circled high above the barn, looking for a safe place to land.

Cowboy stood beneath the shade tree at the far corner of the corral, asleep on his feet, while high in the loft, Ben made love to the woman of his heart.

Their bodies rocked in perfect rhythm, carrying them from one sexual plateau to another—from the moment of first joining, to the beginning of the end. They could no more have stopped than they could have quit breathing. Somewhere within the act, a knowing came upon them that this pleasure couldn't last.

It started first with China, building low and hard and fast. She arched, meeting the power of his thrust with a strong need of her own, and as she did, she lost herself. It burst within her in a blinding flash of pleasure so vast she thought she would die.

The scream in her throat came out as a groan, and she locked her legs around Ben's waist in a subconscious act of holding on to the feeling.

Ben's endurance was just about gone, and when she pulled him the rest of the way in and then couldn't let go, he gave up to the feeling and spilled himself into her in shuddering thrusts.

The silence that came afterward was as powerful as the act had been. They clung, one to the other, stunned by their joining until their skin began to chill. He needed to get his weight off her body, but he couldn't find the strength to move. Finally he rose up on one elbow to look down.

Her hair fanned the mattress beneath her head like a puddle of dark silk. Her eyes still reflected the shock of climax. But her body was limp, satiated by the power of their lovemaking.

"You take my breath away."

She looked up at him and saw the reflection of her own face in his eyes; then she sighed. "It was good?"

He groaned. "No. *Good* is not a word for what you did to me. I may never walk again."

"Good," she said, and then wrapped her arms around his neck. "At least then I'll know where to find you."

He groaned and then laughed. "I love you, China Brown. Do you doubt me now?"

"No."

He nuzzled his face against the curve of her neck. "Then I'll give you something else to think about between now and the rest of our lives."

"What's that?" she asked, then moaned as he rolled the tip of her breast between his fingers.

"One of these days, when all this mess is over, we're going shopping. I'm going to buy you the biggest diamond I can find, and then you and Mom are going to plan our wedding. You once told me that you didn't know where you belonged. Well, I'm telling you now, my love. You belong with me."

They made love again in the loft before climbing back down. And while China held his promise close to her heart, there was a part of her that didn't know if it would ever come true.

The woman stormed into the cabin, her frustration level at an all-time high. She needed an outlet for the anger that burned deep in her gut, but she couldn't play the game. It had been months since that sketch had come out in the *Dallas Morning News,* but there was too much at stake to take a chance, which left her with only one option. There had to be a witness somewhere—someone she'd known nothing about—but time was on her side. All she had to do was wait and one day she would know who it was.

A new lead in the Finelli murder came in the form of a telephone call to a journalist at the *Dallas Morning News,* offering information for money—a lot of money. The journalist was busy, trying to meet a deadline.

"This is not a tabloid, buddy. We don't pay for news."

"Your loss," the caller said, and hung up.

The journalist hung up, but there was a niggle of curiosity, wondering what the man had been trying to sell. It wasn't until that night, as he sat in his apartment with a box of pizza in his lap and a long-neck beer on the table by his feet, that he realized what he'd probably turned down.

Ronnie Boyle, the anchor for the ten o'clock news, was smirking like the proverbial Cheshire cat. Even though the journalist doubted that Channel 7 was in the business of paying off snitches, he wouldn't put it above the likes of Boyle. He upped the volume on the remote and took another drink of beer as Boyle began to speak.

"This evening, Channel 7 has learned that there is a surviving victim of the serial killings here in Dallas. A pregnant woman, who officials now believe was just an innocent bystander to the murder of Chaz Finelli, is in seclusion and waiting to do her part in bringing the killer to justice. The baby she was carrying died on the scene, but she survived, due to the gallant efforts of the doctors and nurses at Parkland Hospital. Her identity is not being released, for obvious reasons."

"Well, hell," the man muttered, then swallowed his last bite of pizza and turned off the TV.

Out on the English ranch, China was in the living room alone when the bulletin was announced that there was new evidence in the serial killer case. She bolted to her feet and then yelled out Ben's name.

He came running, his mother right behind him.

"What's wrong?" he asked.

"The TV. Just listen to what they're saying."

They sat, as the journalist had done, listening to Ronnie Boyle knock down the carefully laid blocks around their world.

Before he'd even finished the bulletin, Ben was on the phone to his captain, struggling with disbelief.

"Someone sold her out!" he yelled. "She might as well stand on a street corner with a sign on her back that says Shoot Me."

"They didn't give her name," Floyd said, although that was a weak excuse and he knew it.

"Well, hell, Captain, if someone knew there was a witness, then they're bound to know her name. As soon as enough money is offered, that will be common knowledge, too."

"Maybe so," Floyd said. "But it's done, and there's nothing we can do except what we've been doing."

But Ben wasn't buying that. "There's something I can do," he said. "I'm putting myself on round-the-clock guard duty with our only witness, and don't start telling me that detectives aren't bodyguards. You tell it to the governor. He's the one riding your ass to solve this case."

"Don't tell me what to do," Floyd snapped. "You've got yourself involved personally, and we both know it."

"Hell, yes, it's personal!" Ben yelled. "I'm going to marry China Brown, but I can't do that until the woman who shot her is behind bars, and she'll never be behind bars if we don't protect China."

China was shaking so hard she couldn't stop. She needed to run—to hide—but there was nowhere to go but to Ben.

He saw the panic on her face and grabbed her, then wrapped her in his arms.

"Either grant me the authority for what I want or fire me," he said.

Floyd cursed. English was just crazy enough to do what he said. The last thing he needed was to lose a good man, as well as their only witness.

"Fine," he snapped. "But this is temporary, until we can come up with a better plan."

"The plan is to find that woman," Ben said. "There are no other options."

He hung up in Floyd's ear and then tossed the phone onto the sofa and held China instead.

"It's going to be all right, honey, I promise. I'm not leaving here again until this is over."

Then he looked at Mattie, who'd listened in horror to what had happened.

"Mom, call Dave. If he wasn't watching the news, tell him what happened. We're going to have to set our watches in shifts."

"Oh, my God," China moaned, and turned in Ben's arms. "Mattie, I'm sorry, so sorry. I never should have come here."

"You hush," Mattie said, as she reached for the phone. "You're part of our family, and we protect our own."

"Mom's right," Ben said, as his mother left the room to make the call. He sat down on the sofa and pulled China into his lap.

"I suppose we've been kidding ourselves that this wouldn't happen. We've been fortunate that it took them this long to get onto the fact that there had to be a witness for the composite to even be made."

China thought about what he said, and as she did, her panic began to recede. He was right. It was an inevitable part of this whole ugly mess, and maybe it was time. She was well now—stronger than she'd ever been before. If she was ever going to have a normal life, this had to be over.

"You're right," she said, surprising herself as well as Ben by how calm she felt. "It was the shock of hearing it that frightened me, but I think I'm actually glad. I want this over, and if it means being a decoy for a killer, then so be it."

Ben turned pale. "You're not putting yourself up as any target. Don't even hint at such a thing."

"But I am, Ben, don't you see? It won't take her long to figure out who I am. She's seen my face. All she'll have to do is ask around. It's only a matter of time before someone puts two and two together and remembers the woman under guard at Parkland Hospital, and then someone else will remember the detective who bent all the rules to be with her and… Well, you get the picture."

"Jesus," Ben whispered, and pulled her close. "You're scaring me, China."

"I'm scaring myself," she said. "But I'm more angry than scared. She took something from me that I can never have back. I want to be able to walk through a mall without wondering if I'm going to be shot in the back. I want to buy groceries and go to movies and sit in the park. I love you, but I'm tired of hiding. She took my life. I want it back."

"You're right, China, and understand…I'm with you in this all the way, and I swear on my honor, I will keep you safe."

China shook her head. "I don't need your promises, Ben English, not when I already have your love."

Ben and China weren't the only ones who'd been rocked by the bulletin. Far away, in the middle of Dallas, another viewer had sat glued to the news. When it was over, the remote was aimed and the television went dead. Images of faces from the past began flashing one by one.

Someone survived. But who? The game only involved one man at a time, and except for Chaz Finelli…

Understanding dawned.

The pregnant woman—the one who'd begged not to be shot! But the papers had said two had died that night. So how could…?

The baby! Of course! How stupid I am. It was the baby that died, not the woman.

Son of a bitch! She saw and heard everything. My God, my God, she can bring down the whole house of cards.

Connie Marx was at her computer, her fingers flying fast and furious as she added this latest bit of information to the file she was creating.

A witness! All this time there had been a witness. Anger spiked. Then why the hell would they assume it had anything to do with her? As soon as she asked herself the question, she realized the answer. Until they'd been able to question the victim further, all they'd known was that the killer was a woman. Considering the people Connie knew had been seriously questioned, probably a tall, blonde woman. It was only after the composite had been created that they'd eliminated her from the list.

Connie hit another series of keys, called up a list and hit Print. As soon as the printer spit it out, she moved to a filing cabinet and pulled out a file, then spread the contents on the table, sorting them one by one. Someone in this stack could very well be the killer, and then she stopped and rocked back on her heels.

Or not.

What if the killer was someone who had escaped Finelli's net? What if it had nothing to do with Finelli's blackmail scheme? What if Finelli had been incidental to the larger picture? Of course! After all, the other victims had been a party to strange sexual activities before their bodies were discovered. And their murders had been done execution style, while Finelli's was an act of impulse spurred on by rage. Possibly rage at being discovered. But what had Finelli known that the rest of Dallas did not?

Connie laid down the file and then strode to the window, letting her thoughts run free. If only she could talk to this witness. Ben English had almost promised her an exclusive. He would know who she was.

She started to reach for her phone, then stopped.

No. She'd already made a mess of her life, and this wasn't about her any longer. She was just an observer, waiting to report the truth.

Chapter 17

China's existence had become big news. The next day, all over Dallas, people were talking, speculating as to who it could be. Rumors flew thick and fast that had nothing to do with the truth, but they were enough to stir up the story all over again. The composite of the serial killer was reprinted in the papers and flashed at every televised newscast. It became an all-out media war to see who could top whom. Beauty shops were doing a booming business. Women who had been blonde for years were changing the color of their hair for fear they might be mistaken for the woman the police were looking for.

Charlotte Humbolt, society editor for the *Dallas Morning News,* was sorting through the picture files of Dallas's finest when she came across a handful of pictures of Mona Wakefield that had been taken at a charity event. She grimaced, remembering what a scene the woman had made by showing up in a sheer georgette dress. In the sunlight, the damn thing had become see-through. Toby Walters, the president of Lone Star Savings and Loan, had been gawking at her so hard that he'd misstepped, fallen into a rock garden and broken his leg.

Charlotte grinned, then laid them aside. As she reached for some others, something about the picture on top caught her attention. She looked back at the stack and then picked another one up—a close-up of Mona guzzling champagne. She stared at it for a minute, trying to figure out why it bothered her so much. Again she shrugged off the thought and started to lay it down, and then it hit her.

"I've got to be crazy," she muttered, and her heart began to thump as she shoved aside the mess on her desk, revealing the morning paper beneath.

Then she laid the picture of Mona beside the killer's composite and started to grin. The resemblance was uncanny. She kept thinking of all the times she'd been snubbed by Bobby Lee Wakefield.

She sat for a moment, contemplating the wisdom of what she was about to do, and then thought, *To hell with it* and picked up the phone. Even though she didn't believe for a minute that the Wakefields would have anything to do with murder, it would serve them right to suffer a little hassling by the Dallas police.

She started to use the phone on her desk and then realized it could be traced, so she took the elevator downstairs to the pay phone in the lobby. There were hundreds of people coming in and out of the building on a daily basis. There was no way they could trace the call to her and Senator Bobby Lee would have to do some fancy dancing for the cops, which suited her just fine.

"Hey, Red, phone call for you on two!" someone yelled.

Red Fisher picked up the phone, hoping it was going

to be Ben, telling him he'd changed his mind about staying at the ranch with China and was coming in to work.

"Detective Fisher, Homicide."

"Compare your killer to a photo of Mona Wakefield."

A click, and then a dial tone buzzed in Red's ear.

"Hello? Hello? Who is this?" he asked, but it was no use. The caller was gone.

Although it was pretty far-fetched, they'd followed up on every lead that had been called in to date, and insulted some pretty important people in the process. The way he figured it, they'd already pissed off the mayor. Just because it was a senator's mother, there was no need to ignore the lead. He looked up and yelled out into the room, "Hey, anybody got a picture of Bobby Lee Wakefield's mother?"

A couple of rude remarks came flying back about what they'd like to do with her, but no one had a picture on hand. Red reached for the phone and dialed a friend at a local paper.

"Mike, it's Red. I need a favor."

"Yeah, and I need a thousand bucks to cover my ass at the bank."

"Can't help you there," Red said. "I told you to quit betting on those horses. You aren't any better at picking winners than you are at picking women."

The man chuckled in Red's ear and cursed him lightly. "So, what's the favor you need?"

"Send me a picture of Mona Wakefield."

"Bobby Lee's mother?" Mike asked.

"Yeah, one and the same. And make it a head shot if you've got it."

"Oh, we've got it," he said. "When there's nothing new to be said about her, she makes something happen. I'm not too crazy about my last mother-in-law, but I'm damned sure glad she wasn't anything like Mona. Man, can you imagine having a mother who looks and acts like that?"

Red grinned. "Just email the picture ASAP."

"In the works," Mike said, and hung up the phone.

A few minutes later, Red stood at the printer, watching a photo printing out. He turned it over and then stared in disbelief. The woman was almost a ringer for the face in the sketch. The ramifications of pursuing this were staggering, but if there was even the smallest chance…

He headed for the captain's office.

Aaron Floyd was at the point of no return. His phone had been ringing nonstop ever since he'd gotten to the office with people wanting verification that a witness actually existed. When Red knocked on his door, he was actually glad for the reprieve—until Red tossed the photo onto his desk.

"That's Mona Wakefield," Floyd said.

"Lay it beside the sketch of the killer," Red said.

Floyd snorted. "Are you crazy?"

"Just do it," Red urged.

Floyd reached for the paper that he'd laid aside and opened it. Before he even laid it down, he was on his feet cursing.

"Who put you onto this?" he asked.

"An anonymous caller."

"Son of a bitch."

"No, actually, it was the bitch herself," Red said.

Floyd's thoughts were racing. "Was she ever interrogated?"

"No, sir. To our knowledge, she wasn't in any of Finelli's pictures, so her name never came up. However, now that I think about it, if even half the stories about her are true, it's a miracle she wasn't a part of his files."

"So maybe she was—once upon a time. Check it out."

"Yes, sir."

"Call Ben. Let him know what's happening. He might want in on this."

Red grinned. That was the best news he'd had all day.

Dave and Mattie were in the middle of a spirited game of Scrabble, and China was in the hayloft making friends with Old Katie with a leftover piece of ham from their lunch. Ben was in the front yard washing his car. It wasn't that the damned thing was all that dirty, but it was the only thing he could think of to do that would keep him within seeing distance of the barn. He didn't want China to feel as if she had no freedom at all, but the truth was, right now, she had little to none.

Just as he was turning off the water, his mother yelled out the door, "Ben! Phone! It's Red."

He dropped the hose and ran to answer.

"Yeah…what's up?"

"We got an anonymous call a while ago. It may amount to nothing and it may not. Captain said to give you a call, that you might want in on the interrogation."

"Is it worth anything, or is it just his way of trying to get me to come back to work?"

"It's a picture of Mona Wakefield. Damned if she isn't almost a dead ringer for the sketch."

Ben's mind was turning over everything he knew. "Was she ever one of the names from the Finelli file?"

"No."

"Now that I think about it, and knowing her reputation, it's a little amazing that she wasn't, right?"

Red grinned. "That's why we're partners. I had the very same thoughts myself. So, do you want in on the visit?"

"Oh, yeah," Ben said. "But I'll meet you there. It's on my way into the city. Give me thirty minutes."

"You got it, Ben. How's China taking all this?"

"About how you'd expect. But she's tough, Red. I've never known anyone as focused on making someone pay."

"Except maybe you?"

"Yeah, maybe. I'm on my way."

Ben was stripping off his shirt as he hung up the phone.

"What's going on?" Mattie asked, as he bolted past them on his way to his bedroom.

"Maybe a break in the case, maybe not. Tell China I'll—"

"I'm here," China said.

"Come with me to my room," he said. "I'll tell you what's happening while I change."

A skitter of anxiety threaded its way through her pulse, but she made herself relax and followed him into his room. He was already down to his underwear and reaching for a pair of pants when she entered.

"Is it about me?" she asked.

"It's about the case," he said. "An anonymous tip has turned up a new face. Someone we never interviewed before."

"Does she look anything like the composite?"

"Ever see Mona Wakefield before?" he asked, as he tucked a clean shirt into the waistband of his pants and then sat down to put on his shoes.

"Senator Wakefield's mother? Sure, I guess."

"Think of it, honey…does she look anything like the woman who shot you?"

China's heart skipped. "I can't really picture her face, but she is tall and blonde, that I remember."

"I'll bring something for you to look at when I get back. Dave is here and—"

"Just go," China said. "Do whatever you have to do to make this be over."

He grabbed his jacket from a hanger and then took her in his arms. She leaned against him, then wrapped her arms around his waist and laid her cheek against the front of his shirt. Ben held her close.

"So, did Old Katie let you feed her today?"

She looked up and smiled. "Yes. I even got to look at the babies, except I didn't touch them, like you said."

"Once she gets used to you and they get a little older, she won't mind if you play with them. Now give me some sugar, honey. I told Red I'd meet him at the Wakefield estate."

She lifted her lips, meeting his halfway, and the fire leaped between them.

"Mmmm-hmmm," Ben murmured as he reluctantly let go. "You hold on to that thought until later, will you?"

She nodded, then added, "Be careful."

"I'll be fine, and I won't be long, I promise."

With that, he was gone. China watched him leave, his long strides making short work of the distance to the front of the house. Then he got in his car and drove quickly away, leaving a cloud of dust behind him.

"He's going to have to wash that car all over again," Mattie muttered.

China turned. She hadn't known Ben's mother was standing behind her.

Mattie saw the fear on China's face and gave her a hug.

"You just never mind about what he's doing and come back in here with me. I think Dave's cheating again."

"I heard that!" Dave yelled.

China sighed and then made herself smile. But the rest of the afternoon, her heart was with Ben.

* * *

Red was waiting when Ben pulled up behind his car in front of the Wakefield estate.

"You made it in good time," Red said, as Ben got out of his car and into Red's.

"Had a good reason. Now let's go. I've got a feeling about this."

"Yeah, buddy, you're still reading my mind."

A short while later, they were standing on the portico of the three-story mansion and listening to the chimes of the doorbell as it rang throughout the house. Shortly thereafter, a maid answered the door.

"Afternoon, sirs. How may I help you?"

Both men flashed their badges. "We need to see Mona Wakefield. Is she in?"

"Yes, sir, I'll just—"

"Delia?"

The maid turned. "Oh, Senator Wakefield, these detectives want to talk to Miz Mona, and I was just going to—"

Bobby Lee hid his dismay behind a wide, open smile.

"You just run along now and tell Mother we have company," he said. "I'll see what I can do to help these fine men." Then he stepped aside and pulled back the door. "Y'all come on in now, you hear?"

They followed him into a library just off the foyer, and it was obvious that the Senator was about to give them the full benefit of his good-old-boy routine.

"Don't suppose I could offer you boys a drink?" he asked.

"No, sir," they said in unison. "On duty," Ben added, and then continued before Bobby Lee could stall them again. "Senator, we need to speak to your mother."

"Why sure, but could I inquire as to the reason while she's coming down?"

But Ben was firm in his resolve. "I'd rather wait and speak with her first, sir, if you don't mind."

Bobby Lee smiled, but he wasn't real happy. He liked things done his way, and this detective wasn't cooperating.

"If you'll just take a seat, then, I'll see if I can hurry her along," he said, and left them standing.

Red glanced at Ben. "Quite a place, isn't it?"

Before Ben could answer, they heard angry voices out in the hall, although they couldn't hear what was being said. Moments later, Mona Wakefield entered the room with her son right behind her. She was dressed in a pale-blue designer suit with a skirt that went just past her knees. Her hair was strawberry-blond and cut in a style that cupped the curve of her chin, forming a frame for her elegant face.

Ben's hopes dropped. He felt like he'd stepped into Alice's rabbit hole and was coming undone. This woman looked nothing like the picture that Mike had sent to Red, and he had a moment of panic, wondering if he'd sent the wrong one by mistake.

"Welcome to our home," Mona said. "Please take a seat." Then she turned to the maid, who was standing at the door. "Delia, bring some coffee to the library, please."

"None for us," Ben said. He didn't want the questioning to become a social event.

"Nonsense," she said, and waved the maid away before sliding sensuously into a wing-backed chair. "Now, what can I do for you?"

Ben plowed ahead with the questions, even though he was beginning to doubt.

"As you know, the Dallas police have been working diligently for some time now trying to bring a serial killer to justice, and we follow up on every lead, no matter who is involved."

She smiled. "Yes, I've heard. In fact, several of my acquaintances have been targeted." Then her eyebrows rose, as if in pretend delight. "Surely you're not here to interrogate me?" She looked at her son and laughed. "Bobby Lee, are you playing a joke on your mama?"

He grinned, but it was Ben's opinion that the man looked as if he'd just swallowed a bug along with it.

"No, Mother, it's not a joke, although I must say, it feels like one."

Mona's face was alive with curiosity as she gave the men her full attention.

"I'm sorry. I just assumed...please continue."

"I need to ask you where you were on the night of December 11 of last year."

She rolled her eyes. "Well, mercy, son. I couldn't begin to remember."

"Check your calendar, Mother. If you had a social engagement, I'm sure your secretary had it written down."

"Yes! Of course. If you men will pardon me a moment, I'll be right back."

She rose with the grace of a model and sauntered out of the room, well aware that three pairs of eyes were watching her go.

The moment she was gone, Bobby Lee attacked. "I want to tell you now that I don't appreciate the insinuation that my mother could possibly have anything to do with murder," he snapped. "Why, she doesn't even know how to shoot a gun."

"Oh, but I do," Mona said, as she reentered the room with a book in her hand. "Your daddy taught me how to shoot rattlesnakes before you were born." Then she smiled at Ben as she took her seat. "We lived in Amarillo back then, and you know how snaky that part of Texas can be."

"No, ma'am, but I'm assuming you do," Ben said. "About December 11?"

She rifled through the pages, then ran her finger down a list before looking up.

"I was at a little Christmas party at the country club. I remember arriving a bit late on purpose." She smiled. "It makes for a grand entrance, you know."

"What time did you arrive and what time did you leave?" Ben asked.

"Why, it was almost eight-thirty when the driver let me out, and I didn't get home until after two in the morning. I remember that because Bobby Lee was waiting up for me." She flashed her son a sweet, motherly smile. "It was snowing that night, wasn't it, Bobby Lee? You fussed at me for being out so late in bad weather and were about to go looking for me when I arrived." She gave the detectives a similar smile. "He was all bundled up in his coat and overshoes, ready to look for his mama. Now that's the kind of son every mother wishes she had. Why, he even gave me a wonderful getaway to Hollywood for a Christmas present. Said I needed a change, and he was right. Had a few collagen injections to get rid of some of those nasty old frown lines. I've had the same hairstyle for at least twenty years, so I had one of those makeovers. Got my hair done over. It used to be really long and platinum blond, remember? But this strawberry-blond is so much more me, don't you agree?"

"Mother! These gentlemen do not want to hear about your experience at the hairdresser," he said, and then flashed the detectives a smile. "Sorry, boys, but you know how women are when they start talking about hair and makeup."

"That's all right," Ben asked, suddenly curious as to when this outing had taken place. "Exactly when were you in California, Mrs. Wakefield?"

"It was just before Christmas, because Bobby Lee flew out and spent Christmas Day with me at the spa."

"Yes, ma'am," Ben said. "Just so you'll be aware, we will be checking your alibi for the eleventh."

Mona took offense at the word *alibi* and stood abruptly, signaling an end to her willingness to talk.

"Call the country club and ask for Carl. He can give you a list of who attended."

Just then Delia the maid entered carrying a tray of coffee. Mona waved her away.

"I'm sorry, Delia, but that won't be necessary after all. Take it back to the kitchen." She turned then, her eyes flashing as she glanced at her son before looking at Ben. "Will there be anything else?"

"That's all for now," he said. "If something comes up, we'll be in touch."

They were in the car before they spoke to each other.

"It's a real puzzle as to why Bobby Lee should suddenly want his mother to change her appearance, isn't it?" Red asked.

Ben nodded. "I would also be interested in the time line between the day that composite hit the front page of the *Dallas Morning News* and the day she left for California."

"Partner, do you know what a stink this is going to raise?" Red asked.

"From the looks on their faces, they're already smelling it," Ben said. "You mind writing up the report? I want to get back to the ranch before dark. China isn't sleeping so well these days."

"Nightmares?" Red asked.

"Wouldn't you?"

Red sighed. "Sometimes this job really sucks."

They drove away, unaware of what a tempest their questions had unleashed in the Wakefield home.

Bobby Lee made himself stay on the other side of the desk, because he knew if he got too close to his mother, he would hit her.

"You couldn't just answer their questions, could you?" he screamed. "You had to keep talking and talking, like the white trash you are." He picked up a paperweight and pitched it across the room, knocking a picture off the wall and sending glass flying in all directions.

Mona was devastated. She'd spent her entire life living down her humble beginnings and now, to hear it from her own son's lips, was more than she could bear.

"If I'm white trash, then what does that make you?"

"Unfortunate!" he screamed. "I've spent my entire life trying to live down your escapades. No matter how hard I try, you keep pulling our reputations back down to the gutter where you seem so at home."

Mona paled. The pain of his words were more than she could bear.

"You don't know the depths of my sacrifices for you," she whispered.

"The only thing of depth between us is the shit you keep getting us in. Now we've got the police meddling in our business because you can't keep your pants on your ass. You've ruined everything...everything! I've just run the shortest presidential race in history. Hell's fire, it was over before it began."

Mona lifted her chin, her eyes blind with tears. "That's not the only thing that's over," she said, and strode out of the room.

Bobby Lee cursed and yelled and cursed some more,

blaming his daddy for marrying a sprawling whore and then himself for not being an orphan. Long minutes passed before he began to calm down, and when he did, he realized what he'd done. He stormed out of the library and up the stairs to his mother's room. But she wasn't there. He ranted as he went, calling her name from room to room, but no Mona. It wasn't until he breached the kitchen doors and sent Delia into tears that he learned she was gone.

"What do you mean, she's gone?" he yelled.

"Just that, sir," Delia sobbed. "She picked up her keys and walked out the door without ever going upstairs."

"Did she say where she was going?"

Delia's sobs deepened. "No, sir. She just thanked me for taking such good care of her and told me if I ever had any children to drown 'em."

Bobby Lee paled. This was worse than he'd imagined. He pivoted sharply and headed for the library on the run to call his campaign manager, Ainsley Been.

Ainsley was enjoying a blow job when his phone began to ring.

"Don't stop," he groaned, knowing the answering machine would pick up while the prostitute continued to do her thing.

But his mood went limp when he heard Bobby Lee begin to shout. He shoved the prostitute aside as he scrambled for the phone.

"Hello, hello," he muttered, cutting Bobby Lee off in midcurse.

"Ainsley, Goddamn it, where the hell have you been? We've got trouble, big trouble. Mona was interrogated by the police about the Finelli murder, and now she's gone."

Ainsley blanched. "What the hell do you mean, she's gone?"

"Just that. We had a little fuss after the police left, and she took it all wrong," he said. "I need you to get someone on it. Find her, damn it, and get her back here before the police find out. Hell's fire, do you know what the police are going to think if they know she skipped?"

"Now, Bobby Lee, I'm going to ask you something, and I don't want you to take offense."

"What?" Bobby Lee yelled.

"Does she have a reason to be afraid of the police?"

Bobby Lee groaned. "Hell if I know, but I damn sure do. If this gets out, I'm ruined."

"I'm on my way."

Chapter 18

China was waiting for Ben when he came home and went out to meet him as he pulled up in the front yard and parked.

The sight of her running out the door and then flying into his arms overwhelmed him. She laughed aloud as he swung her off her feet. The sound touched his heart in a way that made him want to cry, and he remembered the day when he'd wanted to be the one to make her laugh.

"This is one fine way to be welcomed home," he growled, and buried his face in her neck.

She smiled. "I thought it had merit," she said, and then kissed him square on the mouth, drawing out the last bit of his good sense.

He groaned. "God, how I love you," he whispered, and then held her close to his heart. No matter what else there was between them, she finished what he was meant to be.

"What happened today?" she asked.

"Let's go inside. There's something I want you to see."

"You brought a picture? Is it her? Did you find the woman who shot me?"

"I don't know," Ben said. "You'll have to tell me."

They started inside as Dave was coming out. "I'm off to go check on the stock. Want me to come back later?"

"Yes," Ben said. "Now more than ever."

Dave's eyes widened. "What's happened?"

"We may have ourselves a pretty good lead."

"You're kidding."

"Senator Wakefield is not laughing," Ben said.

"Wakefield? How in hell does he fit into this?"

Ben pulled a picture out of his pocket and handed it to China. "I think we'll let China tell us."

She took it from him upside down. As she began to turn the picture, it was as if a face from her nightmares began to come into view.

"Well, honey, what do you think?" Ben asked.

China moaned. Her legs went weak. She dropped the picture and covered her face.

Ben grabbed her as she staggered. He'd expected a reaction, but not one this intense.

"China…honey…talk to me. Is it her?"

"I'm going to be sick," she muttered, then tore loose from his grasp and headed for the bathroom down the hall.

Ben went after her, leaving Dave in the hall alone. He bent down and picked up the photo. "Christ almighty," he muttered. "Mona Wakefield. How in hell can this be?"

Mattie came out of the kitchen as China dashed past. "Honey, what's wrong?" she cried, but China didn't stop. When Ben raced down the hall behind her, Mattie knew something had happened. She followed. If something bad was going on in her house, she needed to know.

China was leaning over the sink and washing her face when Ben burst into the bathroom.

"Are you all right?"

China braced herself on the sink with both hands and shook her head no. Ben grabbed a towel and began to dry her off as Mattie came in behind them.

"Somebody better start talking," she said.

China sank down on the side of the tub and put her head in her hands, leaving the talking up to Ben.

"I showed China a picture of another suspect. This is the reaction we got."

Mattie gasped, and then sat down beside her. "Honey, is it true? Did you recognize the woman who shot you?"

China shuddered. "It looked like her. Oh, God, it looked just like her."

"That's all I needed to hear," Ben said. "I'm calling Captain Floyd. We need an arrest warrant."

"Who is she?" Mattie asked.

"Mona Wakefield."

Mattie gasped. "*The* Mona Wakefield? The senator's mother?"

"One and the same," Ben said.

"But, Bennie, why on earth would a woman like her become a murderer?"

"Who the hell knows?" Ben said. "But she's not getting away with it. Stay with China, will you? I need to make a few calls."

"Are you going to arrest her tonight?" China asked.

"I've got to call my captain first, honey. I'll let you know in a bit."

"I want to be there when you go," she said.

"Hell, no," he muttered.

She stood up then, facing him squarely, without any sign of fear.

"I have to, Ben. I need to see her face. I need to see her in handcuffs and know she can't ever hurt me again."

His shoulders slumped. "We'll see," he said softly.

"I'm coming with you while you make your calls," China said. "I have to know what's going on."

He held out his hand. She grabbed it, holding on as if it meant her life.

"You still here?" Mattie asked, as Dave passed Ben and China in the hall.

"I've been in on this ever since Ben brought her out to the ranch, and since it looks like everything's about to hit the fan, I wouldn't miss it for the world."

"That's what I love about you," Mattie muttered. "Bloodthirsty to the end."

Dave took her by the shoulders and gave her a quick kiss.

"So you love me, do you?"

Mattie blushed.

"When are you going to do something about it? We're not getting any younger."

"Is this a proposal?" Mattie asked.

"Would you say yes if it was?" he countered.

"When this is all over, I might," Mattie said, and took him by the hand. "Looks like supper is going to go all to hell tonight. Let's at least make some popcorn. I'm starved."

"Lead the way," Dave said. "I'm right behind you."

They could hear Ben on the phone in the living room as they walked into the kitchen. Dave wanted to listen, but Mattie smiled at him, and he followed her instead.

"Look, Captain, I have a positive identification from our only witness. She says Mona Wakefield is the woman who shot her. How much more do you need?"

China watched, aware that Ben's captain must be arguing a point Ben didn't want to consider.

"I know," Ben said. "Yes, she said she had an alibi, but we haven't checked it out. She was at some country club Christmas party. You know how those things are. She could show up and circulate for a while, then disappear without anyone missing her, do the deed and then come back to the party without anyone being the wiser. Remember China's first description was of a woman in a beaded evening gown and a full-length fur coat? Pretty typical wear for a country club party, don't you think?"

Ben started to pace. China tried to catch his eye, hoping she could glean something from his expression, but he wouldn't look at her. And then he exploded.

"That's just great! And give her time to skip the country? I don't agree."

But Aaron Floyd wasn't caring whether anyone agreed or not.

"I don't give a flying you know what whether you agree or not," he said. "We're not arresting a senator's elderly mother until we bust her alibi."

"Mona Wakefield is a barracuda on the hunt, not an elderly anything. And if your eyewitness's say-so isn't worth anything, then you make your damned case without her."

He hung up the phone and then threw it on the sofa.

"Son of a bitch," he muttered.

China was almost afraid to ask.

"They won't arrest her?"

"Not yet," he said. "Afraid to step on too many political toes, but don't give up on us yet. Red already has the country club list, and Captain Floyd has assigned two sets of detectives to contact the people who were at the party. Before morning, I'll know what Mona Wakefield was wearing, even what she had to eat. If she has a secret, I'll find it."

"Am I still in danger?"

Ben hesitated, then nodded. There could be nothing but truth between them.

"Probably now more than ever," he said. "But Dave and I are here. We'll take turns watching the house. I don't think anyone knows your name, let alone where you are. However, we can't take any chances."

"It's almost over, isn't it, Ben?"

He crossed the floor and took her in his arms. "It's getting close, honey. Hang in there for me, okay?"

"Okay."

"Are you hungry?" he asked. "Suddenly, I'm starved."

She smiled. "That will make your mother very happy. If there's one thing I've learned about Mattie, it's that she uses food as a cure-all."

"And it works, doesn't it?" Ben said.

"Unless you eat too much of it, and then it's a whole other problem," China said, and then laughed.

Mona was driving south without aim. She'd emptied her bank account of cash with the purpose of getting as far away from Dallas as she could. But the farther she drove, the more painful her memories became.

Bobby Lee, her own son, had called her white trash. He'd said he would rather have been an orphan than be tied to her name. My God, how could this be? Hadn't she spent her life for her husband and her son? After she'd been widowed, she'd had plenty of chances to remarry, and some of the men were not only rich but good-looking. But had she? Had she given one thought to her own personal needs? Hell, no. She'd stayed for Bobby Lee.

She'd known from the start that he was special—always trying harder than all the other boys his age. He was never satisfied with second best. Always pushing, pushing, pushing for more. Even during his brief marriage, she'd been at his beck and call, and when that had fallen apart, she'd been there for him, picking up the pieces of his life and helping put a home back together again.

Granted, she didn't have a college education, but that didn't make her stupid. She knew things—lots of things.

She stifled a sob and blew her nose with one hand as she changed lanes on I-35. She needed a plan, but in the meantime, she needed a place to hide. In spite of the fact that her son had cursed her existence, she knew him well. He would want her back, but not because he would be sorry. Oh, no. It would be for the sake of his image, and that alone. He needed to have her back before word got out that his mother had run away from home. She'd already decided that motels would be too obvious. Even if she used cash to pay, he would find her.

It wasn't until she realized she was entering the outskirts of Houston that she remembered her old friend from back home. If Bitsy Chance still lived in Pasadena, she would help her. She and Bitsy went back a long way.

Happy to have a plan, she pulled over at the first gas station she came to and headed for the phone booth just outside the door. Luckily there was a phone book inside and she began to scan the pages, looking for Bitsy's name. To her relief, she found a listing, but it wasn't until she began to dial that she realized the phone book was almost five years old.

"Oh Lord, let her be there," Mona said, as the phone began to ring. On the fifth ring, a man answered.

"Hello," Mona said. "Is Bitsy there?"

"Who wants to know?" he growled.

"I'm a friend of hers from back in Amarillo. Tell her it's Baby Doll."

"Hey, Bitsy," the man yelled. "Some woman calls herself Baby Doll wants to talk to you. Says she knowed you from Amarillo."

Mona heard Bitsy squeal and started to cry, but they were tears of relief.

"Baby! Baby! Is that you?"

Mona swallowed a sob. "Yes, Bitsy, it's me."

"Ooh, girl, I've been following all the fuss about you and your boy. Aren't you just the thing, now? I'm surprised you even remember someone like me."

"Oh, Bitsy, I think I'm in trouble. I need a place to stay."

Suddenly, whatever envy Bitsy Chance might have harbored was gone in a flash. It was just like the good old days when she and Mona had sneaked out on their parents and gone honky-tonking in cowboy bars.

"Where are you, honey?"

Mona squinted through the filthy glass, trying to read the sign on the station.

"I'm in Pasadena at a place called The In and Out."

Bitsy squealed again. "Honey! This is fate! I'm twelve blocks from there."

"Will your husband mind?" Mona asked.

Bitsy laughed. "Girl, that fool's not my husband, and don't you worry. He'll be gone before you get here."

"Don't tell him who I am," she begged.

"Don't worry, and don't move," Bitsy said. "I'm comin' to get you."

Mona hung up the phone and then locked herself in her car and waited to be rescued. She would cry later, after she didn't need to see to drive.

It was six-thirty in the morning when Bobby Lee opened the door to Ainsley Been. Ainsley started talking before he got a foot in the door.

"I'm sorry, Bobby Lee, but it's as if Mona vanished from the face of the earth," Ainsley said.

Bobby Lee groaned, and grabbed the man's arm and pulled him inside.

"This is awful, just awful. Put some more men on it. She has to leave some kind of a paper trail."

"She cleaned out her checking account, Bobby Lee. Was there a lot of money in it?"

"Hell, yes. Probably a good twenty or thirty thousand," he said, and began to pace.

This was worse than he'd thought. He'd expected her to pout and then come storming back this morning with some young buck in tow just to prove she hadn't lost her touch, but if she'd taken all that money, this didn't feel good. It didn't feel good at all.

He thought of all the loose ends of his own life, but he couldn't get past the obvious. The presidential race.

"I've thought about it all night," he told Ainsley.

"Thought about what?" Ainsley asked.

"I want you to schedule a press conference."

"What the hell for? Surely you're not going to talk about this mess?"

"No, I'm going to get myself out of the public eye as much as possible before it all falls down around me. I'm still Senator Wakefield. I still have my pride and my reputation. I can always run for president again another time. Besides, I have to be back in Washington, D.C., by the weekend. I can't leave Dallas with all this hanging over my head."

"What are you saying?" Ainsley asked.

"I'm going to renounce my candidacy for personal reasons and let that be that."

Ainsley groaned. His future was now as bleak as Bobby Lee's. No one would want to hire a campaign

manager who hadn't been able to keep scandal away from
the candidate he was representing.

"Are you sure?" he asked.

"Yes. Do it," Bobby Lee said. "Set it up at the Wyndham Anatole for tomorrow morning before I change my mind. That's where I made my announcement, that's where it will be rescinded."

"Yes, sir," Ainsley said. "I'll call you with the details later."

As he left, Bobby Lee was already in gear, planning his speech. Maybe if he managed to cry as he said it, the press would put a different spin on the news and make him look like the hero, broken and sad, but nevertheless a hero who was willing to put his family before his personal ambitions.

Mona woke up on her back just as a giant-size cockroach skittered across the ceiling above her bed. She stared at it in sleepy fascination, wondering how creatures like that managed to defy the laws of gravity. It wasn't the first time she'd awakened and not known where she was, but it had been a few years since the last occurrence. Then she heard Bitsy hawking and spitting in the bathroom across the hall and remembered where she was—Pasadena, Texas—and that she'd run away from home.

She rolled over and sat up on the side of the bed. Ignoring her nudity, she stood and headed for the bathroom.

"Bitsy, you 'bout through in there? I need to pee," she yelled.

"Give me a second to rinse my mouth," Bitsy hollered.

Mona waited. Moments later, Bitsy opened the door and then stopped in her tracks, her eyes bugged out in disbelief.

"Ooowee, girl, you ain't changed yourself a bit, have

you? You still parade around in your birthday suit every morning, just like you used to."

Mona shrugged. "It's just flesh and bone," she said, and shut the door behind her as she pushed Bitsy aside.

"Yeah, but it always looks different on you!" Bitsy yelled, and then ambled back into her bedroom and took off her nightgown to dress for the day.

As she passed a mirror, she paused for a look. She was almost ten years younger than Mona, but it didn't show. In fact, Mona didn't look much older now than she had in her forties. Bitsy frowned at the bulges and wrinkles on her own body and then shrugged it off. What the hell did it matter anymore? It wasn't as if she were looking for a man. She'd had plenty of them and not bothered to keep a one.

By the time Mona came out of the bathroom, Bitsy had coffee brewing and the television blaring.

Mona sauntered into the living room with a towel wrapped around her. Bitsy jumped up and pulled the shades on her windows.

"Lord, Baby Doll, you have a funny way of trying to hide, paradin' around all nekked in front of the windows and all."

Mona shrugged. "I didn't think."

Bitsy grinned. "Get yourself a cup of coffee and then set down and tell me all about it."

Mona poured the thick brew, but now that night had passed, she was loath to discuss the mess she was in with someone she hadn't seen in years. What if she said something that could ruin Bobby Lee's chances at the White House? No, she'd better just keep her troubles to herself. And she was saved from having to answer Bitsy so soon when her phone began to ring.

"That's probably my boss," Bitsy said. "I called in sick

this morning, but I don't think he believed me. I'll take it in the bedroom and play it up right, okay?"

"Whatever," Mona said, and turned her attention to the morning news on the TV. It wasn't until she heard her son's name mentioned that she sat up and began to take notice. She turned up the volume and then took a sip of her coffee, and, not for the first time, thought of what she'd left behind. Fine clothes, clean sheets and Delia's hot buttered biscuits were the first to come to mind.

"Senator Wakefield has called a press conference for this afternoon at the Wyndham Anatole in Dallas. Sources are saying that they're expecting him to withdraw from the presidential race. If he does, this will be the shortest candidacy in presidential history. He hadn't even announced a platform and he's already falling off it."

"No," Mona moaned, and sat up with a jerk. "No, Bobby Lee, you can't do this to me."

Bitsy came back into the room ready for a gabfest and found Mona scrambling to get up.

"What's wrong?" she said.

"I've got to get home," Mona said. "Bobby Lee's about to make the biggest mistake of his life, and I've got to stop him before it's too late."

"But you just got here!" Bitsy cried.

"Yes, and I can't thank you enough for helping me out," Mona said. "But I've got to get back to Dallas by noon."

"You're crazy. You'll never make it in time."

"I have to," she said. "Everything depends on it."

Within five minutes, she was dressed and gone, leaving Bitsy Chance with an unmade bed, four wet bath towels and a dirty coffee cup. It was Bitsy's opinion that Mona had been rich too long to be fun anymore.

However, money was the least of Mona's worries. When she finally got back on I-35 heading north, she pressed the accelerator to the floor.

China woke up to find herself wrapped in Ben's arms. The last thing she remembered was Ben seeing her to bed. She'd heard the front door open, then close, and knew he'd gone outside to relieve Dave on guard duty. There were dark shadows beneath his eyes, and his cheeks had a gaunt, almost haunted look. China felt guilty, knowing that the stress of her presence in his life was the cause of all that.

She snuggled a little closer, sighing with satisfaction as he unconsciously pulled her closer. It seemed a miracle that the man loved her, but love her he did. He told her on a daily basis and showed her in every way he knew how. All she had to do was trust that it would last and their lives would be perfect. After the killer was put behind bars, of course. For now, that was their top priority.

Just as she was thinking about going back to sleep, the phone began to ring. Ben came awake within seconds and was answering before he'd even opened his eyes.

"Hello."

"Ben, this is Red. We've got our warrant."

Ben was rolling out of bed as he spoke. "Her alibi didn't hold."

"Everyone remembered her there, but no one could vouch for the entire time, or even when she left."

"Did you get an ID on what she was wearing?"

"Yeah. A floor-length sequined gown. A couple of women said it was dove gray. The rest we asked said it was something pale blue."

Ben's heartbeat skidded. A blue beaded gown. "What about a fur? Was she wearing a fur?"

"Hell, yes. In fact, that caused the biggest fuss. About half the women we talked to were animal lovers and berated Miz Mona real fiercely for wearing dead critters on her back."

"Hot damn," Ben muttered. He winked at China, who was now on her knees, following his every word.

"Is the warrant arrest and search?"

"Yeah. The clothes were the clincher for the captain. After he heard that, he said screw the senator, or something to that effect, and told us to go for it. He made a couple of calls, found a judge who doesn't much like Bobby Lee's politics and we're in like Flynn. When can you be ready?"

"What time is it?" Ben asked.

"Almost seven."

"I'll meet you at eight outside the Wakefield mansion."

"We'll be waiting," Red said.

Ben hung up the phone. "We've got a warrant," he said.

"I'm going with you," China cried, and jumped out of bed on the run, grabbing her clothes as she went.

Ben hesitated. "Honey, I don't know if this is such a—"

She stopped, her jeans in her hands. "We've already talked about this."

He sighed. "Then hurry up. There's no time to shower. Just get dressed and see if Mom's made any coffee. I've had about three hours' sleep, and I don't want to run into a light pole before I put the cuffs on that woman's hands."

Chapter 19

Bobby Lee was still in his pajamas when the doorbell began to ring. He grabbed a robe and headed for the stairs on the run. Please, God, let it be word about his mother. But his hopes fell when he saw the two detectives from yesterday and the uniformed officers behind them.

Delia was already there, looking wild-eyed and ready to burst into tears.

"Oh, Senator, these people are looking for Miz Mona. I didn't know what to say."

"You go on to the kitchen," he said. "Tell Cook to bring my coffee to the dining room."

"Yes, sir," she said, and hurried away.

Bobby Lee smoothed back his hair with the palms of his hands and then tightened the belt of his robe.

"Gentlemen, I would appreciate it if you would step inside. You're lettin' in the flies."

"Our business is with your mother, sir. We have a warrant for her arrest."

Bobby Lee's ears began to buzz, and he felt the blood

actually draining from his face. He wondered if, for the first time in his life, he was going to faint.

"You can't be serious," he muttered.

"Oh, but we are," Ben said. "She has been positively identified as the woman who shot Charles Finelli. And, as you know, the gun that was used to kill Finelli has also been linked to a number of other crimes in the city. Now, either you call her down, or we'll go up and get her."

"No, no, you don't understand," Bobby Lee said, as Ben motioned for the officers to proceed upstairs. "She's not here. I swear."

Everyone stopped. For a moment there was total silence. And then Ben took a step forward and grabbed the senator by the lapels of his robe.

"What do you mean, she's not here?"

"We had an argument yesterday after you left. She stormed out, and I haven't seen her since. I've had my men out looking for her all night, but we can't find a trace."

Ben pushed him up against the wall. "If you're lying to us, you'll find yourself arrested for aiding and abetting, for harboring a fugitive and for anything else I can think of."

"I'm not, I'm not, I swear," Bobby Lee mumbled. "As for this other, you've got to be mistaken. My mother wouldn't hurt anyone. She's not capable of something like that."

Ben turned him loose in disgust. "Officers, commence the search," he said, and then turned to Red. "I'm calling in an APB on Mona Wakefield while the senator here shows you her room."

"Yes, of course," Bobby Lee muttered, and started up the stairs just as China walked through the door.

Ben turned. "I told you to wait outside," he said.

"Where is she?" China said. "I need to see her face-to-face, just like before."

"She's not here."

China moaned. "She got away?"

"I don't know what happened," he said, and took her by the arm. "Please, honey, wait outside in the car with the other officer, okay?"

She nodded and had started to leave when she saw someone standing on the stairs. It was the first time she'd seen the senator in person, and he didn't look as good as she'd expected. In fact, he looked as if he'd seen a ghost.

"You're the witness…aren't you? The woman my mother is supposed to have shot."

China took a step forward, moving beyond Ben's reach.

"My baby is dead because of her."

Bobby Lee moaned and then sat down on the stairs, his legs too weak to stand.

"This is all a horrible mistake."

But no one seemed inclined to believe him. "Senator, you were going to show my partner to your mother's room?"

"At the head of the landing, first door on the left. Help yourselves. I don't feel so good."

The officers moved forward, led by Red Fisher, leaving the senator on the stairs.

Ben took China by the arm and pulled her to the doorway.

"In the car. Now."

"I'm going," she said.

"The captain wouldn't be too happy with me if he knew you were here, so let's don't push the issue, okay?"

"Is she going to get away?" China asked.

"Hell, no. Mona Wakefield's face is as familiar in

Texas as McDonald's Golden Arches. She'll turn up, and when she does, we'll arrest her. Wait for me outside. I'll have to go by the station, but we should be home before noon."

It wasn't what she wanted to hear, but it was enough. She went back to the patrol car, while Ben joined the officers in their search of the estate.

Bobby Lee had retreated to the library and was frantically searching for his lawyer's home phone number. Cursing every woman on the face of the earth, he decided to call Ainsley instead. Ainsley answered on the first ring.

"It's me," Bobby Lee said. "The police have a warrant for my mother's arrest, and my house is being searched as we speak. What time did you schedule that press conference?"

"Christ almighty, Bobby Lee, is that all you can worry about?"

"You just answer me, damn it. I know what I'm doing."

Ainsley sighed. "It's set for noon."

"That's too late," Bobby Lee said. "Make it ten."

"This morning? That's only two hours away. I'll never be able to change all of the—"

"Just do it," Bobby Lee snapped. "I'm going to break the news myself, not the other way around. I refuse to look like I'm part of this mess."

"You do this, and you'll be selling your mother down the proverbial river."

"She sold herself years ago," Bobby Lee said. "They're just finally coming to collect."

"All right. I hope you know what you're doing."

"I always know what I'm doing," Bobby Lee said, and hung up in Ainsley's ear.

Then he went to his room to dress, bypassing the destruction of his mother's quarters. He didn't want to know what they found. The way he figured it, the less he knew, the more innocent he would appear. By the time he was ready to come back downstairs, he had everything all figured out. By God, he was going to come out looking like a hero again or know the reason why. It wasn't going to be easy, but he was about to announce to the citizens of his fair city that when he'd discovered her duplicity, he'd turned in his own mother for her horrible crimes.

After that, he had one last chore to attend to, and then everything was going to fall back into place. So he wasn't going to run for president. So what. The more he thought about it, the more he began to convince himself that it had been his mother's dream, not his, all along.

As fate would have it, Mona had a flat tire just outside of Austin. She pulled off the highway into a rest stop and popped the trunk, although she didn't have the faintest idea of how to remove the spare, let alone take off the flat tire. But she reminded herself that she'd come from hardy pioneer stock. Her great-great-granny had walked across the country from Boston to Texas, following her family wagon to a new land. If that woman could walk several thousand miles and live through Indian and Mexican wars, then by God, Mona could figure out how to change a flat tire.

She rolled up the sleeves of her designer suit and leaned into the trunk to study the setup. The tire seemed far too small, therefore it must be flat. But just to be sure, she got the manufacturer's book out of the glove box and began to read. Before she'd gotten past the directions on how to change the digital clock to daylight savings, a trucker was pulling off the highway and coming to a stop behind her.

"Thank You, Lord," she said, and stood up, pasted a smile on her face and sauntered toward the man.

He got out of his rig, thinking this was his lucky day. Before he knew it, he was showing her how to take the spare out of the trunk and where to place the jack to make sure the car didn't tip.

"I don't know what I would have done without your help," Mona said, playing helpless to the hilt.

"It's my pleasure," the trucker said, as he tugged on the doughnut, but it wouldn't come out. "Dang thing's stuck on something," he said, and leaned a little farther into the trunk.

He gave it another couple of tugs, and as he did, the layer of carpeting inside the trunk came up in his hands.

"Something had spilled on it," he said. "Looky here. It plumb glued the carpet to the spare. Don't look like it's ever been used, or you would have found this before."

Mona nodded, pretending great interest, but she didn't really care. All she wanted was to be on her way.

"I'll straighten the carpet," she said. "You just take that little old tire and do your thing, okay?"

The trucker grinned. He was going to do his thing, and he hoped that she'd be willing to do another little thing or two when he was through.

Mona knew what he was thinking, and she'd play hell before she bumped bellies with some stranger. She hadn't ever been that hard up. She leaned into the trunk and began pulling the carpeting back down. As she did, a flash of something shiny caught her eye. She lifted up the carpet again and peered under, and as she did, her heart skipped a beat.

A gun. Jesus Christ, it was a gun.

But where had it come from? This car was hers. She'd

bought it off the showroom floor less than a year ago. No one drove it but her. There was no way this could have...

A strange look crossed her face. She glanced toward the trucker to make sure he hadn't seen, then calmly smoothed the carpet back down. A few minutes later, he was finished.

"Just put that dirty old flat right in here," Mona said. "And tell me, what do I owe you for your help?"

The trucker tossed the flat and the jack inside the trunk and slammed the lid.

"You can't drive over forty or fifty miles an hour on one of these things," he said. "As for what you owe me, well, I'll just let you decide." Then he rubbed his hand down the front of his fly and grinned.

Mona smiled. "Why don't you just crawl up in that big old truck of yours and stretch out in your cute little bed and I'll see what I can do."

When he grabbed her by the hand and headed for the truck on the run, she thought she would break a heel. But her chance was coming. She needed to put some time between her and this moose, to get lost in the traffic without having to worry about him following her and she knew what she was going to do.

The trucker climbed in, then pulled her up. He was tearing off his pants and climbing into the sleep cab as she slid into the seat. Mona took one look at the limp flesh hanging between his legs, yanked the keys from the ignition, and jumped out of the truck.

She hit the ground with a thump, felt the heel of one pump give as she landed, but was too full of adrenaline to care. She hauled back her arm and flung the ring full of keys as far out into the grassy pasture as they would go. She had one glimpse of the sunlight on metal as they spiraled out of sight, and then she began to run.

The trucker was pulling up his pants and cursing as he practically fell out of the truck, uncertain what to follow, the bitch or the path of his keys. But she was already in the car and driving away before he had his pants zipped, which left his keys. He headed for the pasture, cursing with every step.

Mona vaguely remembered his warning about not driving too fast, but she didn't have the time to waste. She stomped the accelerator to the floor once again and held on for a very rough ride, unaware of the fate that awaited her in Dallas.

Hours later, as she hit the city limits, she realized she had come back too late. The radio stations were full of the news. Dallas's favorite son had withdrawn from the presidential race. Her despair was cut short by the horror of the news that followed.

There was a warrant out for her arrest. According to the news, her own son had been the one to turn her in. Hurt beyond belief, an instinct for self-preservation led her to the cabin on Lake Texoma. She hadn't been there in years, but it would be a good place to hide while she figured out what to do next. She wasn't going into hiding as much as she was retreating to lick her wounds.

All the way through the city, she kept imagining everyone who passed her would know who she was. Fear kept her moving, even though the car was low on gas. She'd missed the turn to the cabin and had to retrace her steps. By the time she pulled up, the gauge was registering Empty.

She got out, her legs shaking, her stomach rumbling from hunger. But it couldn't matter. She would think about that later on. All she wanted was a bed and a shower, and if the utilities weren't on, she'd bathe in the lake.

It didn't occur to her until she turned the knob that the

door would be locked. She started to cry, pounding on the door in frustration. It was the last straw. As she pounded, something fell from the ledge above her head, landing at her feet with a clink. A key. Of course! The spare key.

She opened the door and slipped inside, expecting almost anything except what she found. Instead of furniture covered in drop cloths and a layer of dust, everything was spotless, and if her eyes didn't deceive her, it was new, certainly newer than when she'd been there last.

She turned on a light and then walked through the rooms, looking in closets and poking through drawers. They were full, as if someone were living here. At the thought, she spun and raced toward the door, locking it firmly and then sliding the dead bolt, just in case. It seemed obvious that Bobby Lee had rented the thing out and hadn't told her. This was a fine mess. Someone could come back at any time, and then she would be found out. This wouldn't do.

But she was so tired and so filthy. The least she could do was shower and maybe find a change of clothes. She could eat, leave some money behind for the food that she took, and then get to the lake bait shop for gas before it closed. She was too tired to drive, but it didn't look as if she would have a choice.

Frantic, she raced into the bath and stripped off her clothes. Minutes later, she came out of the shower, dripping water and heading for the bedroom in search of something clean.

The first bedroom had furniture, but the closets were empty. But when she went into the other, she knew she'd hit the jackpot. Makeup was on the dresser, as if the woman who lived here had just laid it down and walked out of the house. The closet was full of dresses. Mona shuffled through them in haste, searching for something comfortable, but to her surprise, she couldn't find anything but lingerie and evening gowns. It didn't make sense. These weren't the types of clothes she would have expected a lake dweller to wear. She closed the door and headed for the armoire, hoping she might find some jeans or slacks inside.

She flung back the doors and then screamed before she realized what she was seeing. At first glance it appeared she'd uncovered a stash of decapitated heads, and then she cursed herself for panicking when she looked again and saw it was nothing more than some long blond wigs on hair stylist's dummies.

"Heavens," she muttered, as she fingered several strands. "Talk about trashy. All these wigs, and not one of them of good quality."

She continued to search and was about to go back to the closet for another look when she found a pair of jeans and a shirt in the last drawer down.

"Thank goodness," she muttered, and yanked them out, then began to put them on. To her surprise, they actually fit. The waist of the jeans was a little large, but the leg length was almost perfect. The shirtsleeves came all the way to her wrists, which was uncommon, considering her height.

It wasn't until she crammed her hands in the pockets and pulled out a handful of receipts that she realized her surprises weren't quite over. Curious, she sat on the edge of the bed and began to unfold them. One after the other, she read in silence. But the longer she sat there, the greater her understanding grew.

She looked up, her gaze centering on the clothes hanging in the closet, the wigs sitting in the armoire on faceless plastic heads, then back down at the receipts in her hand. She thought of the gun in the trunk of her car. The police were looking for her for murder because her son had turned her in. She thought back to the vacation he'd sent her on and the makeover he'd insisted she have. Her stomach turned. She needed to throw up, but there was nothing in her stomach to regurgitate. She dropped her head between her knees and remembered the day he was born. All that blood. All that pain. All those sleepless days and nights of his childhood—and it had come to this.

"Oh, God…oh, dear God, what have I done?"

After a while, she crawled on top of the covers and rolled herself up in a ball. Whatever happened to her was going to have to wait until tomorrow. She was too tired to do anything but sleep.

It was all over the national news. A warrant had been issued for the arrest of Mona Wakefield, Senator Bobby Lee Wakefield's mother.

Ariel Simmons was sitting in a Motel 6 when she heard the news and started to laugh. Thank God it was over. But the longer she laughed, the worse she felt. Before long, she was crying. It wasn't over. It would never be over. Her reputation was ruined, despite no longer being a murder suspect. The people who came to hear her preach were few and far between, old people with little to no money to donate to her ministry. It didn't pay to preach when the only people who came just wanted to hear the Word of God. It was the ones who thought they could buy their way into heaven who had been paying her bills.

With their absence, she was reduced to places like this, rather than the opulence to which she'd been accustomed. Finally, she wiped her eyes and went to the bathroom to wash her face. This was the last stop on her tour, not that it mattered. When tonight was over, she'd been giving some thought to moving south—maybe Florida—someplace where she could get lost in the crowds and create a new world, even a new identity for herself. If she sold her home in Dallas and the rest of her holdings, she would have enough to live on comfortably for the rest of her life.

The more she considered it, the better it sounded. After all, as long as there was life, anything was possible.

It was dark when the shot came through the window near the chair where China was sitting. One second she was screaming and the next thing she knew she was on the floor and Ben was on top of her, telling her to stop. She sucked in a breath and clung to him in horror as he ran his hands across her body in frantic sweeps.

"Tell me you're all right. Tell me it missed you."

"I'm fine," China said, and stifled the need to shriek.

"God," Ben groaned, and then pushed her up between the sofa and the wall. "No matter what you hear, don't move, do you hear me?"

"Ben! Bennie! Are you all right?"

Ben could hear his mother's footsteps as she started down the hall.

"Mother! Get back! Get down on the floor and stay there until I tell you it's okay."

He could hear her starting to cry, but she did what she was told, although her need to know her loved ones were all right outweighed the prudence of keeping silent.

"Bennie, are you and China all right? What about Dave? He's outside, isn't he? Oh, dear God, what if he's—"

"Don't either of you move. I've got to go."

Seconds later, China watched him crawling belly-fashion across the floor and then into the kitchen, where the lights were out. She knew he was going out to danger. All she could do was pray.

It was impossible for the shooter to know if the shot had connected. One second the girl had been right in the sights and the next she was gone. One thing was certain, he needed to finish the job.

He started running in a crouch, circling the ranch house, searching for a way to enter, when all the lights in the house went out. A silent curse slid through his mind. This raid was a bust. He'd taken a shot at the woman. Maybe he'd gotten lucky.

Something rustled in the grass off to his left. He pictured the cop inside the house and thought of the one he'd left unconscious out near the barn. What if there were more? He couldn't afford to take a chance.

Within minutes, he was gone.

Ben found Dave's limp body just as he heard the sound of a motorcycle starting somewhere toward the highway. The shooter was getting away.

Dave moaned, and it was the prettiest sound Ben could have heard.

"Dave, buddy, where do you hurt?"

"My head. I think I hurt my head. What happened?"

"I'll explain later, but I need to get you in the house."

Within the hour, the ranch was crawling with the police, from Christopher Scott, the Navarro County Sheriff and every deputy he could raise, to part of the homicide division of the Dallas P.D. Everyone knew why it had happened, but the shooter was gone. The good news was that China Brown was still alive.

Sheriff Scott was waiting for Ben as he came up from the barn.

"Your shooter is gone, Ben. We found tracks, also

where he stashed his bike, but we need daylight for anything else."

"I know, Chris, and thanks for coming out," Ben said.

"Just doing my job," he said. "Although I don't relish something this ugly happening on my watch, if you know what I mean."

"Yes, I do."

"I'll leave a man on guard up around the highway, although I don't expect another attempt tonight."

"Thanks. And thanks for getting an ambulance out here so quick for Dave."

"He's probably got a concussion, but he'll be all right," Scott said. "Did Mattie go with him?"

Ben nodded, thinking of China alone in the house. "I'd better go check on China. The last few months have been pretty hard on her. This didn't help."

"Anything I can do, don't hesitate to call," Scott repeated, and then he was gone.

A few minutes later, there was nothing left to indicate the turmoil they'd just been through but a few drops of Dave's blood on the front porch and a yard full of tracks. A couple of the deputies had tacked a piece of plywood over the broken window. Something that would be dealt with tomorrow. For now, Ben needed to hold China in his arms and reassure himself she was still in one piece. He couldn't get past the image of her smiling at him as she sat down in her chair, and then the glass shattering all around her as she started to scream.

He entered the house calling her name.

She came out of the kitchen, carrying a knife. Shock still lingered in the nervousness of her expression. Ben locked the door behind him and then took away the knife.

"Here, honey, let me have that, okay?"

She handed it over without a word.

Ben smoothed the hair away from her face, wishing he could make that look in her eyes disappear as easily.

"The sheriff left a deputy on guard, but the shooter is long gone."

"It's not over. It will never be over until I'm dead."

"Don't say that," he said, and then picked her up and held her close. "Don't ever say that again."

She sighed. It seemed inevitable. No matter how hard the good guys tried, the bad boys would win in the end.

"I don't want to die," she said. "Not anymore. I haven't wanted to for a long, long time."

"And I don't want you to, either, honey. I won't let that happen. I promised. Remember?"

She cried herself to sleep in his arms, and then Ben held her while she slept, with her head stretched across his lap and one hand clutching the fabric of his jeans. He sat propped against the headboard with one hand on the middle of her back and the other beside his gun. Tears ran freely down the middle of his cheeks as he waited for dawn. He was scared. As scared as he'd ever been in his life. If something didn't happen soon in their favor, it was going to be damned hard keeping that promise he'd made.

It was midmorning by the time Ben and China got to Commerce Street. Ben's stomach was in knots as he pulled into the parking lot of the Dallas P.D. He needed to check in with his captain, apprise him of everything that had happened last night and try to figure out where to go from there.

"Come on, honey. Maybe this won't take too long, and then we'll go check on Dave. Mother said he was okay, but I want to see for myself."

China hated herself for the gut-wrenching fear of getting out of Ben's car, but she was so tired of hiding that

she could almost wish it was over, regardless of the out-
come. She clung to Ben's hand as he hurried her inside.
Once there, she began to relax. Everywhere she looked
she saw uniforms and badges and officers with guns.
Safe. In here, she was safe.

He introduced her to Captain Floyd, who promptly
decided she was too thin and needed to eat. He set her in
his own office with a Coke and a box of doughnut holes.

"The chocolate-covered ones are the best," he said, and
handed her the remote to his TV. "Why don't you kick
back, watch a little TV, have yourself a snack? If you get
tired, stretch out on my couch. We'll take our meeting to
the room across the hall."

"Thank you for being so kind," she said, and then
smiled.

At that point Floyd was lost. He cleared his throat
gruffly and then frowned.

"Yes…well, come on, English. Let's get this show on
the road. I want to know everything that happened last
night, and I want a full report from the Navarro Sheriff's office ASAP."

Ben winked at China and then followed his boss across
the hall, where the task force had assembled for an update. The main focus was on Mona Wakefield. She was
still missing, and China had been shot at last night. The
nails were getting tighter in Mona's coffin.

China set the pastry aside, but she kept her drink, oc-
casionally sipping as she flipped through the channels
for something to watch.

Time passed and she dozed. The program changed, and
a replay of Senator Wakefield's press conference began
to air. In the back of her mind, she heard what was happening but couldn't bring herself to care until she heard

a reporter shout over the background noise, trying to be heard.

"Bobby Lee...Bobby Lee...are you going to—"

She came up on her feet, her eyes wide and filled with fear, her heart pounding so hard she could scarcely breathe. Instinctively, she took a step backward and splayed her hands over her belly, just as she had that night on the South Side of Dallas.

"No!" she screamed. "Don't shoot! Don't shoot!"

She might as well have screamed "Fire," because every cop on the floor, including Ben, was in the office with their guns drawn before she woke all the way up.

It was obvious to them all that no one was in sight, and they were ready to attribute it to a bad dream when she started to cry.

"Oh, my God, oh, my God." She covered her face with her hands. "I didn't remember until now. Oh Lord, all this time and I didn't remember."

"What?" Ben said, and took her hands away from her face. "What didn't you remember?"

"The photographer. He yelled out at that woman. When she heard him, she turned. The flash started going off on his camera. She was in such a rage. She pulled a gun and started shooting. Then she shot me. But I didn't remember until just now that Finelli called her by name."

"What, honey? You mean you actually heard him call her Mona?"

"No," she moaned. "He yelled, 'Bobby Lee.' Three times and real loud. That's when the woman got mad. That's when she pulled the gun."

A moment of stunned silence passed over them, and then everyone started talking at once. China dropped back onto the sofa, and Ben followed her. He took her by the shoulders and looked her straight in the eye.

"Are you telling us that Finelli called that woman Bobby Lee?"

"Yes."

He looked up at his captain. "Well?"

Floyd stared, struggling with the implications of what she'd just said, and then he yelled, "Avery! Somebody get Matt Avery."

When a young officer appeared, China recognized him as the one who'd helped her compile the composite of the killer's face.

"Avery, if you have a picture of someone, can you scan it into your program and then make the changes you normally do?"

"Yes, sir."

Floyd yelled again. "Somebody get him a head shot of our beloved senator. I want to see what comes out of this pot."

Chapter 20

It was magic. One minute Bobby Lee Wakefield's face was on the screen, and then, with a few keystrokes from Officer Avery, he'd become a she, right down to the long blond hair and come-hither eyes.

"China?"

"Yes."

"Jesus," Floyd whispered, and sat down with a thump.

"This could explain why Bobby Lee decided to take the credit for turning his own mother in. It certainly shifts the blame, doesn't it?" Red said.

Floyd shook his head in disbelief. "But he's a football star and a war hero and a Goddamned United States senator. This doesn't make sense." He looked at China again. "Are you sure about this? I mean...you picked out his mother before."

"And no wonder," Ben said. "Look at the resemblance. They could be twins. As for making any sense, killers never do. However, if I remember anything about Psych 101, killing men who are into perversion could be a symbolic way of trying to kill himself."

"But Finelli wasn't into that, was he?" China asked.

"No, honey. He may not have known about the other victims. But catching Bobby Lee in drag would have been the picture of the century. No telling how much money he would have made off that one single shot."

"Instead, Finelli made the headlines," Floyd said, and then wiped a shaky hand across his face as he stared at the image on the screen. "Go get the son of a bitch. I'll have the warrant by the time you arrive."

China stood.

"You wait here, little lady," the captain said.

"Let her go," Ben said. "She's earned it." Then he took his cell phone out of his pocket.

"Who are you calling?" Floyd asked.

"Just keeping a promise to someone I know."

Connie Marx was coming out of the shower with a towel around her head when her phone began to ring. She crawled across her bed and grabbed it, letting the wet towel fall to the floor as she did.

"Hello."

"Connie?"

"Yes?"

"This is Ben English."

She froze. "Yes?"

"You know where Senator Wakefield lives?"

Now her heart was skipping beats. "Yes, of course. Is it Mona Wakefield? Are you going to arrest her?"

"No, not her."

There was a moment of silence, and suddenly she knew.

"You're kidding," she muttered.

"We're on our way there now," Ben said.

"Oh, my God, this is great."

She hung up in Ben's ear and was scrambling for her

clothes before she remembered she needed a cameraman to make this all work. She grabbed the phone again and dialed the station where she used to work, disguising her voice so no one would suspect.

"I need to speak to Arnie White, please." Then she hit the speaker button and continued to dress.

"This is Arnie."

"Arnie, this is Connie. You still hungry?"

He knew exactly what she meant. They'd shared one passion, and that was moving up to bigger and better things.

"Oh, yeah. What's happening, doll-face?"

"This is big, Arnie. Real big. Get a camera and meet me at Senator Wakefield's estate as fast as you can. We're about to get the hottest piece of news in Texas history on tape."

"I'm already gone," he said, and hung up in her ear.

She smiled. Justice. She'd waited a long time for justice, and now it was about to come.

Bobby Lee was on the phone, checking in with his office in Washington, as he heard the sounds of a number of arriving vehicles.

"I think I've got company," he said. "Just follow through on that EPA lobbyist and I'll talk to you when I get in. Yes, tomorrow around noon. We'll have lunch."

Although he wasn't expecting guests, after the bombshell he'd dropped yesterday, it was to be expected. And he wasn't about to turn the media away. Not when he was riding the airwaves on a sympathetic high.

But it wasn't the media who Delia admitted, and when he saw China Brown at the head of the group, his stomach started to roll. She knew. He didn't know how, but she knew!

Ben took the senator by his hand and twisted it around behind his back. One handcuff went on with a snap.

"Bobby Lee Wakefield, you are under arrest for the murders of Charles Finelli and Baby Girl Brown. You are also under arrest for the murders of Tashi Yamamoto, LaShon Fontana and—"

When the other handcuff snapped around his wrist, Bobby Lee's mind went blank. He could see the detective's mouth still moving, but he could no longer hear the words. His world had narrowed to the woman who was pointing her finger, saying things he didn't want to admit.

"You shot me," China said. "I did nothing to you, and you still shot me as if I were a stray dog."

"No," he mumbled. "Not me. It wasn't me. You've got it all wrong. It was my mother, remember? You identified her already, and you were right. She's crazy white trash. Who knows why she did it, but she was always into sex. Every kind of sex with all kinds of men."

"You lie!"

Everyone turned.

Mona Wakefield stood in the doorway like an avenging angel, her hair a mess and still wearing her son's clothes. She tried to push her way past the officers, and they immediately stopped her.

"Let her pass," Ben said, and then from the corner of his eye, he saw another car arriving out in front. It was Connie Marx. She hadn't wasted any time. The way he figured it, she'd earned at least this much redress.

Mona's legs were shaking almost as hard as her voice. Seeing all these officers in her own home and knowing why they'd come was almost more than she could bear. She couldn't look at Bobby Lee. Not yet. Not until she'd said what she had to say.

She stopped in front of Ben and then handed him a fistful of receipts.

"I found these in my son's clothes at our cabin at Lake Texoma," she said. "I believe there's a receipt, in his name, for a particular gun that the serial killer is known to have used—the very gun I found beneath the spare tire in my car. The car I so graciously loaned to my son whenever he wanted to be on his own. There's also a closet full of dresses at the cabin, some that I dare say will bear traces of blood, and an armoire full of interesting, though cheap, blond wigs. Not at all my style."

"Mother! What are you saying?" he gasped. "You can't blame me. I'm your son."

Mona flinched, and then she slowly turned to stare her son in the face. The death penalty. He would get the death penalty. Texas was not a forgiving state in matters of justice. Man or woman, young or old, if the courts sentenced you to die, then die you did. Her lips began to quiver as her eyes filled with tears.

"Not anymore. As far as I'm concerned, you are now the orphan you always wanted to be."

"No," Bobby Lee wailed. "I didn't mean it. I never mean what I say, you know that. Tell them I'm sorry. Tell them and make it okay."

She stared at him as if she'd never seen him before, and, truth be told, she wondered if that was true. In her mind, had she made him the son she'd always dreamed of, rather than the bastard he'd always been? It didn't matter now. Nothing mattered. She turned away, and as she did, she saw a woman standing near the wall. Immediately, she knew who she must be.

"You...are you the woman he shot?"

China didn't answer—couldn't answer.

"You are, aren't you?" Mona sighed, and the tears

began to roll. "I don't know what to say to you. Because of my family, you lost your child. I understand your pain, because I just lost mine, too. I'm sorry. So sorry." Then her shoulders slumped, and for the first time, Mona Wakefield looked every one of her sixty-eight years. "Detectives, do your thing. I will be making a statement to the press in the morning. I assume the charges against me will have been dropped by that time."

"Yes, ma'am, and thank you for coming forward," Ben said.

"Had I known what I harbored, I would have done it sooner."

The room became a turmoil of shuffling feet, along with the sounds of Bobby Lee Wakefield's shrieks and promises to repent. China stood for a moment, pinned against the wall by the crowd of people and a woman with a camera.

"China?"

She turned. Ben was calling her name, a worried expression on his face.

"I'm okay," she said, and pushed her way through the crowd and walked out of the house.

Lifting her face to the sunshine, she closed her eyes and drew a deep breath of air. A light, sweet scent filled her nostrils, telling her that somewhere nearby there were lilacs in bloom. The warmth on her face, the sound of a bird chirping in a nearby tree…the peacefulness of it all filled her heart.

She could walk a street when she wanted to.

Shop in a mall if she chose.

Walk in the sunshine and never have to fear she'd be shot in the back.

It was over.

Epilogue

Spring was moving on toward summer. Bluebonnets were in bloom and everything had turned a vivid shade of green—from the pastures on the English ranch to the trees along the highways. Everywhere the eye might see, the earth was alive and flourishing.

China sat on the back porch, watching Ben cut hay in the pasture beyond the house. Behind her, the house was quiet, the rooms echoing only with the sounds of her own footsteps now that Mattie and Dave had married and she'd moved up the road to be with him.

There had never been a question of China leaving. She belonged here now, just like she and Ben belonged together. There were days when she saw the hunger on his face, the times when she knew he held his tongue for fear of pushing her too fast. She loved him with a passion she hadn't believed existed. But he wanted his ring on her finger. He wanted to call her more than China, more than the woman of his heart. He wanted to call her wife.

It was strange that she'd resisted. She couldn't imagine being anywhere else or with any other man. Something in her was changing, though. She could feel it day by day. She glanced at the position of the sun, judging the time against when she would need to prepare a meal. It would be hours yet before Ben would come in from the field.

Restless, she stood abruptly, dusted off the seat of her shorts and started toward the barn to see Cowboy. As she walked, she stopped at the gate as she always did, burying her nose in the burgeoning bank of the honeysuckle and inhaling the rich, sweet scent. As she did, a flutter of motion caught her eye, and she lifted her head to look.

There, hanging from what appeared to be a tiny gray thread, was a splitting cocoon, and emerging from the hanging sarcophagus was a small butterfly, its wings still wet and folded against its body.

It was a miracle, this witnessing of rebirth, and she held her breath as she watched the butterfly crawl to a nearby branch and hang, like a piece of silk in the wind, while it waited for its wings to dry. Little by little, the wings began to flutter, then open, revealing shades of vivid yellow framed by whorls of shining jet. It was like staring into the pattern of a stained-glass window and seeing light through all the pieces.

China held out her finger and, as if sensing the warmth of her skin, the butterfly crawled on and then stayed there, postponing its moment of flight.

Somewhere in the back of her mind she was a child again, hiding from Clyde beneath her mother's front porch. She could see that small brown worm inching its way through the grass, could remember feeling as ugly and insignificant. She'd lived her life in that frame of mind, never seeing herself as a vibrant woman but through the eyes of a bitter man. He'd called her ugly and tried to drown her the way people drown animals they no longer want.

Even though she'd grown and flourished, there was a part of herself she'd kept hidden away. And it had hung in the back of her mind just like the cocoon was hanging on the bush, unaware that all the while, her thoughts were changing—changing.

As she watched, the butterfly suddenly lifted from the end of her finger, fluttering upward like a helicopter lifting off from a pad. Then, caught by a passing breeze, the bright yellow butterfly disappeared beyond the house.

She stood there in shock, looking around at all there was before her, and then slowly lifted her hands to her face. They began to tremble as she felt her features, sculpting them anew in her mind. Then, suddenly, she had to see for herself if what she felt was really true.

She bolted into the house, running through the rooms until she came to the mirror in her room. She stood, staring at the woman who looked back.

Her hair was thick and long and tied at the back of her neck with a piece of ribbon that was as blue as her eyes. Her face was flushed beneath a light tan, and there was a smile on her lips that came from within. She reached out toward the mirror and laid trembling hands on the glass, but the woman she saw wasn't there. She moved her hands to her own face and felt the heat of her skin, and then closed her eyes in quiet joy.

Somewhere between the loss of a child and the arms of her man, she'd turned into something grand—a woman who was beautiful because she was loved.

She moved back, loath to tear herself away from the joy on that woman's face, and then she smiled. The woman smiled back, as if to say, *It's okay. I'll always be here.*

China laughed and walked out the door, her stride lengthening with each step she took. By the time she cleared the yard and headed toward the pasture where Ben was cutting hay, she was running.

Ben saw her coming. Fear leaped within his heart when she began to run. And then he saw her face and realized she was laughing. He didn't know what had happened, but he wanted to share her joy. He stopped the tractor in the middle of the field and crawled out of the cab in haste. As he started toward her, it seemed as if she were flying as she leaped one windrow of hay after another, bounding from place to place, like a butterfly darts from flower to flower.

He caught her, laughing, although he didn't know why. And when she dug her hands through the sweat-dampened ends of his hair and told him that she loved him, he knew something had changed.

"What happened?" he asked.

But there was no way she could explain the way she felt inside. So she did the only thing she could. In so many words, she handed him her heart.

"Bennie, if I asked you something serious, would you tell me the truth?"

"Always."

"Promise?"

He grinned. "I promise."

"I'm beautiful to you, aren't I?"

Breath caught in the back of his throat, and his eyes filled with tears.

"Yes, baby, more than words can say."

She laughed, and then threw her hands up over her head as if she'd scored a major victory.

He didn't know what was happening, but he was beginning to like it.

"Then don't you think you should marry me quick before men start lining up at the door?"

His lips tilted upward as joy began to fill his heart.

"China Brown, are you proposing to me?"

She grinned. "Yes."

He picked her up and then turned in a slow, silent circle, savoring the sound of her laughter and the soft, sexy curves against his chest.

"So, is this a yes?" China asked.

He started to smile.

"It's yes!" she crowed. "The man says yes!"

"I don't know what happened to you, but whatever it is, I am eternally glad."

China kissed him soundly, savoring the truth in her heart.

"It was nothing," she said. "I just saw a butterfly."

* * * * *

Dear Reader,

I am so excited that one of my favorite stories, *Protective Instincts,* is finally available again! I loved writing this story. There is nothing like a sexy hero and a determined heroine to set the pages on fire. I love New York City, so the setting of this one was so much fun to incorporate into the mystery.

Settle in with a nice cup of hot tea and get ready for plenty of twists and turns! Be sure to visit my website, www.debrawebb.com, for news about upcoming books!

Enjoy!

Debra Webb

PROTECTIVE INSTINCTS
Debra Webb

Prologue

"Now who's in control, Ned?"

The razor-sharp edge of the dagger she held glistened in the light. He tried to speak…to beg, to tell her he would do anything she asked, but he couldn't. He could only mumble through the scrunched-up panties she'd forced into his mouth. Why had he let her into his apartment? He should have realized something was wrong…but she'd distracted him.

"Oh, that's right," she said, her voice condescending, as she trailed the metallic tip down the center of his chest. A crawling shiver followed its path. "You can't talk right now, can you?" She smiled a sick, sinister smile he'd never seen on her before.

He needed desperately to swallow. He tried, gagging reflexively on the nylon choking him. His eyes burned. He was a grown man and he was going to cry. Why the hell was she doing this?

A sheen of sweat coated his skin. His heart pounded harder, making his chest ache, as she walked all the way around him. *Please, please,* he prayed, *let this be just an-*

other of her games. He didn't want to die like this, naked and tied to a chair. He didn't want to die at all.

"If they found you like this," she continued, her tone casual, as if tying up a man at gunpoint and then waving a dagger in his face was an everyday affair, "maybe they'd recognize you for the pervert you are." She checked the rope binding his wrists behind his back. He groaned and tried to pull away.

Ned closed his eyes and fought another sting of tears. Surely she couldn't mean to—

"Look at me, *Dr.* Harrison," she ordered.

He opened his eyes. She stood in front of him now, the tip of the blade pressed against the flesh directly over his heart. It thundered savagely. So hard he could scarcely draw a breath.

What had he done to her that was so bad? She'd enjoyed the sex just as much as he had. And, as he always did, he'd ended the brief affair on an upbeat note and she hadn't complained. Why now?

"All those women, Ned." She shook her head in disapproval. "You're a user," she snarled. "You strike when your prey is the most vulnerable. You're nothing but scum."

He whimpered, the sound small and desperate. No! He wanted to scream. He was a great man. He'd achieved far more in his psychiatric practice than he'd ever dreamed possible. How could this happen now? They'd all been willing. He hadn't forced any of them. They'd liked it... wanted it...

The tip of the blade pierced his flesh. He felt the warm blood bloom, then ooze down his chest. Felt the tears spill from his eyes. Something like a sob escaped his aching throat. This couldn't be happening to him. Not now.

She laughed, the sound brittle and harsh. "You bastard.

You're not a man, you're a wimp. A real man wouldn't have to prey on vulnerable women. A *real man* wouldn't cry when faced with the truth." She poked him a little harder, drawing blood again. A muffled cry emerged from him. "You're sick. That's what you are. What's next for you—little girls waiting at the bus stop?"

He stilled. The realization hit him like a mallet between the eyes. Damn. So that was what this was all about. She was pissed off because— Dear God, could it be that simple? He snorted, then laughed as best he could with those frigging panties shoved halfway down his throat. What a stupid bitch. What the hell had she expected?

Fury darkened her face. "Are you laughing at me?"

He tried to control himself, but he just couldn't stop. If he hadn't been tied to the chair, he would have doubled over with the laughter bubbling up inside him.

"You son of a bitch."

He laughed, then coughed, almost choking. This was all about one stupid little slut.

"Go to hell!" she snarled, her eyes wild.

She lunged, jamming the dagger into his chest.

His body jerked as his startled gaze collided with hers.

She looked as surprised as he was.

Shaking her head, she backed away from him.

He blinked, then stared down at his chest. The jewel-handled weapon was buried to the hilt.

Shit.

He looked up at her one last time as the narrow focus of death closed in around him.

Chapter 1

Elizabeth Young imagined that Dr. Ned Harrison was every bit as good-looking in death as he'd been in life. The navy-blue pinstripe suit and red power tie had probably been his favorites. The white linen that draped his coffin, along with the six tall candles surrounding it, made an impressive display. But the most effective ploy was the huge choir assembled behind the distinguished-looking priest. The choir's grand entrance, as well as the blessing, had been nothing short of awe-inspiring. And Elizabeth wasn't even Catholic.

It was the perfect send-off for such a highly regarded, nationally renowned psychiatrist. The brooding medieval architecture of the Holy Trinity Church lent a dramatic atmosphere for his final public appearance.

No one who knew him, least of all Elizabeth, would be at all surprised to find Ned's picture on the social page of tomorrow's issue of the *New York Times*.

The city would mourn the loss of a brilliant doctor, and a great number of its female inhabitants would mourn him for completely different reasons.

Elizabeth surveyed the crowd around her as the priest continued to chant mass in solemn, hushed tones. More than half those present were women under forty, fashionably dressed, all beautiful and probably all wealthy.

Though Elizabeth was neither rich nor glamorous, she would bet her next month's earnings that the one thing all the females in this room had in common was that they had slept with the deceased.

Including Elizabeth.

She shifted on the hard wooden pew, knowing full well there was no getting comfortable physically or mentally. What on earth had possessed her to come to Ned's funeral mass? She glanced around at the other women, all facing forward in somber attention, and wondered what *their* reasons for putting in an appearance might be. Maybe rather than mourning or merely showing their respect, they'd all come for the same reason she had—to make absolutely certain that he was really dead.

Of course the visit the homicide detectives had paid her had pretty much driven the point home. The two men had been fairly cordial at first, but the questions had soon turned openly accusing, as had their attitudes. Elizabeth shuddered at the memory of one detective in particular. She hoped she wouldn't have to go through that again. She had a new life here....

Another shudder quaked through her. She'd almost allowed him to ruin everything. How could she have been so foolish?

"Can you believe she wore that dress to a funeral?"

Elizabeth turned her attention to the woman sitting next to her, her one trusted friend. "What?" she whispered.

Gloria Weston angled her head to the right in a gesture that made Elizabeth want to hunker down out of sight.

"Over there. The blonde in the devil-red dress," Gloria elucidated beneath her breath.

Elizabeth strained to look without actually moving her head. She frowned. "Do you know her?" The woman looked vaguely familiar to Elizabeth, but she couldn't quite place her.

Gloria shook her head. "She looks like that model who had all that trouble last year. I don't know. She's probably just another one of Ned's hussies."

Elizabeth cocked an eyebrow. "What does that make us?" she murmured.

Gloria snorted softly. Fortunately no one seemed to notice the rude sound. "Fools," she retorted. "Just like the rest of them."

Elizabeth didn't want to think about that—or the telephone call she'd gotten from Ned late Friday afternoon. The slimeball. He'd called two or three times last week, begging her to have dinner with him. "Just to talk," he'd assured her. "I'm not ready to let you go," he'd added in that charismatic voice of his. What a jerk. She knew what he wanted all right, and she had no intention of falling into that trap again.

No way.

But on Friday she'd gone to the restaurant, anyway. He'd made her an offer she couldn't refuse. Her pulse quickened at the thought of the videotape. It was the only reason she'd gone. And then he hadn't shown up. She'd wanted to kill him. Who'd have thought that a few days later she'd be attending his funeral? It was eerie. She shivered. What if the detectives had found...?

No. She resisted the urge to shake her head. She wouldn't think about that. They would definitely have mentioned that little fact.

"Look." Gloria nodded toward another woman who sat

two rows up. This one had coal-black hair cut in one of those sleek, face-hugging styles. She sported a dress that defied any description Elizabeth might have attempted. "That's Vanessa Bumbalough," Gloria said, one hand over her mouth to muffle the words.

The name didn't ring a bell. The woman sat next to a man who resembled the late John Lennon in profile. He hadn't bothered to remove his sunglasses. Elizabeth's brow furrowed in question as she leaned fractionally closer to her friend. "Who's Vanessa Whatever-you-said?"

The man sitting directly behind them cleared his throat. Elizabeth cringed. Gloria ignored him. "She's a new phenomenal fashion designer. She's been all over the papers lately. Don't you ever read?" Gloria made an impatient face. "Apparently her designs stole the show at this season's big fashion debut. The whole industry's up in arms. She's hot, hot, hot."

Ned wouldn't have chosen her otherwise, Elizabeth mused. The man had a reputation to maintain, after all. She winced at the idea of just how gullible she herself had been. How could she have thought that Ned Harrison was really interested in her? She wasn't beautiful in the classic sense of the word, though she wasn't exactly chopped liver, either. She possessed no real social graces, and couldn't tolerate contact lenses, leaving her no alternative but to wear glasses. Even worse, she'd done the unthinkable by giving up a prestigious job at a ritzy interior design firm and taking what most would consider blue-collar work in a city where one's profession was the single most qualifying factor for being a part of the *in* crowd.

Screw the in crowd. Elizabeth was happy just as she was. Well, for the most part, anyway.

She glanced at her friend. Gloria was one of the city's beautiful people. Petite, a head of fiery-red corkscrew curls, pixie features. Not to mention she had one of those awe-inspiring power jobs on Wall Street. Wherever Gloria was, everyone always flocked to her and wanted to know the inside scoop. People loved her. She was a smooth operator, as street-smart as she was business-savvy, and a real sweetheart, especially if she liked you. She was the first friend Elizabeth had made when she arrived in the city. She'd met her at one of Brian's, her ex-fiancé's, infamous parties. Gloria had been there for Elizabeth ever since…through everything. The breakup with Brian, leaving the firm and having to find a new, low-rent place to live. Elizabeth owed her. Big time.

Ned "the Casanova Shrink" Harrison had almost cost her that friendship. And he definitely was not worth it.

Then again, he hadn't deserved to be murdered, either. Elizabeth didn't like the trickle of guilt she experienced on the heels of that thought. It was true that she'd felt just a little glee upon reading of his abrupt demise in Sunday's paper, but then she'd caught herself. That she'd spoken with him only hours before his unfortunate date with destiny was definitely unnerving. What if he'd actually shown up for their dinner date and laid on the charm? What if she'd fallen under his spell one last time?

Last being the operative word. She shivered as her mind conjured up the murder scene the newspaper had described in grim detail.

Dying in such a humiliating manner was overkill, she reasoned, no pun intended. Sure, there'd been a moment or two when she could have killed him herself, but the truth was she was an adult. It wasn't like Dr. Harrison had taken advantage of a helpless child. She'd made a conscious decision to enter into a sexual relationship with him. As had, she presumed, the rest of those assembled here today. She scanned the seated crowd of women who could easily inspire an issue of *Vogue* or *Glamour.* The mass ended and the priest began the eulogy. His opening remarks bemoaned the great man New York City had lost. Elizabeth wondered for a few moments if the kindly Father would have waxed so eloquently if he'd had a loved one who'd been one of Ned's conquests.

"Look," Gloria murmured, then inclined her head toward the aisle that separated the rows of pews. "Remember her from the party the other night?"

Elizabeth peeked past her friend to the woman in question as she scooted in at the end of a row. The rustle of silk and lightweight wool accompanied the efforts of those already seated to accommodate the newcomer. The woman was tall, impossibly thin and, of course, beautiful. Supermodel material. Elizabeth did remember her. If memory served, she was an actress. Soaps, that was it. She'd just landed some bit part in a soap. Elizabeth nodded in response to her friend's expectant expression.

She remembered the party, too. She hated those kinds of parties, but Gloria dragged her to them, anyway. Hardly a weekend night went by without some sort of party Gloria insisted they simply could not miss. Luckily they'd only run into Brian a few times. But no matter where they went, the crowd was always the same: a little too wild for Elizabeth's liking. Gloria called her a party pooper, when the truth was, Elizabeth was simply a homebody. She wasn't into the party scene the way Gloria and her other friends were.

Besides, it had been only ten months since she and Brian parted ways. That was entirely too long in Gloria's opinion for Elizabeth to still be afraid to go out on a limb with someone new. But Elizabeth didn't see it that way. In spite of her mother's desertion, she'd been raised in a small town where people mated for life, not

for one night. Although, she'd be the first to admit that
Brian had not been the love of her life. Rather, he'd been
a means to an end. She just hadn't seen it until it was too
late. She had regrets, but only a couple. Moving to New
York had been the right thing to do. Breaking out on her
own with the only real skills she possessed was also the
right thing to do, even if it had been scarier than hell at
first. But she'd survived.

She'd survived Ned Harrison, too, hadn't she? How
could Gloria have expected her to look for a new love
when Elizabeth had gotten so tangled up in Ned's web
of deceit?

Elizabeth shook off the disturbing thoughts. She was a
survivor. That was what her daddy had always said, and
her daddy had been a very smart man.

Moistening her lips to conceal the tiny smile thoughts
of her father evoked, Elizabeth straightened and focused
her attention on the priest's words. She was here. She
might as well pay attention. She darted a look at her
friend. Gloria appeared to have finally settled in now
that she'd scrutinized the crowd. A mixture of affection
and respect bloomed in Elizabeth's chest. Gloria was in
a league of her own. It seemed impossible that Ned, the
heartless bastard, had fooled her. Well, maybe even Gloria had her vulnerable spot.

Lord knew, Ned Harrison was an expert at finding
those spots.

Elizabeth drew in a heavy breath. They'd both survived Ned—but would she survive his murder?

Special Agent Collin MacBride paid little attention
to the priest's words as he continued his evaluation of
the attendees. The group was a veritable cast of who's

who from the city's high society and the up-and-coming. Mostly women. No surprise there.

Mac watched one woman in particular. Elizabeth Young. He shifted slightly so that he could see her better. Tall, slender. She wore a black dress, though not the kind one expected to see at a funeral.

Then again, none of the women present were dressed in proper mourning attire. Things had definitely changed since his days as an altar boy. He saw enough long, shapely legs and silk fabric here to feel as if he was watching a fashion runway loaded with Victoria's Secret models, rather than a nave filled for a funeral service. Amid the variations of in-vogue sameness was Elizabeth Young. Oh, she wore the little black dress rightly enough, yet she was decidedly different.

Tall, even wearing flat-heeled shoes, she didn't walk with the same confident glide as the others. No nail polish, very little makeup. He'd gotten a pretty good look at her when she first entered the church. He'd been standing in the shadows near the massive double doors. She and her friend, one Gloria Weston, had hurried to find a seat as if they feared they might miss the opening act of the hottest new Broadway play.

Elizabeth Young wore glasses, the small, gold-wire-rimmed kind. Oddly enough, there was something appealing about the prim look they gave her, along with her neatly braided hair. He cocked an eyebrow at the direction his meandering thoughts had taken. He'd definitely gone too many hours without sleep. Anytime he looked at a possible suspect and found her appealing in some way, he needed to recharge his batteries. Years of training and field experience weren't supposed to just fly out the window. Where was his usual control? Down the toilet, obviously, with his patience for bumbling homicide detectives. He gritted his teeth when he considered how badly they'd screwed up.

Next to him, Luke Driver edged a bit closer and in a low voice said, "She doesn't really look like the type who could bury a knife into a man's chest."

Mac glanced at his brand-new partner, a kid fresh from the Farm. Luke had a lot to learn that only experience would teach him. "They usually don't," he returned, putting forth a concerted effort not to show his impatience. What the hell did he think? That a killer walked around with an identifying mark stamped on his forehead?

Driver shrugged, too cocky to be embarrassed. "I mean, she just doesn't look like the type who screws around with some guy, then sticks him."

Still waters ran deep more often than not, Mac considered, but said, "Harrison's murder was an emotional kill, an act of passion. You saw the videotape. Miss Young is certainly capable of the necessary emotion."

"Man, is she," Driver muttered wistfully.

Mac clenched his jaw as the images he'd watched on that videotape quickly played in the private theater of his mind. Oh, yeah, Elizabeth Young was definitely passionate. His pulse quickened as his mind focused on one particularly vivid image of her nude body. Streaks of gold highlighted her lush brown mane of hair as it glided over her skin with her rhythmic movements atop her lover. Small, firm breasts jutting forward, begging to be tasted. She might not have that high-class walk down pat, but she damn sure had the art of sex down to a science. Mac's groin tightened before he could stop his reaction.

Mentally cursing himself, he looked away from her then. Elizabeth Young wasn't just a suspect; she was the prime suspect in this high-profile murder investigation.

The last thing he needed was a genuine case of pure lust. The facts were all he needed. And he had several of those.

Ned Harrison had had a dinner appointment with Elizabeth Young at seven o'clock on Friday night. By nine he was dead. The homicide detectives had found the very private, definitely X-rated videotape of Harrison and Elizabeth Young hidden in his bedroom. There was no way to determine when it had been made. Other tapes had been found, as well, more than two dozen. Ned had been a busy man. All the tapes except Elizabeth's had been safely tucked away in his walk-in closet, right behind his wall of Armani and Donna Karan suits. Each had been labeled with a name and date—all except Elizabeth's.

Mac didn't know yet what made hers different. But he would find out. *That* she could count on. It was an absolute miracle the detectives hadn't given away that ace in the hole. At least they'd had sense enough to keep the tapes to themselves when conducting their hasty interviews and spilling their guts to the media.

As if that fiasco wasn't enough, the so-called rush-rush forensics report that should have been ready yesterday was stuck in a political bottleneck. He'd had to fight like hell to get jurisdiction over this case. It was Wednesday already and he hadn't even been allowed to interview any witnesses or suspects. Hell, he hadn't even gotten the detective's report until this morning. He hated delays; he hated screwups even more. One brash detective had already royally screwed up by pushing Miss Young until she went on the defensive—the absolute wrong thing to do. What did they teach these guys in detective school?

Mac folded his arms over his chest and seethed. Now, five days after the man's murder, he'd finally gotten the word to proceed as lead on the case. If he could just get his hands on the damned autopsy report, he'd be in business.

Yep, he hated delays, hated not knowing the facts. Simple things, like whether or not Harrison had had sex before he died or if he'd been drinking. The only two things he did know at this point were the approximate time of death and the apparent cause of death. Brannigan, the shoot-first-ask-questions-later detective from the NYPD working on the case in supposed cooperation with Mac, was running down the history of the dagger. Was it a part of Harrison's personal collection? Or had the killer brought it with her or him?

Mac had a gut feeling that it belonged to Harrison. He owned an extensive collection of antique swords and daggers. Too bad one of his toys had been used against him.

Some hobby, Mac mused. He imagined that the weapons gave the guy a sense of power. He wondered how powerful he'd felt when one was jammed between his ribs.

Mac hadn't liked Ned Harrison. He liked him even less now that he was dead. It blew Mac's ongoing case all to hell. Mac, as a member of a special task force, had been watching Harrison for weeks, hoping for a break in the case concerning illegal Internet activities of a group known only as the Gentlemen's Association. Harrison was the first of the group they'd been able to pinpoint and identify. Now he was dead, leaving Mac back at square one. The Bureau wasn't very happy about that, which only added to the maelstrom of the past five days.

It was definitely possible that Harrison's death was a well-planned hit designed to look like a crime of passion. The head of the Gentlemen's Association might have learned that Harrison had been compromised. But Mac couldn't see how anyone could know that the feds were on to Harrison. Mac had been too careful. It made more sense that it was just what it appeared to be. But before he scrapped Harrison as a lead and moved on, leaving the final mop-up details to the local homicide detectives, Mac intended to be sure there was nothing else to be garnered about this association from Harrison's life or his death.

He'd gleaned every bit of information about the man that his past offered. Harrison had risen above his orphaned beginnings. Both he and his only sibling, a twin brother, had done well for themselves despite a bad beginning. His brother's death four years ago had left Harrison alone in the world since he'd opted not to marry and have a family of his own. But men like Harrison were too selfish to give enough of themselves to have any kind of real family.

"Our lady is on the move," Driver warned beneath his breath.

Mac jerked to attention, his gaze seeking Elizabeth Young. She was working her way to the end of the row, muttering *excuse me*s to those seated between her and the aisle. Now just where the hell was she going? Heads turned as she dashed down the aisle, past Mac and into the vestibule.

He glanced at Driver, giving him an unspoken command to stay put. Mac slipped quietly into the large entry hall. He watched, remaining still and silent, as Elizabeth Young pushed up her glasses and swiped her eyes, then wrapped her arms around her middle. She was trembling. Had her heinous deed finally pinged her conscience? Or maybe she was considering everything the cops had openly accused her of in the past two days.

Without making a sound, he stepped closer and instinctively offered her the crisply starched handkerchief from his coat pocket. He never could tolerate a weeping female. "Are you all right?"

Elizabeth stared at the white handkerchief for several seconds before she reluctantly accepted it. "Thank you," she murmured without looking at him. "I'm okay."

Another step disappeared between them. "Did you know him well?"

Her head shot up at that question. She looked straight into his eyes, then blinked. "What?"

He inched closer. "Dr. Harrison," he offered, coming closer still. Close enough to watch the pupils of her eyes dilate when she realized she was alone with a stranger who was suddenly in her personal space.

"I mean," he explained carefully, keeping his voice low, soft, "you're so upset, I thought maybe you were family or maybe his girlfriend."

Her fingers clenched the white cotton. She didn't even breathe—at least, not that Mac could see. She looked like a deer caught in the headlights of an oncoming car, frightened but too shocked to react.

She shook her head finally, the movement strained. "No. I...I'm...a former patient."

Mac nodded, then shrugged one shoulder. "I suppose losing your therapist can be overwhelming."

Her gaze narrowed at the hint of sarcasm in his voice. Dammit. He hadn't meant to let it slip out. She looked him up and down for the first time. "I'm sorry, I didn't get your name."

Mac smiled, the one the ladies always told him they liked. All confidence and charm. If Miss Young liked it, she showed no outward indication. "Collin MacBride." He started to offer his hand but decided against it, since he was more than a little certain the offer wouldn't be well received.

She was clearly suspicious now. She pushed her glasses higher on her nose and asked, "Were *you* one of his patients, too?"

Smart lady, Mac admitted. She was watching closely for any signs of lying. She might look like the naive librarian who needed to get laid, but she hadn't fallen off the turnip truck just yesterday. "No," he confessed. "Just a friend."

She shoved the handkerchief back at him without having used it. "Thank you, Mr. MacBride, but I should get back."

"Wait." He stopped her before she could escape. She looked back at him from the entryway to the nave, reluctance slowing her. He cranked up the wattage of his smile. "You didn't tell me your name."

Something flickered in those amber eyes, fear, anger, both maybe. "No," she said, her voice tight with something like disdain. "I didn't."

She left him staring after her. The all-natural, almost tomboyish gait made his gut clench.

Mac's smile widened. *Let the games begin.* She had until tomorrow morning and then she was his.

However smart she thought herself to be, whatever cover-up skills she'd learned since the last time she'd stabbed a man in the chest, it wouldn't be enough. Mac would not give up until he knew everything she'd seen, said and done where Ned Harrison was concerned.

Elizabeth Young had herself a new shadow.

Sad...so sad.
We want to weep, but the tears won't come.
We miss him already.
It's all their fault. All those pretty bitches.
One of them...no, no, all of them stole him away. They

made him weak. Made him want things he shouldn't. Now he is lost. And we are sad.

    They will pay.
    They all will pay.

Chapter 2

She'd had more than enough time for the shock to fade and the reality of Harrison's death to steep her conscience, Mac decided. That was assuming she had a conscience. Considering the bout of tears she'd suffered at the funeral, he was relatively certain she still had one. Driver had been right in that respect. Mac really didn't see her as a cold-blooded killer. But jealousy could drive people to do things they normally wouldn't. Or maybe she'd found out what Harrison was doing with his videotaped sessions. That would piss anybody off.

It was 8 a.m. and Mac had opted to leave Driver back at 26 Federal Plaza to work on yanking Brannigan's chain regarding the origin of the murder weapon. Quite honestly, Mac preferred questioning a suspect alone the first go-around.

He'd arrived at Elizabeth Young's small Leonia apartment at 7 a.m. sharp. On the Jersey side of the Hudson, the apartment was actually the attic-turned-living-space portion of an older home owned by an elderly woman who lived alone and no longer needed the additional space. According to the landlady, who acted as a sort of answering service, Miss Young had already left for the job site this morning. Another two steps in the wrong direction for Mac. The most effective interviews were conducted on the suspect's home turf where they were the most comfortable. Who'd have thought she'd be up and at 'em so damned early?

Mac checked the street and number he'd jotted on his notepad again. Almost there. He drove past some of the city's finest cast-iron architecture with the ornate facades and oversize windows until he reached the SoHo address the landlady had given him. He parked in a nearby alley and walked to the entrance of the four-story building. One second turned to five as he studied the top-floor windows before going inside. When he entered the lobby, he found scaffolding and indications of ongoing plaster repair on the walls and ceiling. An ancient warehouse turned residential lofts, eight in number and with price tags to match the upscale address, no doubt.

He boarded the old-style freight elevator and set it into motion. Though in a state of refurbishment, the building, as well as the location, was a far cry from Elizabeth Young's own current home address.

He already knew her poignant Cinderella story. Her defense attorney would use that saga to sway sympathy from the jury when the time came. Small-town girl falls in love with big-city boy and follows her heart in hopes of making all her dreams come true. Then, as dreams have a way of doing, they'd crashed down around her. The love of her life had turned out to be a lying, cheating, smooth-talking womanizer. Poor Elizabeth had suddenly found herself on her own in the big, bad city.

The elevator came to a stop, groaning loudly in protest. Somehow, though, Mac thought with a twinge of respect that annoyed the hell out of him, she'd managed to land on her feet. She'd found an affordable, yet tolerable place with reasonable rent, and she'd fallen back on the trade she'd learned from her father—painting. Not the artsy kind, but the plain old, elbow-grease-required, interior-redecorating sort.

In the past eight months she'd built up a solid reputation and enough business to merit hiring a helper. Mac walked down the corridor toward the open door on the right. There were two large lofts on each floor, one on either side of the centrally located elevator. Since the other door was closed, it made sense to go for the open one first.

He supposed her helper was about somewhere. She'd picked herself a real winner there, too. Mac wondered if she had any idea the con artist she'd hired had a rap sheet as long as his arm. But then, her own rap sheet was nothing to scoff at—which was another thing they had to discuss. According to Detective Brannigan, she didn't like to talk about her past. Mac felt fairly certain she wouldn't care for any of his questions, especially after the report he'd read this morning.

The preliminary report from the medical examiner stated that Harrison had had sex just prior to his death. The only substantial clue as to the identity of the person with whom he'd had sex was a single pubic hair that didn't belong to the deceased. Well, that and a few healthy scratches on his neck that were only a couple of hours old at the time of death. DNA testing was already under way. All they needed was a comparison sample to try for a match.

Miss Young wasn't going to like that, either.

Mac paused in the open doorway and surveyed the scene before him. Beaumont Devers, better known as Boomer to his friends, stood on a ladder applying long brush strokes of white paint to the wall around the expansive windows. According to his file, he was just over six feet in height and a wiry 140 pounds. His twenty-second birthday had come and gone a month ago, but his crime-ridden teenage years had left their mark on his thin face. A white scar, which stood out despite his fair complexion, stretched downward from his hairline through his right eyebrow, leaving it with a permanent part. He'd buzzed his blond hair to the point of baldness. A number of nasty-looking tattoos adorned any visible flesh below his neck. The tattered jeans and black T-shirt completed the untrustworthy picture.

Mac couldn't imagine what Elizabeth saw in the kid, unless it was a kindredness of spirit. And there was no time like the present to ask. His gaze slid across the empty room to her location facing the wall farthest from him. She rolled the paint onto the wall with broad, even strokes in a sort of zigzag pattern, carefully covering the newly replastered surface with a fresh coat of pristine white paint. Her hair was secured high on the back of her head in a long ponytail. The kind little girls wore when they jumped rope. She wore baggy overalls and a plain white T-shirt. A red shop cloth, stained with a bit of white paint, hung from her right rear pocket.

The image was incredibly innocent-looking and tugged hard on his protective instincts. Another image, one from the videotape, abruptly appeared before his eyes. He blinked, shattering the illusion, but not before it had its usual effect. Even with her head thrown back in ecstasy, she looked somehow vulnerable, innocent.

A muscle pulsed in his jaw. Looks could be deceiving, he reminded that idiotic part of him that stupidly found her appealing. He was halfway across the room, his leather soft-soled shoes silent on the dirty hardwood floor, before she sensed someone's presence and turned around.

"Miss Young," he said as if she should have expected him. "I hope this isn't a bad time."

She looked startled, then annoyed. There was a tiny splatter of white paint on the lower edge of one lens of her glasses, and those amber eyes beneath widened in surprise. Mac heard the ladder creak as Boomer turned to see what the intrusion was about. To his credit he kept his mouth shut. Mac hoped he stayed smart that way.

Elizabeth stared, dumbfounded, at the man standing before her. She remembered him without effort. What was his name? Something MacBride. He wasn't the kind of man one forgot easily. Tall, good-looking, exuding a charm and confidence that any woman would find attractive. What was he doing here? She frowned. The bigger question was why was her heart suddenly pounding as if she'd never been this close to a handsome man before?

New York City was full of handsome guys. But this was the first time a total stranger had affected her so…so deeply. She squared her shoulders and ignored her silly reaction. Nerves, that was all it could be. She'd had a hell of a week so far. Enough to shred anyone's composure.

"We met at the funeral," he offered, apparently taking her silence as a sign that she didn't recognize him.

He extended one broad hand and smiled that cocky, oh-so-masculine smile that was a perfect complement to his polished appearance. The dark-blue suit screamed tailor-made, the white shirt was spotless and crisply starched, and the tie burgundy and probably Cardin. The black leather loafers, no doubt of Italian craftsmanship, were the only deviation from his cutting-edge attire. For stealth, she decided. That was how he'd sneaked up on her the way he had. Those damned soft-soled shoes hadn't made a sound.

Get it together, Elizabeth, she ordered herself, then promptly passed the paint roller and handle to her left hand so that she could swipe her right on the leg of her coverall before accepting his. *Be cool.* He was probably just an insurance salesman. Didn't those guys always hang out at funerals?

The jolt of electricity that passed between them as their palms touched startled her all over again. She jerked her hand back and instantly went on the defensive. "Do you make a habit of looking up all the women you hit on at funerals, Mr. MacBride?"

One side of that full mouth hitched up a little higher. "Only on occasion, Miss Young."

She resisted the urge to rub her still-sizzling palm against her leg again. He was looking at her—no, not just looking, studying her and seemingly contented not to say anything else. Who was this guy? When she could bear the scrutiny of those piercing blue eyes no longer, she said, "So what's the occasion?"

He reached into his interior coat pocket and pulled out a black leather case. Her frown deepened with growing confusion—and then suddenly she knew. He was a cop. Damn. Why hadn't she thought of that? Just what she needed—more questions she couldn't answer.

He displayed his credentials for her perusal, then tucked them back into his pocket. "*Agent* MacBride," he clarified for her benefit in case she hadn't read the fine print on his Federal Bureau of Investigation ID. "I'm looking into the murder of Dr. Ned Harrison. Your landlady said you'd be here."

Ice slid through her veins, followed by a draining sensation that almost buckled her knees. "I've already answered the detectives' questions. I don't know anything else." Dammit, why did her voice have to sound so shaky?

The paint roller felt suddenly too heavy to hold. She swiveled stiffly and placed it in the pan. Her thoughts raced around in her head like a competitor at the Daytona 500 as she straightened. She'd have to talk to Mrs. Polk about giving out her whereabouts to strangers. But that wouldn't have stopped this man, she rationalized, if he'd shown his official ID. Mrs. Polk had no recourse but to answer his questions. What did he want with Elizabeth? She'd told the others everything she knew. There was nothing else that needed telling. Not if she could help it, anyway.

"I just need to clear up a few discrepancies," he offered nonchalantly. "Routine procedure."

Déjà vu hit like a blow to her midsection. The blood on her hands, her ex-brother-in-law screaming in pain. The police handcuffing her and forcing her into the patrol car. Routine procedure often included unjust incarceration. She couldn't afford to miss any more work. The developer would refuse to pay her the remainder of her contract if she failed to finish on time. She had to have these two lofts finished by the end of next week.

She moistened her lips and adopted an outer calm she in no way felt. "All right. I don't know how I can help you, Agent MacBride, but I'll do what I can."

Boomer was watching, his mounting uneasiness radiating clear across the room. She wanted to say something to reassure him, but at the moment she could only stare into the eyes focused so intently on her. Those haunting memories from the past she'd worked so hard to put behind her kept clawing at her shaky bravado.

"According to Harrison's appointment book, you were

scheduled to have dinner with him at seven o'clock the evening he was murdered."

It wasn't a question. He already knew the answer. So did the detectives who'd interrogated her on two different occasions. But he wanted to analyze her answer. She could see it in his overconfident expression. He checked his facts carefully, made his own measured evaluations. He would never take anyone else's word for anything.

Judging by the set of his broad shoulders and the intensity of his gaze, he already knew more about her than she wanted him to know. Far more than the other detectives had bothered to glean. He'd read her file, made calls, had her pegged as a suspect. Had known exactly who she was when he approached her in the church. Dammit, she didn't need this right now. Didn't want to go through this kind of life-shattering, emotion-twisting investigation again.

Why had she lost control during the service? She'd never convince anyone that it had nothing to do with Ned's death and everything to do with fear for herself. Selfish she knew, but the truth. It must have looked as if she'd been overcome by grief—or guilt. And the tape. Hell. What if he'd found the tape? The other two men hadn't mentioned it. Maybe Ned had thrown it away or locked it up somewhere.

"Miss Young?" he prodded.

"That's right," she heard herself say, her voice sounding as if it came from someone else. "But Ned—Dr. Harrison—never showed up at the restaurant."

MacBride slipped his hands into his trouser pockets and inclined his head, his relentless gaze never deviating from hers. "The maître d' confirmed that Harrison never arrived. Where did you go when you left around eight?"

Breathe, she instructed. *In and out.* "Like I told the other gentlemen," she explained, her impatience showing a little, "I went home." She tried not to sound curt, but it was hard not to. She hadn't done anything wrong and she hated being made to feel as if she had. How could this man or anyone else see her as a suspect? Just because of a broken dinner date she hadn't even wanted to accept? Ned, the bastard, had screwed her one last time before getting his, hadn't he?

No, she decided on second thought, that wasn't it. Mac-Bride was basing his theory on her past. *You could never outrun it,* she reminded herself in a moment of inner clarity. *The past always caught up to you.*

He took a step closer. She drew back a step. "Can anyone vouch for your whereabouts?" His tone was calm, but she could feel the fierce determination beneath the innocuous words. "It would be very beneficial if someone could corroborate your statement."

"What's up, Elizabeth?" Boomer planted his long lanky form right between them. She hadn't even heard him climb down from the ladder.

"Who's the suit?" He glowered at MacBride with obvious disdain.

"It's all right, Boomer," she said quickly in hopes of heading off any trouble for the kid. He was loyal to a fault, always her protector, especially when they worked in rougher neighborhoods, which she'd had to do a lot of in the first few months of getting her business off the ground. But he needed to stand clear of this one. "Agent MacBride is with the FBI. He has some questions about Dr. Harrison's death."

Boomer didn't look impressed. He folded his skinny arms over his chest and continued to blatantly size up the agent. "Just let me know if he gives you any trouble. He don't look too friendly to me." He gave their guest one final glare before stalking back to his work.

Elizabeth almost sagged with relief. Things were bad enough without Boomer getting involved. From the unyielding expression on MacBride's face, she was pretty sure he felt nothing that even remotely resembled relief. Indifference or disapproval quite possibly, but definitely not relief.

"The answer to your question is no," she said pointedly. "I don't have anyone who can verify my whereabouts. I'm sure that was in the detectives' report. My landlady was out that night."

Of course he had known that, but rather than comment, he jerked his dark head in Boomer's direction. "Do you know your assistant has a record a mile long?"

Oh, yes. Condescension, as well as disapproval. He not only knew it all, he was above it all. A blast of indignation melted some of the ice paralyzing her from the inside out. "I'm not as naive as you apparently think, Agent MacBride," she replied sharply, her voice too low for Boomer to hear. "I did a thorough background check before I hired him."

One dark eyebrow climbed upward a notch. "You don't mind that he's had a half-dozen drug charges, including possession with intent to sell? Or that he's done time in one of our less-friendly prison facilities?"

Rather than bank her temper, she allowed it to shore up her courage. "Everyone deserves a second chance."

He nodded knowingly, something new, primal, in his eyes. "Ah, yes. How could I have forgotten? You would be a heavy supporter of second chances, wouldn't you?"

Elizabeth looked at him then, really looked at him. She no longer saw the cocky, handsome man in the thousand-dollar suit, who was perfect from the thick black hair he wore in that short, spiky style that drove women crazy all the way down to the expensive leather shoes. What she saw, instead, was a man who'd had his whole life handed to him on a silver platter. Money, the best schools, probably had never worked a day in his life until he'd signed on with the Bureau. And now he shone like a new penny, chasing bad guys and making the world a safer place. A hero...who didn't know the first thing about what it was like to be down on his luck.

Guys like him didn't need second chances. His world was perfect. He probably worked murder cases just to keep life interesting.

"I'm not ashamed of my past, Agent MacBride," she informed him hotly. "I did what I had to do."

"I see."

She didn't miss the effort it took for him to keep a patronizing smile off his face. "Sure you do." He had no idea what her life had been like, and he sure as hell didn't know how she felt. "How could you possibly have a clue?"

"Of course the drugs weren't really *yours*," he offered, a bitter edge to his words that was impossible to miss. "But then, are they ever when an addict gets caught?" He smiled then, and it wasn't pleasant. "And taking a butcher knife to your brother-in-law was certainly a clear case of self-defense. Am I right, Miss Young?"

A new burst of fury flamed inside her. She would not justify herself to him. She'd done this song and dance twice already. He shouldn't even be here. He knew *nothing* about her. "Golly, mister," she tossed back. "You must be psychic. How else could you read my mind so well? Or maybe you've got a crystal ball in your pocket."

He leaned toward her, the briefest flicker of anger in his eyes before he reined it in. The man was a master at concealing his emotions and thoughts. He'd likely spent a lifetime building that level of control.

"Did Harrison do something that made you take that

dagger to him?" he murmured harshly, his breath hot on her face. "Were you about to be dumped *again?*"

Maybe he wasn't so good at restraining his emotions. He was angry—she didn't have to see it in his eyes because she heard it in his voice. She resisted the urge to flee and held her ground. "I told you I went home when he didn't show," she repeated, emphasizing each word and praying he wouldn't see the lie in her eyes. Before good sense stopped her, she added, "And, for your information, I stopped seeing him weeks ago."

He leaned closer still. Her breath caught. His nostrils flared, a feral gleam in his eyes. "As a patient or as a lover?"

She shivered in response to his cold, lethal tone. How could he know that unless he'd seen the tape? Her heart banged painfully against her sternum. No one knew. No one but Gloria, and she would never tell. Elizabeth grabbed back control. Maybe he was guessing. "We weren't—" She started to deny the notion, but he cut her off with a slow shake of his head.

"Don't lie to me, Elizabeth," he warned, the use of her first name only adding to the unbearable tension. "I saw the videotape."

She stumbled back a couple of steps, barely missing her freshly painted wall in her effort to get away from those words—the very words she hadn't wanted to hear. Oh, God. Ned had promised to give her the tape. That night. He was going to give it to her at dinner. He'd said he was sorry. He hadn't meant to hurt her—he'd really liked her. He'd sworn that he'd make it up to her. He'd lied. He'd refused to give her the tape, and then…

She blinked back the tears brimming. She'd believed him one last time and he'd lied to her. And now this man knew. He'd seen her…

As if he actually could read her mind, that relentless gaze traveled slowly down her body, and in spite of everything, heat kindled in its wake. Damn her traitorous body! Her pulse reacted as he retraced his path, then looked directly into her eyes once more. "You can't hide from me, Elizabeth. I'm very good at what I do. You don't want me for an enemy."

"I'd like you to leave now, Agent MacBride," she told him, her voice oddly devoid of emotion and far steadier than she'd believed possible. She had to think. Had to talk to Gloria. Probably needed a lawyer.

"All right. Have it your way." He reached into his pocket.

She gasped.

A grin tugged at one corner of his mouth. "Don't worry, Elizabeth. I've never shot a suspect who didn't shoot at me first."

The urge to slap that smug expression from his face was almost more than she could restrain. He handed her a business card. "I'll see you in my office at five. Today. Don't be late."

Before she could argue, he turned and strode away. She watched, stunned, until he'd left the loft, then she stared down at the card. Her hand trembled.

This couldn't be happening. Not again.

Her heart thundered violently in her chest, making it ache.

Dizziness swamped her. Her body flooded with adrenaline.

She couldn't breathe. Oh, God. A panic attack.

The trembling that had started in her hands quaked through her suddenly unsteady legs. She closed her eyes, took a long, deep breath and let it out to the count of ten, then repeated it.

This was supposed to be behind her. She hadn't lost control over a threatening panic attack since...since her third session with Ned. At least he'd been good for something.

Then he'd seduced her. Elizabeth forced her eyes open and banished those painful memories. She had to move, had to walk off this excess adrenaline.

Back and forth. Back and forth. From one end of the loft to the other. Boomer probably thought she'd lost her mind, but he didn't say anything—just did his job. *Breathe. In...hold...out. Again.*

Ned had taken advantage of her, used her. And now he was dead. She couldn't change that. The trouble was, it looked as if he was taking her down with him. Why hadn't she stayed until he'd given her the tape? She should have done whatever he asked, anything for the tape. But no, she'd stormed off, knowing she'd have no choice but to go crawling back when he called again. She'd been angry. She'd had no way of knowing she'd never see him alive again.

Mac hesitated a moment after pulling back out onto the empty street. His gaze drifted up to the fourth floor where he'd left Elizabeth. He pounded the steering wheel with the heel of his hand. He'd done a bang-up job of recovering the ground the detectives had lost. He called himself every kind of fool. Cool, he was supposed to have played it cool. Give her space, let her tell her story. Gently guide her.

Dammit.

If he could have kicked himself in the ass, he would have. His body hummed with adrenaline. He gritted his teeth and denied the other sensation the sparring had elicited. It was that very reaction that had made him push harder than he'd intended, to go over the line. He'd shaken her but good. The hell of it was, he was just as rattled as she was.

Perfect. Just perfect.

He blew out a disgusted breath.

By five o'clock when she arrived at his office, and she would come, she would most likely have an attorney with her, and then he'd get nowhere even faster. He'd have to try to regain some of the ground he'd lost, attorney present or not.

Mac glanced in the direction of a dark sedan parked on the opposite side of the street in a neighboring alley. But just in case she decided to cut her losses and make a run for it, someone would be watching.

His cell phone rang at the same time that a horn blared behind him. Mac pressed the accelerator and started forward while fishing in his coat pocket for his phone. He answered the call using his earpiece.

"MacBride."

"You're going to love this."

It was Driver. "What've you got?"

"We traced the dagger to an antique shop over on West Fifty-fifth."

"Yeah." Mac knew there was more. He could hear it in his partner's voice. Anticipation spiked.

"It was purchased as a gift for Harrison," Driver told him, dragging out the moment, "by a Miss Elizabeth Young."

Some of Mac's tension eased instantly at the news that at least one loose end was tied up. "Good work." He glanced at his watch and ignored an uncharacteristic twinge of regret that followed directly on the heels of the relief. She'd already lied to him, so he shouldn't be surprised by this latest development. But he was. She'd gotten to him on some level. He didn't like it. Not in the least. "See you in thirty," he told his partner.

Mac dropped the phone back into his pocket. A satisfied smile slid across his face. This would definitely work to his advantage. He couldn't wait to see how Elizabeth planned to talk her way out of this one. He shook his head as he thought of the pretty lady who could win herself an Oscar for her portrayal of innocence and suffering. She would use the hardships of her past as a smoke screen. But she hadn't fooled him at all. Well, maybe he'd been thrown off balance for a moment or two, he admitted. Not now, though. Now he was focused and fully back on track. She wouldn't be able to tap-dance her way out of this one.

"Gotcha," he muttered.

Chapter 3

Elizabeth waited impatiently in Chico's Cantina. One-fifteen. Gloria was late. She let go an unsteady breath and fiddled with the straw in her cola. She had to get hold of herself. She couldn't let MacBride get to her this way. He'd been worse than those two detectives put together. Something was different about him. More intimidating. A subtle ruthlessness that frightened her. He wouldn't give up until he knew everything.

She hadn't done anything wrong. Sure, there'd been moments when Ned's actions had made her want to kill him, but she hadn't. Thinking about it wasn't against the law. Likely dozens of women, especially former patients, had probably thought about it more than once.

Maybe one of them had actually done it.

Elizabeth went rigid. Could one of the women who'd come to his funeral have been his killer? Was that why MacBride was there?

He suspected *her.* That was why he'd been there. Something frigid seeped into her bones. He'd discovered the dinner date and the videotape of her and Ned

together, and he'd put it all together and come up with
murder. She sipped her cola to wet her desperately dry
throat. How long would it be before he found out about
the two big arguments they'd had? Very public arguments in the lobby of Ned's office building—and at that
party. She'd slapped him during the second one. He'd
grabbed her by the shoulders and shaken her and she'd
slapped him again.

And she'd…God, she'd told him he'd be sorry. Had
anyone heard her say it? It had been a threat, there was no
way to interpret the words any other way, but she hadn't
really meant it. Everyone said things like that in the heat
of anger. She wouldn't be the first or the last—except
maybe where Ned Harrison was concerned.

Had she been the last person to threaten him out loud?
In front of dozens of witnesses?

But she hadn't killed him.

Dammit.

Elizabeth pressed a hand to her lips and closed her eyes
long enough to pull herself together. The evidence would
be stacked against her. She was an outsider. Despite having lived here almost two years, she was still an outsider.
It would be much easier and certainly less messy to pin
the rap on her. She could barely afford her rent at the moment. A high-dollar attorney was out of the question. And
if she was stuck in a jail cell, she'd lose her contract on
the rest of the lofts and any prospects of future income.

She had no family who could help. Her sister, Peg,
would sympathize, but it was all she could do to keep a
roof over her three kids' heads. Too bad that scumbag
she'd been married to hadn't had any life insurance. Then
when he'd careened off a bridge and into a river while in-
toxicated, at least he would have been worth something.

Instead, her sister'd had a tough time scraping together the money to bury the worthless bastard.

Elizabeth swiped her eyes and forced herself to think calmly. She wasn't guilty. Surely the real murderer had left some sort of evidence. She knew Ned had been with someone else. It was why he hadn't shown up at the restaurant for their dinner date. Had that woman returned later and killed him, or was it someone else entirely? Maybe she'd even been hiding in the apartment while Elizabeth was there. There was no way to know. She'd thought he was alone when she confronted him. But someone had definitely been there shortly before her abrupt arrival. She'd seen the tousled sheets, smelled the musky scent of sex.

The son of a bitch.

She drew in a deep breath and again focused on calming her racing heart and jangled nerves. When she'd left Ned Harrison he had been very much alive. But MacBride would never believe that. If she admitted that she'd gone to his apartment, he would use it against her. Besides, she was pretty sure no one had seen her. Why give the authorities any more ammunition than necessary? She'd be a fool not to recognize that she was at the top of the suspect list already.

She couldn't tell MacBride anything and risk being charged with Ned's murder. The truth didn't always set you free. Elizabeth knew that better than anyone.

The bell above the door jingled, drawing her back to the here and now. Gloria stood just inside the entrance and scanned the small cantina. Elizabeth waved and her friend rushed over, a briefcase-size purse hanging on one shoulder, a folded newspaper tucked under the opposite arm.

"Sorry I'm late." She dropped into the seat across from Elizabeth. "Last-minute BS on a conference call that shouldn't have lasted more than five minutes." She beamed a smile and lifted one eyebrow triumphantly. "But I saved the account. Everyone, including Murphy, was suitably impressed."

Murphy was Gloria's boss. She continually surprised the man. He knew how good she was and how hard she worked; she'd worked for him for three years now. But somehow she always managed to amaze even him with one more unexpected coup. Gloria insisted it was the luck of the Irish. But Elizabeth knew differently. Her friend was smart and relentless, and had a sixth sense about market maneuvers.

Wriggling out of her elegant suit jacket, Gloria called out her drink order to the passing waitress.

Elizabeth smiled for the first time that day. One of the things she liked most about Chico's was that everyone was treated the same. It didn't matter if you arrived wearing a power suit or baggy denim overalls. People from all walks of life frequented the place. Elizabeth could look around now and point out the stock traders like her friend, the computer geeks, the starving artists and the electricians and plumbers who were much like herself. No one, particularly the cantina staff, seemed to pay any attention to the differences.

"Sounds like your day was better than mine," Elizabeth commented thinly, thoughts of MacBride's visit drawing the black clouds back over her head.

Gloria studied her closely as the waitress plunked her diet soda before her. "What happened?"

Elizabeth clutched her hands together in her lap and swore she would not get emotional. She had to stay calm. "An FBI agent paid me a visit today."

Surprise claimed her friend's features. "An *FBI* agent?"

Elizabeth nodded. "You remember after the funeral

yesterday I told you about the good-looking guy who'd been so nice to me? You know, he gave me his handkerchief, like guys in the old movies we watch?"

A predatory gleam flashed in Gloria's eyes. "Oh, yeah. You said he was really something."

Elizabeth nodded grimly. "He is. He's an FBI agent and he was there watching me."

Disbelief registered. "He told you that?"

Elizabeth shrugged. "In a roundabout way."

Gloria shook her head. "This is insane. How could they suspect you?"

Elizabeth stared at the red-and-white checked tablecloth. God, she didn't want to have to tell Gloria this. The subject was still a little tender between them. But she lifted her gaze back to her friend's and confessed, "He asked me to have dinner with him…the night of his murder."

A beat of silence echoed, blocking out all other sound.

"Ned asked you to have dinner with him?" The color of excitement that had tinged Gloria's cheeks only moments ago faded. "You didn't agree. Not after…"

Her words trailed off. She didn't have to say the rest. Elizabeth knew.

Dammit, she knew.

She blinked back the tears she'd sworn she wouldn't allow to fall. "He said he'd give me the tape."

"The tape?" A stillness settled over Gloria.

Elizabeth nodded. "He promised he would give it to me if I'd have dinner with him." There was no need to tell her the rest. Ned had hurt them both badly enough. She wasn't about to add insult to injury by telling Gloria that he'd gone on and on about how much he cared for Elizabeth. It had been a lie, anyway.

A line of confusion or maybe irritation creased Gloria's usually smooth brow. "And you believed him?"

"I was afraid," she said, her voice trembling. "I didn't know what he'd do with it if I didn't take it when he offered. There's no telling what he might have done if—"

"You're not the only woman he taped," Gloria said bluntly, her voice painfully hollow as all emotion except one—desperation—visibly drained out of her. "He probably had one on all of us."

"Maybe he destroyed the others," Elizabeth hurried to assure her, but they both knew that wasn't likely.

Gloria snorted a dry laugh as she shook her head, her gaze distant, no longer focused on Elizabeth. "That low-life bastard. I should have known he couldn't be trusted."

Elizabeth frowned. "How could you have known?"

Gloria gave a start, as if she'd forgotten where she was. She seemed suddenly nervous. "No, no. I...I meant that neither of us should be surprised by anything the cops uncover about him."

"That's true," Elizabeth agreed slowly. She didn't have time to analyze Gloria's sudden edginess before they were interrupted.

"You ladies ready to order now?" the college-age, scantily clad waitress asked as she paused at their table. Actually, *paused* wasn't an adequate description. Her feet were planted firmly on the floor next to their table, but her hips never stopped swaying, the pencil in her hand poised above her pad.

Gloria ordered her usual salad with dressing on the side. Elizabeth ordered the same, since she wasn't very hungry, anyway. When the waitress sashayed off, Gloria, appearing to relax a bit, propped her elbows on the table and focused on Elizabeth.

"All right, so tell me what the fed wanted."

Elizabeth wrapped her arms around herself, feeling cold and far too much like the way she had that day eight years ago when she'd been in a too-similar situation. "That's easy. He wants to prove that I killed Ned."

"But you didn't kill Ned," Gloria countered, the edge back in her voice. "He can't pin anything on you without evidence."

"He knows we were supposed to have dinner together that night." Elizabeth resisted the urge to look away. This was Gloria. Her best friend in the whole world, no matter what had gone down between them where Ned was concerned, Elizabeth could trust Gloria.

"Did you have dinner together?" she asked pointedly, her eyes giving evidence of the hurt hovering just beneath her strained composure.

"I went. For the tape," Elizabeth added emphatically. "He didn't show. I waited about an hour and then I left."

"Someone at the restaurant saw you, I presume."

Elizabeth nodded. She sat up straighter, feeling oddly ill at ease with the tone of Gloria's voice. What was the deal here? Was Gloria upset about Ned's calling her? Elizabeth had thought they were past all this. The cards had been laid out on the table. Both of them had been taken in by the man. After much shouting and more tears, they'd reached an understanding…and put it behind them.

Until now.

Damn him. If Ned had to die, why didn't he just do it the old-fashioned way? A simple heart attack or massive stroke. Or, hell, even a taxi accident. Lord knew, the cabdrivers in this city were more than a little reckless.

"You told the fed that he didn't show and that you went home, right?"

"Yes, but I don't think he believed me."

A new wariness slipped into Gloria's surprisingly unsympathetic expression. "Why wouldn't he believe you?"

Elizabeth's heart threatened to burst from her chest. She wet her lips and forced out the words she didn't want to say. "Because I lied."

Gloria huffed a sound of disbelief. "Damn it, Elizabeth, why did you do that?"

"I was angry, okay?" she tossed back. The people at the next table turned and stared. She took a breath and ordered herself to be calm once more, then began again, quietly, for Gloria's ears only. "I wanted him to know that he should never call me again. I was tired of him hurting us. So I went to his apartment. I banged on the door until he answered." She shook her head. "He was pulling his clothes on, insisting he was running late." She clenched her jaw to slow the emotions mounting all over again. "He was so apologetic. But I knew he was lying."

"What'd you do?"

"I stormed into the apartment, straight to the bedroom. The sheets were tousled." Her gaze locked with Gloria's. "He'd called and pleaded with me to meet him for dinner, then kept me waiting an entire hour while he had a romp in the sack with someone else."

Gloria closed her eyes, shuddered visibly. "Bastard," she hissed. "I'm glad he's dead."

Elizabeth scrubbed her hands over her face. "We argued. I told him never to call me again. And then I demanded the tape." She made a sound, something along the lines of a laugh, but pathetically lacking in humor. "He just laughed at me. He…" She chewed her lower lip to stem the tears threatening. "He was going to use it to blackmail me. He told me I'd get it when he was through with me." She shrugged, still scarcely believing her own stupidity. "I couldn't believe it."

Gloria's breathing had grown as rapid and shallow as Elizabeth's. "Tell me exactly what you did then."

"I slapped him and he…he tried to…" She frowned, trying to remember the exact sequence of events. "He grabbed my arm and I fought to get away. Then I ran out."

"Okay," Gloria said, visibly grappling for her own composure. "You listen to me, Elizabeth. You do exactly what I say. Do you hear me?"

She nodded.

Gloria released a shaky breath. "You stick to your original story. He didn't show, you went home. Don't tell the cops anything else. This is a high-profile case. They'll want to solve it as soon as possible. Pinning the rap on you would be the fastest route." She reached across the table and placed a reassuring hand over Elizabeth's. "What about the tape?"

God, she could just die. "That's the worst part. He wouldn't give it to me…and the cops found it. That FBI agent, MacBride, told me he'd viewed it."

"Damn."

"My sentiments exactly." Elizabeth stared down at their hands. What a mess. She might as well face it. She was doomed.

"Look," Gloria said, drawing Elizabeth's gaze back to hers. "You didn't kill him. They can't prove you did. Having sex with a man doesn't make you guilty of murder."

Elizabeth smiled. Her friend was right. Regardless of how it looked, she was innocent. "True," she agreed. She studied Gloria for a long moment, trying to see what it was that nagged at her. She supposed her friend was just afraid for her…or angry that Ned had once more hurt her. "I really didn't kill him, you know."

Gloria squeezed her hand. "I know you didn't. The

cops are just looking for an easy out. If they had any real evidence, they'd arrest you."

Been there, done that, bought the T-shirt, Elizabeth thought grimly. "He brought up Billy and the drug charge." Gloria knew the whole sordid story about Billy, the brother-in-law from hell, and the time Elizabeth had claimed her sister's drug stash to save her from a beating. Elizabeth had never even tried drugs, but she had a possession charge on her record because she'd gone the distance for her only sibling.

"Well," Gloria said after a few seconds of consideration. "That still doesn't make you a murderer."

Elizabeth wrapped her arms around herself again, feeling cold. "No, but it puts me at the top of the suspect list."

Gloria frowned suddenly, as if she'd just remembered something important. "You said this MacBride guy is from the FBI?"

Elizabeth nodded.

"Why would the FBI investigate a simple homicide case?"

Not sure she could answer that one, Elizabeth could only speculate. "They must think his murder is connected to others or—" she spread her hands "—to some other criminal activity where the feds have jurisdiction."

"Or maybe we've just seen too many TV dramas," Gloria teased, acting more like her old self now. "Maybe the cops asked for their help since it's such a high-profile case. The media will be all over every aspect of the investigation."

"That could be, I suppose." Another thought occurred to Elizabeth. She shook her head in frustration. "It'd be just my luck that they think I'm some sort of serial killer."

Gloria started to smile, then gasped and pressed her hand to her chest. "Speaking of murder, I almost forgot." She quickly retrieved and opened the newspaper she'd tossed on the bench seat next to her. "Look at this."

She pointed to a headline that read *Fashion Designer Found Murdered.* Elizabeth skimmed the brief article. The details were gruesome.

"Remember her?"

Elizabeth glanced from the unnerving article to her friend. "Should I?"

"Look at the picture." She tapped the photo to the left of the article.

Recognition dawned. The long-legged, raven-haired beauty at the funeral. The one with the John Lennon look-alike for an escort. "Oh, my God." She looked up at Gloria. "She sat a couple rows in front of us at the funeral."

Gloria nodded. "The scuttlebutt is that someone in the industry did in the hottest new competition."

"My God," Elizabeth repeated. She stared at the article again. Who gave the press permission to print such grim information? Weren't these sorts of details supposed to be kept hush-hush? The woman's throat had been slashed. "What kind of person could do that to another human being?"

"Yeah, really." Gloria tapped the newspaper. "That's the murder your FBI agent should be investigating. Not wasting time on some jerk who only got what he deserved."

Elizabeth refolded the paper so she wouldn't have to look at the woman's picture. It was definitely too much right before lunch. "I'll be sure to tell him that at our five-o'clock meeting."

Gloria tensed. "You have to talk to him again today?"

Elizabeth nodded. "At 26 Federal Plaza." Seeing Gloria's gaping expression, she added, "I think he's trying to intimidate me into a confession."

"Don't tell him anything he doesn't need to know," Gloria warned again. "In fact, I'll talk to a friend of mine about a good attorney for you, if you'd like."

A worried sigh escaped Elizabeth. "I hope it doesn't come to that."

When she spoke, Gloria sounded a lot more confident than Elizabeth felt. "I don't think it will. But it would be nice to have the right name to toss around. It might even get the feds off your back."

"Good idea."

The waitress zipped by, pausing only long enough to deposit their salads and ask if they needed anything else, to which they both replied no.

Elizabeth dribbled ranch dressing over her salad, noting that Gloria did not. Her friend was extremely calorie-conscious. Elizabeth supposed it paid to be when you spent twelve hours a day behind a desk. Gloria had made the comment on several occasions that the asses of her female co-workers got wider every day. Gloria had no intention of following that trend. Elizabeth supposed the one good thing about her line of work was that she got plenty of exercise.

She smacked her forehead with the heel of her hand. She'd almost forgotten again. "How's your niece?"

Gloria appeared taken aback by the question. "She's fine. Why do you ask?"

"You mentioned she was having some trouble a couple of months ago, and I keep forgetting to ask how she's doing," Elizabeth explained. Gloria seemed quite put off, which puzzled Elizabeth. The two of them usually talked about everything. Her niece, apparently, was as touchy a subject as Ned.

"You know how it is when you're eighteen and a freshman in college," Gloria said dismissively. "You think nobody knows anything but you. Since her father's death last year, she's sort of withdrawn from everyone, especially her mother. It hasn't been easy, but she's managing."

Elizabeth remembered that terrible night Gloria had called. Her brother-in-law, an NYPD detective, had been killed in the line of duty. His wife and daughter were devastated. Not long after that, Elizabeth's father had died. God, that had been a lousy month.

"I'm glad she's doing better," Elizabeth said, feeling guilty for bringing up the subject, yet knowing she'd feel guilty if she hadn't. "It's tough to lose your father, especially at that age." At any age, Elizabeth thought. She still missed hers. They'd been so close.

Gloria picked at her salad. "She's all my sister has left." Her tone had turned somber. "We have to protect her at all costs."

Elizabeth paused, a forkful of salad halfway to her mouth. Her friend's swift mood changes were immensely disturbing. They were so unlike Gloria. "Of course you have to protect her," Elizabeth agreed gently. "Let me know if there's anything I can do to help."

Gloria smiled, but the expression didn't reach her eyes. "Just keep me up-to-date on what's going on with your fed." Her faint smile widened to a genuine grin. "And remember, if things get too hairy, you can always seduce him."

Elizabeth almost choked on a cherry tomato. "Yeah, right," she muttered when she'd stopped coughing. "I don't think MacBride is seducible." She remembered vividly his steely gaze and precisely controlled responses. He wasn't the kind of man a simple girl like her could get to...even if she wanted to.

"Oh, honey, that's the country girl in you talking,"

Gloria scolded, the words and the tone so very Gloria. "They're *all* seducible. Trust me."

"I'll bear that in mind," Elizabeth replied. She refused to analyze the warm glow that accompanied the ridiculous suggestion. Gloria had no business putting ideas like that in her head. That was the last thing Elizabeth needed. An affair with another man she couldn't trust. Especially considering this one suspected her of murder.

And had seen her naked having sex with another man.

Elizabeth blushed to the roots of her hair. How would she ever face MacBride this afternoon? She had to find a way to keep him from getting to her....

The newspaper didn't do our work justice.
We will have to leave a stronger impression next time.
One pretty bitch down.
One by one we will make them pay.
All of them.
We won't rest until it's done.

Chapter 4

"I'll have to see your ID, sir," the guard posted in the entry hall said as Mac stepped off the elevator.

It wasn't as if he hadn't flashed his ID in the lobby before he boarded the only elevator in the building that went all the way to the top floor. Rather than informing the rookie of that, Mac fished in his pocket for his badge and showed it again.

The youthful cop, whose badge read Ledbetter, flushed. "Sorry, sir, but a reporter managed to get inside last night before the homicide detectives got here and we've all been instructed to double-check IDs."

"No problem," Mac muttered as he ducked beneath the police tape that marked the penthouse apartment off-limits to anyone other than authorized NYPD person-nel. He hadn't needed Officer Ledbetter to tell him that the perimeter had been breached sometime shortly after the discovery of the body. The morning's headlines had screamed that loud and clear. It only made bad matters worse that the breach had occurred before the arrival of the crime-scene techs. No telling what the eager reporter had contaminated in his haste to get the story.

Mac paused long enough in the doorway to slip on latex gloves and paper shoe covers. Every detective and agent was taught to carry extras just in case. One never knew when they'd be needed. As he prepped for entering the crime scene, Mac noted that the handles of the elegant double doors that separated the posh Upper East-side penthouse from the entry hall were sooty with fingerprint powder.

The whish-whish of someone else's paper shoe covers echoed from down the hall. Mac surveyed his surroundings as he made his way in the direction of the sound. A grand dining room and great room flanked the hall on either side a few feet beyond the main doors. A small powder room and guest bedroom lay on the right beyond that, then the hall took a slight turn to the left and opened up into an extravagantly appointed sitting area that bordered a massive master suite.

This was where the murder had taken place.

Mac paused, his gaze landing on the spray of blood fanned over the wall above the headboard. No matter how many crime scenes he'd examined in his ten-year career, the initial sight of spilled blood always rattled him.

The victim would already be in the capable hands of the medical examiner, but telltale signs of the final battle for life she'd waged were clear to all who entered.

Through the floor-to-ceiling windows, which displayed a magnificent Manhattan view, brilliant sunlight poured into the room, gleaming on the plush, sand-colored carpet. Despite the two techs working vigorously, collecting everything from carpet fibers to dust on the glittering chandelier, the room felt vast and empty. The stark white walls framing the room were marred only by the blood that trickled down like garish streamers toward the rumpled bed.

Judging by the spray of blood above the bed, Mac surmised that the victim had been dragged there for the final affront. The tousled condition of the turned-down covers indicated that she'd likely been in bed before or after the intruder arrived. He thought about the undamaged doors, handles and lock assembly he'd viewed while slipping on his gloves and shoe covers, and decided that *intruder* wasn't the right word. Whoever had done this had been allowed in by the victim. Since the front doors were the only means of entry and windows were not likely since they were on the thirtieth floor, he had to assume that the victim knew her killer.

"Agent MacBride?"

Mac turned toward the familiar voice coming from the doorway behind him and bit back a curse. Detective Brannigan. The last person he wanted to see. He hoped like hell the guy wasn't the lead on this investigation, because he was the one who'd bungled the Harrison investigation before it had hardly started.

"Officer Ledbetter told me you were here," Brannigan said as he moved into the room. "I'm the lead on this investigation. What interest do you have in this case?"

Perfect.

Brannigan resented like hell that the Harrison case had been taken from him, he wasn't going to be happy about Mac's presence here, period.

"Vanessa Bumbalough was one of Harrison's patients. She also attended his funeral." Mac surveyed the enormous room once more, noticing that the techs had paused in their work to listen, apparently, to the exchange.

"That's correct," Brannigan said. The fury that burned

in his eyes belied his even tone. "But I can't see how that ties into her murder."

Mac thought about the condition of the room. The overturned bedside table, the twisted bedcovers, the blood. Then he considered the rest of the house—immaculate, every little thing in place. In the lull the techs turned their attention back to their task of collecting any evidence they'd missed on their first sweep, which would have taken place late last night shortly after the discovery of the body.

"Were there any witnesses?" Mac asked rather than responding to Brannigan's comment regarding the victim's connection with Harrison.

The middle-aged detective shook his head, sending his triple chin into a sluggish side-to-side motion. "No one saw or heard anything. The doorman insists that no one other than residents entered the building yesterday. He checked the log."

"I assume there was more than one doorman during the twenty-four hours prior to the body's discovery."

Brannigan shoved his hands into his trouser pockets. "Yeah, there were four and we interviewed all of 'em. Doormen and anyone else who worked on the premises in the last forty-eight hours."

"The other residents?" Mac knew he was pushing his luck now. Brannigan was more than a little ticked off.

"We're working on that right now. It takes time to cover this many apartments."

"Of course."

"We're also talking to the people she worked with," Brannigan went on as if he felt the need to prove himself. "With all the hoopla surrounding her splash onto the fashion scene, it could have been a competitor."

Mac looked around the room again. "Maybe."

In a tone just shy of seething, Brannigan said, "And maybe it was a jealous lover. We're still looking for the guy who accompanied her to Harrison's funeral. From what we've learned, she recently dumped her longtime lover for him. We haven't located the jilted lover, either, but we will."

Mac nodded, affirming the detective's conclusions. "That would be the most logical avenue to follow."

Brannigan shifted his considerable bulk from one foot to the other. "I suppose you want details," he said irritably.

Mac lifted a skeptical eyebrow. "Are there any that weren't in the newspaper this morning?"

Brannigan's retort didn't bear repeating and once more snagged the attention of everyone in the room. He glared at the techs, who immediately returned to the task at hand. "We got that little mystery solved. One of our new guys has a cousin who's a reporter. That won't happen again."

Vanessa Bumbalough had been found in a skimpy negligee, tied to her bed and her throat slashed. All that information had been in the paper.

"There was one thing," Brannigan said after a moment.

Mac waited, trying not to let his impatience show. Brannigan would give him the details in his own time. There was no telling when he'd see the ME's report. Payback for stealing the Harrison case. But Mac did what he had to do.

"The reporter didn't get a chance to see this," Brannigan explained smugly, "before he was ousted."

"What would 'this' be?" Mac asked when the detective hesitated.

"The victim had also been gagged—with a pair of panties."

Mac tensed, the ME's report on Harrison slamming

into his brain, rocketing him into a higher state of alert. Harrison had had a pair of panties shoved into his mouth to silence him.

"Not the fancy, sexy kind, either, mind you," Brannigan added. He rocked back on his heels, seemingly tickled to know something Mac didn't. "They were the cheap nylon kind. The killer shoved them so far back in her throat that she'd surely have choked to death even if he hadn't slit her throat."

Mac absorbed that information, knowing full well that Brannigan had already made the connection with Harrison. "What makes you think the killer is male?" There was more. Mac could feel it. Brannigan's whole demeanor was far too cocky.

The portly detective shrugged nonchalantly. "Well, the ME did mention that he thought the victim had been sexually assaulted. We won't know the full details until we see the preliminary report, of course, but that was his initial conclusion."

When Mac had gleaned all he could and had tolerated all of Brannigan's gloating he could stomach, he made his way back to the elevator and down to the lobby. He glanced at his watch as he settled behind the wheel of his sedan. He still had time to drop by the morgue and take a look at the body before he returned to his office and prepared for his meeting with Elizabeth Young. He needed to know what kind of struggle the victim had put up. If, as Brannigan suggested, she had been sexually assaulted, he wanted to know details. Had she first submitted, then changed her mind? Or was the act a flat-out rape from the get-go? If she hadn't resisted, that would lend credence to the idea that she knew her attacker.

One thing was certain, if Miss Bumbalough's killer was male and there was a connection to Harrison's murder, then that sure as hell let Elizabeth Young off the hook.

Mac eased his sedan into the flow of traffic and thought about that for a moment. Maybe it wouldn't let her off the hook. Maybe she and the killer were a team. Of course, connecting Harrison's murder with this one, even though the victim was one of his patients and had attended his funeral, was a stretch even with the cheap panties.

It could be coincidence. But Mac's instincts were humming. He had a feeling that, somehow, the two were connected. He mentally ran through the similarities. The victims had been restrained, both had been gagged with cheap panties, and now there was the possibility that both had participated in sexual activity prior to death.

Coincidences? Maybe.

Too soon to tell. But he would find out. Because whether Brannigan liked it or not, Mac wouldn't let it go until he knew for certain the two cases weren't connected.

Elizabeth stood outside the building at 26 Federal Plaza and took a deep, bolstering breath. She had to do this. Had to be calm and collected, as well as strong. She'd left work early this afternoon and stopped at home long enough to change into the one and only suit she owned. A black broomstick skirt and matching single-breasted jacket. It was the only remaining ensemble from her days with Brian and the firm. Everything else she'd burned in a bonfire one night after too much wine with Gloria. She'd learned very quickly that even in a not-so-upscale neighborhood people called the police when they saw suspicious activity.

She'd almost gotten arrested for the act of liberation. Ultimately the cop had felt sorry for her since she'd just been dumped and lost her job on the same day. So he'd ushered her and Gloria back into her apartment and made them swear they would sleep it off before undertaking any other activities. The next morning she'd awakened with the kind of headache one got from drinking cheap wine and with a closet that was considerably barer. She suddenly wished she could go back to that night, or at least the morning after. That was the morning she'd made the decision to go see the shrink Gloria had recommended for the panic attacks she'd suffered with for nearly a year. Which led her to this place.

Elizabeth braced herself for the worst and entered the intimidating building.

After consulting a directory she crossed the cavernous lobby and hesitated at the turnstiles that blocked the elevators which would take her to the twenty-seventh floor.

"I'll need your name and a picture ID, ma'am," the guard informed her brusquely.

She dug out her driver's license and held it up for his inspection. "My name is Elizabeth Young. I have a five-o'clock appointment with Agent Collin MacBride."

The guard checked his list and then nodded for her to pass. Elizabeth thanked him and tucked away her license. Once through the turnstile she had to turn over her purse to a female guard, who rummaged around inside it before sending it through an X-ray machine similar to those at the airport. Elizabeth stepped through the metal detector and waited patiently for her purse to be returned to her.

She exhaled a heavy breath as she pressed the button for the elevator. The doors slid open immediately and the moment she selected the proper floor the doors closed and she was whisked upward.

The blue-carpeted reception area on the twenty-seventh floor was sparsely furnished and rather cold-looking except for the enormous FBI seal decorating the far wall. The seal boasted of pride and demanded respect and managed to undo every scrap of bravado Elizabeth had mustered.

She moistened her lips and held on to the shoulder strap of her purse. Might as well get this over with. She marched up to the receptionist's desk and said, "Hello, I'm—"

"Miss Young?"

The voice jerked her around as efficiently as if its owner had grabbed her by the arm and pulled.

"I'm Agent Luke Driver," the man said. "We've been waiting for you. If you'll come this way please."

The blood roaring in her ears, Elizabeth allowed Agent Driver to direct her down a long corridor to the sixth office on the right. He opened the door and stood back for her to enter ahead of him.

Elizabeth studied his face for a moment before she did so, but she found no comfort, no assurance that all would come out right. She was on her own here. She should have listened to Gloria and called that attorney. But she couldn't afford a fancy attorney. If she could get this matter straightened out without having to go into hock for a retainer, she would.

Forcing one foot in front of the other, she walked into the office and Driver closed the door behind her. She glanced over her shoulder and wasn't surprised to find that he hadn't followed her inside.

Agent MacBride was not behind his desk, nor was he anywhere in the office. She really was on her own. Thankful for the reprieve, Elizabeth used the time to learn what she could about the man. She read each and every one of the accolades hanging on his walls. Plaque after plaque. Certificate after certificate. There were numerous pictures of him receiving commendations. But there wasn't the least sign of family or loved ones. No pictures on the desk or wall of anyone other than those related to work. Nothing.

Like the man, the office was elegant. She wondered vaguely if all FBI agents had mahogany desks and credenzas, expensive leather upholstered chairs and a view that looked out over the city he served and protected. Somehow she doubted it. These luxuries were probably his personal belongings. They matched his thousand-dollar suits and Italian-made shoes.

She then wondered what kind of house he lived in and just how much an FBI agent was paid. Not this much, she'd bet. Nope. Collin MacBride was exactly what she'd suspected—a rich guy with a need to prove his worth. Once more Elizabeth scanned the many plaques and pictures that attested to his accomplishments. Just what she needed. A refined greyhound with the simple-minded tenacity of a pit bull.

The door opened behind her and she turned to see Agent MacBride step into the office. The air felt suddenly charged, and the size of the room diminished instantly.

"Miss Young, I apologize for keeping you waiting." He skirted his desk and gestured to one of the chairs.

Without preamble she sat. She tried to moisten her lips, but her mouth was too dry to make a difference. The pounding of her heart was almost deafening as she forced herself to focus on the man who walked around his desk to settle into the leather chair behind it.

He was tall, at least six-two. And just as handsome and well dressed as she remembered. He had the build of an athlete, but with a little more bulk to fill out his designer suit. She felt a flare of heat in her midsection, startling her. She blinked, frowned and tried to analyze the reaction. Before she allowed herself to admit the surge of heat for what it was, he spoke again.

"Have you thought about our earlier visit?" he asked in that smooth voice that spoke of breeding and an Ivy League education.

Had she thought about it? Fury seared away all other emotion. What the hell did he think? "Actually," she said, not bothering to keep the fury out of her tone and lying through her teeth, "I haven't had time to think about anything but work. Was there something in particular I should have thought about?"

He smiled, but it was venomous. "Do you recognize this?" He tossed a photograph to her side of the desk.

Gingerly she reached for it. Her breath caught when she recognized the object pictured in the eight-by-ten print.

The dagger.

The one she'd found at the junk store on Fifty-fifth. The one she'd bought Ned as a thank-you for helping her with her panic attacks. The gift she'd given him before she'd recognized him for the monster he was.

"I thought you might," MacBride said smugly.

Her gaze shot to his. "So what if I do?" Her words were flinty with a fear she couldn't name. Somehow some part of her knew this was bad. Very bad. She pitched the photograph back on his desk as if merely holding it would further condemn her.

"That's the murder weapon." He picked up the picture and pretended to study it. "It was buried to the hilt just left of the victim's sternum." He shook his head solemnly. "Slid right between the ribs, punctured a lung and nicked the pericardium." He shrugged then. "He couldn't have lived more than a few minutes. Not even long enough for help to arrive had someone called for it."

The trembling started in Elizabeth's hands, but quickly spread to her entire body. She stared at her fingers as if she could still them by sheer force of will, but she could not. Her stomach roiled and for one beat she was certain she'd be sick.

"Except no one called for help. Whoever plunged this dagger—" he tapped the photo "—into Ned's chest left him there, naked and dying."

Elizabeth lifted her gaze to meet his. "I didn't do it." She struggled to swallow back some of the desperation tightening her throat. "I swear I didn't kill him."

Those blue eyes bored more deeply into hers, that relentlessness she'd recognized yesterday flashing like a neon sign. "All I want from you, Elizabeth, is the truth."

The truth.

God, he knew she'd lied.

How could she hope to fool this man?

Gloria's words echoed in her ears. *Stick with your original story. Don't tell the cops anything else.*

She drew in a ragged breath. "I've already told you everything I know."

Lights pulsed behind her eyes. Nausea burned bitter and hot in her throat. She'd never before had a migraine, but the abrupt chord of pain in her skull now was no ordinary headache.

That unyielding gaze never deviated from hers. He didn't even blink, just kept watching her. "I don't think you have."

The trembling escalated. Unable to sit there another second, she lurched to her feet. "I've told you everything. This…this harassment is pointless. I can't help you, Agent MacBride."

She whipped around and headed for the door. She had to get out of there. The pain was excruciating, the trembling almost violent. If she didn't leave now, she might not be able to under her own steam. She would not give him the pleasure of seeing her collapse beneath the pressure.

Before she could jerk the door open, he was standing next to her, one broad palm plastered against the slab of wood that stood between her and escape.

"If you think of anything you need to tell me, my cell number is on that card I gave you."

She closed her eyes and struggled to hold herself steady. "I won't think of anything." Forcing her eyes open, she met that blue gaze. "You shouldn't be wasting your time on me, Agent MacBride. You should be out there looking for the killer."

"What is it you're afraid of, Elizabeth?" he asked softly, the gentle tone a vivid contrast to the fierceness in his eyes.

Shaking her head in denial, she glared at him with all the disdain she could marshal. "I'm innocent." She'd meant to hurl the words at him with the fury smoldering inside her, but she'd fallen well short of the mark. All she'd managed to do was sound desperate.

"Then you won't mind submitting to certain tests," he suggested in that same smooth baritone.

Tests? Her mind raced with the possibilities. Had she touched anything? Left prints or some form of DNA that would tighten the noose already around her neck?

She remembered slapping Ned. Maybe she'd scratched him. He'd grabbed her brutally. Shaken her. Had she lost a loose hair on his clothing?

Her heart slammed mercilessly against her rib cage. That was it. She'd watched enough forensics shows to realize what he was up to.

"Elizabeth? Is there a problem?"

Her gaze locked with his once more and she shook

her head. "Call my attorney." She rattled off the name of the legal eagle Gloria had given her. "You can discuss it with him." She couldn't take any more. She couldn't do this. Not again. Not alone.

He leaned in closer, fully into her personal space. "I'll call him, Elizabeth, but that's not all I'm going to do."

She swallowed, hard. Grasped the anger that swelled just enough to give her the strength to demand, "Is that a threat?"

He smiled and her foolish heart skipped a beat. This close she could feel the pleasure it gave him to have her trapped so firmly in his net of suspicion. She wanted to pound on that broad chest and rant at him. She wanted to shake him until he realized she was telling the truth. She did not kill Ned Harrison. She was innocent. Why couldn't he see that?

But she couldn't do any of those things. All she could do was stare into those intense eyes and fight the urge to admit defeat.

"No threat," he said on something that could have been a sigh but sounded more like a chuckle. "Just fair warning." All signs of amusement or gentleness vanished then. That chiseled jaw hardened like granite and his unflinching gaze seemed to go straight through her. "I'll be watching you, Elizabeth," he warned with all the determination and confidence of a fire-and-brimstone preacher. "If you make one mistake, I'll know it." The corners of those firm lips tilted upward, hinted at a smile. "And you will make a mistake. They all do."

For two long beats she stood frozen, staring into those accusing eyes, and then he moved. The instant he backed off she flung open the door and hurried to the elevator.

By the time she reached the street the panic had

gripped her in its vicious talons. The pain in her skull all but blinded her.

And she realized, beyond a shadow of a doubt, that he knew.

He knew she was lying.

Chapter 5

Elizabeth had little choice but to work sixteen-hour days for the past two days. She'd fallen seriously behind on her schedule with the funeral and the interrogations related to Ned's murder. Not to mention the worry and guilt slowing her usual pace. She'd never survive as a criminal. She just wasn't cut out for a life of deception.

It was Saturday and she hadn't heard from Agent MacBride since their meeting on Thursday evening. She hoped she never heard from him again. A little shiver chased over her flesh, reminding her that she might not have heard from him, but she'd seen his people watching her. The moment she pulled out onto the street each morning, a dark sedan slid in behind her and followed her to the job site. Boomer, too, had noticed the feds hanging around.

MacBride had warned her he'd be watching.

But what if it wasn't him or his men? What if it was whoever murdered Ned? She shuddered at the thought. Borrowing trouble wasn't going to do her any good. She'd worried enough for several lifetimes during the past week. Besides, Boomer was certain her tail was "fibbies," as he called them. He swore he could spot a federal agent from a mile away—they all looked the same. Same fancy suits, same designer sunglasses and the same superior attitude.

Boomer was right about the attitude, she decided as she put the lid back on the fresh bucket of paint she'd had to open an hour or so ago. MacBride had enough cocky male attitude for a dozen men. That much testosterone in one guy could be a little scary. She shivered again. Only this time it had nothing to do with fear and everything to do with awareness.

Okay. Time to call it a day. Whenever she started fantasizing about the guy attempting to pin a murder rap on her, it was definitely time for a break. It was late. She was tired. She'd have to work tomorrow. Working on Sunday was her least-favorite thing to do, but finishing up this loft was essential. She'd just have to grin and bear it come morning. She glanced at her watch. It was well past ten and she'd obviously gotten punchy. Too little sleep and far too much pressure bore ruthlessly down on her. A decent night's sleep would do wonders for her ability to think straight. The final finishing touches could wait until morning. But she wouldn't ask Boomer to help on Sunday. He likely still had a social life.

"I'll finish up here," she said to Boomer when he noticed her putting away her tools. "You go on ahead and I'll see you on Monday."

A frown creased his brow. "I'll just hang around and walk you out," he offered, ever the protector.

She shook her head. He'd already put in far more hours than his meager salary covered, but he'd insisted on helping her catch up. "No. Really. I'll be okay." She shrugged.

"Who's going to bother me with my very own federal agent watching?"

He crossed to the opposite side of the room and peered out the window. "He's still out there, all right." Boomer expelled a couple of inventive curses. "I don't know why you put up with it. They got no right watching you like this."

"It's okay." She ushered him into the dimly lit hallway and pointed to the elevator. "Now go. I'll be fine."

Reluctance slowing his step, Boomer shuffled to the only exit. He hesitated before boarding the antique lift. "Don't let 'em see you sweat, Elizabeth." His gaze settled on hers. "We both know you didn't kill that prick." He pushed open the iron bars that served as a door to the elevator, then paused to look back at her once more before boarding. "But he deserved exactly what he got."

Boomer stepped into the elevator and pulled the bars closed before setting it in to motion. His gaze remained steady on hers until he was out of sight. She shuffled back into the loft, exhaustion clawing at her.

How often had she complained about Ned in front of Boomer? She hadn't told him everything, but she'd gone on and on about how he'd used her, how he'd hurt her.

A new kind of iciness crackled inside her. Surely Boomer hadn't—

No! She refused to believe that. MacBride's innuendo about Boomer's past was playing on her mind, that was all. She knew Boomer. He wouldn't kill another human being any more than she would.

Elizabeth moistened her suddenly dry lips and made quick work of putting away the tools of her trade. She refused to dwell on a concept as ridiculous as that. The whole idea was just another indicator of how badly she needed a good night's sleep.

Shortly after Boomer's departure, she was ready to go, as well. She glanced out the window to see if the sedan was still there. Yep. Right there in the alley across the street. The driver had backed in so that he could pull out behind her without any real effort. She wondered if they'd been trained to do that very thing to ensure that they didn't lose their surveillance target while turning around. Probably.

As the old lift lowered to the still-under-construction corridor that would eventually serve as a lobby for the building, she couldn't help thinking what a monumental waste of time the surveillance of her movements really was. If the feds expended half as much effort on finding the real murderer as they did on watching her, they might have solved the case by now.

By the time she stormed out of the building, she'd worked up a pretty good head of steam. Instead of climbing into her old beat-up truck, she marched across the street and right up to the sedan parked in the alley.

She banged on the driver's window. "Why do you keep watching me?" she demanded, any good sense she'd possessed now lost to exhaustion and fury.

For a few seconds she wasn't sure whoever was on the other side of the tinted glass intended to respond, then the door opened. She fell back a couple of steps. What if Boomer had been wrong? What if this wasn't one of MacBride's henchmen?

Agent MacBride himself emerged from the vehicle. He towered over her with only the car door between them. To her utter chagrin, her gaze swept him. The usual elegant suit jacket was missing. The crisp white shirt he wore beneath remained free of wrinkles and stretched tautly over his incredibly wide shoulders. The top two buttons of his shirt were open and the navy tie hung loose at his throat.

His short hair looked as if he'd run his hands through it repeatedly, leaving it tousled in a manner that could only be called sexy. But by far the most unnerving feature was his relentless gaze.

"I told you I'd be watching, Elizabeth."

Damn her treacherous emotions, but she shivered at the sound of his voice. She wrapped her arms around herself and glared up at him, determined not to allow him to see another indication of weakness. "This is ridiculous. Why aren't you chasing the real bad guys, instead of harassing me?"

He eased around the door and shoved it shut behind him, putting his big body mere inches from hers. "We both know why I'm watching you, don't we?"

Anger flamed inside her. "Did you call my attorney?" She definitely had, as much as she'd hated to—the retainer alone had set her back two months' rent, but her landlady had been understanding and offered to allow her to pay the rent a little late. Thank God there were still a few compassionate people around.

"Do I need to call your attorney?" he countered smoothly. "I thought maybe we could settle this between us."

Her breath stilled in her lungs as that fierce gaze settled on her lips. What was he doing? Was this a new strategy? Had he noticed her attraction to him physically and decided to play on it? Was he that desperate to pin this on her? Or maybe he simply thought she truly was guilty.

"I'm tired, MacBride," she admitted, too exhausted to fight this battle now. "Just leave me alone, okay? I don't need this crap."

She gave him her back and headed toward her truck on the other side of the street. Damn him. She was sick to death of being accused. What was it about her that

made people believe she could commit a crime so heinous? Even the sheriff back home had initially believed
her sorry-ass brother-in-law, not her. But, with her prod-
ding, he'd dug more deeply, finally discovering the real
truth. She was innocent. Just like now.

Who knew? Maybe it was a guy thing. Maybe they
had to side with each other, protect the brotherhood at all
costs. If there was a woman anywhere nearby to blame,
that was the preferred route.

"Did he help you do it?"

MacBride's voice stopped her dead in her tracks mid-
way across the street. She turned slowly, afraid to ask
what he meant by that statement and equally afraid not to.

"What the hell are you talking about?"

The streetlights were few and far between, but there
was just enough moonlight combined with the yellow
glow of the nearest street lamp to allow her to see the
knowing expression that tipped those sensual lips into
the vaguest hint of a smile.

"Your assistant, Boomer. Did he talk you into it?
Maybe the two of you have something going on and he
got jealous of your relationship with the good doctor.
Those younger guys are like that, you know. Is he the
one who tied up Harrison?"

White-hot fury exploded inside her. She clenched her
hands into fists and shook with the effort to restrain the
fury when she spoke. "This isn't going to work, Mac-
Bride." She scarcely recognized the icy voice as her own.
"I didn't kill him and neither did Boomer. If you have
some kind of evidence that leads you to believe I'm guilty,
then arrest me. If not, leave me the hell alone."

She spun away from that all-consuming blue gaze and
started forward again. This just kept getting worse and
worse. He was like a dog with a bone. He just wouldn't

let it go. All she had to do was reach her truck, climb in, and she was out of there. She would not waste another moment of her time on this man or his silly suppositions.

"But you can't prove you actually went home after being stood up at the restaurant."

The words were spoken softly, yet there was no denying the determination in his tone. He wasn't going to let this go until he knew everything.

She hesitated once more and summoned the necessary courage to face him yet again. "That's right." She looked straight into those assessing eyes. "I don't have anyone to vouch for my whereabouts. I can't prove anything. You'll just have to take my word for it."

Enough already. If he had evidence he would arrest her. But this intimidation had to stop. She'd had all she could take.

"All right."

Startled, she stared up at him. "You believe me?"

That shadow of a smile again. "I didn't say that. You said I'd have to take your word for it. I can do that if—" he paused "—you're willing to repeat those words during a polygraph."

Fear paralyzed her. She couldn't take a polygraph. He would have proof of her lies then.

"Is there a problem?" He inclined his head and studied her more closely. "If you're telling me the truth, then you have nothing to lose and everything to gain."

"I...I thought polygraphs weren't admissible in court," she retaliated. The blood froze in her veins. This was it. She was done. He had her. He would never in a million years believe her story now. She'd lied. Once labeled a liar, she would be doomed.

"You say you're telling the truth. I'm simply offering you an opportunity to prove it," he said, effectively avoiding her question.

"I'll...I'll have to talk to my attorney," she stammered.

He moved closer—back into her personal space. She couldn't have moved had her life depended on it. The fear had nailed her to the spot. She couldn't move. Couldn't think what to do or say next.

"All I want from you, Elizabeth, is the truth. If you're really innocent as you say you are, then you must know that your uncooperative actions are slowing down this case. You're essentially helping a murderer to continue walking the streets. If you want to clear your name, then help me."

"I...can't help you. I don't know anything."

Mac stared down into those frightened amber eyes and it was all he could do not to reach out to her, not to comfort her. She was scared to death, and every instinct screamed at him to reach out. These kinds of feelings were totally unacceptable. He gritted his teeth and got himself back under control. She was a suspect, the primary suspect, in a murder investigation. He needed her cooperation. Losing his focus was not an option.

"Did you have sex with Harrison that night? Did you go to his place looking for him when he didn't show up at the restaurant? Did you have a fight? Maybe you didn't mean to kill him. Maybe it was a game that got out of hand. I know about the kinky sex he enjoyed, the games he played."

She shook her head, her whole body tense with the urge to flee. But something, the fear maybe, held her firmly in place, right where he needed her.

"I didn't—"

"Don't lie to me, Elizabeth," he pressed. "You've already lied to me once," he ventured. He'd known from the moment he first laid eyes on her that she was hiding something.

She blinked. "Why would I lie to you? I didn't kill him."

He tried to read the other emotion whirling in those wide, fearful eyes, but he couldn't. "Is it the videotape? Are you afraid that your relationship with Harrison is going to be exposed to the whole world? Is that it?"

She shook her head again. "He...he used me. It was a mistake." She looked away then. "I made a mistake." This time when her eyes met his, they were filled with certainty and fortitude. "But I didn't kill him."

"Are you the one who scratched him when you argued?" Mac went on. "Is it your pubic hair we found on his body?"

The bravado vanished in an instant. "I told you I didn't go to—"

"Why don't I believe that?" he asked, cutting off her denial. His gut told him she was telling the truth about her innocence where the murder was concerned, but there was something more. She was lying about something and he had to know what it was.

She held up her hands, palms out. "Enough." She backed away a step. "You can arrest me or you can let me go home. Which will it be?"

His cell phone vibrated in his chest pocket. "Go home," he told her as he reached for the infuriating cell. "But remember, I'll be watching."

Without responding to his blatant threat, she stormed away. He let go a disgusted breath and flipped open the phone. "Yeah," he barked.

"Mac, we've got another one. Brannigan just called. I'm on my way there now."

Mac's frown deepened. "Where?" He didn't have to ask what. He already knew. There'd been another murder.

"Mercer Street. Willidean Delinsky." Driver rattled off the exact address. "She goes by the name Deana Dell. She's that supermodel who got busted for drugs early last year. You know the one who does the Sass ads."

Sass was a designer perfume that was all the rage with younger women. Mac definitely remembered the model. Blonde, glamorous. She'd been at Harrison's funeral wearing a red dress that turned every head in the place. "What's the connection?" He knew there was one, otherwise Brannigan would not have let them in on his turf. Considering her presence at the funeral, she at least knew Harrison on a social level.

"She's one of Harrison's patients. Brannigan found the appointments in her calendar."

Mac swore. "I'll meet you there."

The scene was every bit as gruesome as the one two days earlier involving Vanessa Bumbalough. The modus operandi appeared to be exactly the same. Only this time Mac got to see the victim before her body was removed. She'd been tied to her elegant bed, sexually assaulted and then murdered in the same manner. The spray of blood adorning the wall testified to the violence.

As he stood back and viewed the undisturbed crime scene, his predominant thought was that this was an execution. Someone had demoralized and executed this woman. This was no random act of sexual violence. This murder had purpose and calculation. Again, the home was undisturbed elsewhere. Not a single item looked out of place. Absolutely no signs of forced entry. This building didn't have a doorman but whoever had entered the premises had been allowed to do so by a resident who pressed a simple button and disengaged the lock barring the entrance. Brannigan already had officers canvassing the residents to see if anyone had buzzed in a visitor today.

The ME had put the time of death at six to eight hours ago. Of course this was only an estimate; they wouldn't have more concrete details until after the autopsy. The victim's live-in boyfriend had come home late from the office and discovered the body. Brannigan was still grilling him in the next room. But Mac didn't need to hear any of the interrogation. This had nothing to do with the boyfriend.

This was about Ned Harrison.

He was sure of it. He'd felt that nudge at the Bumbalough crime scene, but now it was more than a nudge. Someone had murdered Ned Harrison and now, whoever that was, appeared bent on killing his patients. But why? What did Vanessa Bumbalough and Deana Dell have to do with anything? Why these two patients? What did they have in common besides Harrison?

Those were the answers he needed.

The possibility that these two women would not be the last abruptly surfaced in the flood of scenarios crashing into his consciousness.

Elizabeth.

She had been Harrison's patient.

A cold hard fist of fear jammed into Mac's gut. She might very well be hiding the answer to all this and not know it. He thought of the videotape of Elizabeth Young and then the ones of the two dead women. Was it simply being a patient of Harrison's that marked these women for death, or was it the videotapes? Each one had likely already been viewed by the Gentleman's Association, whose membership was spread out across the country like a disease building toward an epidemic. It could be any one of those sick bastards. If someone high enough in the association had realized that Harrison was under federal surveillance, his death may have been ordered.

But why the women?

There had to be something more.

And somehow Elizabeth Young was the key. He was certain of it. His protective instincts surged. Whether or not she was guilty of murder, she most likely needed protection.

He motioned for Driver to step into the hallway with him.

Once out of earshot of the crime-scene techs and any of Brannigan's men, he said quietly, "I want you to go straight to Elizabeth Young's apartment and stay there until I relieve you."

Driver frowned. "But what about—"

"Go now." Urgency had tied his gut in knots. He didn't want her alone. "I'll be there as soon as I can."

None too pleased to have to give up a crime scene for a simple stakeout, Driver nodded and headed out without an argument. He had a lot to learn, but he was a good kid.

Relaxing a fraction, Mac returned to the master bedroom where Deana Dell's body was being prepared for removal by the ME. The ordeal to come would serve as further violation and injustice to her physical remains, but it would help identify her murderer.

She and Vanessa Bumbalough were the only witnesses they had.

Elizabeth climbed out of the tub, quickly dried off and wrapped a clean white towel around her. She felt better already. She'd needed that long, steamy soak.

Deciding a cup of hot cocoa was in order, she padded into the kitchen. As she poured the milk into the pan to warm, she attempted to block all thoughts of Agent MacBride.

But she failed miserably.

If he forced the issue, she would have no choice but to take the stupid polygraph test. It was too late at night to call her attorney, but she knew that if she refused the test, it would be taken as a sign of guilt.

She was screwed if she did and screwed if she didn't.

She shivered when she thought about the way Mac-Bride had looked at her lips. Her fingers instinctively went there, tracing her mouth, her mind struggling with the question of why he would have looked at her that way. As if he wanted to kiss her, as if he was attracted to her. But that was impossible. He only wanted one thing.

To pin a murder rap on her.

All this surveillance crap was nothing but intimidation. Her attorney had confirmed her suspicions, but she hadn't really needed him to. She'd already been down that road.

It was these other feelings that worried her. She hadn't been attracted to a man sexually since Brian. Sure she'd had an affair with Ned, but that had been about pure physical release and nothing more. She'd needed someone in that way to prove it hadn't been her fault that Brian dumped her. Ned had known it and he'd taken advantage of her.

But this was different. This was almost overwhelming. Maybe it was nothing but a combination of all the events that had befallen her in the past year. Maybe she was simply vulnerable. She needed someone to take care of her. She was so damned tired. And Agent MacBride was strong and had that take-charge mentality down to a science.

She poured her warm milk into a cup and slowly

stirred in the cocoa mix. All this time she'd been telling herself she could make it on her own. That she didn't need anyone to support her.

Dammit, she didn't.

She was doing fine. If she hadn't gotten behind on her schedule with all this insanity surrounding Ned's murder, she would be fine, financially and otherwise.

She did not need anyone taking care of her. She was strong and self-reliant. She always had been.

This would pass and she'd be fine again. She sipped her cocoa and wandered into the living room. It wasn't as if it was the first time she'd been faced with seemingly insurmountable obstacles to overcome.

Feeling better already, she set her cocoa on the table next to the sofa and clicked on the television. She might as well catch the news before she hit the sack. Although it was April and the weather was pretty good for this time of year, a sudden winter storm wasn't unheard of. When self-employed, you had to stay on top of anything that might set the work schedule back.

Before she could sit down, her telephone rang. She answered on the second ring.

"Hello."

A beat of silence, then the distinctive click of the party at the other end of the line hanging up.

"Jerk," she muttered. She hated telemarketers. Why the hell would they call so late? And when they did, they always wanted to speak to Mr. Young, assuming the man of the house would be more receptive to their pitch. She'd tried to tell previous callers there was no Mr. Young, but they didn't seem to believe her. Apparently the new way to handle the situation was to simply hang up when a female answered the phone.

"There ought to be a law against it," she hissed.

Then she remembered. The *law* was too busy intimidating innocent people like her.

She was so caught up in her law-bashing session that the knock on the door made her jump.

Taking a deep breath, she forced herself to remain calm. Then anger took over once more. Now he was knocking on her door? Mrs. Polk would not like her having visitors at this hour. The elderly woman didn't want anyone living above her who partied or had late-night guests. Elizabeth couldn't blame her. She was an old woman who supplemented her income by renting out her unused upstairs. She didn't need any additional stress in her life. Hell, who did?

This was ridiculous. She would not have anyone, not even federal agents, knocking on her door at all hours of the night. Too furious to think rationally, she went in search of her robe, then stomped over to the door in her bare feet, unlocked it and jerked it open.

The tiny landing atop the private rear stairs that led to her apartment stood empty. She stared out over the narrow alleyway that separated Mrs. Polk's small frame house from her neighbor's. The moonlight that managed to penetrate the darkness and surrounding trees did little in the way of illumination. Elizabeth blinked and looked again. Nothing. Too dumbfounded to be afraid, she stepped out onto the landing and squinted into the darkness to survey the steep set of stairs leading to the drive where her truck was parked. Nothing. No one.

Had she imagined the knock at her door? There'd been only one. Maybe a passing car backfired.

A shudder passed through her. She was obviously more exhausted than she'd realized.

After closing and locking the door, she had another thought. What if the jerk had called and knocked on her door just to make sure she was home? Maybe MacBride thought she'd slipped out.

Indignation burst inside her. She strode to the front window and stared down at the street. A dark sedan sat at the curb directly across the expanse of pavement from the house.

"Damn you," she muttered, wishing he'd been at the door so she could have told him just what she thought of his mind games.

A smile slid across her face. His cell phone. That was how he'd called from the car. She let the curtain fall back into place and rushed to find her purse. Dumping the contents, she rifled through the mess until she found Mac-Bride's card.

She'd punched in the number and heard the first ring before she allowed herself time to have second thoughts. When she would have hung up, he answered.

"MacBride."

Renewed fury flared inside her. "Look, you pompous jerk, I don't appreciate being harassed in the middle of the night."

"Elizabeth?"

"Don't pretend you don't know what I'm talking about," she went on. "I can't stop you from watching my house or my job site, but I will not tolerate you calling my house and hanging up, or your knocking on my door and then disappearing. Just leave me alone!"

Before Mac could ask what the hell she was talking about, she hung up. He replayed her words in his mind. Someone had apparently called her and hung up and then knocked on her door and disappeared.

Why the hell would Driver do anything as ridiculous as that? If he'd wanted to ensure the suspect was indeed at home, he should simply have asked when he called, not hung up.

Something dark and foreboding crawled up Mac's spine. He dialed Driver's cell and held his breath until his partner answered.

"Driver."

The noise in the background made Mac frown. Horns blowing. People arguing. "Driver, what the hell is going on? Elizabeth Young—"

"I was just about to call you," Driver shouted into the phone. "I've been in a little fender bender. I'm trying to talk the investigating officer into releasing me now."

Driver wasn't even at Elizabeth's house.

Mac's blood ran cold. Then who the hell made that call? Who knocked on her door?

Chapter 6

Despite driving like a bat from hell and zooming through the Lincoln Tunnel, which would have been impossible had it not been the middle of the night, it still took Mac far longer to reach Mrs. Polk and Elizabeth's apartment than he'd have liked. He didn't bother to covertly park on the street, choosing, instead, to roar straight into the driveway and skid to a halt right behind her beat-up old truck.

He was out of his car before it stopped rocking and took the exterior stairs up to her door two at a time. Despite his hurry, he took note of each vehicle within a block of the house on either side of the street. The surrounding homes were still and dark. Mac knew this section of the small town. Low crime, mostly blue-collar workers, all probably tucked in for the night in anticipation of church on Sunday morning.

Sucking in a deep breath to calm the thrashing in his chest, he pounded heavily on the door. He refused to consider that he might be too late already or that…he was overreacting. He shook his head as he let go a ragged breath of fatigue. He shouldn't have left her without surveillance. Every instinct had warned him that something far beneath the surface was going on and that she was the key. For more than forty-eight hours, he or one of his men had watched her every move.

And what had he done tonight? He'd left her on her own.

The door opened just as he raised his fist to pound on it again. Relief, mixed with a kind of vague defeat, gushed through him at the sight of her.

Her hair mussed and her glasses askew, she stared at him for a moment before recognition flared. In the next beat, her eyes widened in surprise, which was quickly followed by unbridled fury.

"What are you trying to do? Wake the whole neighborhood?"

Highly trained agent that he was, he couldn't even respond when faced with the fact that she stood in the doorway wearing a T-shirt that scarcely reached the tops of her thighs. Backlit by the interior light behind her, the gentle curves of her slender figure were clearly silhouetted beneath the thin cotton fabric.

Before he could stop himself, he gazed down the length of her, all the way to her neatly manicured toes. But it was the return trip that ultimately shattered the last of his defenses. Back up those long, toned legs, over a slim torso and small breasts that jutted firmly against the flimsy fabric covering them and on to a slender throat that curved upward into delicate cheeks and full lips. When his gaze at last came back to rest on hers, the look of rage in those amber eyes jerked him from the trance of lust he'd fallen victim to.

"I'm calling the police." With those snapped words, she executed an about-face and left him standing there like the unwelcome guest he was.

His own temper flaring, Mac crossed the threshold uninvited and slammed the door behind him. "I am the police," he snarled.

The frightened-rabbit expression that captured her pretty face sent him hurtling back into reality. What the hell was wrong with him? He never lost it like this.

Elizabeth couldn't believe her eyes, much less her ears. Maybe it was her, but she didn't think so. MacBride was behaving strangely, and she didn't know whether to run for her life or slap some sense into him. Either way she was reasonably sure he had no intention of backing off.

"What is it you want, Agent MacBride?" She planted her hands on her waist and marched straight up to him, lifting her chin defiantly. How dare he barge into her home in the middle of the night! It was bad enough she'd endured his shenanigans with the phone call and the anonymous knock on the door. "I'm sick and tired of you and your people following me around." When she was toe-to-toe with him, she poked him in the chest with her forefinger. He flinched. That mere touch sent an electrical charge surging through her, but she quickly recovered. "This is blatant harassment."

"You called me, remember?" he growled.

She shivered as the sound of his voice shimmered over her already exposed nerve endings. "Only because you called first and hung up like a kid playing a prank." She huffed a sigh of exasperation. "And let's not forget you knocking on my door and then vanishing like Houdini. What'd you think? That I'd sneaked out the back door to go murder someone else? I don't even have a back door." Control snapped. "Why are you doing this?"

As she fought to regain her composure, something changed in his eyes, and that lean, chiseled profile softened just the tiniest bit. "That's just it," he said. Even his voice was softer. "I didn't call you and I damn sure didn't knock on your door until just a few seconds ago."

Mac watched the confusion claim her, lining her smooth brow, parting those luscious lips. "One of your men then," she refuted. "I opened the door—" she gestured to the one he'd slammed only moments before "—and no one was there." Her gaze arrowed to his. "You said you'd be watching. I saw the car."

"I didn't follow you home tonight, nor did any of my men. Can you describe the vehicle you saw?"

She trembled, shook her head in answer to his question, as well as in denial of the possibility that obviously scared the hell out of her.

Someone had been watching her, all right.

"I…I don't understand."

Mac squeezed his hands into fists and resisted the urge to reach for her. Every moment with her was a battle for control. His immediate instinct was always, always to protect her.

"Is there anyone in your neighborhood who would do this sort of thing as a joke?" he asked, determined to keep this discussion on track. "A friend who gets off on scaring others, maybe?"

Her head moved jerkily from side to side. "All the neighbors are older, like Mrs. Polk." She laughed, but the sound held no humor. "No way could one of them have knocked and gotten down the stairs and out of sight before I opened the door. I mean, I hesitated before opening it, but not that long." She seemed to wilt beneath the weight of the realization that she'd just dismissed the safest, most reasonable possibilities, leaving only one alternative.

Mac crossed to the door, opened it and moved out onto the small landing to survey the situation from her vantage point. He peered over the side and concluded that even jumping over the railing wouldn't have been a big deal for a younger person, an athletic type. He knew he could do it easily. But if her neighbors were around Mrs. Polk's age, seventy or so, there was no way one of them could have taken that leap. He glanced up and down the narrow alley that separated the house from its neighbor. With the numerous overgrown shrubs and small detached garages, there were plenty of places for someone to hide. A quick jump over the rail and simply darting back under the stairs would be sufficient camouflage.

He stepped back inside and closed the door. During his short absence Elizabeth had donned a tattered terry robe. With her arms wrapped around herself, she looked incredibly vulnerable and very much like a frightened little girl in need of a hug.

But she was no little girl. Those full lips were parted slightly as if she was on the verge of asking something but feared the answer. She'd straightened her glasses and thrust her fingers through her hair, leaving the silky mass hanging loosely around her slender shoulders.

Mac bit back a sigh. Beating himself up for noticing every little thing about her would accomplish nothing, but somehow he had to get a grip and pull it together.

Right now was the perfect time to strike. She was vulnerable. But it took every ounce of determination he possessed to force himself to do his job. "It's time to stop playing games, Elizabeth. Tell me what it is you're hiding and we'll get this mystery solved." He stared directly into her eyes. "You won't be safe until this thing is settled. I know it and I think deep down you know it."

The delicate line of her jaw hardened just a fraction. "Are you admitting that you believe me when I say I didn't have anything to do with Ned's—" she blinked rapidly "—with Dr. Harrison's murder?"

He wanted to believe that she was capable of a slick move like this—that the whole phone-call-knock-on-the-door thing was a hoax designed to garner sympathy—but he knew better. No way could she fake that kind of fear. He'd seen it in her eyes when she realized it hadn't been the authorities outside her door or on the other end of that call. She'd been truly frightened. Still, on the off chance that he was a bigger fool than he already suspected...

"No," he told her flatly. "I'm admitting that I believe someone else knows your secret and that maybe that very secret is putting you in the same kind of danger Harrison found himself in."

Bingo. Direct hit. Her breath caught and the stark fear glittered in her eyes once more. Now all he had to do was move in for the kill.

Stepping closer—into her personal space, a move he already knew unsettled her—he pressed, "Tell me the truth, Elizabeth. I can't help you if you don't." She tried backing away from him, but he just kept moving nearer until she backed into the sofa and had no choice but to admit defeat. "Do you know where I was when you called tonight?" he asked.

She couldn't breathe, couldn't think, couldn't escape those penetrating blue eyes. *Please,* she wanted to cry, *just leave me alone. I didn't do this awful thing!* But she couldn't speak. She could only stare into those accusing eyes and pray he wouldn't see the truth in her own.

"I was at the scene of a ten fifty-four. Do you know what a ten fifty-four is, Elizabeth?"

He was closer, yet she wasn't sure he'd moved. But something about his savage demeanor made her feel as if he was right on top of her, waiting. Waiting for the truth.

"A homicide," he said in answer to his own question. Emotion shuddered through her. Another murder.

God, she didn't want to know this. Why didn't he just leave? It couldn't have anything to do with her. She blinked back the sheen of tears that threatened to wreck the remnants of her already shredded composure and stared back at him in defiance. "What does that have to do with me?"

"Did you know Deana Dell, the model?" he went on, ignoring her question, his face mere inches from hers. "She was one of Dr. Harrison's patients, too, just like you. Maybe you saw her at the funeral."

The blonde. She knew instantly. In the devil-red dress. A model. Living large and fast. Elizabeth remembered her now. She'd read about her and her trouble with drugs, last year maybe. She'd instantly wondered if the model had been covering up for someone else, too. But at the funeral Elizabeth hadn't gotten a good look at her face. Hadn't recalled who she was then.

And now it no longer mattered.

She was dead.

Homicide.

That meant murder.

Dear God.

Her stomach rolled over.

"That's the second one of Harrison's patients to die since the funeral," he said pointedly. "Don't you find that strangely ironic?"

The room tilted and then started to spin. Nausea boiled up in her throat. She was going to be sick.

Mac stumbled back a step as Elizabeth pushed away from him and ran from the room. Restraining the need to go after her, he took a moment to calm the crazy mixture of emotions raging inside him. But he couldn't take any chances that she might make a run for it. There was a window—no fire escape, though. In four steps he'd crossed the room and entered the small hall. As he reached the closed bathroom door, his concerns were allayed by the sound of her violent retching.

Guilt stabbed him right in the gut as he leaned against the wall next to the door. He'd forced that on her, had pushed her to the edge. Damn. Sympathy wasn't supposed to enter into this. Where was his usual detachment? Why the hell couldn't he maintain a proper distance?

He released a weary breath and refused to consider the answer to either of those questions.

Eventually he heard the toilet flush and the water running in the basin, then a minute or so later she opened the door. "I'd like you to leave now," she announced with a good deal more strength than she looked capable of managing.

"I need some answers first."

She ripped off her glasses and rubbed her eyes, then glared at him. "Don't you ever give up? I'm telling you I don't know anything!"

He stepped nearer to her. Didn't miss the flicker of uncertainty in those amber eyes. "Yes, you do. And I'll keep coming back until you tell me everything."

She pushed her glasses back into place and shoved her hair from her face with trembling fingers. "You're wasting your time, Agent MacBride."

Another thought poked its way through the jumble of theories whirling in his brain. "How did your ex-fiancé take your affair with Dr. Harrison?"

She blinked, taken aback by the question. What was he fishing for now? Didn't the man get it? She didn't know anything relevant to his case. "Brian and I broke up months ago."

Mac shrugged, the move casual, but his expression was anything but casual. "That may be, but he had to be pissed off when he learned he'd been replaced by a hot-shot shrink. Wasn't Harrison a friend of his?"

A frown worried her lips. She'd seen Ned at some of the parties she and Brian had attended. She'd even seen Brian talk to Ned from time to time, but then, he talked to everyone. Not once in their nine-month relationship had she heard Brian mention Ned. Ned certainly never mentioned Brian other than in the context of how her breakup with him added to the stress that brought on her panic attacks.

"I don't...think so," she admitted in all honesty. "I suppose you could call them casual acquaintances."

MacBride was watching her so closely that she could almost feel his eyes on her. She tugged the lapels of her robe tighter around her, but it wasn't her body that held his attention, she knew. He was studying her face, analyzing her responses, looking for signs of deception. She knew what he was after. Someone to nail with this murder rap.

"It's late, Agent MacBride," she said, squaring her shoulders and moving slightly away. "I'd like you to go now."

For one long moment she was sure he intended to argue the point, but to her surprise, he didn't.

"I'll be outside all night," he said, instead. "When I go, one of my men will take over. Don't even think about trying to give us the slip."

She nodded, too grateful for the presence now to react to his order.

With one final, lingering look, he turned and made his way back into her living room. She followed, suddenly conscious of her meager furnishings and less-than-spectacular housekeeping skills. She wasn't exactly a slob, but she wasn't neat, either.

At the door he hesitated once more. "This door doesn't have a peephole or a dead bolt. Think about getting both installed. In the meantime, at least ask who's there before you open the door."

Oddly, she was pretty sure his words were well meant. That he cared what happened to her.

Yeah, right.

He only wanted to keep his prime suspect alive and well until he could nail her for murder.

"Thanks for the advice," she retorted, a hint of sarcasm lacing the words.

That sea-blue gaze bored into hers. "I'm serious, Elizabeth. I don't want you to end up dead. You were one of Harrison's patients, too."

With that profound statement, he left.

For several seconds after the door closed, she could only stand there absorbing the impact and ramifications of his words.

Two of Ned's patients had been murdered in the past seventy-two hours. Coincidence? Apparently the FBI didn't think so.

Cold, bony fingers of fear clutched her throat. Maybe MacBride was right. Maybe her life was in danger. Before the thought fully formed in her mind, she turned the button on the knob locking the door. She hurried over to the front window and drew back the curtain. Just as he promised, MacBride backed out onto the street and parked directly in front of the house. A relief so profound slid through her that her knees almost buckled.

Vanessa Bumbalough was dead. Deana Dell was dead.

Who would be next?

Elizabeth half stumbled to the sofa in her haste and snatched up the phone. She punched in Gloria's number and paced the floor as she waited for her friend to answer. *Please, God,* she prayed, *let her be home. And safe.*

When a groggy hello came over the line, Elizabeth blurted, "We have to talk!"

Mac waited patiently for Driver to answer his cell phone. "They find anything else?" he asked without preamble.

"Nothing. The MO appears to be exactly the same as the last one. No sign of forced entry, probable sexual assault after being tied to the bed and panties shoved into her mouth. The only signs of struggle are in the bedroom. The techs found dozens of different prints. The lady apparently had a lot of guests. Since she and the Bumbalough woman ran in the same circles, there's no telling how many sets matching the previous scene they'll find."

A lot of nothing leading nowhere. Mac rubbed his eyes and stared up at the light in the window of Elizabeth's apartment. He had a bad feeling about this. A very bad feeling.

"I'm going to keep up the surveillance on Elizabeth Young tonight," he informed his partner. "I'll need relief around 8 a.m. I want you to track down a Brian Novak of Design Horizons and have him meet me at my office at nine."

Driver snorted. "Tomorrow's Sunday, Mac. How can I—"

"I don't care if it's Christmas," Mac shot back. "Death doesn't observe weekends or holidays. Have the guy at my office at nine sharp."

"Will do," Driver replied sheepishly. "Anything else?"

Mac exhaled a weary breath. "That's it. Call me if they find anything new."

He closed his phone and dropped it on the console. It

was going to be a long night. Shifting until he found a comfortable spot, he considered the layout around Elizabeth's apartment. She had no security, and the surrounding area was an intruder's wet dream. Everyone went to bed early and likely didn't hear as well as they used to. If someone wanted her, getting to her would be easy. She worked long hours and probably slept like a rock during the few hours of rest she got.

If she was the innocent she insisted she was and the latest turn in this case evolved into what he suspected, she could very well be in grave danger.

Whether she was a suspect, a material witness or simply a woman in jeopardy because she got mixed up with the wrong guy, Mac was duty bound to protect her.

The scary part was, who was going to protect him?

He was plunging headfirst into personal involvement. Something he never did.

But there didn't appear to be a damned thing he could do about it this time. Some part of him was hell-bent on saving the woman, whether he saved himself or not.

Elizabeth slept maybe two hours the entire night. Even before sunrise she was pacing the floor. At six she'd forced herself to bake her Sunday favorite—blueberry muffins—and she'd made a strong pot of coffee. The way she felt at the moment it would take the entire pot to get her through the day. But she had to work. She simply had no choice.

She pulled on her jeans and a T-shirt, rolled on a clean pair of socks and then slipped on her sneakers. Another cup of coffee and she'd be good to go.

She stilled, her gaze drawn to the front window. How was MacBride faring? she wondered. She moved to the window and peeked around the edge of the curtain. He was still there. The driver's-side window had been lowered to let in the cool morning air. As she watched, he scrubbed a hand over his face. She could just imagine how he felt. Exhausted. Hungry.

"Dammit," she uttered.

No matter how many times she told herself that her most recent problems were entirely his fault, she just couldn't help feeling sorry for him sitting out there in a cold car after having no sleep.

Admitting defeat with a mighty exhale, she filled a thermos with coffee and wrapped a couple of muffins in a napkin. The least she could do was feed him. He had, after all, spent the night watching over her. The thought made her shiver with an awareness she could no longer deny. She was sexually attracted to the man.

What an idiot she was. Outright asking for trouble.

Ignoring the alarm bells jangling in her head, she pulled on a jacket and marched out the door, down the steps and across the street. He'd caught sight of her before her sneakers hit the pavement, and he was climbing out of the car.

"Is everything all right?" he asked, those blue eyes surveying her from head to toe.

Just like last night, she could feel his eyes roaming her body, leaving heat everywhere. And damned if he didn't look fine with a night's growth of beard shadowing that chiseled jaw. "Everything's just peachy," she lied, forcing the forbidden thoughts to the farthest recesses of her mind. "I thought you might be hungry."

Actually he appeared ravenous. But then, she hadn't noticed that look in his eyes until after he'd given her the once-over. She shivered and scolded herself for allowing such a silly notion. Rich guys like MacBride didn't bother with working girls like her. Well, working girls in the sense of blue-collar types. Which was what she was. She'd been born into a blue-collar family and she was damned proud of it.

"Thanks." He reached for the thermos she offered. "I hope this is coffee."

She shrugged one shoulder, attempting to come off as indifferent. "Black. I didn't know if you liked cream or sugar."

"Black is perfect," he said, unscrewing the top while his eyes and full attention never deviated from her.

She pushed a tremulous smile into place. "Muffins," she explained as she thrust the still-warm baked goods at him.

He set the thermos on the roof of his car. The lid that served as a cup was filled with steaming coffee and clutched in his left hand; with his right he reached for the muffins.

Her heart banged against her ribs when his fingers brushed hers. She silently railed at herself once more. "I have to get to the job site," she said, her voice quavering like that of a sophomore hoping to be invited to the prom.

He sipped the hot coffee, then asked, "On Sunday?"

Shoving her hands into her back pockets, she offered another of those careless shrugs. "Sometimes it's necessary." Unlike him, she had to really work for a living. Even so, she didn't have money to throw around on elegant clothes and fancy cars. She stole a glance at the dark sedan he drove. Foreign, pricy, luxurious. She'd bet those leather seats were heated, too. Must be nice, she mused. And here she'd felt sorry for him out here in his sixty-thousand-dollar car. How many ways could she prove herself a fool?

For a time they stood in silence. He consumed the

muffins and drank a good portion of the coffee without commenting on the quality or palatability.

Finally he tossed the napkin that had contained the muffins into his fancy car, then screwed the lid back on the thermos and handed it to her. "That was great, thanks."

She accepted the thermos, careful not to allow her fingers to graze his. She was already in enough trouble here. "It was the least I could do," she said before she thought. A flush heated her cheeks. "I mean…you did keep an eye on my place last night and I was pretty shaken up."

Those twin blue laser beams cut right through her pretenses. "You didn't think of anything you needed to tell me?"

Here they were again, right back at square one. "I'm telling you—"

His cell phone buzzed, cutting off the rest of her words. He reached into his breast pocket and pulled out the slim device, quickly opening it. "MacBride."

She looked away, not wanting to intrude. It could be his girlfriend. Or his wife. Her head turned around so fast it almost gave her whiplash. In search of a wedding ring, she lowered her gaze to his left hand.

No rings whatsoever.

She emitted a little snort of self-disgust and forced her attention to the ground where it belonged. What an absolute idiot she was! He was the enemy. She was a pathetic woman who'd been dumped by her fiancé and taken advantage of by her shrink, to whom she'd paid top dollar to climb inside her head. He had, in turn, used what he'd learned to get inside her pants.

It just didn't get worse than this.

"Give me the address again." The steely tone drew

Elizabeth's attention back to him. He listened intently, his face devoid of emotion. "I'm on my way."

She waited, her nerves jangling, as he snapped the phone closed and put it away. His voice had sounded so ominous. Maybe there'd been a break in Ned's case. This whole nightmare couldn't be over soon enough for her.

He lifted his gaze to hers and said the last thing she wanted to hear. "There's been another murder. Cassandra Fowler."

Her heart took off at a gallop, the blood whooshing in her ears as it roared through her body. Even though she didn't recognize the name, he didn't have to say the rest. She already knew.

He glanced away briefly, then zoomed in on her with such ferocity that she almost stumbled back from the force of it. "Another one of your former lover's patients."

Tension thickened between them.

"It's time to come clean, Elizabeth," he said grimly. "Before anyone else has to die."

Chapter 7

Lucky Strike bustled with activity at noon on Sunday. The cool downtown eatery was on Grand between Broadway and Wooster. Though incredibly hip, it wasn't the kind of place a girl had to worry about dressing up for. A good thing, too, since Elizabeth had walked straight from her job site. She'd felt a panic attack coming on and had needed the long walk. Her private fed had followed in his dark sedan, taking care to keep his distance. As soon as she'd arrived, the waitress had shown her to one of the wooden tables in the back and taken her drink order.

Despite all that had occurred the night before, as well as that morning, Elizabeth had managed to complete the final details on the job this morning. If she could get the second loft on the floor finished by the end of the upcoming week, she'd have it made. For a couple of weeks, anyway.

She fingered the mug of coffee and forced herself to focus on the events of the past week. As much as she didn't want to, she had to consider that something very sinister was happening and somehow it related to Ned and his dirty little secret. Her dirty little secret.

The bastard. Even in death he haunted her.

She repressed a shudder and once again wrapped her mind around the concept of serial murders. Whoever had killed Ned could very well be the one killing his patients, seemingly one by one. This time the shudder would not be repressed, and her whole body shook with it.

Maybe she should have ordered a stiff drink, instead. She felt suddenly cold and alone. She glanced around the lively dining room with its French copper bar, seemingly carefree patrons and attentive staff, but she couldn't shake the feeling.

There was always the off chance that the murders weren't even related, she debated.

"Yeah, right," she muttered. Maybe she could have gone along with that theory after the first woman was murdered. And maybe even the second. But the third...

Three women.

Three of Ned's patients.

In some instances the third time was considered the charm, but in this situation Elizabeth could only conceive that it was a sign. A sign of bad things to come.

She was a woman.

She was one of Ned's patients.

If there was a list with those two common factors, she would be on it.

A shiver crept over her skin. How could this be happening?

She moistened her lips, then clamped down on her lower one to stem the fear welling up in her throat. What had any of those women done to deserve to die?

If her initial conclusion at the funeral was true, then they had all likely slept with Ned, just as she had. But he was dead; he wasn't killing anyone. He hadn't had a fi-ancée or even an ex-wife or girlfriend that she or Gloria knew of. Jealousy couldn't be the motivation. Some of his patients probably had husbands or significant others who could have done the killing. With one murder perhaps, but surely three different men wouldn't have decided on the same route of revenge against the former lovers of Dr. Ned Harrison. And why would one man kill his, as well as someone else's, cheating partner?

This couldn't be about scorned lovers.

She stilled. Or maybe it could.

Who said the murderer was a man? It wasn't con-firmed yet that the victims had been sexually assaulted.

Maybe some woman who'd secretly been in love with Ned had decided to kill him and all his hussies. The term Gloria had used to describe them brought a wan smile to Elizabeth's lips. The realization that she could very well have hit on the answer chased away any real humor.

Three women were dead. God only knew who might be next.

"There you are."

Elizabeth looked up at the sound of Gloria's voice. The corner of her mouth instantly rose, but the automatic re-sponse melted away when her gaze landed on the woman standing next to her friend.

"Elizabeth, this is Annabelle Ford." Gloria ushered the other woman forward. "Annabelle, Elizabeth Young, my best friend."

Annabelle extended her hand and Elizabeth had little choice but to shake it. The woman's touch was warm and firm with confidence, as was her smile. "It's a pleasure to meet you, Elizabeth. I'm so sorry it has to be under the present circumstances." Her voice wasn't unpleasant, just a little gravelly.

Elizabeth studied the tall, thin woman for a long moment, wondering vaguely who exactly Annabelle Ford was and why she was with Gloria. Her light-brown hair was cut in a fashionably short style that framed her somewhat angular face. Brown eyes that appeared both intelligent and sincere assessed her with equal curiosity.

"Nice to meet you, too," Elizabeth eventually remembered to say.

"Did you order already?" Gloria asked as they took seats, one on either side of Elizabeth at the square table.

She shook her head. "Just my drink." She sipped her café mocha once more, noting from the corner of her eye that Annabelle was still scrutinizing her.

When the waitress had taken drink, as well as food, orders all around the table and rushed away to place it, Gloria leaned forward and kicked off the conversation in a quiet tone.

"I don't know what's going on, but after you called I did some thinking."

Elizabeth had actually called her friend twice in the past twelve hours. Once around midnight after her run-in with MacBride and then again this morning when he got the call that another woman was dead. She and Gloria had decided to push the meeting they'd planned for dinner this evening up to lunch. Neither of them could stand the suspense a moment longer. All that had kept them from meeting that morning was Gloria's overnight company from the party she'd attended and Elizabeth's need to finish up that one loft.

"This can't be coincidence," Gloria went on. She sat back in her seat and shook her head. "My God, three women...all Ned's patients." She inclined her head toward her companion. "That's why I called Annabelle."

Just when Elizabeth was about to ask who Annabelle

was, Gloria told her. "Annabelle is—" she swallowed with difficulty "—was Ned's attorney."

"And his confidante," Annabelle put in, that husky voice modulated to a discreet level. "I've known Ned since our college days. We shared a great deal. He was an outstanding man." She fell silent and her gaze grew distant.

For just a second, Elizabeth couldn't help wondering if Annabelle had been one of Ned's lovers, too. When she'd spoken of their relationship, there'd been a smidgen of intimacy about her tone. But Annabelle didn't strike Elizabeth as Ned's type at all. She was really tall, at least six feet. Her slim frame lacked the curves Ned's women usually possessed. Who knew, though? Ned clearly was not a man of high morals, so maybe his standards didn't always dictate the voluptuous type. And admittedly, Elizabeth didn't quite fit that mold, either. Maybe she and Annabelle had something in common.

"She knew Ned better than any of us," Gloria rushed to add. "On the way here, she told me some very startling secrets about our old friend."

That tweaked Elizabeth's attention. She propped her arms on the table and leaned into the circle, speaking directly to Gloria. "How about this newsflash. Whoever is doing this may have both of us on his list, as well."

"Precisely," her friend agreed. "This is why we have to do something."

Elizabeth gave her a palms-up gesture. "Do what? I spend half my time looking over my shoulder. I'm scared to death someone is already watching me." She leaned closer still. "I told you what happened last night."

"Someone besides the FBI, you mean?"

This query came from Annabelle. Startled that Gloria had shared this with a stranger, Elizabeth could only stare at the woman.

"Don't be angry, Elizabeth," Gloria said. "I had to tell her everything. She can't help us if she doesn't know everything."

Where had she heard that before? Elizabeth mused. Mac had used the same line on her, but for totally different reasons. She shook herself. When had she started calling him Mac? "Yes," she said bluntly in response to Annabelle's query. "I feel like someone besides the FBI is watching me."

Annabelle placed a hand over hers. Elizabeth gritted her teeth against the instinctive reflex to jerk her hand away. "I think you might be right," Annabelle said. She looked from Elizabeth to Gloria and back several times as she spoke, her gaze direct, insistent. All attorney. "Have you ever heard of the Gentlemen's Association?"

Both shook their heads.

Annabelle sighed. "Well, it's not something you're going to enjoy hearing about, but I feel I must tell you." Her gaze took on a kind of desperate quality. "Ned shared this information in confidence with me, but he's dead now and I'm almost certain it may be crucial to your continued survival."

Her words frightened Elizabeth. "What is this Gentlemen's Association?"

Finally releasing her hold on Elizabeth, Annabelle went on, "The association is a coast-to-coast group of men, all wealthy professionals much like Ned, for whom life has become tragically boring because they have it all.

"They have all the money they could ever wish for, social status, anything they want. So the thrill of the hunt, of the challenge is gone." She shook her head sadly. "I watched this very need eat away at Ned. None of his accomplishments were ever enough. His life lacked the primal kind of excitement that comes from a new conquest. So he joined this association."

Elizabeth felt her blood turn to ice when the next logical thought occurred to her. "The videotapes."

Annabelle nodded. "They make these tapes, each attempting to outdo the other, and then play them on the Internet via private chat rooms for the entire association's viewing pleasure."

Gloria's gaze locked with Elizabeth's. "He did that to us." Her words were scarcely a whisper but filled with the same emotions whirling through Elizabeth.

Anger, humiliation. The feelings almost overwhelmed her, but she fought them. She had to hear all of this. Had to find a way to protect herself. And her friend.

"Once you become a member of this association, there is no turning back. The only way out is death."

Elizabeth felt her face drain of color. "You think they killed him?"

Annabelle nodded grimly. "I firmly believe that's the only logical answer. Ned had a weakness, ladies. He became addicted to these darker needs. The more perverse the better. I believe that addiction cost him his life. This association is responsible for what he became."

A frown furrowed its way across Elizabeth's brow. "But what about the women? They don't even know this association exists. Why kill them?"

Annabelle seemed to ponder the question for a moment before responding. "There's always the possibility that the two aren't related. But Ned told me only a few days before he died that he thought someone was watching him. He feared he'd done something to displease those in power." She shrugged. "I have no idea what he'd done or thought he'd done. I only know he was afraid."

"Oh...my...God," Gloria muttered slowly.

Both Elizabeth and Annabelle stared at her.

"That's why the FBI is involved. We should have known it would be something like that."

Sex, videotapes, the Internet. It made sense to Elizabeth. "You could be right."

"Think about it," Annabelle said, picking up the ball and running with it. "If the association thought that Ned's affiliation had been compromised and the FBI had an eye on him, they would certainly want to neutralize the threat. What better way than to execute him?"

Elizabeth shook her head in confusion. "But what about the women?"

Silence reigned for what felt like an eternity.

"They must think one of you knows something." Annabelle gave a decisive nod, warming to her theory. "Obviously they're not certain who knows what, so they've decided to take out all of you, one at a time. Or perhaps the other murders are simply to cast suspicion elsewhere."

"That's crazy!" Elizabeth hadn't meant to sound so vehement. But the whole thing was ludicrous. This was real life. Why would some anonymous association risk killing dozens of women over one jerk they'd already taken out of the picture? "The risk is too great."

"I don't have all the answers," Annabelle admitted with an urgency that struck a chord of dread deep inside Elizabeth. "The only thing I am certain of is that both of you—" she glanced from one to the other "—are in serious danger."

"What do we do?" Gloria directed her question to Annabelle, her tone filled with every bit as much urgency as Annabelle's.

A stillness settled over Elizabeth as realization dawned on her. Annabelle was right. There was no use pretend-

ing otherwise. Either one of them could be next. "There's
only one thing we can do," she said.

The other two turned to her, their faces expectant,
hopeful. Even Annabelle looked as if she feared she might
somehow be on that list. Who knew? Maybe she was.
When it came to animal attraction and raw sex, type
wasn't always an immediate concern.

"We fight back." Elizabeth felt the weight of her own
words. She'd been there once, had prayed she'd never
have to go back, but here she was, eyeball deep in a battle to prove her innocence. And quite possibly to protect
her life. "They already think I'm guilty," she continued
solemnly. "All they need is one real piece of evidence. If
they can't prove I did it, they'll move on to the next likely
suspect." Her gaze slid to Gloria's. "Can you prove where
you were that night?"

Gloria's pupils dilated slightly. "I…I—"

Elizabeth cut her off. "The point is, they won't stop
until they have someone to prosecute. If not me, then
you." She turned to Annabelle. "Or you." She paused,
gathering her courage before she said the rest. "The way
I see it, the real problem is staying alive until the police
either nail someone or we do it for them."

The three simply stared at one another for a minute
that became two.

"How could we possibly—"

"That was my thinking." Annabelle interrupted whatever protest Gloria was about to launch. "We can't trust
anyone else. We have to work together, just the three of
us, and solve this mystery." She pressed a hand to her
throat. "Our very lives may depend upon it."

Gloria held up both hands. "Wait. Wait. Wait. How are
we supposed to do that?"

Before anyone could answer, the waitress arrived with

their order. Elizabeth had pretty much lost her appetite at this point, but she needed energy for work, as well as for what lay ahead where this murder investigation was concerned.

As soon as the waitress had moved on, Annabelle said, "We need the connection between Ned and the association."

Elizabeth laughed. She couldn't help it. It just popped out. She fiddled with her fork to avoid the expectant looks from the other two. "If the FBI couldn't find enough evidence to take them down, which obviously they hadn't, how are we supposed to?" It was her turn to insist on a reality check. She'd been thinking more along the lines of checking out everyone who knew or associated with Ned. People they knew, not some ghostlike organization they couldn't even prove existed.

"My sentiments exactly," Gloria reiterated.

Annabelle sat in silent consideration for a moment before telling one more secret she knew about her dearly departed client Ned Harrison. "The FBI will be searching his computers, at the office and at home, but they won't find anything."

Apprehension inched its way up Elizabeth's spine. "What do you mean? How do you know that?"

"The association's business is conducted in cyberspace, the Bureau will try tracking where Ned has been, but they won't find anything, because he used a special system for his little hobby."

Elizabeth didn't know much about computers, but she did know that, like a telephone, anything a person did on the computer could be traced. Somehow a trail was left. "So where is this system he used?" Elizabeth felt her pulse quicken at the idea of bringing down this association. Her stomach roiled at the thought that the members of the demented group had likely seen her videotape. She tamped down the urge to gag. She didn't even want to think about some of the games Ned had prodded her into playing. God, how could she have been so stupid?

"At his office there's a secret room. It was a part of the original architecture—a bomb or storm shelter of some sort. It's like a vault. But when the building was renovated some forty years ago, it was filled in, or at least that's what the blueprints said." Annabelle smiled knowingly. "Apparently the contractor on the job at the time decided to save himself a little money and just boarded it over. Anyway, Ned discovered it when he had the office remodeled a couple of years ago and decided to make it a vault for his most private files." She sighed as she peered down at her salad. "Eventually he turned it into a media room for his forbidden pleasure."

Elizabeth shivered at her choice of words.

"You've seen it?" Gloria asked, appalled.

"Well, I haven't actually seen it, but he did tell me about it. He had some sort of shield installed so that the room's presence couldn't be detected. It's all quite high tech."

"We have to go there!" Gloria exclaimed, an extra portion of desperation in her voice.

Elizabeth shook her head. "No. We have to go to the authorities." MacBride's image loomed large in her mind. He would know what to do, she was sure of it.

"How do we know we can trust the authorities?" Annabelle said offhandedly. "What if one or more of them belong to the association, as well? After all, they haven't brought the association down in all this time. I happen to know that Ned has been affiliated with the group for more than a year now. What's the holdup?" Her fierce dark eyes settled on Elizabeth. "I'll tell you why—because they're *men*."

"We can't trust men on this issue," Gloria said. "We get the goods on the association and we take it to the press. We could blow the whole thing wide open, then the authorities would have to take action."

"Not we," Annabelle corrected. Again she looked from Gloria to Elizabeth. "His office is surely being watched. One person slipping past anyone who might be watching will be problematic enough. But all three of us..." She gave her head a brisk shake. "It would never work."

Seemingly endless seconds of tension-filled silence passed as each digested what that meant.

"I would have done this myself as soon as I was notified of Ned's murder, but the police were everywhere," Annabelle said. "I couldn't risk it. I couldn't be sure the man in charge wasn't involved." Anger etched fierce lines into the features of Annabelle's face. "I wanted so to find whoever had done this to him."

Elizabeth and Gloria exchanged a look of uncertainty.

"Even if I had been able to get into his office I couldn't have managed," Annabelle went on. "I was in an accident a few years ago. My right shoulder and my left arm were severely damaged. I have almost no upper-body strength. The hidden door is extremely heavy and there is no automatic opener. Ned explained that the mechanism would be too easily detected. Therefore the entryway has to be opened and closed manually."

"I'll do it," Gloria offered without hesitation. "I can do it."

Elizabeth shook her head. "No. I'm stronger than you. I'll do it."

"I said," Gloria argued, her Irish temper flaring in those green eyes, "that I would do it."

"I'm accustomed to *manual* labor," Elizabeth pointed out. "I know I can do it. If you get in there and then you can't—"

Gloria heaved a sigh of exasperation. "Fine. You do it."

"Time is of the essence," Annabelle suggested. "We shouldn't waste any. We need to act now."

"Just one question," Elizabeth wondered aloud. "Why did Ned tell you this? Wasn't it dangerous for him to tell anyone?" She watched Annabelle closely as she responded.

"He wanted me to know—" her voice faltered and her eyes grew suspiciously bright "—in case something happened to him."

Well, Elizabeth didn't know this Annabelle from Adam's house cat, but she did know Gloria. She trusted Gloria. And if Gloria thought she was okay, then she must be. Besides, what choice did they have? Annabelle knew far more than the two of them put together. And knowledge was power.

Brian Novak was not accustomed to being rousted from bed like a common criminal. His money generally bought him a blind eye. But, Mac mused, there was a first time for everything.

"You know, Agent MacBride," Novak said, his hangover obvious in his rusty voice, as well as his disheveled appearance, "my attorney will be calling your superiors first thing tomorrow morning." He reached for the crystal decanter on the sideboard that served as a bar in his spacious great room. "I'm quite certain there is a law against this type of behavior."

Agent Driver had worked half the night and all morning to locate Novak, who'd recently moved into a criminally expensive midtown high-rise. Not one of his colleagues or cronies seemed to have his new address, but Mac had his own ideas about that. Finally Driver had managed to run down the secretary at Novak's design firm. Being young and new to the firm, she had been more easily intimidated and she'd rolled over on her boss like a playful puppy.

Now, at half-past noon, Mac finally had Novak's attention. He'd asked him where he'd been on the Friday night the doctor was murdered.

Novak took a sip of his whiskey and made a sound of approval before smiling at the question. "You think I killed Ned Harrison?"

What Mac really thought was that Novak had a connection to the Gentlemen's Association, but he hadn't wanted to press his luck by bringing up that theory unless it became absolutely necessary. Right now Novak was the only possible thread they had left on that case, and even that connection was thin. Too thin. Unlike with Harrison, they had no hard proof. Even with Harrison the only true evidence they'd managed to gather in months of work was one intercepted telephone conversation. Mac had clung to that link, knowing Harrison would eventually make another mistake.

"Yes," Mac said in answer to Novak's question and to the man's utter surprise. "Actually, I do." Driver stood silently on the other side of the room. He'd learned the first week on the job with Mac not to show any emotion. No matter how startled he might be at what he witnessed.

"Please, gentlemen—" Novak gestured to the sofa and chairs "—make yourselves comfortable. This discussion could prove interesting."

Mac didn't have any hard evidence connecting the murders of the women to Harrison's, but in his gut, he knew they were connected. Harrison's murderer might have been a woman, but a man had killed those women. The preliminaries on the first two victims had confirmed sexual assault. The killer had left behind seminal fluid, which could ultimately identify him. Mac wondered if Brian Novak was that stupid.

He dumped Elizabeth, so he must be. That notion seared Mac's brain like a hot blade. He blinked it away, refused to allow her into his thoughts right now.

Mac took Novak up on his invitation and settled on the sofa. Driver remained standing near the door. That routine was another thing he'd learned. When two agents attended an interview, one always stood to maintain the intimidation factor.

"Do you have an alibi or don't you?" Mac prodded.

"I was at a party," Novak said smugly. "Ned was supposed to be there, as well, but I guess he ran into a snag, so to speak."

The man's treatment of Elizabeth Young aside, there was something Mac didn't like about Novak. Maybe it was that beach-bum tan or the windblown way he wore his blond hair. Could be the earring—or even the blatant way he stared at Mac. From his manner of dress to his posture, the man clearly thought he was God's gift to women. Men, too, Mac decided. He hadn't missed the way Novak had sized up Driver and himself when they arrived. Poor Elizabeth. She hadn't had a chance against a smooth operator like this.

Mac clenched his jaw and attempted again to banish her from his mind. For the hundredth time he marveled at just how much difficulty he was having with this case…with her.

"I'd say he did," Mac replied, not the least bit amused by the man's gallows humor. "Why don't you give me the names of people who can verify your whereabouts?"

Novak drained his glass and set it aside. "Certainly."

As Mac jotted down the information, Novak rattled off more than a dozen names and telephone numbers. When Mac had crossed the "t" on the last one, he lifted his gaze to the other man's. "I don't see Elizabeth Young on your list. Aren't you two involved?"

Mac knew that his question must have confused Driver, for Driver was aware that he knew differently. But this bozo didn't.

The truth was, Mac wanted—no, needed Novak's take on the relationship. What did that make him? A masochist?

"That relationship ended months ago," Novak said with a practiced laugh. "Your people really need to sharpen their investigative skills."

Mac nodded and made another note on his trusty pad that had absolutely nothing to do with Novak or Elizabeth or this case. "And what exactly was the nature of your former relationship?"

Novak took a deep breath and then slouched back on the couch, allowing his shirt to fall open and offering up his well-defined chest for display.

"Well, let's just say I did Elizabeth a favor." Novak inclined his head. "I gave sweet little Elizabeth the opportunity to grab the brass ring and she went for it. She couldn't wait to get out of that pathetic little dump of a town. I helped her get what she wanted and she made it worth my while."

Mac tensed before he could stop himself. Every muscle in his body jerked with the need to pound the hell out of this bastard.

A knowing smile lifted one side of Novak's mouth as he leaned forward and braced his arms on his knees, his gaze focused intently on Mac. "She's very good."

Fury sent Mac's blood rushing to his head, throbbing there in time with the stampede in his chest. His fingers tightened around the pen as if it were Novak's neck.

"She's always a little hesitant at first," Novak went on, pretending to be oblivious to Mac's reaction. But he knew. He knew and he enjoyed it immensely. "But once you get her started, man, is she hot."

Mac stood, his control slipping away fast. "I'll get back to you as soon as I've checked out your alibi."

Novak pushed lazily to his feet and led Mac to the front door, which he opened.

Mac wanted to kill him. He'd never in his life before wanted to kill a man over a woman, but he wanted to tear Brian Novak limb from limb.

Driver was already heading down the corridor to the elevator, but Mac hesitated in the doorway. "I wouldn't leave town if I were you." His gaze locked with Novak's pale-gray one. "There will be more questions."

Novak leaned against the door frame as if being visited by the FBI was an everyday occurrence. The bastard didn't even have the good sense to be worried.

"Take her, Agent MacBride," Novak said softly, knowingly. "You won't be sorry."

With his pen and pad in his pocket, Mac's fingers curled into tight fists of rage, but somehow he held himself back. "Thanks for your cooperation."

Mac stormed away without a backward glance. As angry as he was, the only thing he could think about was that videotape and the images it held. By the time he reached the elevator, he was as hard as a rock from merely thinking about Elizabeth Young and what Novak suggested.

He stepped into the waiting car and Driver punched the button for the lobby. "Quite a character, huh?"

Mac's only response was a grunt. He couldn't think clearly enough right now for a proper one. Every ounce of blood in his body had raced to his loins.

He had to close his eyes against the truth he wanted to deny.

Novak had seen it. Had rubbed it in.

Mac wanted Elizabeth. He wanted her riding him slow and easy at first, and then hard and fast, her head thrown back in ecstasy. He wanted her touching him, kissing him. He wanted to feel her lips, her tongue on his skin. And then he wanted to take her with such intensity that she wouldn't even remember a jerk like Brian Novak when it was over.

He wanted her all to himself.

Suspect or not.

Mac shook himself. He'd lost it. That much was clear. "Driver, I want you to take the surveillance on Young tonight."

His partner was about to protest. Mac saw it in his eyes, but one look at the ferocity in Mac's and he snapped his mouth shut.

"Sure," he muttered. "Sure, why not?"

"It's the right thing to do," Elizabeth told herself under her breath one last time.

Leaving the subway she'd glanced around again. No sign of the guy who'd been watching her. She'd had a hell of a time, but she was pretty sure she'd given the agent the slip. If she'd driven her truck, she'd never have been able to do it. But she'd parked it in an alley and then disappeared in the subway before the guy realized what she was up to. Then she'd ducked into a group of missionaries while he searched for her in the crowd on the platform. He was so certain she'd gotten on the train that he'd climbed aboard for a second to look for her. When he moved farther down the platform, she'd sneaked aboard the car he'd just checked. She'd watched him search for her as the train took off for its next stop.

Then she'd walked the ten blocks over to Avenue of the Americas and to the row of old brownstones now used as offices, Ned's among them. It was really dark on this part of the street. Trees and architecture all but blocked the meager light from the streetlights. But she knew her way here with her eyes closed. What a joke. Look at what it had gotten her.

Nothing but trouble.

With the spare key Annabelle had given her now tightly clasped in her hand, Elizabeth slipped into an alley and then down the backside of the row of brownstones. She tried without success to calm her racing heart, to quiet her breathing. What if she was being watched this very minute? She swiveled her head from side to side. Nothing.

Keeping close to the wall, she moved toward the rear door that would lead into Ned's office. She supposed Annabelle had a key because she'd been his attorney. Since he had no surviving family, his attorney would be the most likely person to settle his affairs. Annabelle seemed just as scared by the murders as Gloria and Elizabeth were. This kind of action seemed their only recourse when they couldn't know who to trust. Elizabeth ignored the little voice that screamed at her that this was all wrong somehow.

She had to do this. Had to help exonerate herself. If they could prove the Gentlemen's Association was involved in Ned's death, then she would be free and clear. But they needed hard evidence.

Taking a deep breath for courage, she pushed away

from the concealing security of the shadowed wall and moved to the door. Though there was no exterior light nearby to worry about, just enough moonlight glimmered down to guide her without giving away her presence. Thank God the police hadn't padlocked his office as they had his apartment. She supposed that made sense since his home—not his office—was the scene of the crime.

She had the key inserted into the lock when she heard it.

A footstep...something...

Before she could turn around, a strong arm snaked around her throat. A punishing hand clamped down on her mouth. The scream she tried to deliver died in her throat.

His angry breath on her cheek sent a shudder of recognition—of dread—through her. She felt his hard body pressed against her backside. Tried to jerk away. Twisted to break free, but he only held her more tightly to him.

His lips close enough to touch her skin, he whispered, "I knew it was you."

Chapter 8

"Open the door, Liz," he ordered, his voice savage and cold.

Even before he'd used that pet name for her, she'd known it was him. An all-too-familiar shudder had quaked through her the instant he touched her...the instant she felt his breath on her skin.

"Let go of me, Brian, or I'll scream!"

He laughed the condescending laugh that punctuated the very essence of his macho mentality. He considered himself above all others, especially her. Why hadn't she seen that when they first met? Why hadn't she picked up on what a jerk he really was?

"So scream," he taunted. "Who's going to hear you?" He reached for the knob, gave it a fierce twist and kicked the door inward. "We're going to talk." Shoving her inside ahead of him, he quickly closed the door behind him.

Elizabeth scrambled to regain the equilibrium she'd lost physically, as well as mentally. Too many possibilities for her to choose just one swirled wildly amid the confusion and irritation clouding her ability to reason. Why was he here? What did they have to talk about?

Brian moved to the long table in the center of the dark interior and switched on one of the brass reading lamps. The dim glow pitched the space into long shadows, but she would have been fine without the light. She had first-hand knowledge of every inch of this room. After all, she'd helped decorate these offices just months ago. How else could she have afforded such an exclusive analyst? She'd worked hard to make Ned's suite of offices into everything he'd wanted. This room was no exception.

Ned's professional library. The walls were lined with book-filled, gleaming mahogany shelves. A single conference-style table, also mahogany, surrounded by upholstered armchairs served as the focal point. Built-in brass reading lamps lined the table, four of them altogether, their dignified appearance disrupted only by the latest technology in telephones sitting square in the middle. The classic reading lamps gave the room a more intimate ambiance than overhead lighting; the telephone with built-in conferencing capabilities was essential equipment.

The far corner of the room was equipped with a small wet bar complete with a dormitory-size fridge, a state-of-the-art coffeemaker and a small marble sink. A Monet print hung next to a shiny brass rack that held mugs and glasses. But the perks didn't stop here. In Ned's office there was another bar, one containing almost any kind of liquor one could want. To most the elegant piece of furniture looked like the matching credenza to his desk, but he had insisted that he needed a means of entertaining certain *special* clients.

She'd learned the hard way just what *special* meant to him.

Ned Harrison hadn't missed a trick. Whatever he

wanted, he got. No matter the cost. He'd once lived in the upstairs portion of the brownstone, but fame had sent him in search of more elaborate housing. Now the rooms above his offices served as mere storage. She wondered briefly if it had all been worth it. Had his primal urges been worth dying for? She'd pretty much concluded that his murder had something to do with those very urges—and the Gentlemen's Association.

Who would ever have suspected? On the outside he'd been all charm and grace and appeared to have the world by the tail. All one had to do to join him in his glorious life was be obedient and submissive to his demands. Yet somehow he'd always managed to make her think it was what *she* wanted. It sickened her now to realize how naive she'd been.

"Sit." Dragging her attention back to the present, Brian motioned to one of the chairs.

He loved tossing out those one-word commands as if she were a dog or other well-trained pet. And hadn't she been?

But those days were over. "No thanks," she threw right back at him, folding her arms in defiance.

Those pale-gray eyes, as hard and icy as a frozen lake, gazed relentlessly into hers as he started toward her. She fought the urge to run. She would not let him have his way. Not again. Not ever again.

"I said sit!" He jerked out one of the chairs and clamped a hand on her shoulder with crushing strength, propelling her into the waiting seat.

For the first time since she'd realized it was him, fear slithered around her, tightening her chest. What was his problem? And what was he doing here, anyway?

Before she could demand some answers, he gave another order. "Tell me what it is you think you know." He propped himself on the edge of the table, positioning himself so that he could look down at her. "I don't want to have to hurt you."

If he'd slapped her, she wouldn't have been any more surprised. As cruel and belittling as Brian could be, she'd never feared him in the physical sense until now. With her heart pumping feverishly and dread dampening her skin, she seized back some semblance of control and dredged up an innocent look. "I don't know anything. What're you talking about?"

Her heart beating relentlessly against her sternum, she held her breath and prayed he would let it go at that.

He smiled, the surface convention utterly sinister. She swallowed. Hard. Was this some sort of game? She'd never seen him like this.

And suddenly she knew.

Brian was a part of this. He was probably a card-carrying member of the Gentlemen's Association as well. God knew he had the penchant for perversion.

"I know what you did, Elizabeth," he said softly, the gentler tone laced with a threatening edge. "The truth is, I don't give a damn that Harrison is dead." He made a sound, half growl, half chuckle. "He took too many chances." Brian reached out to graze her cheek with his fingertips. She flinched, earning herself another of those unnerving smiles.

"I know how he felt about you," he told her in that same low tone. His fingers trailed down her throat. "He thought you were special. Didn't want to let you go like he should have." His fingers splayed around her throat.

Elizabeth was determined not to let him see her fear. Damn him. "Don't touch me like that." Hard as it was, she maintained eye contact, kept him looking at her so he wouldn't notice her left hand inching its way toward the center of the table.

That evil smile only widened. "All you have to do is tell me the secret you're keeping and everything will be fine. I know you know—that's why you're here." The pressure of his fingers increased ever so slightly, raising goose bumps on her flesh. "He wanted you, so I let him have you. But it wasn't easy, you know."

She froze, the thoughts screeching to a halt inside her head. "What're you saying?"

"Marrying you wasn't going to change who I am," he went on mysteriously. "It would have simply provided the kind of image I needed. Until I found you, there hadn't been anyone I would have allowed that privilege. But I knew you'd never suspect." His fingers slid around to cup her neck and draw her closer. "As naive as you were, you could still bring me to my knees with that sweet mouth and that hot body."

Fury burned away every other emotion, including the paralyzing fear she'd felt only a second earlier. She tried to jerk away from him. This was insane. Nothing he said made sense.

"But Ned…" He released her and shrugged. "He was obsessed with you. Just watching you at the parties turned him on. He had to have you. What could I do? He was my best friend."

This just couldn't be. She shook her head in denial of what his words meant. "I rarely even saw the two of you speak. How could he have been your best friend? You didn't even come to his funeral!"

"Our relationship wasn't like that," Brian explained. "It was a private bond." He leaned nearer still, those menacing eyes carrying enough of an arctic blast to form icicles inside her. "Just like the one I know you're keeping from me."

A new thought punched through the pile of others tumbling into her head. "But it was Gloria who introduced me to Ned." She shook her head thoughtfully. "She suggested I see him…professionally." He couldn't be right about any of this. "You didn't have anything to do with it."

Brian stared at her lips now in a way that had once drawn her like a moth to the flame. Abruptly his earlier threat echoed loudly in her ears. He wanted answers—or he would hurt her. She inched her fingers closer to the telephone in the center of the table.

"I'm the one who told Gloria that seeing Ned would be a good idea for you," he said.

His statement stunned her, stole her breath. Gloria—her best friend, the only person in the world she trusted—was involved in this? Any bravado she'd managed collapsed like a house of cards. "I don't believe you," she protested weakly.

He straightened away from her, snapping out of his fixation on her lips. "Well, it's true. I have no reason to lie." He stared down at her once more, impatience registering. "Tell me what you know." When she would have argued, he said, "Careful now, I don't want you to regret anything." Something knowing slid into his expression. "I could always tell the police that I have evidence you killed him."

"I didn't kill him!" How could he say that? Just when she'd thought nothing else could shock her. It was beyond all question now. He was insane.

"Of course you did," he countered.

Her head moved side to side in denial of his ridiculous accusation. "Why would I kill him? You can't possibly have any evidence."

"Because he wasn't going to let you go, even after you discovered his socially unacceptable appetite and was repulsed by it. He wanted to keep you, anyway. We all knew the troubles the two of you were having." That evil smile stretched his lips once more. "You'd be surprised what can be turned into proof."

The way she'd openly avoided Ned, the argument. God. The dagger.

It had been a gift from her. Had Brian planted it there? Horror gripped her by the throat. Surely he hadn't killed Ned!

"A man should always know when to let go," Brian rambled on. "But he just wouldn't let it go. I warned him that keeping you would be a mistake. The longer the relationship went on, the more likely you were to discover our secret. Others were concerned, as well."

Keeping her? Incredulity momentarily overshadowed the fear. This was the twenty-first century. Men didn't *keep* women. And the only appetite she'd known Ned to have was the insatiable one he had for women. He liked to screw around, especially with those who trusted him on a professional level. One woman would never have been enough for him. He'd been far too smooth to ever get caught. He knew how to make a woman think she needed him—believe it had been her own idea. She stilled. But there had been that one secret—the videotapes…and the Gentlemen's Association.

"I don't know what any of this means," she said, her fingers finally touching the edge of the telephone base. Anticipation propelled adrenaline into her bloodstream. She struggled to keep the tumultuous emotions from her eyes.

"Tell me, Liz." Brian leaned in her direction again. "How did it feel to plunge that dagger into his chest?

Was it like the time you stabbed your brother-in-law, or was it all the better knowing you'd sliced straight into his heart?"

"I didn't do it!" The raw, primal sound of her voice startled even her.

"But can you prove it?" he taunted. "Now, tell me what you know."

Her fingers curled around the receiver, and in one swift move she surged upward and slammed it into his skull before he could block the move. He crumpled to the floor.

And didn't move.

A trickle of blood bloomed at his hairline along his temple. Her first instinct was to see if he was dead or alive, but her second overrode it. She ran. Jerked the back door open and ran like hell.

She had only one thing on her mind—finding Gloria.

Brian couldn't have been telling the truth. She refused to believe that Gloria had betrayed her like that. Hadn't they both suffered at Ned's hand? Gloria was just as hurt as she was. They were best friends, for God's sake.

Pushing herself to move faster, Elizabeth bounded onto the sidewalk. Brian could come to any second and chase her down. She felt certain she'd only stunned him. She shuddered at what he might have had planned for her. But why? What did he have to do with any of this?

How could she not have known he and Ned were close?

What did they have in common? Ned was a psychiatrist. Brian was an architect. At least five years separated them in age. Their tastes in clothing, music, in everything, were worlds apart. She couldn't even imagine what they talked about.

The Gentlemen's Association.

The realization struck her like a blow to the abdomen. Brian had to have been a part of it, too. He'd seen the video. Renewed horror rushed through her. How many of *their* lovemaking sessions had he videotaped? Her knees threatened to buckle. Would this nightmare ever end? All these years she'd felt so sorry for her sister living in hell with an on-again-off-again drug habit and an abusive husband. And look at her. She hadn't fared much better.

Elizabeth slammed headlong into a brick wall—or what felt like one.

Kicking and clawing, she wrenched away from the hands grabbing at her, but he was too strong. She couldn't let him get her now. Had to get away. She opened her mouth to scream.

"Stop fighting me!" he ordered.

She went limp as recognition of the voice filtered through her hysteria. Her gaze flew to his face.

MacBride.

"What the hell are you running from?" he demanded sharply.

In the next second Elizabeth realized two things. She had just committed assault and been caught fleeing the office of a victim in an ongoing murder investigation.

A murder investigation in which she was a prime suspect.

She was screwed.

MacBride shook her just hard enough to get her attention. Those strong fingers gripping her arms sent spears of heat through her. "What happened, Elizabeth? What're you doing here?"

"I...I thought I'd left something in the library." She trembled at the idea of having lied to him yet again. She was tired of lying—especially to him. If he ever found out...

Even in the dim light she saw his eyes narrow. "At Harrison's office?"

MacBride was no fool. He knew exactly where she'd been. Had probably known this was where she was headed the minute his man reported her having given him the slip in the vicinity of midtown.

"Yes." She sucked in a ragged breath and shrugged free of his hold, even though a part of her would have liked nothing better than to wilt in those powerful arms. "I…I helped decorate his office," she stammered, grappling for an acceptable excuse, "and I only just realized my paint chips were missing. I thought maybe I'd left them here."

"The work you did for Harrison was months ago, wasn't it?" That scrutinizing gaze bored straight into her.

She lifted her chin and flat out ignored his innuendo. "I guess I must have left it someplace else."

He cocked his head and eyed her suspiciously. "That doesn't explain why you were running for your life. Was someone else here, too?"

God almighty. If by some sick twist of fate Brian was dead, she was done for. Even if he was alive and kicking, she didn't want MacBride to talk to him. The last thing she needed was Brian putting ideas about evidence and motives into MacBride's head. She was already at the top of his list.

"While I was searching I…I thought I heard someone outside, maybe a burglar, so I ran." She held her breath as she waited for his reaction.

"I guess we should check it out, then."

Before she could come up with a reasonable excuse not to, he was dragging her back toward the office. At the door her heart leaped into her throat. If Brian opened his big mouth…

"You left the door open?"

The door stood ajar the way she'd left it, but there was

no sign of Brian. She blinked and looked again just in case. No Brian. Thank God.

She nodded in answer to MacBride's question. "I was too scared to take the time to lock up." Now that was the truth.

"You have a key?"

The slightest dash of surprise flavored his voice.

"I guess I forgot to give it back after the job was done," she offered, moving to the conference table to lean against it. She couldn't trust her ability to stay vertical at the moment. A mixture of relief and trepidation had turned her muscles rubbery.

She imagined that Brian must have noticed that someone had detained her as she fled. He'd likely slipped away unnoticed in the other direction.

Lucky him.

She was stuck here with MacBride.

She shivered when her eyes took in the whole of him as he stood in the middle of Ned's library surveying the place. Agent MacBride was a hottie, that was undeniable. And there was a definite attraction between them. But she damn sure didn't need any additional complications right now. Not to mention the fact that MacBride thought she was a killer.

Staring down at the floor, she contemplated that reality. She still had trouble accepting that Ned was actually dead—murdered. She shivered again and wrapped her arms around herself. She'd never known anyone who wound up murdered. Setting aside the fact that in some ways he'd deserved a bad end, he'd still been a human being and now he was gone.

Standing there in the library she'd helped choose colors and carpeting for, that bottom line crashed in on her. No force on earth could bring Ned back. His life was over and hers might very well be, too, if MacBride had anything to say about it.

"You're certain there was no one else here besides you?"

Careful not to look directly at him, she nodded. "Just me—until I heard the sound outside. Someone must have been poking around in the alley." She'd let him draw his own conclusions. Could have been a homeless person for all MacBride knew.

He bent down and picked up something from the floor. "I guess I overlooked this the last time I was here." He held the item out for her inspection and she knew instantly what it was. Brian's money clip. A fourteen-carat gold showpiece with the initials BWN. Brian Wayne Novak.

MacBride dropped the item into his jacket pocket. "I'll just take it in for analysis by the folks in forensics."

If he questioned Brian...

MacBride's slow, deliberate approach abruptly derailed that worrisome thought. She tried not to look at him, but she simply couldn't help herself. The way he moved, fluid, predatory and with the unparalleled grace of a hunter. The fit of that expensive suit, even with his collar unbuttoned and his tie jerked loose, lent a dangerous element. There he was all polished and smart-looking on the outside, but something deeply primal simmered just beneath. She could see it in those blue eyes. She could feel it vibrating all around him like a force field. That short, silky hair looked as if he'd just raked his fingers through it, and his jaw sported a five-o'clock shadow.

Everything about him screamed sex, blatantly challenged any female within sight or smelling distance to come have a taste.

He stopped no more than two feet away, his long-fingered hands propped firmly on his hips, the lapels of his jacket pushed aside. She told herself not to look into those eyes, not to let him draw her in more deeply.

But then he spoke and any hope of denying the urge was lost. "This was not a smart move, Elizabeth," he said quietly, his voice soft and deadly serious. "Coming here makes you look even guiltier than you already do. Didn't you stop to consider that access to this office was too easy? I've had someone watching 24/7 for just this moment. You'd better start talking."

She blinked once, twice, her mind frantically attempting to focus on his words while the part of her that made her female zeroed in on all that marked him male. Her very skin felt electric, ready to combust. "I told you I—"

"I know what you told me, but it was a lie. Just like the other lies you've told me. I'm giving you another chance here. Tell me what you know, and this will be a lot easier on the both of us."

Summoning her scattered resolve, she looked him square in the eye and said the only thing she could. "I don't know what you want from me, Agent MacBride. I've told you everything I know."

"Did you have sex with Harrison the night he was murdered?" he asked casually, unhurriedly. But he gave himself away when he shifted his gaze from hers, a visible concession to the tension mounting between them.

"No," she said adamantly.

"Then you won't mind submitting a sample for DNA comparison to the intimate body hair discovered at the scene."

Mac knew he'd gotten her attention then. He heard the harsh intake of breath, saw the widening of her eyes.

"My attorney—"

"Your attorney can't make this go away, Elizabeth," he cut in smoothly. "Only *I* can. But to do that I need to be able to eliminate the possibility that you were in Harrison's bed that night."

For an instant she wavered, uncertain. He didn't want that moment of increased vulnerability to pass. "Making that elimination would be a major step in the right direction."

"I guess it couldn't hurt," she said stiffly.

He watched her lips as she spoke, knowing it was a mistake but unable to help himself. There was just something about her mouth, something that drew him, made him want to taste her.

Before he could thwart the impulse, he'd moved closer, his thigh brushing hers as he stood closer than was safe. The resulting charge of the slight contact went straight to his loins.

"See how easy that was?" he offered roughly, fighting hard to stay on track here.

She watched his lips now, her own slightly parted. Was she attracted to him, as well, or was this just one of her maneuvers to distract him?

Her tongue darted out to moisten her lips. Control slipped another notch and he was pretty sure that getting any *harder* would be impossible. But he had her right where he wanted her. He couldn't let the moment go—just yet.

"Tell me why you really came here tonight," he urged, his voice as soft as it was insistent. "Was it Novak's idea or yours?"

Her gaze collided with his. "I'm no fool, Elizabeth. The clip has his initials on it."

"It's..." She shook her head. "It's not what you think."

"How do you know what I think?"

She lifted one shoulder uncertainly. "You think I killed him."

For the first time since he'd met Elizabeth Young, he allowed himself to look at her—the woman, not the suspect. The tomboyish sprinkle of freckles across the bridge of her nose. The way her glasses always needed pushing up or setting straight. The rich amber of her eyes. His fingers itched to tangle in the thick mass of dark hair she always kept pulled back in a braid or ponytail. Long strands had slipped loose now. They clung to her face, appearing even darker against the creaminess of her skin. But it was her mouth that tormented him more than anything else. Wide, full, the bottom lip noticeably heavier than the top.

"You wanted to kill him," he said without thinking.

She chewed that tempting lower lip for a second. "But I didn't."

"Was Novak in on it? Did the two of you plan this together?"

That sent her rushing for cover, but he blocked her path. "He was, wasn't he?"

"I don't know!" She tried to push away the arm that held her back, but only succeeded in shoving him a little further over the edge with her touch.

"Is he involved with the Gentlemen's Association, too?"

Her head came up. She opened her mouth to refute his suggestion, but her face gave her away before she could tell him yet another lie.

"Don't waste your breath, Elizabeth. Your eyes already gave me the answer I suspected." He choked out a laugh. "Do you have any idea how much danger you're in right now?"

The fear and uncertainty vanished with one blink of her long-lashed lids. "From whom? Them or you? You keep pushing me and pushing me like you really believe

I'm guilty, but I see the way you look at me. I'm not blind, MacBride."

And that easily he was lost. He took her face in his hands and kissed her. As his mouth swooped down to claim hers, he felt the little hitch in her breath. She tensed but didn't draw away. He took that as permission to plunder the luscious mouth that had been driving him insane for days.

That was the final rational thought Mac managed. She tasted like chocolate and coffee. Café mocha maybe. And she was hot, so damned hot.

He gently lifted her glasses up and off, leaving them on the table so that he could get back to touching her with both hands. His fingers delved into the thick softness of her hair, and he groaned with satisfaction. He'd wanted to touch her like this from the moment he first laid eyes on her. He took the kiss deeper, thrusting his tongue inside her, wanting, needing more.

Still she didn't surrender to the kiss. He was kissing her. She allowed it but didn't respond.

Images of the innately sexual creature on the videotape flooded his head, and a jolt of jealousy went through him. He wanted her like that, wanted her responding to his touch, to his kiss.

He kissed her harder, demanding a reaction.

And that made him just like them.

He tore his mouth from hers, but couldn't draw away completely at first. Had to hover there. This close he could still feel her pull. He licked his lips, tasting her, feeling her quick little puffs of warm breath on his damp skin. The way she smelled, like a rose beneath the warm sun, made him want to pull her to him again.

But he didn't.

He stepped back, at a loss, for a moment, for words.

She refused to look at him, kept her gaze somewhere in the vicinity of the third button on his shirt. Right about the same location where the knife had entered Harrison's chest. Another dose of reality slammed into him.

"I'll take you home."

At some point he would need to acknowledge having overstepped his bounds. But not right now.

Right now walking away pretty much took all the strength he possessed.

Trust was such a powerful tool. Who would ever suspect? By the time the victim grew suspicious, it was too late.

Far too late.

One carefully calculated strike was all it took. So easy, so quick. The blade sliced deeply into the creamy smoothness of her throat. The gush of blood flowed like a crimson river, propelled by the final frantic beating of her heart. Her entire body tensed and the scream that would have rent the air wilted impotently behind the panties stuffed in her mouth.

We are so proud of ourselves. It's almost over. We are so very close. Only a few more to go.

And vengeance will be ours.

Chapter 9

Elizabeth lay in the predawn darkness and thought about the previous night. A part of her had wanted to go to Gloria's place and demand answers. But how could she do that? It would be an outright admission that she didn't trust her friend. A slap in the face. She just couldn't do that. Gloria was the one person she *had* been able to trust. Brian had to be lying. There was no other explanation. Ned had almost ruined their relationship; it would be just like Brian to try to finish it off.

He was jealous that way. A selfish son of a bitch who cared only for himself.

She closed her eyes and exhaled a heavy breath. She'd been so blind. The whole idea of moving to the big city, of working with the masters at a design firm like Design Horizons. It had been her dream since she was twelve, when she realized what one could do with a mere gallon of paint and a yard of fabric. Her father's work as a handyman had ingrained in her a love of houses and their care. As she'd grown older she realized there was a whole world of possibilities out there. And she was good at designing and decorating interiors. Really good, though she'd had no formal education in the field. Her skill came naturally, like breathing. She looked at a room and saw a bare canvas.

But the break with Brian had ended all that. She had no reputation, no contacts of her own, so she'd had to fall back on the sort of work she could do without any of those things—good, honest hard work. Interior painting could be backbreaking. You had to be good, as well as fast, to earn a living wage at it. She was both, but she was a woman, which was an automatic strike against her. She'd had to work cheaply at first, and being choosy about her work location hadn't been an option. Finding Boomer had proved a lucky break. He wasn't afraid of anything, including hard work.

Now her work was pretty steady. The locations were a great deal better and she'd earned the beginnings of an excellent reputation. She could make it.

Just when things had been looking up financially, if not personally, Ned had entered the picture. Sure, she'd seen him around; the kind of parties Brian attended or hosted catered to the rich and socially privileged. Seeing Ned on a professional level had felt right at first. He'd seemed kind. She'd needed that. All her life everyone she'd depended on or needed had deserted her, one way or another. Her mother had walked out on them when Elizabeth was in kindergarten, her father had died last year, and then Brian had dumped her. According to Ned, the panic attacks were caused by years of uncertainty. His counseling had helped.

The affair had been an accident—at least she'd thought so at the time. Brian's caustic words reverberated in her head. It was hard to believe that Ned would have set out to reel her in like that when he could have any woman he wanted. The memory of the videotape slammed into her thoughts like an out-of-control dump truck on a downhill stretch. Oh, yeah, she shouldn't be shocked at anything she discovered about him.

She flopped over onto her side. But the part about Gloria, she simply refused to believe that. Elizabeth had every intention of chalking up the whole idea to Brian's cruel selfishness. He'd lost his friend and he wanted Elizabeth to lose hers. The first time she'd gotten accolades from a pleased design client, Brian had found a way to ruin it. Despite all the nasty little things he'd done, she hadn't realized until the very end just how selfish he was. Or maybe she hadn't wanted to see it.

But that was over now and she was left wondering if Brian was involved in Ned's murder. Had it been his intent to set Elizabeth up? The fact that whoever had killed Ned had used the dagger she'd given him seemed to support that theory. She considered MacBride's suggestion that she submit to DNA testing. Shuddering at the implication, she curled into the fetal position. She didn't kill Ned, so she wasn't really worried on that score, but what if whoever had attempted to set her up had planted the evidence they'd discovered? She emitted a harsh spasm of laughter. *Okay, Elizabeth, exactly how would someone have gotten any of your pubic hair without your knowledge?*

She thought about her shower or bathroom floor. Sometimes there were loose hairs scattered about when she got around to housework. Lord knows she didn't bother with it often. She supposed someone could have come into her place while she was at work and Mrs. Polk was off playing bridge or something. It wasn't outside the realm of possibility. Nor was the possibility that Brian had saved a couple of her hairs from their time together, she considered. They'd lived together for several months.

But all that was just too farfetched. That kind of thing only happened in movies.

This wasn't a movie; this was real. Elizabeth hugged her knees more tightly to her chest. MacBride was certain she was involved. He knew she was lying to him. He read her so well. And he kissed like no one had ever kissed her before.

At the unnecessary reminder her skin heated from the inside out. She'd tried so hard to block the memory, but it just wouldn't go away. All night she'd awakened every couple of hours, and her first thought each time was of his kiss, his touch. He'd startled her with the move, although some part of her had known it was coming, and she'd frozen at first, unable to respond on even the most basic level.

Who was she kidding? She always froze—at first. It took a great deal of trust just to dive in, and she simply didn't trust any man that much. She'd trusted her father, but he was gone now, then she'd put her faith in Brian, and look where that had gotten her. Her sister had trusted her husband and she'd paid dearly for it. So had Elizabeth. She'd almost gone to prison after taking that knife to her brother-in-law to stop him from hurting her sister yet again. Hadn't it been another man who'd taken their mother away from them? She'd fallen so desperately for him she'd deserted her husband and two small children, never to be heard from again. According to Ned, it was that abandonment that had set the stage for her current phobia. She wasn't entirely sure that was true, since she'd long ago blocked all thought of her mother from her mind. But maybe it was true.

One thing was certain, she couldn't trust MacBride.

He was an FBI agent who considered her a suspect in his current murder investigation. Even if she could muster up the courage to trust him, he would use that trust to prove her guilty. That combined with the undeniable truth that he was one hundred percent male, canceled any hope of her being able to trust him.

No matter how attracted she was to him—and she was definitely attracted—she couldn't let down her guard. Ned had offered some fancy name for her little trust problem, but she didn't necessarily agree with his conclusion. Sure, with a guy she was attracted to she could work up enthusiasm for sex eventually, *eventually* being the key word. She closed her eyes and pressed her forehead to her knees. Brian had called her frigid. They'd fought so many times over her lack of sexual ambition that eventually she'd learned to submit to his needs a little more quickly, but only with conscious effort. Ned had known all the right words to coax her into cooperation. But no one, absolutely no one, had ever made her *want* to jump in with both feet.

Except MacBride.

Oh, she'd gone through the usual routine of freezing up at his first touch. But in mere seconds she'd wanted to throw her arms around him and climb his hard male body. The only thing that had stopped her had been her lack of trust. Yet for the first time in her life, she was certain she could have dived straight in, ignoring the whole trust issue. Just her luck to find the one man who set her on fire with barely a touch and he wanted to charge her with murder!

She uncurled and rolled onto her back to stare at the ceiling, noting the cracks in the old plaster and the fact that the ceiling, as well as the rest of her apartment, needed a fresh coat of paint. She harrumphed. Painters were like hairdressers; they always needed a makeover but were too busy taking care of everybody else to find time to do their own. That was the story of her life. Always wishing for what she couldn't have.

The telephone next to the bed rang, cutting short the self-pity session.

Her heart took a breath-stealing dip. It was scarcely daylight. Who would call her at this hour? Her sister? Something could have happened to one of the kids...

She snatched up the receiver. "Hello."

"Elizabeth?"

She frowned, not immediately recognizing the woman's voice. Something like a moan and then a grating attempt at clearing a throat. "Yes," she answered, trepidation slowing her response.

"Elizabeth, it's Annabelle."

The ache of hopelessness in the woman's voice propelled Elizabeth into a sitting position. Fear ripped through her at her first thought—Gloria. "What's wrong?"

"There's been...another murder," she stammered.

Elizabeth felt herself go numb.

"I heard the call go out on the police scanner," Annabelle explained solemnly. "I checked the address they called out against Ned's patient log."

A tense beat of silence sent Elizabeth's heart into warp speed.

"It's Marissa Landon, it has to be. The officer at the scene reported that the victim was female and that's her address." Another of those moanlike sounds. "Is this ever going to stop? Why can't they do something?"

"I'll call Gloria." Elizabeth scarcely recognized the stone-cold voice as her own. The relief at her friend's safety was there, but the realization that another woman was dead overrode it to a large degree. Thank God it wasn't Gloria. But still, another murder.

"We have to talk," Annabelle urged. "I think there's a new pattern developing here. Did you get to Ned's office yet?"

Elizabeth was already out of bed and searching for clothes. The question stirred the dread that had settled like a rock in her stomach. "We can talk about that when we're all together. Where should we meet?"

"My office." She gave Elizabeth the uptown address. "I'll be waiting."

After disconnecting, Elizabeth punched in Gloria's number and jumped into her clothes as she waited out the rings.

Four murders. It was only Monday. Ned had been dead for just over a week and already four of his patients were dead.

Dear God, who would be next?

Mac was at the office when the call came in. He hadn't been able to sleep, so he'd come in to study what he had on the murders that had been dubbed "The Princess Murders," since all of the victims had been New York society elite.

All three of the women were young, all were beautiful and wealthy, but other than that the only true connection among them was that they'd been patients of Ned Harrison's. After the second murder, Brannigan had started checking female victims against Harrison's patient log as a matter of course. Mac hadn't asked for lead on this case, but he'd asked for cooperation; Detective Brannigan seemed happy to give it, since he was more than aware that Mac could take the case if he wanted it.

Each victim had been bound to her bed and gagged

with a pair of cheap nylon panties. The ritual was the same each time—she was sexually assaulted and then murdered with a single slash to the throat. No sign of struggle in any room other than the bedroom was evident at any of the scenes. Who was this man that the women would allow him into their homes without question? Did he force his way in with a gun?

At each scene numerous prints were lifted, but it would take forever to cross-check them all. The killer's seminal fluid was left behind in each case. DNA testing and cross-matching with CODIS—the FBI's bank of DNA profiles on convicted offenders—was in the works. Mac had made all the right calls to ensure a speedy response on the DNA results.

But now there was a fourth victim. It wasn't that Mac hadn't anticipated additional victims. He had. Whether Brannigan was ready to admit it or not, he had himself a serial killer. And somehow the killings were connected to Harrison.

The one thing about the latest killing that startled the hell out of Mac was the location. The victim was found in her home less than six blocks from Harrison's office—where both Elizabeth and Novak had been the night before. According to the ME she'd been dead long enough to be in full rigor mortis with some cooling of body temperature, which indicated the victim had been dead twelve to fourteen hours.

Mac glanced at the digital clock on his desk as he got ready to head to the crime scene. It was 7 a.m. now. That would, roughly speaking, put the time of death at sometime between 5 and 7 p.m. the previous night. He'd discovered Elizabeth and evidence of Novak, at Harrison's office at approximately 7:30. He was still furious that the surveillance team monitoring Harrison's office had somehow missed Novak's presence. They'd spotted Elizabeth and called him immediately, but they'd missed Novak entirely. The wily bastard couldn't be that good. Catching someone with motivation to get inside Harrison's office had been the whole point of surveillance versus locking down the damn place. They needed a break in this case. With the proper surveillance he could have pinpointed Novak's exact time of arrival. Hell, maybe he'd just beat it out of the guy.

Mac was still investigating Novak, but there were several things he already knew about the man. He'd been born to wealthy parents who were still movers and shakers in the financial world. His father had been immensely disappointed when his only son chose to go into architecture and design, rather than mergers and takeovers. Novak had never been in any real trouble, other than one petty drug bust in college and a charge four years ago of soliciting prostitution. Like Harrison, Novak had himself a sick little obsession with the seamier side of sex.

Until now Mac hadn't had any evidence to warrant the subpoena of DNA evidence from either Novak or Elizabeth. But things were different now. They had both been in the vicinity of the crime, were guilty of breaking and entering the office of a recent murder victim whose case was ongoing, and the two were definitely hiding something.

One way or another, Mac intended to know what it was.

He would push Elizabeth Young until she broke.

Before he could stop it, the memory of kissing her erupted inside him, yanking the rug right out from under him. Sending his senses reeling all over again. He'd worked hard all morning and most of the night not to think about her in that sense. To forget the insane move he'd made kissing her. But he couldn't seem to keep it pushed away. The taste of her, the smell of her, kept haunting him.

He shook his head as he exited his office and headed for the elevators. He couldn't stop thinking about her when what he needed to be focusing on was the facts.

Fact one: Elizabeth Young was supposed to meet Ned Harrison the night he was murdered.

Fact two: the murder weapon was a gift from Elizabeth.

Fact three: an illicit affair between Elizabeth and Harrison had ended badly; already several of their mutual friends had given statements to that effect.

Fact four: Elizabeth had a record of drug possession and felony assault.

Fact five: she had no alibi for the night of Harrison's murder.

Finally and the most damning of all: Elizabeth knew he was attracted to her. She'd said as much. *I see the way you look at me.* Which meant he wasn't being objective where she was concerned.

Even in light of all that, he still wanted her.

Elizabeth sat adjacent to Gloria in one of the matching wing chairs flanking Annabelle's desk. The office was nice, not quite as luxurious as Ned's, but on that order. She had an uptown address that spoke of money and prestige.

Elizabeth had no idea what kind of attorney Annabelle was, since she hadn't met her until yesterday, but if accommodations were any indicator, she must be doing well for herself. Elizabeth liked that. Any time a woman could flourish in a man's world, she loved it.

"Look at the last names." Annabelle pointed at the list she'd made of the victims, all former patients of Ned's.

"Damn," Gloria breathed the word. "They're in alphabetical order."

Annabelle nodded in confirmation. "Bumbalough, Dell, Fowler and now Landon. I checked the log of patients and there are four more, including the two of you."

Elizabeth's forehead pleated into a frown. "I'm sure Ned had a lot more than eight patients."

"Definitely," Annabelle hastened to agree. "But these are the ones I've pretty much narrowed the list down to, having had a more personal relationship with him."

Elizabeth and Gloria exchanged uncertain glances.

Annabelle sighed. "Yes, I'm aware that Ned sometimes broke the rules with his patients." She folded her hands atop the clean blotter on her desk. "I didn't really have a problem with his less-than-savory involvement with the association and the darker side of sexuality." She paused, her expression intent, thoughtful. "But I fear that this association business and his crossing the line with his patients delved into far more dangerous territory than he intended."

"How did you figure out that he had become sexually involved with—" Elizabeth swallowed tightly "—some of his patients?"

Annabelle leaned back in her chair and fixed her gaze on Elizabeth. "To be perfectly honest with you, I suspected as much months ago."

"What did you do?" Gloria leaned forward a bit in anticipation of her answer.

"I confronted him, of course. Gave him my professional advice whether he wanted to hear it or not."

"But he didn't want your advice," Elizabeth said, knowing how Ned would have reacted to being told what to do by anyone. He was far too arrogant to allow anyone to boss him around.

Annabelle looked down for a moment before saying more. "He was my friend," she said when she again met their gazes. "I didn't agree with what he did, but I couldn't just walk away, either."

Elizabeth blinked back the tears that had blurred her vision. Ned had used them all. When would she ever wake up and stop allowing men to take advantage of her? Furious with herself, she glanced at her watch. Nine-thirty already. Boomer would be wondering where she was. He knew to get started without her, but she couldn't put off going much longer. Getting behind wasn't an option. She needed to fulfill this contract. She needed the money.

"Did you find the hidden door?"

The unexpected question startled Elizabeth back to attention. With the news of another murder, she'd completely forgotten about the previous evening's mission, even though she'd promised Annabelle an update and had expected the question.

She shook her head. "Brian followed me there or stumbled upon me there, and I couldn't do anything."

Annabelle straightened, clearly surprised. "Brian Novak?"

Elizabeth nodded. "He…" She frowned, trying to remember his exact words. "He accused me of killing Ned and then urged me to tell him the secret I knew." Her gaze connected with Annabelle's. "Do you think he was talking about the Gentlemen's Association?"

"Brian was watching Ned's office?" Gloria asked, her voice, as well as her expression, revealing her shock.

"Apparently." Elizabeth couldn't think of any other explanation for why he would have been there at precisely the same time she was. She shuddered inwardly. "He kind of scared me." As furious as it made her that MacBride had her under surveillance, the sight of that nondescript sedan parked outside her place this morning had been reassuring. It hadn't been him, but it was one of his men.

"Jesus," Gloria muttered on a shaky breath. "This just gets more bizarre by the minute."

"If the police don't stop this murderer..." Annabelle allowed her words to trail off. She didn't have to say the rest. They both knew what she meant.

"What're we going to do?" Gloria looked from Annabelle to Elizabeth. "If there're only four others and two of them are us, we have to do something to protect ourselves."

Her friend was right, Elizabeth agreed silently, dread rocking through her. And Gloria was her friend. She wasn't about to put any stock in anything Brian said. She trusted Gloria, to confront her with Brian's accusations would be wrong. "How?"

"Do you have someone you could stay with at night?" This from Annabelle. She looked from one to the other. "I really don't think either of you should be alone, especially at night." She massaged her forehead as if an ache had begun there. "I can't believe the police haven't noticed this already. They're supposed to be trained to see these details. You should have police protection."

Elizabeth suddenly remembered that MacBride had considered this fact. *But he still thinks you're a murderer,* a little voice taunted.

Elizabeth's entire being trembled again.

"I could stay with my sister," Gloria said uncertainly. "She has her husband's gun."

This time the tremble stayed with Elizabeth. "That's a good idea," she said thinly, trying hard to be steady.

"But what about you, Elizabeth? You could stay with us, too," Gloria urged.

Elizabeth shook her head. If the killer was after her, no way would she endanger Gloria's family. She stilled. What if it was her he really wanted? What if all these other murders were nothing but a decoy? She could be the coup de grâce.

Enough, Elizabeth, she railed silently. *Don't make this about you. It's about Ned…somehow.*

"I'll ask Boomer to stay over." That would work. He'd be glad to. And he was tough. She wouldn't have to worry with him around.

"Just be sure you do," Gloria said, her voice still full of apprehension. "I don't think any of us should be alone." She looked at Annabelle. "What about you?"

The attorney waved her hands in a forget-about-it gesture. "I'll be fine. I have friends I can stay with. So you'll be with your sister," she said to Gloria, "and you'll have *Boomer* to protect you?" She frowned. "Who, exactly, is Boomer?"

Elizabeth laughed, the quick burst of humor easing some of the tension. "He's my assistant."

"An ex-con," Gloria added. "She'll be safe with him."

Annabelle looked a little skeptical, but said, "No doubt."

Something else nudged at Elizabeth. "Annabelle, could Ned have been murdered for his money?"

The attorney considered the question for a moment. "I don't see how. I've started his will through probate. His brother was to inherit everything—"

"His brother?" Gloria asked incredulously. "I didn't know he had any siblings."

Annabelle's expression turned solemn. "Well, he did have a brother, but he died several years ago. No other family left. So in accordance with Ned's wishes his assets will be distributed to various charities."

Well, well, Elizabeth mused. Who would have thought that Casanova Ned would turn into a philanthropist upon his death? Too bad he hadn't shown that kind of compassion in life. She'd never once wondered if he had any family. He just seemed to *be*—as if he'd sprung forth fully grown with no need for any family.

All of them had work to get to, so the meeting broke up and Gloria and Elizabeth walked out together. On the sidewalk Gloria, in vintage Gloria fashion, hailed the first cab that passed. At least a dozen always whizzed by Elizabeth before she could get one's attention.

"Call me tonight," Gloria ordered as she climbed in. "I want to hear Boomer's voice coming across your phone line."

Elizabeth nodded. "Don't worry. I won't take any chances. And you'll be at your sister's."

"Immediately after work," Gloria assured her. The look in her eyes told Elizabeth there wasn't any question. Gloria was obviously as afraid as she was.

When Gloria's taxi had merged with the traffic, Elizabeth walked slowly toward the garage where she'd parked her truck. Others, hurrying to work, brushed past her, and she moved closer to the curb to avoid them. She thought about the woman who'd been murdered last night and tried without success to understand why this was happening. Why would anyone want to kill Ned's patients unless he somehow suspected one of them of being responsible for Ned's death? And that was assuming the murderer was a friend of Ned's.

Was that how Brian fit into all this? Had he killed Ned because of her? She shook her head. Brian didn't care that much about anyone and neither did Ned. Playing sick little games appeared to be what the two had in common. Could their game playing have turned into murder?

She wrapped her arms around herself as that bone-chilling cold that came from deep inside made her tremble. She was on that kill list. If the killer knew about her fight with Ned and the visit to his apartment, he would no doubt consider her a prime suspect. But why kill the others? Maybe he just wanted to be absolutely certain he got the right one.

She'd lived with Brian for months. Surely she would know if he was capable of murder.

A car screeched to a halt at the curb, the abrupt sound jerking Elizabeth back to the here and now. Her heart slammed against the wall of her chest and she started to run.

Surely he wouldn't strike in open daylight on a crowded street. Then recognition flared.

MacBride peered at her from inside the dark sedan. She'd forgotten all about her private watchdog.

"Get in," he ordered.

She waited as a couple of pedestrians pushed past her, rushing for a passing cab. Irritation instantly mounted in her. MacBride had been following her again. "What?" she demanded as she stepped nearer to the curb and the waiting car.

"Get in," he growled, his gaze every bit as fierce as his command.

She leaned down to peer inside the car. Turned toward the passenger window, his left hand on the steering wheel and his right arm braced against the back of the front seat, he looked like a panther poised to lunge at his prey.

"Why?" she asked, uncomfortable with his whole demeanor.

"Get in willingly or I'll arrest you. It's your choice."

The edge in his voice sliced right through her annoyance, changing it to uneasiness. "All right."

Knowing she had no choice, Elizabeth opened the door and slid into the passenger seat. Before she had time to fasten her seat belt, he barreled into the flow of traffic, earning himself squealing tires and impatient honks.

"I'm only going to ask you this once, Elizabeth," he said without glancing her way. "What were you and Novak doing at Harrison's office last night?"

Not that again. "Who says Brian was with me and why do you want to know?"

"I found you there," he said, sparing her a swift but thorough assessment, "around seven-thirty. I have every reason to believe Novak was there, as well."

The money clip. It wouldn't take any time at all to prove it was Brian's. "What difference does it make?" she asked, exasperated. She was so tired of this. She hadn't done anything illegal.

"Because around that time, just a few blocks away from where I found you, Marissa Landon was being murdered."

Chapter 10

Mac drove around for almost ten minutes without speaking. Elizabeth's tension escalated with every passing second. She felt certain he planned to take her to his office, but he didn't. Then she figured he planned to take her to the police station to face those two detectives again, Brannigan and the partner whose name she couldn't recall. But he didn't do that, either.

Instead, he just drove, finally stopping in front of a well-maintained, older building located in the vicinity of Ned's office. The recently renovated architecture was ornate with intricate detailing around the windows and porte cochere. For another tension-filled minute he sat without moving, forcing Elizabeth's pulse rate into the danger zone, in spite of her valiant effort to focus on anything but his silence. She mentally listed the various elements of the structures looming just beyond the sidewalk and patches of grass, but every breath she drew was an effort. Her heart pounded so hard she couldn't imagine MacBride not hearing it.

Just when she thought she couldn't take anymore,

he spoke. "You see that center window on the seventh floor?"

Elizabeth looked upward to the floor he'd indicated. She knew where they were, knew what he was trying to do. When her eyes focused on the center window, she answered, the hollow word a mere whisper, "Yes."

"That apartment belonged to Marissa Landon."

As Elizabeth stared at the dark window with its flower box overflowing with a bright spring mixture of blooms, the reality of what Annabelle had told her settled on her like a sopping-wet quilt. Who would water those flowers now? Marissa was dead. Murdered.

"Do you know what arterial spray is?"

A hard knot formed in Elizabeth's stomach. "I don't want to hear this." The shaking that had plagued her in Annabelle's office started again.

"It's usually found near the victim of brutal violence," he went on cruelly. "The perpetrator has to inflict a wound that involves an artery. Like with Marissa. The slashing wound almost completely severed her head from her body. The carotid artery, as well as the jugular, were sliced clean through. Imagine the depth of evil hostility it took to inflict that kind of violence on another human being."

She squeezed her eyes shut and tried to block the gruesome images his words evoked. "Please, just take me back to my truck. I don't know anything."

Without a word he swerved away from the curb and merged into the traffic again. Her body was ice, her senses numb. She fought back the tears and silently screamed at the indignity, the senselessness. How could she know anyone who would do something so heinous? Surely her suspicions were wrong. Surely Brian couldn't be responsible for that kind of horror. But what if he was, and what if she did know something that would make a difference?

Could she live with herself if even one more person died?

When MacBride parked once more, they were at Ned's office. Elizabeth blinked as confusion jumped into the painful mixture of emotions twisting inside her.

"Why are we here?" Fear raced to the forefront of all else, and she turned to face MacBride. His blue eyes were dark with emotion. "Why did you bring me here?"

"Get out," he ordered. "We're going inside."

She reached for the door handle, but her hand shook so badly it took two attempts to open the door. Her head spun, making her movements awkward, unbalanced. What if MacBride had found the hidden door? What if he knew why she'd come here last night? She glanced quickly from side to side as he ushered her toward the front entrance. Had her being here last night somehow caused that brutal murder? Was Detective Brannigan waiting inside to interrogate her? Her chest ached with the impotent floundering of her heart. She couldn't drag in a deep enough breath. She wanted it to stop—the murders, the suspicions, the fear. She just wanted it to stop.

MacBride used a key to open the front door, then locked it behind them once they were inside. Elizabeth sucked in a shallow breath and tried to calm herself. She couldn't let the panic take over now. She had to stay in control.

The reception area was only dimly lit by the sparse sunlight filtering in through the half-closed shades. The air smelled stale already. The owner was dead, whatever kind of jerk he'd been. Whatever good he'd done in his life, if any, it was over. He was dead and so were four of his patients. And somehow she was a part of it all.

She had to sit down. Elizabeth stumbled toward a chair and collapsed into it. "I don't want to be here," she murmured for all the good it would do. MacBride apparently wanted to punish her, to make her tell him what she knew, which was nothing that would matter. She was certain of it. If she'd thought for one second that anything she'd seen or heard or done would matter...

Except that one thing...

Mac wrestled back the sympathy that rose immediately as she crumpled beneath the weight of fear and guilt. He gritted his teeth, bracing for the charge that would accompany touching her, and took her by the arm to haul her to her feet. "This way, Elizabeth."

She lurched forward, having little choice but to go with him or be dragged behind him.

He took her into Harrison's private office, the one where he saw his patients, and herded her toward the leather chaise longue. He leaned against the edge of the massive desk and crossed his arms over his chest, cranking up the intimidation as he glared down at her.

She sat like a statue except for the fine trembling she couldn't hide. Before he could stop his traitorous eyes, he'd taken in every last detail of the way she looked today. She wore faded jeans and, unlike the overalls she usually donned for work, the jeans fit snugly, hugging her slender figure. The blouse was of soft cotton, short-sleeved and buttoning up the front. One sneaker was about to come untied. But it was the way she wore her hair that unsettled him the most. It hung unrestrained over her shoulders, a cape of rich brown velvet. Her amber eyes stared up at him from behind those delicately rimmed glasses. She was scared to death, sick with dread at what she feared lay ahead.

By God, he intended to have some answers! Five people were dead. One might damn well have deserved a bad end, but the others were victims in the truest sense of the word. Whatever Elizabeth knew, whether she considered it relevant or not, he would have it before they left this room.

"What do you want from me?" she asked, her voice unsteady.

"Is this where you spent all those hours with him?" The question was issued sharply, and Mac wanted to bite off his tongue when he recognized the emotion behind it. Jealousy. Dammit all to hell. He was jealous of a dead man's relationship with the woman who could very well be his killer. He clenched his fists and fought the ridiculous feelings.

"Yes," she replied softly. Her fingers twisted together as she wrung her hands nervously. "Always right here," she volunteered to his surprise. "The first time I came he—" her eyes took on a distant look "—he insisted that comfort was of primary importance. I needed to relax and speak freely, knowing that anything I said or did in this office would never go any further."

Silence screamed for three beats as Mac realized how telling her final statement really was.

"But he lied to you, didn't he?"

She nodded. "His sessions were helpful at first. The panic attacks went away." She took a steadying breath and looked up at him. "But then he took our relationship to another level. He knew I needed more work to make it financially, so he offered to let me decorate his office. He was very kind to me." She blinked as if attempting to reason out the unreasonable. Her voice sounded machinelike, flat and emotionless. "That's when he…" She lapsed into silence, unable or unwilling to go on.

"He seduced you," Mac said from between gritted teeth.

She moved her head in what he took for a nod. "I didn't mean for it to happen. But he knew all the right things to say and…I needed to hear them." She stared at her clasped hands for a time. "It was a mistake. I should have seen through his machinations."

The blast of fury that roared through Mac forced him to his feet. Harrison had used her, just as he had all the others. But for Elizabeth it was different. The playing field hadn't been level—she was too naive to have any clue about the kind of world she'd allowed herself to be lured into. She wasn't like the others. Another jolt of anger shook him when he considered that he was falling for that same sad Cinderella story he'd predicted she would use to rationalize her actions.

He'd taken the bait, hook, line and sinker.

"So you killed him." He hurled the accusation at her, even though, at this point, he was pretty sure she was innocent—of murder, anyway.

Her head came up and her face flushed. "No! How do I get that through to you, MacBride? I didn't kill him!"

His name on her lips sent something like desire curling through him, which only increased his fury. "But you know something about his death, don't you?" He moved nearer to her, towered over her to achieve the effect he desired. It worked. She retreated as far as her position on the chaise would allow.

"I don't know…" She shook her head, her brow lining in confusion. "I don't know who killed him."

"You went to his place that night, didn't you?" Mac outlined the scenario that had been forming in the back of his mind. Her startled gaze connected with his. "He stood you up and you were angry." She looked away guiltily and he knew he'd hit the mark. "Did you have a fight? Is that how he got those scratches?"

She shook her head.

"Was he using the tape for blackmail? Is that how he got to you?"

She bolted out of her seat, putting herself toe-to-toe with him. Anger glittered in her eyes. "Yes! Gloria and I found out about the videos and what he'd been up to with…with all of us." She blinked once, twice, clearly shocked she'd said so much.

"And how did Gloria feel about that?" He'd already checked out Gloria's alibi. It was airtight. She'd been at dinner and the movies with her niece. But then, he supposed, the niece could be lying. "Did she want him dead, too?" What woman wouldn't after what Harrison had done to them?

"How do you think she felt?" Elizabeth spat. "But we didn't kill him," she countered, some of the bravado going out of her. "We were victims. Don't you get it?"

That was the trouble. He did get it. It took all his willpower to restrain the impulse to take her in his arms. He urged her back down onto the chaise, then sat beside her. "Just tell me what happened, Elizabeth," he said gently. "That's all I want from you."

For a long time she just sat there staring at her hands. Mac wished he knew the right words to say to somehow make her feel at ease. But no words could make any of this right.

"I'd sworn I wouldn't ever speak to him again," she began wearily. "He'd hurt us too much. Almost cost Gloria and me our friendship. But he kept calling. He sounded so desperate. Finally he said he would give me the tape if I'd have dinner with him one last time." She shrugged with the same weariness he heard in her voice.

"I was desperate to get that tape. We knew he had one on each of us. Gloria found out somehow."

Gloria seemed to know a lot of things, Mac mused. He'd read Brannigan's report on his interview with her; maybe he needed to question her himself. But Brannigan had been thorough and he'd verified all statements. Funny they hadn't found a tape of Gloria Weston. Mac wondered how she'd managed to get hers from Harrison.

"Anyway, I went to the restaurant." Elizabeth laughed, a dry, humorless sound. "Like a fool. Of course he didn't show up." She shook her head. "I was so angry. I wanted to tell him just what I thought."

"So you went to his place." Mac had hoped that wasn't the case, but deep down he'd suspected as much. That was what had her running scared. She'd been so close to the murder without even knowing it.

She nodded. "I had to knock several times before he answered. When he did, it was obvious he'd been in bed with someone." She pressed her fist to her mouth as the tumultuous emotions shook her again. "I didn't think. I was furious. I just pushed past him and went straight to the bedroom. The sheets were tousled. The whole room smelled of sex. I screamed at him that I couldn't believe he'd kept me waiting while he screwed someone else."

The idea that Harrison may have threatened her physically or even hurt her in some way tore at Mac's gut. Before he could ask about that, she went on.

"I demanded the tape. He wouldn't let me have it." She exhaled a ragged breath, then chewed her lower lip for a moment. "We argued and he grabbed my arm and tried to make me listen to what he had to say."

Mac tensed as fresh rage gripped him.

"I fought him." She frowned. "I think maybe I did scratch him." She splayed her hands. "I don't know. It all happened so fast." A defeated sigh hissed past her lips. "He wouldn't give me the tape, so I gave up. I warned him to stay away from me. Then I left."

His jaw aching from clenching it so tightly, he asked harshly, "But no one saw you come or go?" He already knew the answer to that. Brannigan's men had questioned everyone in the building.

"I don't think so."

Mac scrubbed a hand over his face, the receding adrenaline leaving him weak. "Why didn't you tell me this in the beginning?"

"I was afraid you'd think I killed him."

Well, she'd been right to think that, although he'd considered her a prime suspect, anyway. "You're sure no one else was there with Harrison when you left?"

She mulled that over for a moment. "I'm pretty sure. I mean, I didn't go into the guest room or bathrooms." She closed her eyes, most likely retracing her movements in her mind. "I didn't go in the kitchen, either, but you can see beyond the island from the living room and I didn't notice anyone. But I was pretty upset."

Mac considered all she'd told him. There definitely could have been someone else there. "I'm still going to need that DNA sample from you. It's the only way I can prove you weren't in bed with him that night."

"Fine." She stiffened slightly. "Does it have to be…"

He knew what she was thinking and let her off the hook. "No. It can be as simple as a saliva swab." The pubic hair wasn't the only DNA evidence they'd eventually collected from Harrison's bed.

Her relief was almost palpable. "Okay."

"Tell me about last night."

Elizabeth had known that was coming. She'd made it through the initial part of her confession, but this part was going to be a little trickier. Her story would sound so farfetched. But what the hell. She had nothing to lose at this point and she was definitely out of options. Besides, MacBride wasn't going to give up until he had the truth. She had to respect that about him. He was trying to bring at least one murderer to justice.

"We had a kind of conference," she began.

"Who?" he interjected.

"Gloria, Annabelle and I."

"Annabelle Ford? Harrison's attorney?"

She stole a quick glance at him and almost shivered at the intensity in his eyes. And he was close. Closer than she'd realized. She resisted the urge to scoot away. Being afraid was over. She had to do this right. If anyone else died and it was in any way her fault for not telling all…

"Yes, Ned's attorney. Gloria called her when the third woman was murdered. We decided to see if we could put our heads together and figure out who was doing this."

MacBride sat perfectly still, his head inclined as he listened to her relate the details of her first meeting with Annabelle and Gloria. When she mentioned the Gentlemen's Association and the secret room, something changed in his eyes, but he masked it so quickly she wasn't sure she'd seen it.

"I guess Brian was watching me," she suggested for lack of any other explanation. "We hadn't really seen each other except at an occasional party in months. I can't imagine how else he would have known. Even Annabelle and Gloria didn't know when I planned to make the attempt at getting in."

"Did he threaten you in any way?"

Elizabeth could feel the tension vibrating in the man sitting beside her. Something she'd told him had hit a nerve. She shook her head in response to his question.

"Not at first. But then he started to make me uneasy. He tried to force me to admit I'd killed Ned." She quickly gave him the condensed version of the conversation. "It was like he thought he could make me say what he wanted to hear."

Mac couldn't stop himself. He had to touch her. He placed his hand atop her clasped ones. "Listen to me, Elizabeth. I can't elaborate much on the Gentlemen's Association, but I can tell you that the people involved with that group are not to be trusted."

She looked up at him, her eyes wide with surprise behind her glasses. "So you do know about them?"

He nodded. "Did Novak say anything else about it? Something maybe you forgot to tell me?" Mac would damn well have Novak picked up this very day. His mention of the Gentlemen's Association to Elizabeth was enough for probable cause.

After a moment's thought she shook her head. "No. That's all he said before I hit him."

He couldn't help the smile that broke loose at the idea of her crowning Novak. The self-serving bastard. "Okay. Shall we try and locate that secret room?"

She nodded jerkily and his protective instincts surged. Their eyes met and he knew in that instant she was without doubt completely innocent. He reached up to touch her face. He heard her breath catch, but she didn't draw away.

The ring of the cell phone shattered the moment.

It took a second ring for him to pull himself together enough to answer. "MacBride."

"Mac, it's Driver."

He stood and moved away from the temptation she represented. "What's up?" The urge to loosen his tie had him reaching for his throat. The room was suddenly too damned hot.

"That guy Novak."

"Yeah." The newest addition to Mac's I-wanna-pound-him list.

"Well, his body was found in Central Park about an hour ago."

The tangle of scenarios and possibilities fighting for attention in Mac's thoughts stopped dead. "You're sure it's him."

"Brannigan's partner ID'd him. It's him."

Mac let go a heavy breath. "I'm on my way."

"Wait," Driver said before he could hang up. "You haven't heard the most bizarre part."

Mac braced himself for cause-of-death details. He always hated that part although those were the very details that gave an investigator the most information about the killer.

"The ME called your office this morning. It seems he found a match to the DNA evidence collected from the female victims in the Princess case."

Before Driver continued Mac was certain it had to be Novak, even though he wasn't sure how the ME had run across a DNA workup on Novak unless he'd been previously entered into CODIS under an alias.

"Remember all the DNA evidence that had to be checked out from Harrison's apartment? Well, Harrison's DNA had to be cross-matched to eliminate body hair, etc."

"Get to the point, Driver." Mac was getting impatient here. He knew the drill. It had to be Novak.

"Well, the specimen in the first two victims was a match. The last two aren't completed yet, of course."

"A match to whom?" Mac snarled. Dammit, why didn't he just spit it out?

"To Harrison," Driver said. "The DNA in both cases is a perfect match to Dr. Ned Harrison."

Chapter 11

Elizabeth stood numbly by as MacBride spoke quietly to the caller. She was afraid to even imagine what had happened now. But it was surely bad. The tone of his voice left no doubt. Cold, flat. Whatever news he'd just received, it was not something he'd wanted to hear.

Elizabeth thought of her friend. MacBride had people watching her, but what about Gloria? She needed protection, too. She remembered what Annabelle had said that morning. Four more. Four more female patients she had reason to believe had carried on a personal relationship with Ned. Two of which were Gloria and Elizabeth. She shuddered. What if that was what the call was about? What if another victim had been found?

MacBride ended the conversation. As he closed his phone and dropped it back into his pocket, she told herself she had no choice but to trust him. The suspicions Annabelle had offered were relevant to the case. Elizabeth had come clean with him about everything else that happened last night and he'd listened. He'd covered her hand with his own, comforting her. She should tell him this part, too. She warned that more vulnerable part of herself not to read too much into his comforting gesture, but she just couldn't help it. She was drawn to him, seriously drawn to him. Somehow the attraction went beyond the physical.

Right, Elizabeth. You're doing it again. Falling for the wrong guy. Who probably felt nothing for you but sympathy.

But he felt something. Elizabeth had noticed the way he looked at her, had seen the hunger in his eyes. She saw the emotion in his eyes as he turned to face her now. There was a dread, not at seeing her, but at telling her the news he'd just received. Why would he care how it affected her if he didn't feel something for her? He'd rescued her from Brian even after she'd given the guy watching her the slip. MacBride had likely sensed where she would go when the other man hadn't had a clue. He was tuned in to her on a very primal level. Or maybe he'd simply had someone watching Ned's office. A good thing, too, whatever the case. She felt reasonably sure that Brian would have come after her if he hadn't seen MacBride outside with her. Brian had clearly snapped out of the dazed state the whack on the head had sent him into and managed to slip away unseen. Tracking her down wouldn't have been a problem for him—except that MacBride had been watching over her. Like a guardian angel.

He moved toward her now, drawing her full attention back to the moment. Those intense blue eyes were guarded, which made her even more nervous. "Novak didn't mention talking to anyone else or expecting to meet with anyone else last night?" he asked, his words measured.

A tendril of trepidation coiled inside her. They were back to Brian again. "No." Where was he going with this?

"I don't know where he went afterward. He…he didn't call or anything." A burst of irritation chased away the trepidation. "I'd have had a few things to say to him if I'd heard from him." She was sick to death of being vulnerable—to MacBride or anyone else. Annabelle's theory nudged her again, shaking her newly found bravado.

"I'm not accusing you of anything, Elizabeth," Mac said more softly as he came nearer still. "But there's been another development and we need to know if Novak mentioned meeting or speaking to anyone else."

Development? A chill raced over her. He meant another murder. "Who's dead?" Her voice gave away the fear building in her. "Don't try to hide anything from me, MacBride," she added with surprising strength.

He touched her. Placed his hand on her arm, nothing complicated or serious, just a touch. But the feelings the gesture engendered were entirely serious.

"Novak is dead. His body was found in Central Park a little while ago."

Mac hadn't wanted to tell her like this, but she'd limited his options. She wanted, needed to know what was going on.

"How?" Her chin trembled ever so slightly and it was all he could do not to take her fully into his arms.

"I can't answer that for you just yet. But considering the speed with which these murders are occurring, I'd like to place you into protective custody for your own safety."

Fear, followed quickly by uncertainty, danced across her face. "I…I can't. I have to work."

"Elizabeth, it would be best—"

"Is someone watching Gloria, too?" she demanded abruptly.

Mac's worry began to manifest itself in an annoying

ache behind his eyes. "Brannigan has one of his men keeping an eye on her, if that's what you're asking."

Her eyes glittered. "I want to know if someone is watching her every minute of the day and night."

He wondered if shock was setting in. She'd gone from wanting to know how Novak was killed to whether or not Gloria Weston was being protected. The way she demanded a more precise response after he'd already given her an answer made him wonder if there was something more he should know. "Are you trying to tell me something, Elizabeth?"

A tremor went through her. "Annabelle has a theory. The murders—" she cleared her throat of the emotion thickening there "—have occurred in alphabetical order. Bumbalough, Dell, Fowler, Landon. Annabelle thinks there are approximately four others she can pinpoint as having had a sexual relationship with Ned. Gloria and I are among those four. She thinks he won't stop until... we're all dead."

Mac had already suggested to Brannigan and his newly formed task force that the killer might be working in a non-random manner. The only difference in Mac's theory was that, judging by the number of videotapes they'd found in Harrison's apartment, there were a lot more than only four more potential victims.

"All the more reason for you to go into protective custody," he suggested, keeping the numbers to himself. The alphabetical theory had been shot down to an extent, anyway, when the Landon woman was found. The killer had skipped over at least three names between Fowler and Landon—names that went with tapes they had found.

She shook her head. "I have to finish this job." She looked directly at him, the urgency in her manner relaying just how important this was. "It can't wait. Boomer will be with me."

"And who wouldn't be comforted by that?" Mac said dryly, regretting it the instant the words escaped.

"Look," Elizabeth said hotly, "I know you don't like him, but he's a good guy and I can depend on him."

Therein lay the crux of the matter, Mac realized. Elizabeth Young had been let down by too many people in her life. Her mother, her fiancé, her brother-in-law, even her father, who'd left her all alone when he died, and finally by her shrink. Trust didn't come easily to her. Being able to count on someone would mean a great deal to her. Even if it was a former scumbag like Boomer.

"You're right," he admitted to her surprise. "I want you to know that you can depend on me, as well. I'll see that someone is keeping an eye on Gloria."

Not bothering to hide her amazement, she murmured, "Thank you."

"I'm going to trust you with something, Elizabeth," Mac told her, only now making the decision to offer the information. "The Gentlemen's Association is why I'm here. These guys are nasty business. They're deep into Internet porn, mostly pretty young women like you, but some even younger. They have to be stopped. Harrison was my only bona fide connection. Novak was a close runner-up. Now they're both gone." He cranked up the intensity of his gaze, hoping to relay the utter desperation he felt. "I have to nail these guys, Elizabeth. I don't want anyone else hurt the way you were. I need evidence. Something. Anything to bring these guys down."

"The secret door," she said softly. "I know where it is."

Mac inspected the loft where Elizabeth and Boomer would be working today. He'd stationed Driver in the corridor just outside the door and given him orders not to leave Elizabeth under any circumstances. Boomer, after a show of belligerence toward Mac's orders, had calmed down and told Mac in no uncertain terms that nothing would happen to Elizabeth while she was with him.

Mac didn't want to leave her. Dammit, he had a job to do, and still he didn't want to go. Apparently it had taken just that one kiss to skew his judgment completely.

As he pointed his sedan in the direction of midtown, he forced his attention back to the case. The hidden room had proved to be the break he'd been praying for. The room was completely sealed, shielded from any sort of detection, similar to the way the CIA insulated their buildings. Harrison had covered every base. The room was totally self-sufficient and separate from the rest of his office. The power feed and telephone lines were split from a neighboring system, that of a legitimate business with nine-to-five operating hours. Never in a million years would their system have been checked. No one, not even Mac, would have thought of that. The lines weren't connected to Ned Harrison in any way. Running lights and a few electronics wouldn't constitute enough of a draw to alert the other business that they were being systematically robbed.

This provided new insight into the way others in the association were probably getting away with their evil deeds without being caught.

An entire forensics team was at this very moment going over the room. The elaborate computer system would likely hold all the evidence they would need to lead them to others.

Mac should be back there himself, but first he had to see Brannigan. They needed to discuss this latest turn of events. There had to be a reasonable explanation for

Harrison's DNA turning up at the crime scenes. Harrison was dead. Mac had viewed the body, read the autopsy.

A theory churned in the back of his mind, but first he wanted to hear Brannigan's take.

Since the detective was still at the crime scene, Mac parked near the entrance to the walking zoo. The body had been found next to a park bench where pigeons hung out hoping to be fed by the numerous daily visitors. Vaguely he wondered if the location was significant. Maybe someone thought Novak had talked.

Five minutes later Mac stood next to Brannigan as the ME's office took away the body. The autopsy would be needed for confirmation, though it appeared Novak had been bludgeoned to death. The irony that Elizabeth had hit him on or near the temple wasn't lost on Mac. According to the ME, time of death was possibly within mere hours of that of Marissa Landon. Even the location wasn't that far away from the Landon apartment.

"No signs of struggle," Brannigan said, then added dryly, "other than the pulp his head was beaten into."

"You think someone just sneaked up on him out here in the dark?" Mac queried, not certain he agreed with that theory.

"His wallet is missing," Brannigan said. "But it seems a little overkill for a simple robbery."

Mac made an agreeable sound. "Whoever did this wanted to make sure he didn't survive."

"Well, that takes Novak off the suspect list." Brannigan sighed wearily. "Damn, I thought for sure he might be our man. Especially after he disappeared on us last night. It seems every time a murder has occurred, he managed to be AWOL."

"What about the DNA connection to Harrison?" Mac

asked, getting to the heart of the matter. "How's forensics explaining that little quandary?"

"They're checking to see if it had been refrigerated or frozen prior to use." The older man shrugged, the movement calling attention to the poor fit of his jacket. "Maybe Harrison had been storing up for a rainy day and somebody decided to use his stash to throw us off."

Mac rubbed his chin, absently noting that he needed a shave. "We need to check into the brother," he suggested. "We know Harrison is dead, there's no question. And yes, someone could be planting the evidence. It isn't impossible, but neither is the possibility that the dead brother isn't dead. We haven't seen his body for confirmation. Who's to say the guy isn't alive and well and seeking his vengeance for his brother's death? We both believe Harrison was killed by a woman, so what if the brother believes it, as well? He can't be sure which of the former lovers is guilty, so he takes them out one at a time, knowing that eventually he'll get the right one."

"Hell, Nigel Harrison was supposed to have died four years ago," Brannigan countered. "He's buried in some shit hole down in Mexico. How the hell am I supposed to verify that he's really dead? We damn sure can't rely on any paperwork they send us. And if he's alive, where the hell has he been all this time? No one I've interviewed even knew Dr. Harrison had a brother."

"I want him exhumed," Mac said grimly, fury pumping through him. "We've got four murder victims with Harrison's DNA fingerprint swimming around inside them." The idea that Elizabeth could be next screamed at him. He clenched his jaw until he regained some semblance of self-control. When he'd investigated Harrison's background months ago, he'd learned about the brother, but that detail hadn't mattered—he was dead. But now they had reason to believe otherwise. Especially considering this latest turn of events. "The brother is an identical twin—he could have the same DNA structure. I want to know if the bastard is really dead or if he's alive and avenging his brother's death." The whole scenario was different now.

"So we're going ghost hunting now?" Brannigan mused, only half joking.

"Maybe," Mac allowed, "but we're not going to overlook that avenue just because we *think* it isn't viable. I want to *know*."

Brannigan shoved his hands into his trousers and ducked his head between his shoulders in an uncharacteristically humble manner. "Your people can get an order like that faster than I can. You know the chain of command I'm forced to work with."

Mac reached for his cell phone. "I'll take care of it." He hesitated before entering the necessary number. "If you're not keeping Gloria Weston under surveillance 24/7, I think you should. Annabelle Ford, too."

"We got someone watching the Weston woman 24/7. You think the mouthpiece needs surveillance, too?"

"She seems to know an awful lot." Mac tried to pinpoint his reservations where Annabelle Ford was concerned, but couldn't. "There's something about her that nags at me."

Brannigan scoffed. "She's a freakin' lawyer. 'Nough said."

"Push the ME for DNA analysis on Novak, too," Mac added as an afterthought. "He's about the same size as Harrison was. A little more muscular, but the height is right. He could be the brother. Who knows? With the cosmetic-surgery possibilities out there today, it could be anyone with a similar build."

Brannigan gave him a two-fingered salute and then strode in the direction of the ME's van where Novak's body was now safely ensconced. Mac stared at his cell phone for a second and considered that it would take some powerful influence to get this exhumation under way ASAP. He had a friend or two in D.C., so he might as well start there. Why bother with the bottom when he could start at the top?

Elizabeth paced the room again, stopping every few minutes to peek out the window. Agent Driver was still there, watching her apartment. It was past seven and she was exhausted. She and Boomer had worked until six and had made a good deal of progress. By then she'd been so wired up thinking about all that had happened she'd just had to call it a day. Boomer had offered to come stay with her, but with Driver right outside she didn't see the point. Besides, he probably had a date. Boomer always had a date.

She'd called Gloria to make sure she was at her sister's, and she was. Elizabeth couldn't help feeling hurt all over again as Brian's words echoed through her. He had to have been lying. She refused to believe that Gloria would do that to her. Elizabeth closed her eyes and collapsed on the sofa. No matter that she'd firmly decided to put that behind her, it pushed to the forefront yet again.

Brian was dead.

No matter that he'd been a jerk who hurt her, she couldn't help feeling bad that he was dead. No one deserved to die a violent death like that. She shuddered when she considered that the last two men with whom she'd been involved had come to tragic ends. But then again, she doubted it had anything to do with her. Both had been deeply involved in very dangerous hobbies. A shiver ran through her when she thought of all she'd seen in that hidden room this morning.

Dozens of pictures of women, some far younger than she, in degrading poses. How could she not have seen how utterly sick Ned was? And if Brian were—had been, she amended with another quake of dread—involved with that kind of thing, he was pretty damned sick, too. Where was her intuition on the subject of men? It seemed she was utterly blind when it came to men. Her naiveté had gotten her into real trouble this time.

Did the members of the Gentlemen's Association see women as nothing more than pieces of meat? Or as mere playthings?

The idea that she had been a part of that, even unknowingly, made her ill. She wanted—needed—to be able to depend on Mac. She rolled her eyes. There she went, calling him Mac again. She wrung her hands and tried to reason out the issue. What if she trusted him and he let her down the way everyone else had? But she needed him. She closed her eyes and confessed that truth. She needed him. She wasn't sure she could get through this alone, and her relationship with Gloria was up in the air right now. At the same time that thought went through her mind, she told herself it was foolish. She could trust Gloria. Brian had lied. That was all.

A knock at her door startled her from the troubling thoughts. She stood, propelled as much by fear as by the instinct to answer the door. She peeked out the window. Her heart almost stopped. Driver's car was gone. Frantically she scanned the area surrounding the house. With immense relief she noted Mac's sedan in the driveway.

Letting go the breath she'd been holding, she hurried to the door. As she reached for the lock she remembered what he'd told her about that and asked, "Who is it?"

"It's me," his deep voice resonated through the wood between them.

Something warmer than relief washed over her, and she quickly unlocked and opened the door. "Nothing else has happened?" She was suddenly afraid he'd come here to tell her more bad news. She'd just spoken to Gloria...

He shook his head. "Nothing new. I just wanted you to know that I'd be out there watching tonight."

She nodded mutely. He looked exhausted. She wondered why he didn't just assign another of his men to take over.

"Call me if you need me," he said.

When he would have headed back down the stairs, she abruptly regained her voice. "Could you come in for a while?" He stopped but didn't turn. She snapped her mouth shut and called herself an idiot. What was she doing?

Slowly, as if considering the prudence of that offer, as well, he turned to face her. Those blue eyes directed that very question at her.

She attempted a nonchalant shrug but managed only a stiff jerk of one shoulder. "I just thought we could talk for a while." She folded her arms to hide the way her hands had begun to shake. "I guess I'm a little rattled." She heaved a mighty breath. "Or restless."

"Just for a little while," he relented, moving deliberately toward her. When he stood in the doorway staring down at her, he qualified, "I'll leave it up to you to let me know when it's time to go."

She nodded and stepped back so he could come inside. When she'd locked the door, she turned to find him standing in the middle of the room watching her. She summoned a smile. "Would you like coffee or tea?"

He shook his head, his gaze seeming somehow more potent and focused solely on her.

She told herself she was simply tired. It had been a long day. Hell, it had been a long week. The faces of all those women floated briefly before her eyes. The realization that Ned and Brian were dead. Murdered. And then the undeniable fact that she could be next…well, it all kind of crashed down on top of her at once and she swayed.

Mac was at her side in a flash. "You should sit down."

Elizabeth leaned heavily on him as he walked her to the sofa. Damn. What was wrong with her? Was everything just catching up to her?

"Thanks," she mumbled as he released her.

"Maybe you're the one who needs some tea," he suggested, concerned.

For just a second she basked in the warmth of his genuine concern. It felt so good to have someone worry about her. Then she shook her head and chastised herself for behaving so foolishly. "Please, just keep me company for a while."

He dropped into the ancient overstuffed chair directly across from her and appeared content to simply watch her.

She looked away, suddenly at a loss as to what they should talk about. Here she'd practically begged him to stay and now she'd apparently turned mute. Well, she might not be able to instigate a conversation, but her blood was rapidly reaching the boiling point. Her gaze flicked toward him and she reveled in simply looking. He'd shed his jacket and tie. She couldn't recall ever seeing him without his tie. A couple of buttons were loosened and she could see a tempting V of bronzed skin. A dreamy sensation tingled to life inside her. She almost laughed out loud. What was wrong with her?

Her gaze bumped his and for several beats she couldn't look away. Naked hunger flashed fleetingly in his eyes. That awareness sent need swirling through her. She wasn't the only one having trouble with the building tension. She felt a smile tickle her lips at the idea he could possibly want her. It seemed so…so unlikely, and yet she'd known from the very beginning that something sizzled between them.

With effort she directed her gaze elsewhere. To the faded rug, then the tattered fabric of the sofa.

"You checked in with your friend Gloria?" he said abruptly.

Her head came up. Was it her imagination, or was his voice strained? She blinked and searched his face for any hint of that sexual hunger she'd seen moments ago. But he'd banished it, assumed his professional demeanor.

She bobbed her head, the movement awkward. "She's fine."

He nodded once. "Good."

The seconds turned into minutes as the silence thickened around them again. What had she been thinking? She should have known this wouldn't work. She just wasn't the type to play the part of seductress and he obviously wasn't that interested or he'd make a move.

She closed her eyes in self-disgust. What was wrong with her? People were dying all around them. How could she be thinking about sex?

"Well." Mac stood. "I'll be outside if you need me."

Her eyes popped open and she scrambled to her feet. "Um…okay." She didn't want him to go. It was crazy. She'd never been good at this, always made the wrong choices. But God, how she hated being weak and uncertain, being unable to go after what she wanted. For once in her life she wanted to be the one in charge. She wanted *him.*

Mac paused at the door. "Good night."

Refusing to hesitate long enough to think, she grabbed him by his shirtfront and pulled his mouth down to hers. She closed her eyes tightly and she kissed him. For one terrifying moment all she could think was, this wouldn't work. He resisted…didn't take her in his arms…didn't kiss her back. Defeat tugged at her fledgling determination. She couldn't do this. Then the marvelous textures of his lips and mouth penetrated her senses as he surrendered to the kiss and abruptly took charge.

He devoured her with his mouth, his jaw scratchy and rough but more tantalizing than any sensation she'd ever known. His fingers plunged into her hair as he deepened the kiss. She could feel the fierce energy radiating just beneath the surface of his hot skin. Those skilled hands slid down her back and suddenly he was touching her everywhere at once, stripping off her clothes, baring her skin to his greedy mouth. His fingers set her on fire every place he touched. His tongue laved her body. She was losing control and she wanted him to lose control with her.

She tugged at the buttons of his shirt until her hands flattened fully against the muscled terrain beneath. The heat seared her palms. She moaned and somehow his mouth found hers again, his kiss insanely sexy and breath-stealingly savage. He pulled her body hard against his, kicked the door shut and carried her to the bedroom, all the while his mouth plundering hers. He tasted hot and strong, like dark, fragrant coffee, full of delicious flavor and the promise of relentless energy. She wanted him to sweep her away, to awaken every part of her body and to stimulate her long-slumbering libido. To turn her into the kind of woman who could bring a man like him to his knees.

She wanted to see his vulnerable side, to find his weakness if it took all night long. She wanted to forget everything, to make the world go away for just this one night.

Their mouths mating hungrily, possessively, they stripped off the last of the restrictive garments, touching, teasing each new expanse of skin they uncovered. He felt so incredibly hot and hard. His muscles were beautifully defined, his body perfectly proportioned. His entire anatomy was a source of perpetual amazement. She wanted to learn all of him, wanted to taste the sweet and the salty.

Broad, broad shoulders and a sculpted chest that narrowed into a lean waist and hips. Incredibly strong arms that lifted her nude body against that tempting torso and lowered her to the bed. Long, muscular legs and strong, confident hands. He came down over her and she smiled as she considered the other generous part of him. His thick sex nudged ambitiously between her thighs, and for the first time in her life she opened freely, without undue coaxing.

She wanted this. She wanted him. She stared into the fiery blaze of those dark-blue eyes and knew this was going to be special. Whatever repercussions tomorrow brought, this moment was worth it.

She gasped when his body drew away from hers, but she soon discovered that he had other plans. He trailed hot, wet kisses along her flesh until he reached his ultimate destination. With the first flick of his tongue she melted into a tangle of shivery sensations. Moan after moan drifted from her lips as he positioned her for full access and lapped hungrily at her sensitized flesh. He pushed her closer and closer to the brink until she was writhing and pleading for him to finish it. She felt ready to combust, to implode with the swelling pleasure.

She screamed his name and somehow his mouth came down on hers as he simultaneously drove into her. He thrust fully, deeply and for the first time she was utterly primed, slick and yielding. Muscles that had once resisted this very moment opened eagerly to him, welcomed the marvelous friction of his rigid male body along her skin and thrusting deep, deep inside her. He cupped her face in his hands and kissed her tenderly, his hips setting the perfect rhythm, not too fast, not too slow. The world narrowed until there was nothing but his weight, his breath, his strong hands, and the plunge and slide of his velvety smooth shaft.

The spiraling sensation started so, so far away and then suddenly she was caught up in a hurricane. She reached frantically for him, called his name as his slamming thrusts brought her closer and closer to that moment of final exultation. Something snapped inside her and a pang of longing, fierce and feminine, erupted, shattered some imaginary membrane that had held her captive for so very long, allowing the final burst of climax to rain wildly down on her, capturing her breath and sending ripple after ripple of pleasure cascading through her.

He followed her over the edge, coming with such force that her body arched like a bow, and with one completing thrust he made her forget everything but him and his touch.

Chapter 12

Mac lay in Elizabeth's bed as the sun rose the next morning. They'd made love over and over again during the night. She'd come alive in his arms just as he'd longed for her to do. His gut clenched when he thought about how she could tear him apart with that luscious mouth.

She lay in his arms now, sleeping peacefully, trustingly. Her glasses were on the bedside table and their clothes were spread all over the apartment. His pulse began to race as he inventoried the way her body was wrapped around his. One creamy thigh was draped across his hip. Her arms were curled around his neck. Her sweet face was nestled in the curve of his neck. And those lovely breasts were flattened against his chest. Her long hair splayed over his flesh like raw silk. There wasn't a part of him that didn't ache for her still. Even after hours of mind-blowing sex.

No coddling or coaxing had been necessary. She'd kissed him first and she hadn't slowed down until she fell asleep, exhausted and sated. She'd explored his body without hesitation. After her first climax she'd rolled him over and climbed atop to ride to completion once more. Her appetite and eagerness had matched his in every way. She'd licked and sucked and kissed him until he'd thought he would go crazy or simply die.

And she was his.

His arms tightened around her.

Whether Elizabeth Young suspected it or not, he never intended to let her go.

"What time is it?" she murmured sleepily, those tempting lips moving against his throat.

"Time for both of us to get to work." Mac knew she kept long hours just as he did. On the job early and didn't stop until it was done. That was something they had in common, loyalty and determination. He respected those traits in her. He also respected her ability to make him hard with scarcely a touch even after a night like last night.

"Hmm...I see we're *up* already," she purred.

He rolled her onto her back and smiled down at her. God, he loved how she looked first thing in the morning. All soft and pretty and relaxed. "Honey," he growled, "up will never be the problem as long as I'm within three feet of you."

They made love again and then they showered together. Mac swore as he wrapped a towel around her damp body that he would not let this moment end. He would not let her down.

And no one would ever hurt her again.

Elizabeth couldn't remember ever being this happy. Not even when she thought she had the world by the tail after Brian's proposition that she come away with him. A flash of regret stung her at the memory that Brian was dead, but she forced it away. She'd cared for him, was sorry that he was dead, but never in her life had she felt the way she did at this moment about any man.

She studied Mac's profile as he parked in front of the building where Boomer was already at work. He'd insisted that he would see her to work, and Driver would take over from there for a few hours. After all, he had a case to solve. But he wasn't about to leave her vulnerable. A warm glow started deep inside her at the idea of how protective he was of her. She'd never known that feeling of security with anyone except her father.

This was good. She knew it with complete certainty.

She smiled.

This was very good.

She didn't want it to end.

Mac switched off the engine and turned to her, propping his arm on the back of the seat. "I've debated whether I should tell you this or not, but I feel like I have to."

Fear trickled into her veins. "What?" She didn't want to hear anything bad. She wanted desperately to hang on to this wondrous moment.

"The killer left behind some evidence at each scene. DNA analysis is back on the first two victims."

She nodded, not sure exactly what that meant.

"All of the victims were sexually assaulted." She shuddered visibly and he winced, clearly not happy at having to tell her this.

"Do you think it was Brian?" she asked.

Mac hesitated before answering, and in that moment her instincts warned her that it was far worse than that. "The DNA was a perfect match to Harrison's."

Shock plowed through her. For a moment she couldn't breathe. "But he's dead," was all she could say.

Mac nodded. "Yes, he is. That's confirmed." He searched her face and she knew that the pain on his was related to the anxiety he saw on hers. "Did you know he had an identical twin brother?"

That news startled her all over again. "No. I mean yes. Annabelle told us he had a brother who'd died, but she didn't mention he was a twin."

"They grew up in an orphanage. Both managed to make a better life for themselves—or, at least, it seemed so." Mac tapped the steering wheel as if contemplating how much more he should tell her. "His brother reportedly died four years ago."

Just when she'd thought nothing else could shock her. Ned had never let on about any of that. "If he's dead and Ned is..."

Mac leveled his gaze on hers. "Ned Harrison is dead," he confirmed. "Don't even go down that road. He's definitely dead. But we haven't confirmed the brother's death as of yet. We're working on it. I just wanted you to know that someone out there might be out for vengeance. If he thinks you killed his brother..."

No further explanation was necessary. "I get it." Icicles formed in her chest. "So I should be on the lookout for a carbon copy of Ned," she said sardonically. This was too much. One Ned Harrison was more than enough.

"Not necessarily," Mac countered. "He may have altered his appearance, surgically and otherwise."

Great. Just great. She released an exasperated sigh. "So basically, he could be anyone."

Mac nodded. "Basically. If he's alive."

His fingers trailed along her hairline, sending delicious shivery sensations through her as he tucked a stray tendril behind her ear. It didn't pay to braid one's hair while being kissed by a man like Collin MacBride. She probably had dozens of wisps hanging about.

"Don't take any chances, Elizabeth. Stay close to

Boomer. He's safe. He was in prison when Harrison's brother supposedly died, and besides, unless the identical twin was less than identical, he's far too tall. Don't wander out of Driver's watch. I need you to be careful while I go do what I have to." He shook his head and looked away for a moment. "To be perfectly honest with you, I'm tempted to arrest you and force you to go into protective custody—"

"You promised," she interrupted. "I have to work."

He sighed. "I know. I won't break that promise." His gaze found hers once more. "But I need you to swear to me you won't take any chances. We can't be sure who we're looking for here. It could be someone from the Gentlemen's Association who had a thing for Harrison."

"I won't take any chances, I swear."

His reservations evident, Mac walked her to the door of the loft where Boomer was already hard at work. Driver took up watch right outside the door.

She was pretty sure she wouldn't soon forget his good-bye kiss. If the desperation behind it was any indication, he was as deep in this as she was.

And she was in way too deep.

Around lunchtime loud voices erupted in the corridor outside the loft. Boomer and Elizabeth exchanged questioning looks. But then Elizabeth recognized the voice railing at Driver.

Annabelle.

Elizabeth put her paint roller aside and rushed into the corridor to intervene. In one glance she summed up the situation. Driver was hell-bent on doing his job protecting her, and Annabelle was equally determined to see her.

"It's okay, Agent Driver," Elizabeth said quickly. "Annabelle is a friend."

Giving the resigned man a triumphant glare, Annabelle stormed past him and into the loft with Elizabeth.

"We have to talk," she whispered from the corner of her mouth. Her gaze flickered to Boomer on the other side of the loft.

"Sure." Nerves jangling, Elizabeth ushered her toward the one small area that was separated from the main part of the loft—the bathroom.

Once within the confines of the tiny room, Annabelle blurted her statement in what was probably an attempt at whispering: "Brian Novak is dead."

Elizabeth nodded solemnly. "I know."

Annabelle took her hands in hers. "I'm so sorry, Elizabeth. I just had to be sure you were all right. I know how close the two of you once were." She glanced toward the open door. "I don't want you to worry. I didn't tell them anything about the other night."

A frown of confusion worked its way across Elizabeth's brow. "You didn't tell who?"

Annabelle rolled her gray eyes with something akin to disdain. "That brutish Detective Brannigan. He spoke to me and to Gloria. She called, extremely upset. I rushed over here immediately, since you don't have a cell phone." She cast Elizabeth an annoyed look. "You really should have one, you know."

Elizabeth nodded. "I know. But you didn't have to worry or hide anything about the other night in Ned's office."

Annabelle squeezed her hands knowingly. "Oh, but you're wrong. That ridiculous detective thinks you killed Brian. He thinks you killed Ned, too!"

A little jolt of shock rumbled through her. "What... what makes you think that?"

The older woman huffed a sound of derision. "Why,

the imbecile said as much. He was rambling on about how the FBI had been watching you from the beginning and how they'd taken the case away from him." She released Elizabeth so she could throw up her hands. "He was furious with MacBride for horning in on his prime suspect."

"Me?" Elizabeth could hardly believe her ears. This didn't make sense. She and Mac had—

"Talk to Gloria," Annabelle urged. "She came away from the meeting with the same feeling. You've got to call that criminal lawyer you put on retainer before you find yourself appearing before a grand jury."

"I will." Her words were thin, since it took all the strength Elizabeth possessed to hold back the misery mushrooming inside her. "I'll call him today."

Apparently satisfied with that assurance, Annabelle warned her again to be careful and left in the same rush with which she'd arrived. Agent Driver looked none too happy about the visit, but Elizabeth didn't care. Right now the only thing she cared about was confirming the worst.

If Mac had used her... She closed her eyes and fought back the tears. She couldn't believe that just yet. Mac had protected her. Made love to her as no one else ever had. She'd opened up to him, been the wanton woman she'd secretly longed to be with the right man. It couldn't have been a lie.

She wouldn't let it be.

Annabelle was upset. She'd probably taken it all out of context. Elizabeth knew from experience that Brannigan could be a brash SOB. On that thought, the pain subsided just a little bit.

She would not lose trust in Mac—not without solid proof, anyway.

* * *

Elizabeth forced herself to work another hour. When she'd reached a good stopping point, she gave Boomer instructions for the rest of the day. Not that he really needed any. He worked well on his own and was good to take the initiative.

Now came the hard part. She exited the loft and found Driver propped on the window ledge at the end of the corridor, sipping coffee from his thermos. The window's view was only of the uncommonly wide alleyway between this old industrial building and the next, but at least it allowed sunlight into the otherwise dark corridor.

"I need to go to Gloria Weston's office."

Driver stood abruptly. "I'm not sure that's such a good idea. We'll have to check with Mac on that."

Elizabeth wasn't about to be thwarted. "You can either take me now or I'll use Boomer's van."

"Let me just give Mac a quick call." Driver flipped open his cell and punched the number. After thirty seconds or so it was obvious he wasn't going to reach Mac. "He must be on another call."

"I'd like to go now, please," she informed him, leaving no room for argument. She was going to Gloria's office one way or another. Something wasn't right. Whatever it was nagged just beneath the surface—she couldn't quite grasp it. She kept replaying the conversation she'd had with Annabelle. Something felt wrong.

Driver finally relented. "All right. I guess it won't hurt."

Half an hour later they were on the elevator headed toward the eighteenth floor and Gloria's office. Driver fit right in with all the suits and ties. Elizabeth, however, stood out like a sore thumb. Her jeans and T-shirt, both dappled with white paint, looked vastly out of place.

"You can wait here," she said to Driver when they reached Gloria's door.

"I'll need to check it out first."

Blowing out a puff of frustration, Elizabeth stood back and allowed him to knock and then enter Gloria's office.

"Miss Young would like to see you." She heard him say. Wow, finally, she had her own secretary, as well as bodyguard. All it had taken was a few unsolved murders.

He stepped back into the corridor as Gloria peeked out from her office, her green eyes wide with surprise. "What's going on?"

Elizabeth shot Driver a look that told him to stay put and quickly followed Gloria into her office, then closed the door behind them. "You know Brian is dead."

Gloria nodded grimly. "I can't believe it. Do you know that they think he's the one who's been killing all the women?"

Elizabeth didn't remember Annabelle saying that. "They do?"

"It's hard to believe, I know. But that's the impression Detective Brannigan gave me."

"But he didn't say that," Elizabeth pressed. She had to know how this was going down.

Gloria frowned thoughtfully for a moment. "No, he didn't exactly say it. I just got those vibes from him and the slant of his questions."

"Did he say anything about me?" Elizabeth held her breath, not sure she could cope with the answer if it matched what Annabelle had said.

Gloria flipped her hands palms up in a noncommittal gesture. "He did mention you." She dropped onto the edge of her desk. "It was odd. He didn't exactly accuse you of anything, but I got the impression he somehow thought you and Brian were in on this together." She pulled a cocky face. "But I set him straight on that one. You and Brian hadn't been in on anything together in months."

Her words warmed Elizabeth. "Thanks." She moistened her lips, then gnawed on her lower one for a second. "Annabelle came by. She was extremely upset. She said that Brannigan considered me the prime suspect in Ned's, as well as Brian's murder. And that he'd gotten the impression the FBI thought so, as well. She…she…I don't know. The more I think about it, the weirder the conversation seems."

Gloria shook her head slowly. "He didn't say anything like that to me, but he did ask a lot of questions about you and Ned and you and Brian." Her frown deepened. "Now that you mention it, he did lean heavily toward that line of thinking. He kept bringing up your name each time he talked about Ned or Brian's murder."

That too-familiar chill crept into Elizabeth's bones. "But he didn't mention the FBI's thoughts on the matter?"

"No. I'm sure he didn't." Gloria shrugged. "Then again, I made it clear that you and I are friends. Maybe he held back, knowing I'd likely tell you whatever he said."

That was true. Since there was no reason for him to suspect Elizabeth and Annabelle had any sort of relationship, he would likely speak more freely around her. Anxiety coiled in her stomach. Still, she had no real proof against Mac.

"And don't sweat Annabelle. I've gotten the occasional creepy vibe from her, too." Gloria rubbed her forehead with her thumb and forefinger. "I just wish this were over."

"Me, too." Elizabeth leaned against the corner of the desk next to her friend. Maybe that was what had been digging at her. A "creepy vibe" was a damned accurate description. But she supposed Annabelle couldn't help how she was. Still, Elizabeth had bigger problems than trying to figure out the woman. "There's something I have to ask you, Gloria."

Her friend turned to look at her, her gaze expectant. "You know you can ask me anything."

"When Brian confronted me at Ned's office, he said some hurtful things." She'd sworn she wasn't going to bring this up...but, dammit, she had to know. She was feeling so uncertain right now.

Gloria shook her head. "Well, I hate to speak ill of the dead, but there's no surprise there."

Elizabeth moistened her lips and worked up the nerve to say the rest. "He said that you recommended me to Ned after *he* told you to. That you were in on the whole thing. His using me and then Ned doing the same."

Gloria's expression had gone from calm and patient to outraged in less than three seconds. "You're kidding, right?"

Elizabeth gave her head a little shake. "I didn't believe him, but I wanted you to know—"

"What do you mean, you didn't believe him?" Gloria demanded, her tone filled with hurt. "You're asking me, so you must have believed it to some degree." She threw up her hands and pushed away from her desk. "I can't believe you would even consider his lies as having any basis whatsoever."

Driver stuck his head inside the door. "Everything all right in here?"

The two severe glowers thrown his way sent him ducking back into the corridor.

"Gloria," Elizabeth urged, "I didn't believe him. I—"

"You didn't?" Her friend was angry now. A flush had turned her pale skin a deep crimson. "Oh, really. Well, you could have fooled me. Why would you bother asking if you didn't?"

She was right. Elizabeth stared at the floor, ashamed of herself for believing Brian even for a second. "I'm sorry. I don't know—"

"I do," Gloria snapped, her arms folded over her chest in an unyielding manner. "You have that little faith in our friendship." Mouth set in a grim line, she skirted the desk and began to shuffle through the mound of papers lying there. "If you'll excuse me, I have work to do."

"Let's not leave it like this, please," Elizabeth pleaded. "I was wrong to let him get to me, but I—"

Gloria held up a hand and fixed her with a hard glare. "I can't talk about this right now, I'm too upset. Please, just go."

Knowing a brick wall when she ran into one, Elizabeth admitted defeat. She moved to the door, but hesitated before going through it. "Just remember one thing," she said softly. Gloria didn't respond. "This isn't your fault. It's mine. I'm the one with the trust issues. I jumped the gun here and I'm sorry. No matter what happens with all this insanity, you're still my best friend."

Elizabeth didn't wait for a reply; Gloria was too hurt right now. But they would work it out…somehow.

She sat numbly in Driver's car as he headed back toward SoHo. His cell phone rang and she jerked at the sound. Swiping the infuriating tears from her cheek, she forced a deep breath and kept her gaze straight ahead. She tried not to think, but it was impossible. The events of the past ten days were whirling in her head, crashing down on her with a sense of finality that threatened her tenuous grip on her composure. Ned's deceit. His murder. The police. The murdered women. Brian's preposterous accusations. His murder. Making love with Mac.

God, please let her be able to trust him. To count on that one thing. She couldn't live with another letdown.

"It's Mac," Driver said. "He needs to talk to you."

Her hand shaking, Elizabeth took the phone. "Hello." She cringed at the quaver in her voice. Strong. She had to be strong.

"Elizabeth, listen to me." The sound of his voice was reassuring. "There's been another murder. I've instructed Agent Driver to take you home and to stay with you until I can get back there."

She just listened, too stunned to reply. Some part of her brain niggled at her, reminding her that she really needed to work, but she couldn't quite grasp the initiative.

"Brannigan is sending another man over to keep watch on Gloria."

Her friend's name startled her out of her trance. "Annabelle said there's still one more before he gets to Gloria and me." God, she prayed her information was correct. What was she thinking? She was wishing the danger on someone else, someone just as innocent as they were. "Whoever she is, she'll need protecting, too."

Silence roared between them for a moment that felt like an eternity. Why didn't he say something?

"If Harrison had another female patient whose name comes alphabetically after the latest victim and before Weston, I can't find it in his files."

Fear broadsided Elizabeth.

If that was so, Gloria was next.

Chapter 13

Elizabeth retraced her steps across her suddenly too-small living room. She'd never noticed before that the old wooden floor creaked in a certain spot about three feet from the rear wall. It squeaked smack-dab in the center, too. Guess she'd never really had time to pace the floor that much or to be aware it made any sounds. Or maybe she'd simply been too exhausted by the time she dragged herself home at night. Whenever her panic attacks had struck at home, she'd done her pacing outside. It worked better that way. Now that she thought about it, this apartment had really served as nothing more than the place she slept and showered. It hadn't really been a home.

Her life had been in too much of an uproar and she'd been far too busy attempting to make ends meet to worry about anything else. The worn area rug and meager furnishings had been included with the place, for which she'd been immensely thankful—she'd had nothing of her own.

Nothing but her clothes and a boxful of mementoes from the life she'd once lived in a small Maryland town. It felt like a dozen lifetimes ago now.

She hadn't even bothered calling her sister, the only family she had left, and telling her about the murders or her connection to any of it. Her only sibling had enough troubles of her own. Fortunately for the kids, Peg had straightened out her life since becoming a widow. No more drugs or drinking. She even had a job. While working at the local Wal-Mart might not have sounded like much to most, it was a huge step for Peg. Elizabeth's little sister had never been much for responsibility, and she hadn't really grown up until her third child was born.

But then, Elizabeth couldn't blame it all on her sister. With a mother who deserted them and a father who'd been too busy working to keep a roof over their heads to influence their raising to any degree, what else could one expect?

She knew she was rambling down memory lane, as fruitless as it was, to avoid facing reality.

In the past a situation this stressful would have thrown her into full-scale panic, but strangely she felt an odd sense of calm. Her concern for her friend had overridden all else. Elizabeth turned and started across the room, once more silently willing the telephone to ring. She needed to hear from Gloria. She'd called her office as soon as she arrived home, but her assistant had informed her that Gloria had gone for the day. She'd called Gloria's sister's house, and there hadn't been any answer. And her cell phone was either out of range or not activated.

Uneasiness plugged away at Elizabeth, but she stayed strong. She should have heard from Mac by now. What was going on with the latest victim? Had he gotten in touch with Brannigan about Gloria?

Elizabeth deviated from her usual route and pushed the curtain aside just far enough to see Driver's car outside. She didn't see him in the fading daylight, but she knew he was around, watching the grounds, checking the doors and windows. She'd offered him some coffee, but he'd declined, saying that his wife always made him a thermos of it each morning. Elizabeth wondered vaguely what it would be like to have that kind of relationship. Taking care of each other's needs, always knowing someone was there to depend on. She closed her eyes and thought about making love with Mac. Long nights, cradled in his arms, sated emotionally, as well as physically.

Never count your chickens before they hatch, darling, her daddy had always said. She, of all people, should know that old adage was true. She knew better than to start thinking about forever where Mac was concerned. They'd shared one night, nothing more. When this case was over, assuming she survived it, they would probably never see each other again. He could have a girlfriend... or a fiancée.

The bottom fell out of her stomach. They really hadn't talked that much. What did she actually know about him? He'd been born and raised in Washington, D.C. Had a degree from Columbia. He was thirty-five and he'd been with the FBI for ten years. She had no idea if he had any family or even what foods he liked or what his favorite color was.

The panic she'd been certain wouldn't strike suddenly did. It tightened her throat, made her skin crawl, as her heart kicked into overdrive and unneeded adrenaline shot through her veins. "Walk it off," she muttered, disgusted with her inability to control the reaction. Damn, she hated being vulnerable to her traitorous body. And just when she thought she'd get through this without a problem.

She grabbed the phone and punched in the number for Gloria's sister's house. When she got no answer she tried the cell phone again.

Still no answer.

Still no word from Mac.

She couldn't take it anymore.

She punched in another number and the answer came after the first ring. "Speak."

Despite the pressure building inside her, she almost laughed at Boomer's barked greeting. "Boomer, I need your help."

Forty-five minutes later Elizabeth climbed into Boomer's truck and shouted, "Go!"

He floored the accelerator and the vehicle shot forward like a rocket. She buckled up and collapsed against the seat. She'd made it.

She'd known that Driver would be watching her truck, so she'd waited until he was doing his perimeter search on the far side of the yard and slipped out. Boomer had waited for her three blocks away. Even now Driver was probably knocking on her door, wanting to know if she was all right. But it was too late; she and Boomer were well out of sight. Mac would be angry. He didn't want her leaving the house for any reason.

"Hurry, Boomer," she pleaded. "I'm really worried about Gloria."

Keeping an eye out for the cops, Boomer made Brooklyn in record time. Gloria's sister lived in a cop neighborhood. Half the residents were on the force, as her husband had been. When her husband had died, she'd known she had to stay. Her neighbors were like family; she couldn't possibly leave.

"Just let me make sure someone is there," Elizabeth said when Boomer parked in front of the small, neat cottage. "I'll wave for you to go on if all is well."

"I can come in with you," he offered, his face scrunched with worry. "I don't like leaving you here."

"As long as Gloria is here and safe and sound, everything'll be fine. I'll call Mac and let him know I'm here. He won't like it, but it's too late now."

Boomer nodded reluctantly. "I'll wait for your go-ahead."

"Okay." Elizabeth slung her purse on her shoulder, slid out of the truck and walked to the front stoop. She pressed the doorbell, but not sure if it worked, she followed with a couple of firm knocks. A moment later the door opened.

"Elizabeth?" Gloria frowned at her. "Are you all right?"

"Are you?" Elizabeth countered, quickly sensing the subtle differences in her friend's voice and posture. Something wasn't right.

Gloria started to say yes, but Elizabeth read the lie in her eyes a split second before she admitted defeat. "I can't do this anymore." She opened the door wider for Elizabeth to come in. "I have to tell you…"

Really worried now, Elizabeth waved at Boomer to send him on his way, then went inside the house. Gloria quickly locked the door behind her. "Where's your sister?" Elizabeth asked. The silence in the house seemed to close in around them.

"I sent her and my niece away."

"What do you mean, you sent them away?" Fear inched its way into Elizabeth's being. Things were definitely getting stranger by the second. Maybe she should have kept Boomer around a little longer. "Where are they?"

"I can't tell you, but they're safe from that madman." Gloria moved about the room, peeping between the slats of the blinds at window after window. "It's better if you don't know. I don't want him to find them."

Elizabeth moved to stand beside her friend as she peered out the front window. "What is it you have to tell me?" she asked softly, not wanting to push, but Gloria had said she had to tell her something. Abruptly she wondered where the police officer was who was supposed to be watching Gloria. "Have the cops been by to see you?" she asked, irritation climbing into the mix of emotions.

Gloria spun toward her. "No!" she practically shouted. "I haven't seen anyone."

This was too bizarre. "Gloria, tell me what's going on."

Those wide green eyes suddenly glistened with emotion. "That bastard is after my niece. I had to save her. I don't care if he kills me."

Elizabeth had missed something here. This didn't make sense. "I don't understand."

"Ned, the son of a bitch, took advantage of my niece, too," Gloria spat.

At first Elizabeth wasn't sure what she meant, then it dawned. "Oh, my God. Not Carrie."

Gloria nodded jerkily. "I couldn't believe it." She swiped at the tears falling freely now. "I wasn't really that surprised when he used us, but she's just a kid. Barely eighteen." Gloria shook with rage, her face turning beet-red. "She kept having all those problems after her father's death. Ned was certain he could help." She clenched her jaw, a muscle jerking in her cheek. "He helped all right. Carrie didn't tell me what happened until a couple of weeks ago."

Elizabeth put her arms around her friend and hugged her stiff shoulders. "I'm so sorry. You're right, he was a son of a bitch."

Gloria went completely rigid. "That's why I killed him."

For a couple of seconds her words didn't fully penetrate the wall of disbelief that instantly formed. Then they did, and Elizabeth felt a jolt all the way to her soul.

"Gloria, you can't mean that!"

She pulled out of Elizabeth's arms and stared at her. "I did. I killed him." Her eyes were glassy now. Elizabeth felt certain she was edging into shock. "I'm glad he's dead." She turned away.

Elizabeth tried to gather her wits. What the hell did this mean? Could Gloria be serious? "Tell me what happened," she urged, moving up behind her friend, hoping to lend support with her nearness.

Gloria lifted one shoulder in a shrug. "I didn't actually mean to kill him. I went there to teach him a lesson. I screwed his damn brains out, making him vulnerable, and then I pulled out my dead brother-in-law's service revolver." She laughed, the sound empty, so unlike her usual tinkling laughter. "He was scared shitless. I had him trussed up like a Christmas turkey in that chair, buck naked, and then I tortured him. Mentally mostly."

She lapsed into silence for a time and Elizabeth struggled to be patient. Gloria was definitely close to a breakdown. Elizabeth could feel it.

"He'd taken out that dagger you'd given him. Cleaning it or admiring it, who knows? Or maybe he intended to scare you with it when you showed up." A laugh tore out of her again. "Oh, yeah, I was there when you came over mad as hell that he'd stood you up. I was hiding in the master bathroom, praying you didn't find me. I couldn't hear everything you said…just parts. Then you left and I tempted him into a game he couldn't resist. He loved every minute of it as I tied him up. He even liked it when I stuffed those panties in his mouth. I brought them with me—brand new cheap ones. I knew he'd hate that they weren't silk. But then I picked up the dagger. That's when he got worried. I taunted him with it, drew blood a couple of times just to hear him whimper." She paused for so long Elizabeth wasn't sure she intended to continue. "And then he laughed at me."

Her voice had gone arctic cold.

"I didn't mean to kill him...but I was so angry," she said tightly. "The next thing I knew the dagger was in his chest. I don't even remember doing it." She pulled in a shaky breath and exhaled loudly. "I don't remember anything after he started laughing except the look in his eyes when the knife thrust into him. It made this... awful sound..."

Elizabeth fought back the images her friend's words elicited. "Gloria, I know this is hard, but why didn't you call the police? You could have explained everything."

She whipped around, pinning Elizabeth to the spot with a piercing glare. "And then what? Spent the rest of my life in prison? For killing a piece of scum like him?"

"Okay, okay," Elizabeth said placatingly, holding up her hands. "I understand. Hell, I would probably have done the same thing if it had been my niece."

"You would've?" Gloria's bravado wilted. "God, I can't believe I did it." She peered out the window.

It was dark enough now that, with only the dim slice of moon hanging in the sky, there wasn't much she could see. Just a streetlight struggling valiantly to send its glow across the small expanse of grass.

"It's like a bad movie playing in my head," Gloria said quietly. "I see myself doing it, but I still can't believe I did. It's like it really wasn't me, just someone using my body. I took the tapes he'd made of Carrie and me. I couldn't find yours." She looked at Elizabeth in earnest. "I swear I tried to find it, but I was so upset..."

"It's all right." Elizabeth thought about how Gloria had urged her not to tell the police anything, not to give them any extra information. She'd been trying to protect Elizabeth, as well as herself. But everything had gone wrong.

"Now he wants her dead," Gloria murmured. Her whole body seemed to quiver with a new, building emotion. "Well, I'll see him in hell first," she snarled. "Since it obviously wasn't Brian, I may not know who *he* is, but I'll be here waiting when he shows up."

Ignoring her resistance, Elizabeth pulled her friend into an embrace once more. "And I'll be here with you. If he comes, we'll take him on together."

Surrendering just a little, Gloria burrowed her face in Elizabeth's shoulder. "We have to!" she cried. "If we don't he'll kill us all."

"No way," Elizabeth argued, "because we'll be right here waiting for him. He has no way of knowing we're on to him now. We know what he wants next."

Gloria drew back. "I'm sorry I let the police suspect you. I should have come forward. I should have at least told you." She blinked back a new surge of liquid emotion.

"It's okay." Elizabeth hugged her tightly. "It'll be over soon."

And it would be. Elizabeth could almost feel him coming. Things had been building toward this moment ever since Ned's death. The momentum had been unstoppable. She closed her eyes and prayed that God would keep an eye on them. And that somehow Mac would find her, would swoop in and save the day.

Her courage shored up at the mere thought of him, Elizabeth drew back and looked at her friend. She brushed away the tears glittering on her cheeks. "I think I'm going to stack the deck to our advantage."

Gloria frowned wearily. "What do you mean?"

"I'm going to call us a hero."

* * *

Mac was on the phone with forensics, pushing for a speedy analysis on the latest victim. He had a few last-minute details to handle and then he was going to Elizabeth. He didn't want her in anyone else's care tonight.

Of course her safety was of primary importance, but a major part of him wanted a repeat of last night. He wanted to make love to her over and over…tonight.

If he could just get these damned people to commit to a time.

The intercom buzzed, sending a fresh bolt of pain through his aching head. He could sure use a neck rub about now.

"Agent MacBride, there's a call from Mexico for you on line four. And that other call is still holding on three. When I asked her if she wanted to continue holding, she said it was extremely important that she speak to you."

She? "Who is she?" The receptionist hadn't said a damned thing till now about the caller being a woman. His first thought was Elizabeth. But Driver would have called if Elizabeth had needed anything.

"She wouldn't give her name."

Uneasiness sliding into his gut, he barked a thanks and stabbed the blinking button that represented line three. He could call forensics back later. "MacBride." Nothing. It was dead. The caller had hung up.

Mac swore and poked the final flashing light. He'd been anticipating this call all afternoon. He couldn't risk missing it. He just needed one damned clue as to the identical twin's whereabouts. Just one. If the guy actually was dead, Mac needed to know it.

"MacBride."

"We've got your body, MacBride," said the man who

worked in Mexico as a liaison between the FBI and the CIA, "but I think you're going to be a little startled."

Why the hell not? Mac mused. Everything else about this case had been screwy. What was one more wacked-out item on the list?

"Nigel Harrison may very well be dead, but he isn't buried here. The corpse in the coffin at his grave site is female, and in damn good condition, too. Incredibly well preserved."

A woman. "Do you have any idea who she is and why she would have been buried in Harrison's stead?"

"Sure do. I have a nice thick file on Nigel Harrison. He was a rather naughty boy when he lived down here. When the Harrison brothers were growing up in that orphanage they called home, they became close friends with a girl there. According to one of the overseers who's still on staff there and remembers the Harrison brothers, the three were inseparable. Apparently they started planning their dastardly deeds way back then. Whenever they got caught in something underhanded, none of the three would admit who actually did the deed. Loyalty was the mainstay. The three stayed in contact when they went off to college. Nigel and the girl became lawyers, and Ned became a doctor. All three apparently rose well above their beginnings."

Mac was becoming impatient. He knew some of that already. "So you don't know where the hell Nigel Harrison is or even if he's dead."

"That's right. He supposedly died in the jungle and his body was carried out by the cave dwellers his companion on the journey allegedly hired."

Mac swore viciously. "I have to find this bastard," he muttered. "What you're telling me isn't giving me what I need. Why would he have faked his death?"

"I can't help you with where he's at," the man explained. "But I can speculate about why he faked his death. The corpse in the coffin belongs to a murder victim. Her throat had been slashed. She might have been well preserved, but the morticians down here aren't so good at covering up the cause of death. I imagine Nigel Harrison faked his own demise to conceal his handiwork. From the looks of the wound, he all but decapitated her."

Realization slammed Mac. "Do you have a positive ID on the woman?" Hell, she could be anybody, but he had a sneaking suspicion it was someone very close to the Harrison brothers.

"That I can give you, as well. Since her practice was in California and they fingerprint everyone who applies for a driver's license, her prints were on file. It's a positive ID."

Mac wished he could reach into the phone line and give the man a shake. "Well, do you have a name?"

"Oh, yeah. Sure. She was the girl who befriended the Harrison brothers in the orphanage. Her name was Annabelle Ford."

"It's Annabelle," Elizabeth whispered as she peered through the door's peephole. "What do you want to do?" She punched the "end call" button on the cordless phone. She'd have to try Mac again in a few minutes. She couldn't keep holding on. Maybe she should have given the receptionist her name, but she'd feared it would set off some sort of alarm, since Agent Driver had no doubt already called in. She didn't want anyone but Mac to know her whereabouts. "I don't know, Gloria." Elizabeth tried to rationalize her hesitation. "I know you trust Annabelle, but there's something wrong about her. The longer I think about it, the stronger the feeling."

Gloria chewed her lip thoughtfully for a moment as a fourth knock echoed, startling them both even though they'd known it was coming. "I…I guess we should let her in. She's a lawyer—she could help. She could have news."

Elizabeth still hesitated. "How well do you really know her?"

Gloria cradled her face in her hands for a moment, then shrugged. "Not that well, but it seems like she's tried to help us."

Maybe so. Pushing aside her nagging reservations, Elizabeth opened the door. "Hurry," she urged the older woman. "Come in. We don't want anyone to see us here."

Annabelle hurried inside, the same look of desperation on her face that no doubt was on Elizabeth's.

"There's been another murder," Annabelle said quickly. "I'm really getting worried. I'm not sure the authorities are going to be able to stop this."

Elizabeth hugged herself. "I'm wondering that myself." She studied Annabelle, tried to pinpoint the rub. What was it?

Annabelle looked from one to the other, a worried expression on her face. "Are you two all right?"

Elizabeth and Gloria exchanged a hopeless look. "Well," Gloria began, "it's…"

"It's just that we're sick about this latest victim," Elizabeth said quickly. She suddenly didn't want Annabelle to know the truth. "It could be either one of us any time now. Wouldn't we be next?"

Annabelle's gaze turned wary. "Good idea to feel that way." She focused on Gloria. "But something isn't right here," she said slowly. "What's going on?"

"I killed him!" Gloria blurted, a new gush of tears punctuating the admission. "It was me. I…I…" Her words faltered, replaced by a high-pitched keening sound.

"It was an accident," Elizabeth hastened to add as she quickly enveloped her friend in her arms once more. "It's okay, Gloria. We'll tell the police everything. There were extenuating circumstances."

"You don't get it," she wailed. "I screwed up! Made a mistake! And now he's after my niece. She's the last one before the two of us."

Carrie Urquhart. Elizabeth shook her head in confusion. "But why wasn't she on Ned's patient log?"

"He agreed to keep her name off the record so her psychiatric care could never come back to haunt her. She's so young. I didn't want her to start out with that hanging over her head. You know some of the big corporations and even some of the universities look for crap like that."

That was why Mac couldn't find another name.

"And now she's in danger because of me!" Gloria trembled violently. "She may die for my stupid mistake!"

Elizabeth reached for her to comfort her, but Annabelle reached her first.

"Don't worry, Gloria, you won't have to witness anything bad happening to your niece. You can go first."

Annabelle whipped a long-bladed knife from beneath her suit jacket and held it to Gloria's throat. "I don't mind deviating from the plan."

"What're you doing?" Elizabeth shouted. The stark fear that had momentarily paralyzed her propelled her into action. "Put that knife down!" She wanted to take it away from her, but it was pressed so close to Gloria's flesh. Instantly Elizabeth remembered Mac's description of arterial spray. She shuddered, her knees almost buckling beneath her.

"Did you really think I'd let you get away with it?" Annabelle growled, her usually gravelly voice even deeper now. "I knew if I picked you off one at a time, I'd eventually get the right one. I knew the few who'd made an impact on my brother's emotions. The ones he toyed with the most…who resented him the most."

Elizabeth tried to make sense of the scene. Annabelle was threatening to kill them. Her voice had deepened considerably. She'd called Ned her brother.

Oh, God.

The twin.

"You're Nigel," she said almost to herself.

"Well, give the girl a cigar," he said facetiously, not even attempting to hide the masculinity of his voice anymore.

Elizabeth looked at his meticulous chignon and then at the perfect fit of his suit over undeniable mounds of breasts. The toned legs, free of male hair, below the hem of her skirt. She'd known something wasn't right, but this…

"Get a good look, Elizabeth. It'll be your last." He laughed cruelly. "Just so you know, the hair is all mine. It took me two years to get it this length. Of course the color is different, just like my eye color. Aren't colored contacts marvelous?" he taunted, all the while pressing the knife firmly against Gloria's throat. He inclined his head sheepishly. "But the breasts are expensive fakes. A little surgery here and there and no one could tell we were brothers." His evil smile sickened Elizabeth. "Or that I wasn't a woman. Even you didn't know."

"Why?" Elizabeth asked.

"It was either take over Annabelle's identity or admit that I'd killed her." He lifted one shoulder in a shrug of indifference. "Stupid bitch. Annabelle should have known I wouldn't marry her. But no, she'd wanted children. She was tired of all the games we'd played together all those years, just me, her and Ned. She'd heard her biological clock ticking. Too bad for her. There was no contest as far as I was concerned regarding how to handle it. All it took was a little extra money to the mortician and one dirty cop. But then I had to kill them both. Hell, I'll bet they're still trying to figure out what happened to those two. Then again, maybe not. I did leave them in a rather compromising position. In that macho culture they're not about to own up to one of their own being homosexual. I just couldn't take the risk that one of them might grow a conscience one of these days and spill the beans. Or get greedy," he added with a sinister snarl, "and start attempting blackmail."

Annabelle...Nigel...whoever the hell he was laughed at her horrified expression. Gloria stood stock-still, frozen in fear, or perhaps defeat.

"Why did you come here?" Elizabeth asked, her voice hollow.

"Here in New York?" he demanded as if she was stupid. "Or *here?*" He looked down at Gloria briefly, then leveled that satanic gaze on Elizabeth. "Well, I came to New York to be with my brother, of course. We'd never been apart for long. And everything was perfect until you bitches had to go and ruin it! You made him what he was. All of you. And that filthy Gentlemen's Association," he accused. "I got them, too, and it was so easy."

Elizabeth knew what he meant by that. He'd set her up to lead Mac to the hidden room and, ultimately, to the Gentlemen's Association.

"So he knew," Elizabeth ventured, trying to keep him calm until she could think of some way to help Gloria. "Ned knew you'd killed the real Annabelle."

Another hateful laugh. "Of course. He was glad to be rid of her, too. We'd always liked it better when it was just the two of us. Even now, he's with me."

Elizabeth didn't want to know what he meant. Nigel was obviously insane. She had to find something else to ask, something to keep him talking. Her heart rocketed into hyper mode. "How did you get into all those women's apartments? Did you use a gun?"

He smirked. "That wasn't necessary. All I had to do was tell them Ned had mentioned them in his will and that we needed to talk. It was incredibly easy. They were all so stupid and we're so smart."

"Why…why have you been pretending to help us?"

"Partly because I needed you to help me lead the police to the association since they're the reason my brother is dead. They made him weak…made him stupid. Women like the two of you were the catalysts they used. So just for the fun of it," he confessed smugly. He waggled his brows suggestively at her. "I went in alphabetical order so I could save you for last. You were special to my brother. I owed you that much." As suddenly as this persona had appeared, it changed again. "But now the fun is over. We're through playing," he said grimly. "Time to die."

Out of options, Elizabeth lunged for him, the first bloom of blood sliding onto the shiny blade as it pierced flesh. She grabbed his arm, pulled with all her might. Gloria screamed, snapping from her paralysis and fighting to free herself.

With a lionlike roar Nigel shoved Gloria aside and grabbed for Elizabeth. She felt the pierce of the cold steel on her forearm as they struggled, but she didn't let up. She had to stop him.

Suddenly the knife was poised high above her.

She couldn't move fast enough.

She was going to die.

An explosion rent the air.

Halfway to its destination the knife suddenly dropped from Nigel's limp hand.

He slumped to the floor.

Gloria scrambled out of his way, her hands clutching at her throat where blood seeped like crimson tears between her fingers.

"I need an ambulance!"

Elizabeth swung around at the sound of his voice. It was Mac. He'd shouted the order into his cell phone.

He'd saved them. Her hero had come.

As much as she wanted to dive into his arms, Gloria needed her more. As if reading her mind, Mac dropped to the floor next to her doing what he did best: saving the day.

Mac sat next to Elizabeth in the lobby of the surgical wing of New York General when she received the good news.

"Miss Weston will fully recover," the doctor told her. "The damage was mainly superficial. She'll need some cosmetic work in the future. But otherwise she'll be fine."

"Thank you." Elizabeth blinked at the tears Mac saw shining in her eyes, but still they slipped past her lashes. When the doctor walked away, she turned to him. Her bandaged forearm and her friend's blood staining the front of her T-shirt the same way it marked his shirt served as vivid reminders of the horror they'd survived. "Thank God it's over."

He slid an arm around her and pulled her close. "Amen."

They sat in exhausted silence for a while and then she asked, "Mac, what will happen to Gloria when the grand jury convenes?"

"That fancy lawyer you put on retainer will get her off the hook with no problem."

Elizabeth looked up at him, hope glittering behind the tears. "Are you sure?"

He nodded. "Definitely. If he's only half as good as his reputation, he'll sail through this on a temporary-insanity plea. Gloria admitted to you that she doesn't even remember doing it. She was out of her mind with worry for her niece. She went over the edge."

"Annabelle—Nigel," she amended, remembering those final moments, "kept saying *we,* like Ned was still with him."

Mac made a disgusted sound. "I think he went over the edge long ago—to the point of no return."

Elizabeth shuddered, then nestled against Mac's shoulder and prayed it would be that easy for Gloria to be absolved from what Ned had pushed her to. Her friend had made it past the first hurdle—she was going to recover. Now she just had to get through this. Elizabeth would be there for her.

"What about the Gentlemen's Association?"

"They're going down. The whole task force has descended on that secret room. This group has a lot to answer for, including pushing men like Harrison, who already have a penchant for the unsavory, over the edge."

She sighed wearily. That was good news. She wanted all of them to go down for what they'd done. "What about us?" she asked without looking up. That question had haunted her all those long hours they'd waited to hear about Gloria. Worrying about her friend had kept her from focusing on the other. But now, as relief sent the stress draining away, there it was.

Mac drew back and looked into her eyes. "I happen to know you have a problem with trust and, considering what you've been through, I can't blame you. I'd like to spend some time proving to you that you can count on me."

She smiled, her lips trembling with the effort of holding back the tears that thickened in her voice when she spoke. "I already know I can count on you, Mac."

He pulled her close once more. "Then all we have to do is get to know each other better."

She smiled. "That sounds like the right thing to do."

"Definitely," he said, those amazing lips spreading wide in a beautiful smile. "It wouldn't be proper to marry a stranger."

Her eyes widened. He couldn't mean that. "We hardly know each other," she protested though she actually had no reservations whatsoever. For the first time in her life she was completely certain about a man.

He kissed the tip of her nose. "That's why we're going to do this one step at a time. And then when we're ready, whether it's next month or next year, we'll take the plunge. Deal?"

Her smile broadened to match his. "Deal."

Like all good deals, they sealed it with a kiss. A long, passionate kiss.

"We could leave for a little while now, you know," he whispered as he nuzzled the shell of her ear.

"Hmm...I hate not to be here when Gloria wakes up." Her breath caught when his tongue slid along her throat.

"Well—" he blew on the wet path he'd made and she shivered deliciously "—we'll just have to find ourselves a handy supply closet, because this isn't going to wait."

"Are you always this impatient, Agent MacBride?" she teased.

He drew back and that blue gaze collided with hers. "I almost lost you today," he murmured thickly. "Never have I wanted anything more than I wanted to do my job—until now. Whatever's happening between us, it's special. Very special. I'm not about to waste any time, and I'm damn sure not going to risk losing you now that I've found you."

His words touched her deeply. No one had ever made her feel this way. Mac was right. This was special.

His lips found hers once more, and just like before, the whole world fell away, leaving only her and the man she trusted.

* * * * *